ENFORCE
HER
A Blue-Frosted Rose
Secret Society
Rough Romance
A.M. PROCTOR

Contents

Cautious Content

Adventurous Adults Only

The Blue-Frosted Rose Society, its people, and the rituals are all products of this author's unfiltered and unhinged imagination. This author wrote a fictional story without any hidden agenda or hate towards any group. Your mental health and religious beliefs matter. While Eden's story (pretty much) wraps up at the end, Scout's story ends on a cliffhanger. The next book in the Blue-Frosted Rose Universe will be from Scout's, Bentley's and Torrid's POV, but trust me when I say Logan isn't done breeding Eden.

The contents might take you to dark places and may be triggering for some.

- Non-Con
- Filthy Rituals
- Stalking
- Murder
- Keelhauling
- Kidnapping
- Drugging
- Stalking

- Familial Fat Shaming
- Abusive Parent

It may also unlock new kink levels.

- Bondage
- Rope Play
- Biting
- Forced and Denied O's
- Somnophilia
- Breeding
- Primal Hunting
- Voyeurism

Chapter One

Adulting

Eden

The professor dismissed the class, and I closed my laptop and carefully put it in its bag. Hoisting the bag onto my shoulder, my brain jumped ahead to the parking lot and the harrowing drive home from St. Petersburg to Tampa, where I still lived with my mother. My gut tightened with apprehension. Was this what life was all about? Reduced to dreading gridlocked traffic in a commute that shouldn't take an hour and a half?

Outside the building, I heard a familiar voice shout, "Eden!"

I spun towards the voice with a genuine smile on my face when I should have frowned, considering how she'd dumped our friendship for a man. "Tracy!" Like, she'd totally ghosted me for Darren, and here I was, greeting her like a neglected puppy.

She hurried to catch up to me. "What's up, girl?"

"Not much. What's up with you?"

I greeted her in our usual fashion. A stupid greeting we'd used since we were in middle school together. At this moment, she wanted to know if we were still cool or if I was going to call her out for dumping me. My response told her I was still the lonely pushover waiting for my only friend to return to me, like always.

And yet, it felt great to fall back into our old friendship in just a few words.

"I've missed you," she said as she reached me. "What have you been doing with yourself?"

My shoulder lifted. "Same old, same old. How about you?"

"I moved into the dorms. You were right about Darren. Turned out to be an asshole."

"Darren was beneath you. You deserve so much better. I'm still making the trek home after classes."

Tracy was classically beautiful, and Darren had been too old, with creepy vibes that made my skin crawl every time he spoke to me. Maybe this time it had been a mutual ghosting between us because I couldn't stand to be in Darren's presence for more than a minute.

"Your mom still won't let you move into the dorms? That drive sucks, especially at rush hour. You should come hang out with me till later."

I winced. "I can't. I accidentally answered my dad's call and told him I was driving. He insisted on finding me an apartment today."

Her perfect pouty mouth formed an O. "That's going to piss Mommy Dearest off. But good for you. You need to get out from under her control."

My gut twisted uneasily. Tracy was right, but hearing her talk about my mom like that didn't sit well. Not that I'd ever defend Mom with Tracy. She was the closest thing to a sister I'd ever have. I don't think Mom would ever get over Dad, so the fact that he'd stepped in to help solve my travel problem might make her smash expensive vases like she did when she found out he'd fucked her younger sister. It had been years since the divorce, and Mom was still bitter and ragey about Dad.

"Yeah, I could be fifty-five and it will still be Mom's life mission to control everything I do."

"Sucks to be you, Eden. Well, I've gotta run, but we need to get together sooner rather than later."

She turned toward the dorms, and I continued through the parking lot towards my car, feeling happy that Tracy was back in my life. Losing her friendship had created a vast hole in my soul. Her presence always brought a level of levity to my all too serious life, even if just by a simple text or phone call.

A long, blacked-out limousine pulled up next to me. The window rolled down, and my father leaned out. "Pumpkin."

And there was another of the many holes that riddled my life. I got my red hair, fair skin, and freckles from him, but that's where the similarities ended. My father had charisma that drew people in. Somehow, I never inherited that from him. I never learned how to be the life of the party, nor did I want to be the center of attention.

I stopped walking and plastered a smile on my face. "Hey, Daddy. What are you doing here?"

His driver put the car in park and got out to open the door for me as I came over. "Don't you remember? You agreed to go apartment hunting with me today after class."

I glanced around campus, red-faced, before jumping in the limo. It wasn't like I'd actually know anyone who might be watching. I just didn't want to be noticed any more than I already was. Maybe I *was* shy, like my mom always told people. She had made lots of excuses for me when I was a kid, even when those excuses never felt true.

"I remember. I just thought we'd meet at the places."

But Dad had a specific place in mind and was chattering about how hard it had been to talk the owner of the condo into renting it out. Dad loved a challenge, and his charm and money were hard to deny.

The condo was within walking distance of campus. Dad got out of the car and immediately met the agent at the secure parking area. I acted interested in the assigned space for the condo, but my gaze strayed up the side of the four-story building.

The building was pretty new, but somehow kept the architectural charm of old St. Pete. The agent explained that the owner built the condos in the early two thousands, and they had just gone through another series of renovations.

The interior halls were cramped but felt secure as we walked past a few doors decorated for fall.

The agent used a key to unlock the deadbolt but stepped back to allow my dad to enter first. I gave the man a shy smile as Dad exclaimed, "Get in here, Eden Bean. Check out the view."

I hated that nickname as much as I hated being called pumpkin. It reminded me of a time when I was taller than my classmates. Tall, fat, and awkward. I had worked hard to move past that stage of my life.

Dad threw back the drapes, and light flooded the coastal decorated living room.

"Wow. That *is* a great view," I deadpanned as my gaze traveled the small furnished living room. The view was of the other side of the horseshoe-shaped complex. Each condo had a small balcony that overlooked the pool area. The balcony had good lighting, and I imagined spending hours out there drawing or reading.

"Does the furniture come with it?" I glanced at the agent who lingered in the entryway.

"It was originally a vacation rental. So, the owner would like to keep it furnished as is."

Dad faced me from the small balcony. "You won't have to lug furniture up the stairs." He gave me his classic winning grin that took me back to when he had actually attempted to have a relationship with me after the divorce. It was the same grin he used when he'd tell me we'd go sailing next weekend.

The agent interjected, "There's an elevator at the front of the building." He eyed me carefully as he spoke, noting every roll that might cause me to want to take the elevator instead of the stairs. I folded my arms around myself and pretended not to feel his judgment.

Turning towards the kitchen, I said, "I like the open floor plan."

The kitchen opened onto the living room. One bathroom was in the hallway across from the second bedroom and the master was located towards the back. It had everything I needed already. But best of all, Mom wasn't here to loom over me at every turn.

"What do you think, Eden?"

A huge smile split my face. "It's perfect."

He turned to the agent. "Then we'll take it."

The door opened across the hall, and an older lady with a mole on her nose peeked her head out, holding a tiny yapping dog. The agent greeted her and then introduced me as her new, longer-term neighbor.

Her gaze was guarded, but Mrs. Bennett smiled, showing me a mouthful of crooked teeth and introduced me to her little dog. "This is Prince Charming."

I laughed and did a little curtsy. "A pleasure, Mr. Charming."

The dog, a mixed breed chihuahua, started barking at me, which created a small chorus of high-pitched yapping from inside her condo. Mrs. Bennett put a pudgy hand over his tiny muzzle to quiet him. "He says nice to meet you."

From the glare in Prince Charming's bulging eyes, I believed Mrs. Bennett was mistaken about what her little ankle-biter was saying. More like *nice to eat you*. I immediately liked her.

I waited in the limo as my dad spoke to the agent outside. The condo wasn't big, but the parking area was almost empty. Either everyone who lived here worked, or most of the condos were vacation rentals like mine.

The driver opened the door, and my dad got in. "It's all set. The owner is a business associate of mine, and offered his place the moment he found out you were going to college here."

On the drive back to campus to pick up my car, he handed me the keys to the condo. "Most of the amenities have an access code. I'll text that to you when I get them."

"Amenities?" I felt dumb for not asking sooner.

"There's a laundry on the main floor near the pool. You'll need a key card for the gate and the gym."

"Oh, cool."

He fished out his wallet and used two fingers to slip me a black credit card. "I paid your rent through the end of the school year. It includes power, garbage, and water, but you'll need to pay for the internet, your food and other essentials."

I took the card as guilt snaked through my gut. "I'm looking for a job."

He shrugged. "Look, I know you wanted to be the next Picasso. I'm happy you decided on graphic arts, but that's a difficult career to break into and keep the lifestyle you are accustomed to."

My spine stiffened. "You mean *Mom's* accustomed to. I don't need much to be happy, Dad."

He looked suitably abashed. "I know, honey. Do you want me to call her and tell her you're moving?"

My eyes popped as dread gut-punched me. My knee stopped bouncing. "No." I threw my hand out. "Lord, no. I'll tell Mom."

We would fight about it, but she'd be less violent without Dad's help. I dreaded telling her, but a part of me was also excited about the confrontation to come. Was today the day I stood up to her? Would I find my voice and tell her she should have treated me better when she had the chance?

The car pulled up behind my old Honda, and I reached for the door.

Dad said, "I'm sorry."

I turned my flood of confusion to him. "For what?"

He lifted a shoulder. "For the way I handled things with your mom. For letting her push me out of your life. I hope we can spend more time together now that you have your own place."

I took a fortifying breath. "Sure, Dad and thank you... for this."

"See you again soon?" he asked with a hopeful smile on his handsome face.

"Yeah, absolutely. Call me." Because I'd never call him. I no longer possessed the emotional capacity to love him as a dad again. Not after he abandoned me to deal with the messy state he left my mother in. Seeing him today reminded me that if I didn't change my emotional direction, I'd end up as distant as he was when I was a child. The only difference would be he had the money to toss at his problems, I didn't.

The driver opened my door, and I fled one uncomfortable scene for one I dreaded even more. I had a forty-five minute drive home to imagine every scenario with my mother. My heart pounded and a fine sheen of sweat wet my brow when I pulled into the driveway.

The second I opened the door of my childhood home, my mother said, "You're late."

I kept moving even as she followed. "I got an apartment close to campus."

"I've been calling you." She paused. "You what?"

"I'm moving out. I can't do this drive anymore." *I can't do* this *anymore.*

I got my height from my mother, but she seemed to grow taller as I faced her in the hall outside my bedroom of twenty-two years.

Her hands went to her hips. "How in the hell are you going to afford an apartment?" We've had this argument a thousand times since I started college.

I stepped back and put my hand on the door. She hadn't hit me in years, but that didn't mean she wouldn't slap me now. "I've got it covered, Mom. It's all settled and taken care of. I'm moving out this weekend." Guilt grew with every word I spoke, blooming feverishly on my face with every word.

Her eyes narrowed into suspicious slits. "I know who covered you. He's great at covering women. If you think Dan's going to swoop in and be the caring dad that he should have been all your life, you're going to be sorely disappointed, Eden."

My face had always been transparent, even though I held my tongue. I closed the door slowly because in her state, even a normal door shutting might be mistaken for a slam. "I know, Mom."

"You'll be back. He won't keep his promises. He never does."

The door clicked softly as mom took her tirade down the hall to the living room. She was probably on her way to find her phone so she could scream at his voicemail. He never answered her calls, but Aunt Mandy would. And Mom would continue to punish her younger sister for seducing my dad while I hid in my room like always.

Today was not the day I stood up for myself.

Logan

Logan Lurch

My phone chimed, and I automatically pushed away from my wall of monitors to give it my full attention. The caller ID told me it was one of my Blue-Frosted Rose brothers.

"Hello." It wasn't really a question.

"Hey, Lur..." He cleared his throat, and rethought calling me Lurch. He started over. "Logan. It's Dan McKenzie." Him not calling me Mr. Dalton had been a minor slight. We might be society brothers, but we were not on a first name basis.

"Yep."

There was a pause, but Dan got the message and jumped right into the reason for the call. "Hey, ya, my daughter is moving into Sam's place. Three-B? She goes to college in St. Pete. Can you keep an eye on her for me?"

I spun back to my computer, found Dan's file, and moved it to the center monitor.

"Eden?" I asked as I opened the file. Dan was one of my local BFR brothers and we had met a time or two over the years, but he was not what I'd call a friend.

"Yeah, she won't be any trouble. She's an introverted artist—"

"Yeah, I got her." The program I created to safeguard the BFR daughters online was feeding me all the information I needed about her. I rarely needed to open the files unless there was a disappearance or kidnapping. Powerful enemies of Society members posed a risk of exploiting children for ransom or blackmail. Because our members were prominent members of society, we were extra careful with our loved ones.

"Thanks, man. I appreciate it. She's been sheltered, and I worry about her out there alone."

"No problem. I'll keep eyes on her."

I hung up on the man, who was still lamenting about his precious little girl. Lord, these dads would go on and on about how special their daughters were if I let them. Spoiled and privileged, these girls had fathers that were unaware of their online activities until mistakes were made and I revealed the truth.

Online, Eden was just like all the rest of them. Typical girly Google searches about hair and makeup tips. She'd had two fairly recent cyber-attacks that the program stopped. I clicked on the sub-folder and opened another window on a separate monitor. I fed the information into my database of known threats and let it run as I browsed our girls' porn history.

She thought going incognito on her phone would keep this shit a secret. A BFR daughter didn't have secrets. I found nothing but the usual bullshit. Eden enjoyed men who talk dirty. She masturbated to mostly ASMR stuff on Pornhub.

I closed her file as the database found a match. A small local group that specialized in trafficking teenagers. Small but bold. They attempted to contact her twice. Even after my program wiped her information off their server.

Being bold put them on my radar. My long fingers skipped over the keyboard as I duplicated her online profile and shoved it in their face. If they have the balls to contact the redhead again, I'll set them up and forward the trap to my contact at the sheriff's office. Hal would take it from there and put these guys in jail, where they belong. People who preyed on the vulnerable deserved what they got.

I moved Eden's information into priority mode, so I'd be notified immediately if she did anything outside her normal routine. I blew up her profile photo and sat back to study it. There was a light in her blue-gray eyes that made me wonder about the person behind the camera. Who made her smile like that? Or was

Eden just an outgoing girl who looked at everyone with that bright curiosity?

The girl didn't have a lot of photos of herself on her profile. Most of the pictures were of things. The buildings, flowers and faces she found interesting and a few drawings she must have done.

Daddy said she was an artist. He wasn't wrong. The girl had a way of bringing life to her sketches. A quick check revealed her major was graphic arts with a marketing minor.

"Condo Three-B," I drawled.

My gaze went to the hardwood floors at my feet.

I'd better get busy.

I lifted the hood on my lightweight shirt, shouldered my bag of goodies, and grabbed the thick ring of keys from the peg as I left the penthouse to go to the stairs.

The Blue-Frosted Rose Society owned this entire city block, but this building was my responsibility. Not the day-to-day maintenance. They employed people for that. I just lived here and ran the unseen security.

My footsteps were stealthy as I moved down the empty hall. We only had ten percent occupancy, but Mrs. Bennett had four little dogs who'd pop off at the slightest noise. She was the last person I wanted to chat with. My key to Three-B was ready by the time I stopped at Eden's new residence.

It was Saturday morning, and she'd be moving in today, so I didn't have time to waste. The dogs across the hall never heard a thing as I opened the door and flipped on the lights.

We had surveillance in the common areas of the building, but I needed more than the usual for this girl. When I gave my word to put eyes on someone for a brother, I never failed.

I owed my life to the Blue-Frosted Rose Society. When Mr. Dalton found me, I was in juvie, on my way to jail after I'd attempted to murder my biological father. I was fourteen, and my dad had been awarded custody, again, by the state after losing me when I was a child.

I touched the scars that marred the right side of my face and forever ruined my vision after his second attempt at killing me. Contacts helped my impaired vision in my right eye.

Drugs took my mother, and my dad had been going through a "rough spot." At only two years of age, I don't remember the neglect that caused our first separation. But the pain, fear, and betrayal of that second time never left me.

I moved from room to room, putting up my hidden cameras. They were the best money could buy. She'd never find them. She'd never know she was being watched, not even in the bathroom.

The foster system did me good. Sure, I had some issues. I learned a lot of things kids never should, but mostly, I only encountered good people. But the state believed in second chances and my father jumped through their hoops to win me back when I turned twelve. It was good for a while, but things gradually went downhill, and I don't believe in giving people a third chance. Life wasn't baseball, and the bastard had tried to kill me first.

I screwed the air vent back into place in her bedroom as my phone alerted me that someone pulled into the parking lot below. The hidden cameras were overkill. I already had this place on lockdown, but I liked watching.

I collected my gear and headed to the door. Slipping out on silent feet, I locked up and hurried to the stairs just as the elevator doors opened and Eden stepped out carrying a box.

Grayish blue eyes lifted and widened as I jerked my chin away from her to hide the hideous side of my profile.

"Oh, hello."

Her cheerful voice almost made me turn back to her and offer to carry her box, but the less she saw of me, the better. I grunted a response that made me cringe internally as I swung open the door to the stairs and retreated to my lair.

Her offended voice followed me up the stairs. "Okay, so not all my neighbors are friendly. That's cool. You do you, boo boo."

Fuck, even when she was being snarky, she sounded like a goddamned angel.

I spent the next hour monitoring the surveillance cameras, watching her get settled in as I attempted to do my other work.

My BFR phone rang, and I answered, "Yeah."

"Lurrrrrch," the male voice shouted in my ear, and I pulled the phone away until he finished. Mickey Dalton was just about the only person who could get away with calling me that to my face. After his father rescued me from juvie, he became my brother in more ways than one.

He continued enthusiastically. "You prepared for the Dionysus ritual tomorrow night?"

"You know I am," I rumbled back immediately. Who would miss the chance of having an entire congregation of freaks lick honey off their dick?

"I hear you're babysitting Dan's brat. You gotta let me know if the carpet matches the drapes."

I glanced at my muted cameras. The girl was in the bedroom, putting her clothes in the closet as she danced to silent music. "She's a natural redhead, Mick. I'm sure it does."

He gave an impressed, "Damn," and then continued, "her daddy is going to be there tomorrow."

I smiled at the image of Dan kneeling before me, mouth open and ready to receive. This job had its perks.

"And you?" I asked Mickey.

"Fuck, yeah. Judy is going to try to fit that anaconda you sport all the way down her throat."

I laughed. "Good luck to her."

He mirrored my chuckle. “I don’t know. She’s been training for this ritual. Hey, gotta run. I’ll see you tomorrow.”

Judy was my brother's long-term girlfriend. Mickey wasn’t the type to settle for just one woman, but he recently talked about bringing her into the society. She would have to be special for him to make a commitment like that.

“Yep.”

He wouldn’t see me tomorrow because I’d be sequestered until the ritual, and then I’d be covered from head to toe in robes and a hood. The only skin needed for this ritual hung between my legs.

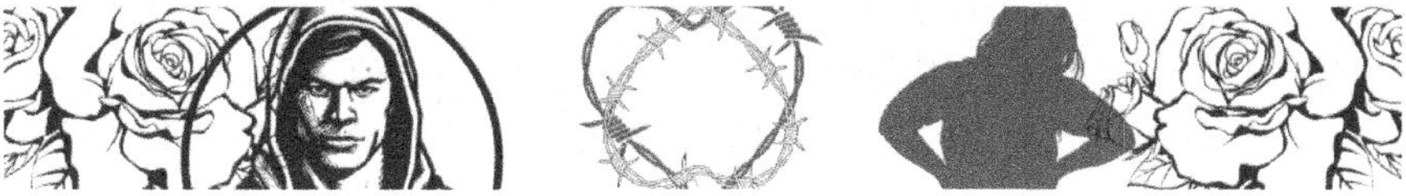

Chapter Two

Freedom

Eden

My very own place. Funny how four paltry words created a hurricane of conflicted emotions inside me. Excitement gave way to a sense of being grown. Adulting gave way to fear of failure. Fear conjured my mother's disapproving voice. *The cutlery is mismatched.*

A huge grin took over my face. "The cutlery is mismatched!" I cringed at my loud voice, but my mother wasn't there to yell at me for having a big mouth.

The grin gave way to giggles as I danced around the kitchen holding a single teaspoon in both hands. "Mismatched and big mouthed," I sang out tunelessly as I skipped in circles in the small kitchen.

I had an enormous mouth, thanks to my father's side, but there was no one here to point that out.

"Freedom."

The way I said that tickled an ancient memory, though I couldn't recall anything but the tune. I pulled out my phone, and after a quick search, I found the old song by George Michael that soothed the itch.

I put it on blast as I finished unpacking. The lyrics of the song spoke to me so much that I set the tune on repeat as I learned it. I got distracted and went down the internet rabbit hole only to learn that George Michael had died, but he had written this song as an autobiography of sorts in the early nineties.

The lyrics had a different meaning for him than they did for me, but I felt a connection with the man through his words. I hoped he lived as his authentic self before he passed away and I vowed I'd find my authenticity as I made my way in this world.

The light had faded, and it was Saturday night in St. Petersburg. There was no one here to shame me for what I was about to do as I got ready to hit the local food scene. I put on some light makeup and twisted my mess of hair into a ponytail.

Maybe I would have a beer, too.

It wasn't as if I had to drive anywhere, but comfortable walking shoes were a must when prowling downtown St. Pete.

I pulled out my phone in a sudden urge to call Tracy to see what she was doing tonight, but my phone listed several missed calls from my mother. She had even left a voicemail.

My stomach felt heavy as I debated with myself. Should I listen to the voicemail or just call her back for the live version? I *had* promised to call her to check in.

I tucked the phone back in my bag as I entered a Mexican restaurant. My mother was best dealt with on a full stomach.

An hour later, I headed back to my new home feeling like an adult for the first time in my life. Like I finally made something of myself, but my brain reminded me with a sinking feeling that daddy paid for the condo and my dinner tonight with that little black card he'd given me. While I appreciated everything he'd done for me, I wondered if I'd ever be able to escape the safety net he'd designed for my life.

I was completely deflated as I entered the alley behind the building. Even though it was darker than I expected back here, I straightened my spine and kept going.

First off, no one kidnapped big girls like me, and I was pretty confident that I could fight off a dark alley attacker.

Something scurried through the overgrowth ahead of me, and my heart stopped as my brain conjured images of an oversized rat attacking me.

Bad men? Not scary at all. Florida alley rats? Absolutely terrifying.

I hurried towards the streetlight at the corner of the building but jerked to a stop the moment I rounded it.

I almost screamed as a group of ten feral cats scattered in every direction as my sudden appearance startled them as much as they frightened me. Cats didn't scare me. It was the image of a million rabid rats that my fearful brain flashed at me before I realized they were cats.

An ominous figure stood up by the dumpster, and my hand flew to my mouth. He was holding a can of cat food in one hand as he frowned and scowled at me from under his hood. Sure, it was October, but it was still too early to be wearing a hoodie in Florida.

The light cut across his mouth and chin in such a way that it shadowed the upper part of his face but accented the features of his mouth, jawline, and Adam's apple. He was older than me; in his thirties, if I were to take a guess.

This must be my tall, grumpy neighbor from earlier.

My tension eased, but only slightly. This man's energy was full of annoyance and contempt.

"I, ah, just moved in." I pointed to the building like a fool. "We, uh, I saw you earlier by the elevator. Remember?"

The guy was menacing, but not creepy. Well, maybe he was a bit creepy, too, but from what I saw of him, he was interesting to look at. His jawline had a royal cut, but his pursed lips curved into a disapproving frown that seemed all wrong. I longed to see his eyes so I could confirm the emotions I felt from the rest of his face. He had a Roman nose, and his chin had a dimple, though I didn't know if it was because of the frown or if it was just the way he was built. Maybe it was a scar that divided his chin.

He just continued staring at me. He was so still, my gaze moved to his shoulders and chest to check that he was breathing. And tall guys shouldn't be built like this man. He wasn't bulky by any means, but unless he was wearing multiple layers under that hoodie on a humid evening, he wasn't rail thin either.

That was why I stared at him much longer than I should have.

Mr. Grumpy Pants clearly wasn't in the mood to chat, and the longer we stared at each other, the more foolish I felt.

I waved at the empty and partially eaten cans of cat food that were strewn around the dumpster. "Sorry, I disturbed your cats' dinner."

I practically ran for the entrance of the building, and I didn't stop when his deep, gravelly voice came across the distance I put between us.

"Not my cats."

My fingers shook so badly I had to enter the code for the back door twice before it unlocked.

They were still trembling when I decided to skip my mother's voicemails and just call her directly.

She picked up on the first ring. "Finally! What, are you too good to pick up your mother's phone calls now?"

"Sorry, my ringer was on silent, and I wasn't paying attention." I was grateful for all the excuses my mind was delivering.

"I left several messages, Eden. I was about to call the police to see if you were arrested."

"Why would I get arrested, Mom?"

Her answer was snappy. "I don't know Eden, you tell me."

"Mom, I know you're worried that I'm going to go wild like you did when you were in college, but I'm not you. You were popular, and I've got one friend." I tried to sound as reassuring as I could, but it sounded whiny even to my ears.

"Tracy's mom called me, and she's not answering her mother's calls, either."

"I'm sure she's fine, too, Mom."

Her voice took on a mocking tone. "Oh, of course she's fine. She's popular and lives in the dorm. You do not know what life is like there, Eden. You belong at home with me."

"Mom, I can't live at home forever, and that drive was downright dangerous."

"Whatever, Eden. The next time I call you, you had better answer. I don't care where you're at or who you're with."

"Mom, I can't pick up the phone in the middle of class."

"If you want to keep living there, you will. Ignore me again, and I'll jerk you out of that apartment so fast it will make your head spin." And there was the threat. While she couldn't cancel the rental she could cut me off completely until I returned home. My dad might support me financially, she was all I had emotionally.

"Okay, Mom. I'll pick up when you call."

"Fine. Now, I've gotta go. Check in tomorrow night, so I know you haven't been murdered."

"I will not get murdered, Mom. I love you, bye."

"I love you, too."

I let out a long breath and released the tension out of my shoulders. I needed to unpack my books and settle in with a smutty, action-packed comfort read.

Escapism was my primary coping mechanism, and dark romance was my escape of choice. Sometimes I needed to lose myself in a story that made me feel more than just guilt, inadequacy, and shame. I longed to feel that giddy feeling of falling in love, even if the primary love interest wasn't the nicest guy, or even real.

Logan

Logan Lurch

I woke early for a Sunday and headed downstairs to the on-site gym. Most of the few permanent residents were retired BFR members and their families. Sundays were for lazy mornings and Bloody Mary breakfasts at the poolside bar, so I had the workout equipment all to myself.

I yanked off my hoodie and forced myself to look at the mirror as I stretched. Focusing only on my form, I silenced my brain every time it wanted to chat with me about my flaws. If I let it, my mind would lament about how worthless I was. It would scoff at the lean muscle I'd worked so hard to build and replace the image in the mirror with the skinny, gawky kid I used to be.

You'll be nothing but this worthless, weak victim who still bears the scars as proof.

That was bullshit, I thought, as I moved to floor exercises like push-ups, planks, and sit-ups. I'd survived my father's abuse not once, but twice, and the last time I hadn't been weak. This skinny, gawky kid had fought back and won.

Sure, but where did that get you?

It got me here. Gave me status. It got me my last name. I became a Dalton.

They never really accepted you, Lurch.

I never really accepted *them*. As hard as Mr. Dalton tried to get me the help I desperately needed and included me in his family, I never actually embraced him, and now he's dead and his sons are scattered and living their own lives. Todd, the youngest Dalton, was married with a child. He was going to be the most powerful man in BFR.

You'll never find anyone willing to marry and breed with you.

Now that was true. I just wasn't made for family. I didn't have the emotional capacity back then, and now I enjoyed the freedom of being single too much to change.

It wasn't until I moved to the weights that I realized I wasn't alone anymore. Eden was already on the treadmill, power walking. My face tightened as unease spread through my body. I wanted to work out alone, not with some kid gawking at me.

I resisted the urge to put my hoodie back on. It was too late to hide my face. Besides, the way she kept glancing at me before jerking away told me she'd already seen more of me than I was comfortable with.

She looked like she was the one who wanted to hide from *my* eyes. She had twisted her red hair in a messy bun, and it was already darker at her temples with sweat.

I turned away, deciding to mind my own business, and went back to my workout.

How long had I been in my head?

The music blasting in my ears was the reason I hadn't heard her come in, but the fact that I didn't sense or even see her told me I'd lost the battle to keep my brain's negativity at bay.

Had she spoken to me when she came in?

Had I just been sitting there, lost in my own world as I ignored her?

Well, you are that creepy guy, Lurch.

I added another weight, just for that thought, and got to lifting. I was on good terms with my alter ego. Lurch was the big bad wolf. He'd do the shit the loner Logan wouldn't dare do.

Need your cheating wife taught a lesson? Lurch was your man. He'd snatch her coming out of the salon you paid for, drug her, and wait patiently in the dark for her to wake up naked in the BFR dungeon next to the man she cheated on her husband with. Three days with Lurch, she'd run back home to her husband, feeling blessed to still be alive.

The man, not so much. You didn't fuck with the Blue-Frosted Rose Society and live to talk about it.

My brain happily served up an unending supply of faces in various states of torture, rape, and death. All the terrible things I've done for my secret society. Instead of shame, my dick thickened from the memories.

Realizing I was back inside my head, I glanced at Eden, who had moved to the stair climbing machine. She was huffing, puffing, and sweating, but her gaze was locked on the front of my workout shorts. I wasn't even fully erect, but the comfortable shorts couldn't hide much, even when soft.

I tried to ignore her gaze as I switched my position to focus on another group of muscles, but her eyes kept prickling my skin as she traced the lines of my body with them.

Eventually, I pulled my earbuds out and glared at her. "You know, if I wanted to be gawked at while I worked out, I'd go to a popular gym."

Her eyes popped wide as she jerked with surprise at my voice. "I'm sorry. I wasn't staring." Her brows scrunched together as she turned the machine off and reached for her towel. "Well, I guess I was, but honestly, I didn't see anything."

She wiped the sweat from her face and met my gaze once more. It impressed me that she didn't lock onto the right side of my face with a horrified expression.

My lips turned up. "I find that hard to believe."

Her gaze flicked down to my shorts and widened before jerking towards the door. "Well, at least I'm not the creep who gets sexually aroused watching himself workout in the mirror."

She snatched up her gym bag and bolted towards safety as a laugh left me.

Was that what she thought I was doing? My laughter continued as the door slammed shut. She thought I was so vain that I wanted to fuck myself while I worked out. I was amused as I finished my workout. I wiped the sweat off the gym equipment and myself before donning my shirt and lifting the hood.

Stepping out in the pool area, I donned my sunglasses, and my good eye found Eden in the pool, doing laps. She was wearing a very modest one-piece swim dress that looked like it belonged on one of the senior citizens lounging by the bar waiting for it to open, not a twenty-two-year-old siren like Eden.

I understood society, especially the BFR extended family, bestowed body issues on beautiful young women, but that swim dress was hideous and did nothing for her but billow and frump. I wanted to see her in a two piece that rose high on her hips to accentuate her round ass.

She popped up and wiped the pool water out of her eyes before she saw me. Her face transformed into a stern glare. "Now, who's staring?"

My lips twisted up, and I lowered my shades to give her a good look at my eyes. "Me. I'm staring."

The glare fell off her face, and I added, "I like what I see, and I'm not afraid to say so, unlike some."

Her pretty mouth fell open with shock as I pushed my glasses back into place and walked away.

"Creep."

I tried to ignore her parting shot, but now that we had dialogue, I had to own the last word. "Careful little angel, you don't want to summon a demon with that pretty little mouth." I turned so she could see my smirk. "You might find it full of regret."

There was something about this girl that made me want to rise to her challenge. Show her what happened to little girls who got too mouthy. She really needed to tread lightly with me or she might just meet Lurch in that dark alley behind the building.

Chapter Three

Honeyed Lips

Logan

While I looked forward to tonight's Dionysus ceremony at the church in North Tampa, I never enjoyed going out in public during the day. It was my misgiving to endure the wide eyed stares and whispered comments, but I steeled myself to endure the humiliation for the payoff later.

I never forgot to pull my light hood over my ball-capped, unruly waves and slide on my sunglasses to veil my face before opening the door to my apartment. I ducked through the threshold and used the key to lock the deadbolt.

Anyone who dared break in and lie in wait for my return would live the rest of their lives with nightmares if they got away. I patted the nine-millimeter stuffed in my pants at the small of my back. I wasn't just ugly; I was dangerous when provoked.

I took the stairs down the four floors to the ground because my neighbors wouldn't love being alone in the elevator with me. I was faster than the elevator anyway, and my ride was waiting out front.

"Watch it!" A female voice snapped as I burst out of the side door, narrowly missing the young blonde woman with the heavy door. Her lips parted in a silent *oh* as her gaze lifted up my body. Her eyes widened when they landed on my face in the shadow of my hood.

I turned away to hide the hideous scars that deformed my profile even though I wanted to question the young stranger as to why she was entering my building through the side door. She was around Eden's age, and since she had the passcode, I assumed it was a friend of hers.

"Pardon me," my baritone voice rasped as I sidestepped her and hurried to the awaiting car so she didn't have to endure my presence any longer than necessary. I felt her shocked stare burn my back all the way across the parking lot. A quick glance confirmed she had gotten a good look at my ugly mug. Her hand was still on her delicate throat as she gawked at the open door.

The driver of the stretch limo opened the door for me. "Good morning, sir."

"Good morning, Pilot," I rumbled with ease. Pilot wasn't his real name. It was a code name given to all our most trusted drivers. The Society did this with all our service providers to maintain their privacy. A Pilot wasn't a full member of the Blue-Frosted Rose Society, instead they were trusted employees.

This Pilot had seen all of me and wasn't fazed by my appearance anymore. He had been my driver for the past ten years. He eyed me from the rearview mirror as he shut the driver's side door. "Excited for the ceremony tonight?"

"I'm always happy to serve Dionysus."

"As I'm sure he is happy to receive your offering."

Once a year, I took part in this ceremony at our church in Tampa. This was by far my favorite of the many jobs I did for the Blue-Frosted Rose. The other jobs sometimes required violence, and my alter ego enjoyed that part a little too much.

I liked playing the big, dumb monster they called Lurch. To be able to let go and embody the beast inside could be cathartic. Sometimes the job required giving someone a beat down, and other times it was a dick down. But this wasn't a job, it was a perk of brotherhood.

Today, they provided me with a feast, washed and purified my body with gentle hands, massaged, and oiled me down before the priest blessed me.

The feminine hands of a veiled priestess helped arrange the deep purple robe I wore. Her delicate fingers found the hole at the front, and she reached in to grab my junk as I fit the belt around my hips.

"Oh!" Her exclamation was of soft discovery as she revealed my cock and balls.

Settling the porcelain mask over my face, I glanced down at her through the slits. She leaned back and stared at my dick.

"It's huge."

I inhaled. "Not always a blessing," I mumbled.

She secured the sides of my robe to my thighs with the built-in ties. "Well, you're definitely not a grower."

"Just wait," I said as I plucked the cock ring - a circle of tiny white and yellow flowers - off the table beside me. Working my dick and balls through it, I continued, "It grows, too."

She immediately arranged the flowers on the cock ring to her liking as my dick thickened and filled.

I lifted a sheet of fine silver mesh from the table, and she helped me attach it between the flowers, so that it draped over my bare balls. My cock grew harder the more she grazed it.

"Let me guess. Twelve inches?"

A breathy laugh left me as she picked up the ceremonial bowl of honey and the brush used to coat my tip. "Maybe, if you measure from underneath." My cock was intimidating for a lot of women and a few men but twelve wasn't quite my number.

She dipped the brush in the honey and firmly took hold of my shaft as she painted the cool, sticky fluid on my tip. The texture of the paintbrush was amazing, and it made me think of the paintbrushes Eden had unpacked as she set up her art area next to the balcony yesterday.

"I've heard stories about you."

"Good or bad?"

The priestess leaned in and placed a kiss on the tip of my dick, coating her lips in honey and sending a thrill of sensation coursing through it. "Both."

She stood up and pressed her palms together. "You've strayed too far from yourself, Logan Dalton. It's why the voices in your head are haunting you. Come back to church and I'll help you silence those voices."

Before I could ask her how she knew about the voices in my head, the door opened and a high feminine voice from behind me said, "They are ready for you, blessed one."

I put the crown of silver ivy on my head and lifted the oversized hood before turning to face the voice.

I watched the girl's pretty eyes widen slightly as the priestess, with honey-covered lips, said, "He's ready." She pressed a pinecone-tipped staff into my right hand and a silver chalice of milk into the other.

My dick was the grand star of the evening as they guided me into the chapel. Instead of pews, our church had elaborate cushions, low beds, and sex furniture.

Bodies in various stages of costume and undress undulated and stretched toward me as they chanted a prayer to the Olympian god of wine, pleasure, and wild frenzy.

My cock grew harder as I followed the priestess towards the altar where the priest led the prayer. The space was already filled with the god's powerful unseen presence. His magic crackled over my flesh as I felt his attention on me.

Hours of meditation and preparation made me a vessel for him to fill. He was pleased as he rushed into me.

My spine stiffened, and hands supported me as my steps faltered. I swayed and moaned as immense mystical pleasure filled me. I tilted the mask down as a member of the congregation brushed against my dick. It was so swollen with excitement it was almost painful, swaying in the cool air with every step.

A large Saint Andrew's cross stood in front of the podium, where the priest continued his chanting prayer. Two men standing on either side of the cross pressed my back against the cool padded wood as the congregation lined up around the room. My arms, hips, thighs, and legs were secured tight as a priestess painted more thick, sticky honey on my throbbing tip.

Mickey was the first of a hundred and fifty worshipers. He dipped down and pressed his lips against me before straightening to watch Judy, his pretty girlfriend, grip my shaft and angle my tip to her mouth. This would be uncomfortable and taboo for a normal man. Mickey was a brother, my brother, but he was far from normal. We'd been raised in the world of sexual excess and pagan rituals.

I caught the gleam in his eye as she stretched her lips over my tip. He was a voyeur, and she loved to perform for him. I had been part of their dynamic many times over the years.

Her hot mouth encompassed and compressed me as she slid my length deeper into her throat. My stomach muscles rippled as I pressed my hips forward against the restraints when she inched back.

My eyes closed as she dipped deep once more, and I felt the back of her throat press against my tip.

My blood thrummed in my ears as I felt the Olympian god sing blessings on this fine woman, taking my length into her throat. He wouldn't allow me to orgasm until he felt the lips of every member here, but my balls tightened under the mesh finery decorating them anyway.

She pulled off with a gasp and took Mickey's arm. The way he gazed at her as they moved to drink the milk from the chalice and receive their blessing from the priest put an ache in my chest. If a sadist like my brother could find love, surely there was a chance for me, too.

The priestess gently dried my aching dick and prepared it with fresh honey for the next member in line. The paintbrush's texture gliding over my cock drove me to the edge of insanity. Especially when I imagined Eden under that veil, painting me for the next in line.

It was a stupid fantasy. A girl like Eden would never paint my cock for others to worship. Dan hadn't raised her to be a BFR lady. She wouldn't want to share someone she loved. She didn't belong here, and she could never love the likes of me.

And this is what the priestess meant by me straying from the fold. The small grounding rituals I learned years ago hadn't stopped working. I just stopped doing them. So I forced my mind back to the here and now and silenced the negativity in my brain. Tomorrow, after I recuperated from being a vessel for a god, I'd restart my spiritual journey with some mindful rituals and prayer.

I opened my eyes after silencing the negative thought and saw that the line moved quickly.

Most merely kissed the tip and moved on, but there were always a few who challenged Dionysus's control by attempting to bring me to orgasm. To my surprise, it was Dan and Mandy who came the closest to tempting the god who possessed me.

Mandy was a lovely tall blonde who turned to her partner and asked, "Will you take him in your ass for me tonight, my love?"

Eden's dad met her loving gaze and nodded slowly. "If that is Dionysus's will."

His brown eyes lifted to my mask, and my head nodded my consent even though I knew I would be on my way home after my brief appearance tonight. The congregation wanted Dionysus, not Logan. Once I orgasmed, he'd leave me, and I'd be special no more.

They bent together, and each took a side of my flared tip for a long, lingering kiss that wrenched a groan from my chest.

A tongue flicked seductively against the sensitive underside. I lifted to my toes at the pleasure swirling through my gut. My cock leaked some precum as I swore under my breath. My balls craved release. I was on the edge of explosion only to have the fuse magically stomped out over and over. It was a particular torture I loved to both inflict and endure.

Mandy swiped a finger through the bead of precum as she rose. She lifted her hand high in triumph as my cock was cleaned and more honey painted on it.

The priest announced, "A small blessing from our most beloved god!"

A cheer rose from the congregation. It wasn't the full blessing of an orgasm, but even precum meant their devotion excited the god. The full explosion belonged to the priest tonight.

When the last of the congregation had coated their lips with honey and moved on, the priest approached me with another priestess, who carried a silver tray with a pair of textured gloves and lube.

The priestess next to me gently removed the decorative flowers and fine mesh as the priest donned the gloves. A clean chalice was held close as his veiled priestess poured a generous amount of lube between his palms.

The cold lube made me jerk as he took hold of my inflamed cock with both hands. His hand stroked up and down my shaft slowly as his voice lifted.

"Oh, we call to thee, Dionysus. Bless us with your pleasure as we enter the frenzy."

The priestess at his side let her robe fall off her shoulders, revealing ample breasts with large, dark nipples. At her lead, the rest of the congregation disrobed, and soft moans filled the large space of the chapel.

I felt the god loosen his hold over my body. A groan left me as the priest twisted the textured glove over my tip, moving faster now. He used both hands as he brought me closer to completion. Pleasure pooled in the base of my spine. My balls tightened as my hands clenched into fists in preparation. Seeing the finish line, the priest began chanting in Latin as he stroked faster.

My toes curled, and my legs shook. I pressed my lips together as I fell off the cliff and sweet bliss erupted through my quaking body. My priestess caught my ejaculate in the ornate chalice as the priest continued to milk me. I fought the bonds as the sensation became too much, but the priest kept stroking me as his assistant poured more lube on my shaft.

"Please... stop..." It was a tight whisper. Barely audible, but I knew my plea fell on deaf ears. I would cum two more times before the ritual could be over.

I knew pleasure came in all types.

A blissful release.

A frenzied orgasm.

And painful madness.

My cock attempted to shrink away from his demanding hands, but the priest wasn't having it and only slowed when it grew once more. His smile was one of triumph. To fail would bring a dark cloud over the rest of the festivities. My stomach muscles tightened and rippled as I jerked and hissed, but the priest drove me hard to my second orgasm.

More lube was applied, and his priestess massaged my balls as I whimpered and pleaded. "No... please... fuck."

Her lubed finger slipped back to massage the space between my balls and anus. I had no control over my body as her finger rimmed my hole. I bucked and jerked as the priest made my overly sensitive dick hard for the third and final time.

"Come on, Logan. You've got this," my priestess encouraged as I lost control of my voice.

The finger rimming my anus pressed hard. "He's tight."

Yeah, because I'm usually the top.

She pressed into me and stroked my prostate.

"Please... Oh gods, please..." I cried out as my aching balls rallied under the priest's demands.

My scream was deafening as my cock kicked, and I exploded a third and final time. I sagged against the restraints as the priest carried his chalice of cum to the podium.

My mask had slipped over my eyes in my struggles, and I only had vision in my right eye, which had been damaged when my father burned me. I could only see blurry bits and pieces of the frenzied orgy happening among the congregation, but the sounds of fucking were loud in my ears.

Two large men pushed forward and unbuckled the restraints, and I adjusted my mask. The priest blessed and then lifted the cup to his lips and let my semen slide into his mouth. His throat bobbed once, twice and a third time before he set the cup down and lifted his robes to reveal his erection to the crowd.

A cheer erupted from the congregation. His priestess fell to her knees and took him in her mouth.

Strong arms supported me as I limped out of the chapel to change and head home.

Eden

Tracy texted me early Sunday to invite me to come see her dorm and meet her friends. They were having a small party, and she wanted me to bring over some wings and a few bottles of rum.

How she knew I had daddy's credit card was like a sixth sense, but I've never been able to say no to her. I just hoped Dan didn't look too closely at the monthly bill as I passed the black card to the girl ringing me up at Hoots Wings. They had the best wings one could want near Downtown St. Pete, and the delicious smell that filled my car had my mouth watering.

It tempted me to drive home, curl up with these wings, and finish the book I'd started reading days ago. Maybe I'd see my mysterious neighbor again and entice him into my home with food. Would these wings be enough to make him happy for once? Or maybe I'd have to entice him in other ways. He did say he liked what he saw when I was swimming. Even though this man was too old for me, I liked what I saw in the gym.

But Tracy would never forgive me for ghosting her, and I really needed to make an effort to keep her close. So I resisted the temptation to hide and drove to the parking garage at the dorms.

I texted Tracy the moment I parked, and she brought two guys down with her to help me carry the food in. Two virile and hot dudes with sexy, muscular arms who appreciated the wings I brought. I was suddenly glad I hadn't gone home. Tracy introduced them as James and Robert as they grinned at me.

I should have eaten before I came, so I wouldn't overeat in front of these guys. I must have cringed as I greeted them, because Robert's brows drew together, and James's smile faltered. *Oh, for fuck's sake.* It didn't matter how many wings I ate, neither man would be interested in me. Not when they had Tracy fawning all over them. I handed them the bags and carried the rum to the dorm.

People crowded the hallway leading to the common room and Tracy seemed to know everyone by name. She greeted them like they were long lost besties and introduced me as her oldest and dearest friend which made me feel important and valued. But my smile felt too shy as I attempted to memorize names to faces while keeping up with her.

I was used to being second fiddle to Tracy's outgoing personality, and she was cool with my introverted ways. When I finally stopped trailing her and found a wall to hold up, it felt natural to both of us.

James kept smiling at me every time I glanced at him. His gaze made me blush. I couldn't seem to get away from him long enough to eat any wings at all.

What would the waitress at Hoots think if I swung by for lunch tomorrow after class? Maybe she wouldn't be working, and I could slip in and out without being noticed as the girl who'd picked up a hundred wings the night before.

I was drinking water to stay sober when James finally approached me.

"Hi," he said as he flashed his pearly whites.

My face heated again but I felt like I kept my cringe internal. "Hi."

He leaned against the wall next to me. "Having fun?"

"I'm not much for crowds."

Tracy had said a small party, but it felt as if everyone who lived here was in attendance.

"Yeah, it can get a little crazy around here at times, but it's not like this every night."

I glanced over at him, and he turned to face me, shoulder pressed against the wall. His presence and confidence were taller than he was, but at least he wasn't shorter than me. My height was always an issue with the opposite sex. Men didn't enjoy looking up at their women, but it wasn't like I was overly tall. Just taller than the average girl. And heavier.

"You go to USF?" he asked with a sexy smirk that had my eyes lingering on his sensual lips.

"Graphic design with a marketing degree."

His smirk transformed back into a smile, and I met the twinkle in his eyes with a blush that no amount of makeup could hide.

"So, you're an artist? Cool. I wish I could draw."

I sipped my water before asking, "What's your major?"

"M.S. in Conservation Biology."

I frowned, and he laughed. "What? I don't look like a biologist to you?"

My mouth formed a cringy grin. "I don't even know what a biologist should look like, so..."

"They all look like me. Ready to change your major yet?"

"Do I look like the type of girl who'd change her major to chase hot guys?"

He shifted against the wall and asked, "You think I'm hot?"

"Don't play dumb. You know you're hot."

He leaned closer. "Tracy says you're her oldest and best friend. I wasn't expecting you to be so damn sexy."

He was lying to me. Not about Tracy; that part was true. The way this guy looked at me made my chest constrict. Awareness narrowed my vision. This guy was too cute for the likes of me, and I couldn't help the suspicion that filtered into my thoughts. James was a stereotypical fuck boy who found what he assumed was an easy target.

"I've gotta go. I have an early class." I could lie too.

I immediately started searching for Tracy, but James took my hand in his. "Don't go just yet."

My body stiffened as his blue eyes pleaded with me to stay. Those eyes held a promise of a wild night that made my heart race.

Would a wild night be worth being used by a man like James? He looked like he knew how to please a girl, but I had been fooled by hot gym guys in the past. Sure they were fit and could thrust, but I rarely got off.

I pressed my red cup into his free hand and said, "No, I gotta go."

I walked away a little taller than I had been when I entered this party. Old Eden would have said, "Okay." She would have let him lead her back to his dorm and take her clothing off as she blushed and crossed her arms over her breasts. She would have accepted the stained sheets he soiled with other girls and let him add her stains to his collection.

Not tonight, dick boy. Adult Eden wanted a man to work for it.

I searched through the crowd and caught a glimpse of blonde hair in a circle of friends. "Hey Trace, I've gotta go. Great party."

She pouted, "Oh no! I haven't had the chance to hang out with you at all tonight."

I grinned. "That's okay. Your boy, James, kept me company." The girls standing around her found James still leaning against the wall where I'd left him. He lifted my red cup with a grin in response and a few of the girls giggled.

I turned back to Tracy. "We'll hang out later." Although I knew it would be a while before Tracy grew bored enough with her new friends to call me, I was okay with that. It had been the nature of our friendship long before college.

I turned back to her. "Oh, and call your mom. She's been talking to mine, and it's causing her to think I've gone wild."

She grinned, and her face became stunning. "Oh, but you have. Hanging out with a boy all night at a dorm party, you bad girl."

I laughed. "Okay, I'm way too sober for this. Gotta go. Bye, girl!"

Tracy turned back to the small group of girls she was hanging with. One girl asked as I walked away, "Didn't she bring the rum?"

Tracy giggled. "She brought it. That's the first step. Getting her to drink it would have been a miracle."

Tracy knew me better than most but hearing her say that made me feel like a prude. I've had a few drinks before. So what if I didn't like getting sloppy drunk? I hated feeling out of control in a crowd. Maybe I *was* a prude, and I should own it.

I parked my car and walked the short distance towards the side entrance of my much quieter new home. The silence soothed my frazzled nerves and I felt grateful that my mother forbade me to move into the dorms at the beginning of the semester. She knew I'd wilt in a communal living arrangement like that.

The stray cats were milling around the dumpster, but Mr. Grumpy wasn't there. For some reason, that upset me as much as it did the cats. Mr. Grumpy wouldn't call me hot. No, he'd say something more truthfully, as he smirked with that look in his eye that made my stomach go all twisty. It would probably be something mean. I'd probably let something cheeky slip out which would make me want to run away and hide. Would he chase me? God that thought made me tingle in low places.

I straightened my shoulders and went inside. Tonight had been an enormous success for me. I went to a party and talked to a cute guy most of the night and refused his advances. I was finally an independent woman.

So why did I feel like I wanted to binge an entire gallon of mint chocolate chip ice cream as I cried and watched sappy movies all night? I couldn't because I didn't have ice cream or cable yet. Instead, I curled up with a sketch pad and drew my feelings until my eyes burned with the need for sleep.

Chapter Four

Reject

Logan

The beginning of the work week had me rubbing my face with the palm of my hand. There had been a few security threats and online rumblings regarding the Blue-Frosted Rose Society that my team dealt with swiftly. It was the nature of people to share incredible experiences. Not everyone got along or agreed with the nature of our secret society. Sometimes people took the rituals too far and feathers got ruffled.

Most of the time, all they needed was a gentle reminder of their vows and a safe avenue to vent and hash out their feelings. Our team was busy deleting correspondence and playing mediator after Sunday night.

The security footage from this morning was playing out on one of my monitors when I noticed Eden leave her condo and head to the elevator. The time stamp in the corner and the way she was dressed told me she wasn't heading to class but to the gym.

Funny. I didn't remember her working out this morning.

I had been in the gym for an hour by the time she opened the door and froze. She backed up but left the door cracked, watching me. At first, I thought she didn't want to interact with me, but the longer she watched through the door, I realized I was wrong.

Sometimes my workouts were merely stretching and lifting, but today I had switched it up with a full-body workout. It started with jumping jacks and skips to get my heart rate up, then moved to squats and lunges before morphing into vigorous burpees. I had been so focused on moving my body to the music blasting in my ears that I hadn't noticed my little stalker watching from the door.

But she watched me for a good thirty minutes before she forewent her own workout in the gym and swam instead. I remembered seeing her in the pool as I crossed the courtyard between buildings. There were more people out there than I wanted to deal with, so I had tugged my hood forward and kept walking. Eyes lingered on me in the footage. People leaned to whisper to each other as they speculated about the hooded man with the scarred face.

The condos were owned by BFR brothers and used mostly to set family members up in relative comfort or as vacation retreats. Few people knew who I was, what I did, and why I lived here, and that's how I preferred it.

I switched the footage to show the interior of Eden's home as I continued to scan through the sea of information my team sent me this morning. She had left her phone on the kitchen counter, and I watched it light up repeatedly as she received multiple messages from someone. It had been the perfect time to install the tracking and recording software.

My lips tightened at the missed opportunity. There would be others, but I did not know who needed her attention so badly that they continuously messaged her. It annoyed me. I wanted to know so damn badly who they were and why they were so demanding of this girl.

Then my phone lit up with a call from her father. I almost let it go to voicemail, but after all the notifications Eden had just received, I picked up.

"Yep."

"Hey... Logan. How are you?"

Dan had that kind of charisma that made people feel like he was their best friend, but I had no friends.

"Your kid is doing fine."

"Oh? That's good. She's a gem. That wasn't the reason I was calling, though."

He paused, waiting for me to ask, but I remained silent because I don't do bullshit banter. He fumbled with the phone but then said, "You left after the ritual Sunday night."

"I always leave after events like that."

He was silent, and I heard Mandy encouraging Dan in the background. "Ask him." Dan shushed her.

"Dan?"

"Yes?"

"Do you want me to fuck you in the ass?"

Dan sucked in a shocked breath at my direct words and flat tone but cleared his throat and said, "We were wondering if you'd like to join us. We'll be in town next week for a few days..."

"No."

Silence stretched on the phone. The type of silence that came with rejecting a man who wasn't used to hearing the word no.

"Why not?"

My hackles rose because I heard, *how can you not be attracted to us considering you're ugly and we are not?* I took a soothing breath, said a silent affirmation and shoved my thoughts aside as my gaze lifted to the video of Eden's bathroom. She was stark naked in the shower, washing her hair, suds gracing her curves.

"I'm not interested in being the third for anything but thank you for asking."

"We just thought... since you were... but you nodded at the ritual." He finally accused me like I had led them on.

"That wasn't entirely me, Dan." I paused and shook my head. "It doesn't matter. The answer is no. Maybe you ought to spend some time with your daughter when you come. She doesn't have many friends and seems a little lonely."

"That's her mother's fault. The bitch is crazy and wouldn't let Eden live her life."

I sighed. "Well, she's trying to live it now."

I hung up the line, not allowing him to come up with any more excuses and explanations.

I fast forwarded the video feed to the current time and found Eden at her desk in the living room by the window. She was hunched over her computer with a textbook spread open as she worked on a project.

A file came through the program from my top enforcer, Bentley. It was coded red. I opened it immediately. A face with hard eyes popped up, along with a brief report. Carl "The Chaos" Dixon was a low-level member of a rough gang that normally haunted central Florida.

So why had he been snooping around our Tampa chapter? Was he connected to the recent security breaches we'd caught? It didn't feel connected. Did we have two threats instead of one?

Bentley had Carl in custody, and my second in command would get the answers we needed.

Eden

Sweet Angel

I worked on my assignments until lunch time. Upon opening my refrigerator, I mumbled to myself, as I removed a left-over box from dinner two nights ago. "I really need to go to the grocery store."

As I transferred the chicken and rice into a bowl and opened the microwave door, I added, "And learn to cook."

This couldn't be difficult to make. It was just rice with veggies and chicken. I was sure I could learn how to handle raw chicken without killing myself with salmonella. Did people really die from that?

The amount of life experience I was prepared for was tiny compared to the people I'd met last night. Tracy's dorm was more adult than I had originally imagined. She even had an espresso maker that she used to make espresso martinis. I'd had a sip and put it down, deciding I wasn't an espresso girl. I wasn't much of a drinker either, even though part of me envied the way others could let go and get smashed without thought of consequences.

Parties just weren't my scene. Tracy called me earlier to tell me she woke up in some random dude's bed and all she can remember is that he ate her ass. My lip had curled. She didn't even catch the guy's name, and he put his tongue on her poop chute. Talk about salmonella. Could one even get that from licking butt holes? Was that even pleasurable?

I wasn't a control freak, but I also didn't want to be that out of control, either.

I picked up my phone and dialed my mother. She had texted like nine times earlier while I was swimming. At least she understood

I couldn't take my phone in the pool and calmed down after a few replies.

When she answered, I said, "Hey mom, what are you doing?"

"Just making lunch. Why what's up?"

I sighed. "I need to go grocery shopping, but I don't know what to put on my list."

"Oh, well, do you have the basics?"

I looked around my kitchen blankly. "Basics?"

"Yeah, like sugar, flour, spices?"

I searched through my cabinets. "I have flour, but the bag is open. Does that mean it's bad?"

"Not necessarily. Is there a date on the bag?"

I turned the bag around, searching for the date. "It's three years old."

"Toss it."

The flour went into the trash. "I wouldn't know what to do with it, anyway."

"I have some simple recipes from when I was younger somewhere around here. I lived off ramen noodles back when I was in college, but that was really not healthy of me."

After going through the rest of my staples, mom offered. "Why don't you come over, and we'll head to that Target I love? It's got groceries and kitchen stuff."

I smiled because I loved that Target, too. "Okay."

"By the time you get here, I'll have found those recipes."

Sometimes it felt like the only time my mother and I truly got along was when we were shopping, so I was excited as I got ready to head to Tampa.

Knowing that mom would be decked out to make the other shoppers envious, I slipped on a summer dress even though it was technically fall in Florida. It was almost winter, which was my favorite time of the year. The moment the temperatures dipped into the low seventies, my favorite hoodie came out to play. It was oversized, snuggly, and had the word *bookworm* on it with a graphic of an open book and a steaming cup of tea.

Maybe I'd buy a tea maker today. Did they even have such a thing?

A short pause in doing my makeup for a quick Google search later, and I learned the tea maker was really a kettle for heating water. Cool, I could heat water. I added that to the list my mother helped me create and slipped on my sandals.

I had just locked my door when Mrs. Bennett's dogs started yapping. The door cracked open, and she said over the racket of tiny barks, "Going out, my dear?"

"Yeah, going shopping with my mom. Need some stuff for the kitchen."

"Oh, I have some bakeware that I don't need. I'm happy to give it to you."

I smiled at the older woman even though the thought of baking anything had my throat closing. "I'm not much of a baker or a cook for that matter. I don't know how much use I'd be able to give it."

"I used to bake all the time for my late husband. Muffins, cakes, just about everything you could imagine until my eyes got so bad I couldn't read the instructions anymore."

The wistful look in her eyes forced an offer. "I'd love to take your bakeware but only if you show me how to use it. I'm happy to read the instructions."

She clasped her hands together, and her face lit up. "Oh goody! I'll get them together right now."

"No rush, Mrs. Bennett. I'll be gone most of the day and have classes tomorrow. Maybe we can get together in a few days?"

"That's fine, my dear. Just give me a knock whenever you are ready. I'll crate the little rugrats in the back room, so we'll have some peace."

"Tell Prince Charming I said hello."

The moment she shut the door, I flew down the hallway and pulled open the door to the stairs. I glanced back towards my door and promptly ran into a solid wall of muscle.

"Oh! Excuse me!" I exclaimed as I bounced off the tall man's chest.

He tugged the side of his hood forward and glared down at me. "Be careful."

The way he purred those two words had my heart skipping a beat or two. "I'm so sorry. I was distracted." My face heated, and my gaze lowered to the thin shirt he wore. I did not know they made hoodies for men that were that thin and short-sleeved. And this man had some serious tattoos under that shirt. Tattoos that had lived rent free in my brain since I'd seen them this morning.

He stepped aside and waved me into the dark stairwell. I hesitated and glanced at his darkened face. His lips twitched before he said, "Run along, little girl."

My smarter female instincts screamed to run back to my condo and lock myself inside. But I had no self-preservation skills. I passed him and started down the steps as he stood on the landing watching me leave.

I called out, "You don't have to hide your face from me."

He grunted and climbed the stairs.

I whispered as my feet skipped down and down. "You're fucking hot."

The door at the top of the stairs slammed shut. I blew out a breath as I left, thankful he hadn't seemed to hear what I'd said. *Why did I feel the need to speak to this man?* I'd never say that to anyone, and yet, it just came out of my mouth. Granted, he didn't hear it, but a part of me wanted him to. This dangerous-looking man made me feel reckless inside.

Chapter Five

Stalker

Logan

It had taken a week for Eden to fall into a reliable routine. She left her phone on the charger in the kitchen and was no longer waking up at every sound in the middle of the night. A week was all it took for this girl to turn into an unhealthy obsession for me. She was much too young and innocent for the likes of me. A Pollyanna who didn't deserve a monster stalking her.

It was four in the morning, and I could finally sneak into her condo and put the tracker on her phone. Not only would this program track Eden, but it would forward all her texts and call recordings to a file on my computer.

Overkill? Maybe.

I took a deep inhale as I put her phone down in the darkness. Her place smelled sweet, like vanilla and cinnamon. It made me think of sunshine on a brisk, clear day.

Her sketchbook was open on the couch. She had been obsessively drawing in it every night after long chats on the phone that were driving me insane because I couldn't hear both sides of the conversation.

I parted the pages and froze as I recognized myself under the streetlamp by the dumpster. I remembered that night clearly. It was the first time the scrawny gray kitten had let me hold him. My features were soft as I snuggled the ratty little waif to my scarred cheek. *I didn't look like that, did I?*

I flipped the page and felt my gut make a tiny jump. It was a close up of my gym shorts. My lips twisted into a smirk as self-satisfaction bloomed inside me. My dick *was* my best feature, after all. She'd made the soft shorts almost transparent, and my dick looked good under her lead. A little small, but the girl was using her imagination.

She had been avoiding my gym times after that day, but I could see I had made an impression on the young woman. Maybe I needed to change it up to catch her working out again.

The next page was a closeup of my hands, gripping the weights. Then a drawing of some college kid with a wild look in his eyes. I frowned and scowled toward the room Eden was sleeping in.

I recognized the look of a predator when I saw it, and this kid was clearly a threat to Eden's heart. His type liked to play games and only saw women as a conquest. That didn't mean he was a bad person, it just meant he was playing in territory that belonged to me. This was my playground. Instead of swing sets and slides, a monster lurked behind cameras and keys.

My gaze cut to the hall. I really shouldn't risk it, but I slunk to the closed bedroom door anyway. I couldn't guarantee that she wouldn't be awake on the other side. The thrill of possibly getting caught by her made Lurch excited. My hand twisted the knob slowly. The door was silent as it opened because I had oiled the hinges while she was in class.

Her scent was stronger in this room. I approached carefully. Her face was relaxed as I stood over her, watching her chest rise and fall with deep, even breaths.

My cock sat at half-mast in my leisure pants, begging me to touch it while my alter ego, Lurch, was conjuring images of pulling it out and caging her with my body. I slipped my hand inside my pants and fisted myself as I leaned closer, careful not to disturb her.

That's it, baby girl. Breathe me in and dream of only me.

My hand stroked my erection, sending pleasure coursing up to meet the thrill of standing over her as she slept. Our breath mingled. Hers the steady inhale and exhale of someone in deep sleep. Mine, the treacherous predator stalking her dreams.

If she woke now, she'd be traumatized, but a part of me wanted her to do just that. I'd hurt her if she did, and I didn't really want to scar her like that. Lurch did. He really wanted to force the pretty young woman to submit to us. He ached to feel her struggle underneath us and hear her screams twist into confused moans.

Collecting my precum on my fingers, I held it under her nose for a few seconds before wiping it on her pillow next to her head. I couldn't resist the urge to leave part of me with her. I'd take care of myself later. It was time to go. After making sure everything was exactly where she'd left it, I locked her front door and headed upstairs.

I sat down in my chair in front of my computer monitors and pulled up the footage recorded hours earlier. Eden in the shower, water pouring over her as her soapy hands slid over her gloriously naked body. Her hands slowed as they lifted her breasts, thumbs simultaneously moving over her large nipples until they tightened for her.

Her face tilted towards the ceiling as she pinched and plucked at the peaks. One lazy hand slipped up to caress her neck and jaw as the other hand moved lower. It was clear to me by the look on her pretty face the moment she touched her clit.

I paused the video and zoomed in. Lips parted in a tiny gasp of pleasure. Eyes closed in bliss. Hand loosely gripping her jaw.

My neglected cock pulsed, grabbing my attention. My hand automatically slipped under my waistband to fist myself as I burned the image on the screen to memory. I left the video zoomed in on her face as I hit play.

"That's it, baby girl. Show me how to stroke that clit the way you like."

Her scent still lingered in my nose as my dick thickened and throbbed under my attention. Every time her full lips parted in a pant or gasp it drove me closer to completion. I adjusted the video as she moved her position. Her face was pressed against the tile as her free hand moved to join the one working her pussy.

"That's a good girl. You're so fucking beautiful like this." My words came out in short pants as my hand quickened on my dick.

"Are you going to come for me now?"

Her eyes squeezed closed as if in answer to my question.

"Yeah, you are. You're gonna come just for me. Aren't you?"

My abs tightened as my body rushed forward with her.

Her expression as she toppled over the edge...

I hissed as my cock kicked out my own pleasure.

"Yeah, baby, we just came together. Too bad only one of us was aware of this precious moment we just shared."

I got up and headed for the shower. It was four-forty in the morning, and I needed a few hours' sleep if I planned to catch my girl for her morning workout.

Eden

Sweet Angel

I was hitting the elliptical machine hard this morning when Mr. Grumpy sauntered in and made direct eye contact with me as he pulled his shirt off. His dark hair artfully flopped across his scars as if he'd spent his life training it to hide that side of his face. The tattoos on his chest were both a display of terrifying death twisted in gorgeous artwork. It wasn't often I admired tattoos but whoever created these images enhanced this man's beauty with the shading and highlights.

This man's facial features seemed to be made up of several different people. Well, his left side had handsome parts, but his right side was downright heartbreaking. The scars were old and covered most of the side of his face. The crescent moons that started from his hairline at his temple and arched over his forehead and cheek. One of the half circles cut across his brow and eye and there was a deep scar on his cheek that was almost a full circle. What could cause such damage? What had happened to him?

I wanted to ask, but I didn't even know his name, and he'd probably snap at me anyway. He was a grumpy man. His lips pulled back in a barely there smile as he started stretching. Why was I so captivated by this man?

I mean, a flexible six-foot, four-inch man with dark hair that seemed to have its own personality, lifting weights wasn't hot, was it?

Not hot like James was. James had confidence, youth, a classically handsome face, and a little more bulk on his side.

Not at all like James, who had been pursuing me via text messages this past week. I couldn't figure out what James saw in me or what he wanted from me. He spent a lot of thumb power trying to convince me I had him all wrong. That he wasn't the fuckboy

I pegged him to be. He was looking for a long-term relationship and didn't want to have sex unless he was sure I was the one.

Our texts had turned slightly suggestive, but he seemed to be playing hard to get. At the same time, James confidently told me in text that he'd wreck me with his enormous dick. When I called him out, he'd simply said he didn't mean he'd wreck my vagina. Did he mean he'd ruin my asshole then? I didn't ask, and he didn't tell.

My gaze slipped to Mr. Grumpy's mature bulge as he started lifting weights. He was wearing soft pants today, but no amount of clothing could hide what he was packing.

I'd never had a big one before, and I was kind of looking forward to finding out what James could do with his, even though I hadn't seen it yet. The way James played hot and cold, confused me. He'd randomly ask me what I was wearing in text and then ghost me after some hot exchanges. The next text would come days later asking me how my day went. Rereading the thread of messages made my head spin. I was beginning to think he had mental issues he hadn't disclosed.

My gaze moved back to the man sharing the gym with me. Mr. Grumpy's body was... seasoned... and corded. Did he work out like this because of his job, or was he trying to make up for his flaws? This mysterious man was obviously much older than me. Did he have a wife, children?

His gaze cut to me in the mirror, and I jerked my eyes away for as long as I could keep them off him. When my unruly eyes returned, he was still staring at me. I offered him a smile. His lips twitched, but the look in his intense gaze made me turn off the machine and reach for my towel. I was curious, but not *that* curious.

The door to the gym opened, and an elderly couple entered. They jerked to a stop when they saw Mr. Grumpy putting his weights away. The silver-haired man said to his wife. "It's okay, it's just Logan."

Logan pulled his shirt on, lifted his hood, and faced the couple. "It's all yours, Mr. and Mrs. Smith."

"Don't rush out on our account, Mr. Dalton. We hardly ever see you."

Logan's smile was wide as I gawked back at them from the door. "That's how I prefer it."

I rushed out the door as he moved towards the exit. There was no way I wanted to chat it up with Logan Dalton after we'd spent the last forty minutes working out in complete damn silence.

When I got back to my place, I put my phone on the charger and noticed I had missed a text from my dad.

Miss you. Call me sometime.

It was the second text he had sent me this week. Guilt made me shift on my feet. The least I could do was call him back. I pulled the phone off the charger and hit the call button as I drifted towards the couch.

"Hey, Daddy."

I winced as he responded, "Hey, Pumpkin. How's the new condo?" That nickname was worse than Bean. As a redheaded man with the same attributes I'd inherited from him, he should have known better.

I should have called him last week to thank him. "It's great, Dad. I love it here. Thank you so much for doing this for me."

"Eden, you shouldn't have had to drive back and forth from Tampa and St. Pete all this time."

"It was okay, but this is much better."

"How's your mom handling it?"

I had finally gotten a handle on my mom's obsessive phone calls by texting her repeatedly throughout the day. I would copy and paste *good morning* from the day before. Then I copied and pasted, *I made it to class* and then *home from class.* I never forgot to text her *good night* promptly at nine every evening, whether I was actually going to bed at that time or not.

"She's starting to accept that I actually moved out."

"You're an adult, Eden. She's had twenty-two years to prepare for this. You should have started college a long time ago. Listen, I'm going to be in town next week. I'd love to come by and spend some time with you."

"Sure. I can cook dinner, and we can catch up."

I cringed as I said the words. I could barely boil water and I'd just promised to cook a whole ass dinner for my dad.

"A home-cooked meal would sure hit the spot."

Panic gripped me. A home-cooked meal? I didn't even know what that meant. Was it like southern comfort food or Italian?

"Great, well, text me your itinerary for next week. I have to get ready for class."

We said our goodbyes, and a quick Google search put me at ease. I felt dumb. It was exactly what it sounded like. I wondered if I could get away with make-it-yourself subs? I could get the meat and cheeses from Publix and set up the little bar between the kitchen and living room.

I was still tense about my dad's visit when James called.

I hesitated before answering it with a short pause before I said, "Hello?"

"What's wrong?"

I loved that he immediately picked up on my stress. He seemed to have a knack for reading my voice, or maybe he was a good guesser. I wasn't sure, and I wasn't going to ask.

I sighed and looked down at my hands. "My dad's coming over next week and wants a home-cooked meal."

His laugh made my lips turn up. "Let me guess. You've never used the stove for anything other than heating leftovers."

I lifted my gaze to the ceiling and sighed. "I've never used the stove for anything."

His laughter grew. "Please don't tell me you plan to order out and hide the takeout boxes."

My lips twisted to the side as I held back my mirth. "I was considering Cracker Barrel."

"Their chicken and dumplings rock, but why don't you let me help instead?"

My brows drew together as I considered this option.

"It's really easy to make at home. I used to make it all the time and nothing beats my grandma's southern recipe. I don't have to stay to meet your dad if you don't want me to."

My eyes widened. "You'd want to meet my dad?"

"Of course, I want to meet your family, Eden. I really like you, in case you weren't sure of my intentions."

Warmth bubbled up in me at his statement. I really hadn't been sure of anything concerning James. "Why?"

I could hear the frown in his voice. "Why, what?"

"Why me?"

"Why not you? You're beautiful and honest and sweet."

Instead of disagreeing with him and pointing out my insecurities and secret dark thoughts about fighting my mother, I simply smiled and said, "Thank you."

I also agreed to let him teach me how to make his grandma's chicken and dumplings. We settled into making plans for a trial run at my place this weekend, and I took pleasure in the fact that we'd found something to do together. I often felt that we struggled to find something in common to talk about when we chatted.

We came from separate worlds. He had a loving, supportive middle-class family. I had estranged and borderline abusive, wealthy parents. He had three siblings. I was an only child. His parents loved each other. Mine hated one another. He wanted to meet my father. The thought of meeting his family created a nervous flutter in my gut. After sitting with my thoughts and emotions I determined this was an excited feeling. An opportunity to learn how functional people do family. They say opposites attract.

Chapter Six

Bloody Carl

Logan

This girl had me all twisted up. She had consumed me without even trying. My mind refused to let her go, even during meditations and prayers for solace. It didn't matter that the feelings were one-sided. That my alter ego already considered her mine and watching another man move into my territory was enraging.

I was playing the long game, but I was losing the short one. This boy was an expert at the short game, and Eden was on the road to heartbreak when he got what he wanted from her.

Lurch wanted to move faster. But if I listened to my dark side, Eden would never be the same. We'd be a cloud that blocked the sunlight that radiated from her. Her sunshine was the reason I was falling so hard, and I couldn't do that to her.

What Lurch wanted to do was illegal and unprofessional, even by BFR standards. Her dad, my society brother, trusted me to keep Eden safe. She was safe from everything except me.

I needed to fuck something up before I ruined everything.

My hand guided my mouse to the BFR tracking program that looked for security breaches. We monitored every member and their immediate family. This program looked for specific keywords in emails, texts and online activity of every member and their families, as well as scanned the media and publications for mentions of rituals and strange gatherings. It analyzed a hoard of data and flagged all threats to the Society. Surely, there was someone who needed to be punished in central Florida.

The Blue-Frosted Rose had remained secret all these years because we eliminated anyone who dared to out us. Technology made sharing information easier. One slip-up would have the world looking at us, and the dark things we did would offend just about everyone. We'd be fetishized and called devil worshipers due to the nature of our rituals. While Lucifer was a valid entity, our rituals did not center on one God. Our religion could be labeled as wiccan. Would they classify us as witches? A sect of rogue witches who bent all the religious rules ever established. All I knew was our magic was real and powerful.

The flagged members popped up on my screen, and I sorted by distance. I was looking for someone close. We had members all over the world, but we had enforcers everywhere, too. I had a remote team because of the sheer number of BFR brothers living in Florida. Tampa was a hot spot because of the home base church, but we also had smaller churches near Orlando and Arcadia. We also owned a sprawling property near Ocala where we hosted monumental events like our annual wild hunt.

I scrolled the list of flagged members and paused on the name Karla McKenzie. Dan's ex-wife had been on our list since she divorced him. My team had been efficient as always. Snuffing out small fires before they grew into problems, but Karla's file hadn't been accessed in a long time. Dan handled her before she became a red flag for the enforcers. She was still an orange threat, but the file below hers was a hot one.

I picked up my phone and dialed my second.

He picked up on the first ring. "Yes, sir."

The background noise of a diner came through with his voice. What day was it, anyway? Thursday. Had it been almost two weeks since Eden moved in?

"Can you talk?"

Less than a month and I'm already fixated on her like I had discovered a new kink.

"Just a minute," Bentley replied immediately. He was used to my long pauses. "Okay, I can talk."

"Give me something I can fuck up."

Now it was his turn to create a long pause. "Do you mean fuck up or," his tone became insinuating, "*fuck up*?" I could just see his smirk as he wiggled his eyebrows on the other side.

"My dick stays in my pants."

"Okay. We have Carl at the warehouse. Belongs to a small-time gang who was sniffing around the Society."

"He's fresh?"

"Yeah, I worked him over a bit initially, but he's a tough nut to crack. Seems to be more scared of his boss than of us."

I checked the time. "I'll be there in an hour."

"Yes, sir."

I hit the end button without goodbyes. Like me, Bent wasn't a man of many words.

I grabbed my gym bag sitting by my bedroom door. Today's workout would consist of blood and fear. I shut off the lights as I made my way to the front door of my pristine condo, but paused as I passed the spare bedroom. We'd already equipped the warehouse with everything I'd need, but my specialty bag called to me today. My blades needed a workout, too.

I put my thumb over the keypad, and the locks clicked after a brief scan. The heavy door swung open easily, and I moved to the walk-in closet. A flick of the lights illuminated all my beautiful darkness.

"Hey babies," I murmured to the inanimate objects of human disaster. Moving past the arsenal of firearms, I opened the glass display case that housed my blades. They gleamed their appreciation before I rolled the leather case and stuffed them in my bag.

The warehouse was in the middle of nowhere Polk County. The sheriff of this county was famous for being tough on crime. He was a good man who wouldn't agree with the terror I was about to rain on this Carl person. But Carl belonged to a gang who terrorized the sheriff's citizens. A gang the sheriff had been gunning for for a long time. Carl could be the key in taking these criminals down, or he might just end up as another missing person. If anyone cared to report the fucker as missing.

I pulled my blacked-out Dodge Ram into the industrial parking area of an old mining property we owned and parked close to the door. Not that the parking lot was busy - it was deserted. I'd beaten Bentley here.

The sound of an off-road vehicle reached me as I opened the door. Satisfaction filled me as Torrid came flying around the corner with murder on his face. I had personally wired the fuck out of this place so that the caretaker would be alerted to anyone hiking or driving on this property.

Torrid knew the moment I turned my truck onto the long dirt road that someone had entered his domain. The man was a better guard dog than a thousand Rottweilers.

Speaking of. "Where's Gaul?"

He shut off the mule and answered with a jerk of his head towards the thick metal door. "Watching the bait."

He glanced at his smart watch, and his heavy brow bunched. Talk about a man looking like his dog. "You expecting company for your fishing excursion?"

I moved towards the door. "Bentley."

"Nice of him to give me a heads up," he complained in a surly, deep voice.

I leaned against the door and crossed my arms. "Keeping you on your toes."

"Bitch, I'm a fucking ballerina."

I dropped my hood and scratched the back of my head. "You in a tutu is not an image I ever wanted to imagine, Tor."

He lifted his upper lip in a smirk. "You're welcome, boss."

Bentley pulled his SUV next to my truck and jumped out immediately. "Been waiting long?"

I pushed off the door with a grunt. "Any amount of time with Tutu Tor is too long, Bent."

Bentley's light blond head jerked to Torrid, and the man said, "I'll tell you later."

I put my thumb on the keypad and said to Bentley standing behind me, "You don't want to know."

The lock clicked open, and the muffled sounds of menacing barking reached us. "How long has Gaul been at him?"

Tor moved past me to open the next set of doors. "All night."

"Sleep deprivation by vicious Rottweiler." Bentley sounded impressed.

As the second set of doors opened, the barking grew louder. "How many days?"

Tor stepped up to the bars of the innermost door. "Two." He gave a low whistle, and the barking stopped.

The dog in question came bounding around the corner, but his happiness at seeing Tor morphed into a low growl as he realized his daddy had company.

Torrid took a leash and muzzle off a hook on the wall and thankfully suited up his canine. The dog knew me, but he was unpredictable and loved his job a little too much.

I understood the 'bite first, ask questions later' mentality. Hell, it was exactly why I was here today.

We went down the corridor and found the fish hanging naked from shackles attached to the high ceiling, surrounded by bars just wide enough for Gaul to get his meaty head through.

My hand went to my nose as the scent of stress and panic mixed with bodily fluids hit me in the face. "Shew, Carl. You reek."

The man barely lifted his head to peer at me through tangled dark hair. "Fuck you."

I moved to the table along the wall and hoisted my gym bag onto it. The zipper felt too loud as I opened the bag and started removing the few items inside.

My blades made a dense thump on the granite slab as I set the leather roll down to remove my rubber apron. I turned and faced the scene of Bentley and Tor removing the bars that had barely protected the man from Gaul's gnashing teeth overnight. His thighs and hips sported the consequences of letting his guard down.

Gaul shoved his muzzled nose right into the man's exposed junk with a snarl the moment he was able to. At least this man kept his junk intact. I'd seen what Gaul's overnight goals were. It wasn't pretty.

Carl screamed and twisted away. "Get that thing away from me!"

I said one word, "Tor."

Torrid nodded and picked up Gaul's leash. "Let's go for a walk."

At the word walk, the dog immediately turned to Tor with a huge grin on his oversized face. From killer to puppy in seconds.

Bentley detached the last panel of bars from the concrete and heaved the heavy thing to the side as I pulled my light hoodie over my head.

Carl stiffened as I kicked off my shoes and unbuttoned my jeans. "What are you doing?"

I met his gaze with a menacing smirk as I lowered my pants, taking my underwear with them. Carl glanced over his shoulder at Bentley, who was unwinding the pressure washer attached to the wall. "Why is he getting naked?"

Bentley merely chuckled and continued preparing the hose.

Carl's wide eyes were red from lack of sleep, but his panic was tangible. "You can do whatever to me. I'm not a rat."

No, he wasn't a rat. But he'd already told me what his greatest fear was. He had probably raped countless women in his career as a criminal, but the thought of getting raped by a man would be his undoing. If I started stroking my dick, he'd sing immediately.

But where was the fun in that?

Eden

The weather was beautiful as I walked to class for the first time since moving into my new home. It was the first day below eighty degrees, and the sticky humidity of summer seemed to have taken a vacation. It would be a brief reprieve, but it was a beautiful day.

All that considered, I was still sweating and out of breath as I walked onto campus.

"Eden, wait up."

I cringed at having James see me red faced and puffing, but my smile bloomed as I turned around. "James."

He jogged up to me, blue eyes sparkling with a friendliness that reminded me of a golden retriever. "Hey. I was hoping to see you today."

I drug my arm over my forehead, wiping away the beads of sweat. "Yeah?"

"What are you doing tonight?"

My head cocked away as I narrowed my gaze at this beautiful man. "Why?"

His grin spread into a smile. "I thought you might want to catch some dinner with me."

I hesitated. "Tonight?"

He backpedaled, "If you already have plans..."

"No. I'm free tonight." Shit, that came too quickly. *What happened to making the guy work for it, Eden?*

"So, seven?"

I nodded, and he said, "Think about where you want to go and text me later."

"You want me to choose where we go?"

"Yeah, that way you'll always be happy with the meal."

I scratched the back of my sweaty neck. "But what if *you're* not happy with the meal?"

He barked a laugh. "I may look complicated, Eden," those brilliant blue eyes dropped down my body and back up, "but I assure you, I eat."

My brows drew together as I tried to figure out if he meant what I thought he insinuated. "Okay?" I glanced behind me at the building. "I gotta go. I'll text you later."

"Cool. See you later."

Resisting the urge to watch him walk away, I turned towards the building and rushed to class feeling giddy, even though it was too soon to feel this way about a man I barely knew. *Fuck my silly heart.* This guy hadn't earned it yet, and a simple dinner date of my choice made my day.

Wait, was it a date? He asked me out, not the other way around. Was he expected to pay for dinner? Should I choose a cheap option or offer to pay half?

Then there was the question of what to wear.

By the time I got home from classes, I was a mental wreck. I decided on a tried-and-true choice, a place I'd been to before because familiarity bred comfort for me.

I texted James: **Do you like Mexican food?**

Yep.

There's a Mexican place not far from where I live.

He replied: **I know it. Meet you there.**

"Okay," I said to no one in particular. "Time to get dolled up."

But choosing something to wear for our first date was a chore. As much as I wanted to impress, I felt frumpy in just about everything I owned. To counter that feeling, I took my time doing my makeup and braiding my hair.

Instead of walking like I should have done, I drove to the restaurant to avoid the inevitable sweat fest that my body enjoyed putting out.

"Wow, Eden, you look amazing."

He was waiting for me outside, wearing the same thing he'd had on when I saw him earlier. Jeans and a tight blue t-shirt that matched his eyes.

"Thanks." It was all I could muster. I'd spent hours on my appearance, and he'd just rolled his hot body down to the restaurant without a care.

I pushed aside the feeling that I had done all the work for this date and asked, "Have you been here before?"

"Lots of times," he said as he opened the door for me.

The conversation was minimal as we sat down and looked at the menu. I was considering what would be the least messy to eat since I usually wore a portion of my meal, no matter where I was.

Yep, I was that girl, and of course I wore my light-yellow blouse with green and blue delicate flowers trimming the neckline.

His voice startled me out of intense concentration. “Have I done something wrong?”

I lowered the menu and met his gaze. “No. Why?”

“Because you’re hiding behind that menu like you’re embarrassed to be seen with me.”

My jaw dropped open. Was he just as self-conscious as me? “What? No. I’m just... trying to pick what I want to eat.”

“The enchiladas are delish,” he offered with a grin that had me doing a double take. This guy wasn’t self-conscious. He was teasing me.

Was *he* embarrassed to be out with *me*? If he was, why in the hell did he ask me out?

“So, you’re an artist?”

Thankful that he interrupted my suspicious thoughts, I nodded. “I try.”

“I can’t draw for shit.”

“Neither could I when I first started. It’s a skill one develops with practice and time.”

The server came, and I ordered the damn enchiladas.

He took a sip of his Jack and Coke and asked, “Well, I won’t be changing my major anytime soon. I just don’t have the patience for art.”

“That’s because it’s not your passion.”

He cocked his head as he put his chin on his fist. My mother would flip out over his elbow on the table. “But it’s yours?”

“Even as a child, I found beauty in the smallest things. Like the way a weathered hand had character.”

“So, you draw hands.”

“I did when I was a kid. I desperately wanted that character to come alive in my sketch.”

He smirked and sat back. "She has a hand fetish."

"I do not."

"That's okay. I have a secret foot fetish."

My toes curled in my sandals and not in a good way. "Weirdo."

He looked mildly offended. "Are you judging me?" Lifting his hand and waggling his fingers for inspection, he added, "How do my hands measure up?"

My gaze followed his hand as he stretched his arm across the table. I could just hear my mother tsking. I took his hand in mine and made a big show of inspecting it. "They are soft, which means you take care of yourself."

His fingers closed over mine. "And?"

"You have big hands."

"You know what that means, don't you?"

I met his gaze. "Size large gloves?"

He smirked. "Big dick."

"Oh." But his grin was contagious, and I laughed.

He let go of my hand. "You don't believe me?" He reached for his waistband and half stood up like he was going to flop his penis out onto the table. "I can show you."

"Don't you dare."

Now he laughed. "You actually thought I would drop my pants right here in the middle of the restaurant? I love how gullible you are."

My throat suddenly felt dry. "Gullible?"

"Yeah, but I like your innocence," he said with a wide grin. "It's sweet."

I took a sip of ice water, and he mirrored my action by swigging from his squat glass of alcohol. When he set it down, he said, "It makes me feel like you have a low body count."

I inhaled and water went down the wrong pipe causing a coughing fit. I wanted to cover my entire face with the napkin instead of just my mouth as my face grew redder and my eyes watered. "Body count? I wouldn't think that would be an issue with you." The words just flew out of my mouth between fits of coughing as I considered how fast I could make it out the door and to my car.

He looked suitably abashed. "I'm sorry. I didn't mean to offend you. It's just, I'm technically a virgin."

My head snapped back to him. "Bullshit."

He lifted his hands. "I'm a flirt and have fooled around a lot, but I've never actually done the deed. I'm saving myself."

Thankfully, our food came and interrupted this line of conversation.

Once I picked up my fork and knife, he asked, "Do you work out?"

I cut a tiny bite but didn't put it in my mouth. "There's a small gym in my building but I prefer to swim."

His smile lit up. "I love to swim, too. There's a pool at my gym. You should come work out with me sometime."

I cut another bite, ignoring the first. "Yeah, that would be fun." *Fun like taking a hammer to the head.* Working out with friends always turned into a round of *train the fat girl* and I looked forward to that like one enjoyed a migraine.

He studied my face a moment before he offered, "Or I can just come swim with you sometime."

Like getting in a bathing suit in front of a hot gym rat would be any better than him standing over me shouting encouragement as I lifted weights for him. "Sure."

"My parents always said that those who play together, stay together."

"Besides the gym, what else do you like to do?"

He smiled again. "I paddleboard."

"I tried that once. Fell off and couldn't get back up on the board. I prefer sailing."

He perked up. "You know how to sail?"

Pride made me sit a little straighter. "I do. My dad has a forty foot, blue water sailing vessel called *Divinity*."

"That is so cool. You've got to take me sailing sometime. See? We found something we both love to do. My parents like to go on cruises together. They have priority boarding with all the major cruise lines."

He leaned in like he had a secret to share, and I mirrored him, eager to hear it. "I want that for my life. I want to still be in love with my partner forty years after we're married and have grandchildren. That's why I'm saving myself."

"I've never thought that far down my lifeline. I just want to graduate college and get a job that will allow me to get out from under my parents' influence."

He sat back, studying me for a moment. "Your parents are divorced?"

I nodded, "Dad is a chronic cheater, and Mom is too controlling."

"I'm sorry."

I shrugged it off. "Don't be. It is what it is. Besides, my dad's guilt got me into that condo. Without the condo, I would have never been allowed to go to the dorm party where I met you. So, there's a bright side to divorce."

"Things do happen for a reason," he agreed before he tipped his glass back and finished his whiskey sour.

The server brought the check, and when he didn't reach for it, I picked it up. "How do you want to do this? I'm happy to pay for my side."

His gaze went to the slip of paper in my hand. "How much is it?"

When I gave him the number, which was bigger than I expected because of his numerous alcoholic beverages, he said, "Let's split it."

I put the bill down and grabbed my wallet as disappointment settled over the meal in my stomach. The black credit card was easy to find; it was the only card in the slots. "Don't worry. I'll get it."

It was a small price to pay for finding out that we had little in common, different goals, and that body count mattered to James. I had a fairly low body count, but I couldn't believe this guy had none. *So, was he a liar, too?*

He leaned back with a grin. "I'll get it next time."

I wasn't entirely sure there'd be a next time. James was cute and sweet but I think he friend-zoned me.

James was hot and probably fun in bed even without putting the technical D in the V, but he wanted things from me. Things I had never allowed myself to consider. I wasn't sure I wanted a husband, children, or grandchildren. I couldn't be good at any of those things, considering my parents as an example.

He walked me to my car, and when I turned to say goodbye, he was closer than I realized. My back pressed against my driver's side door as he leaned in with bedroom eyes. "Thank you for dinner, Eden."

"Thanks for asking me out." *Did I just say that? I'm an idiot.* Where had my careful filter gone? I would have never said that before moving out. But then again, I wouldn't be here if I hadn't.

It looked like he just might kiss me, so I was glad I'd worn flats tonight. Heels would have made me feel more self-conscious than I already did.

His lips grazed mine in a delicate kiss before he pulled back. "We should do this again soon."

The alcohol on his breath had me asking, "You okay to drive home?"

He straightened with a confident grin. "Abso-fucking-lutely. I'll text you tomorrow."

"Okay... Goodnight."

"Sweet dreams, Eden."

I watched him walk towards his car. He seemed okay, but maybe I should text him later just to make sure.

Chapter Seven

Trouble

Logan

Poor Carl lost his bravado right after his shower. If you've ever sprayed your feet off at the self-service car wash, then you could imagine the pain of a pressure washer on the tender bits of the rest of your body.

Carl's low pain tolerance, coupled with his fear of being man-raped, had him tapping out well before my lust for blood was satisfied.

He started singing like he was the main character at an opera the moment my scalpel drew first blood. The fatal flaw with this type of torture was that the victim would say anything to make the pain stop.

His screams and desperate attempts to give the information he thought we were looking for settled into my bones as I continued to work on the man. He confessed to terrible, inhumane acts of violence and deviance against others as he bled from a series of small wounds.

Carl was the worst kind of low life, and the gang he belonged to wasn't any better. They trafficked migrant workers and prostitutes. If his information could be trusted, some were as young as eleven. I had little inclination to stop the torture as I took his left nipple between my thumb and forefinger. My blade was sharp and quickly peeled through skin and trembling flesh.

My phone chimed, and I put his nipple on his forehead as I stepped away from the screaming man strapped to the metal table.

Bentley leaned over Carl and offered him some water. "Why were you snooping around our church in Tampa?"

The man took the offered sip as his eyes locked onto Bentley like he was the Coast Guard search light in a vast ocean of death. "Church? Please... I'll tell you everything... just make him stop."

Bentley's voice was gentle. "No, you'll tell me now, and I'll ask him to leave."

The relief in Carl's voice was evident as the words tumbled from his desperate mouth. He was told to find out what he could about a rival gang. He thought we were a gang like his. It was obvious he knew nothing about the secret society.

I used a towel to clean the blood from my hands before touching my phone. The information my phone provided made me frown. Eden was home from class, but she had a date tonight with that college kid she'd been talking to her friend about.

The phone clacked against the table with such force both men twisted to look at me.

"No, please... you promised." Carl turned to Bent with desperation, the drama of his dire situation playing on his face.

Bentley lifted a shoulder as he met my gaze. "Will you please leave?"

"No," I growled as I picked up my bloody knife.

Carl screamed as I removed his testicles in a swift movement.

Poor Carl didn't realize he was an example, not an informant until it was too late.

Bright blood flowed from the wound between his legs as I laid the sack on his stomach. I loved playing mind games with my victims, but I didn't have time to fuck with Carl.

"Send these to his gang as a reminder why one doesn't fuck with the Blue-Frosted Rose Society."

Carl's breathing was shallow. His complexion grew ghostly. A few more pints of blood loss and he'd slip away peacefully. It wasn't my finest kill, but watching him fade away soothed the noise in my soul.

It wouldn't last. Bentley would dispose of the body. Carl would soon be forgotten. The itch to kill again would return sooner than normal because I couldn't savor Carl's death.

And whose fault was that?

I showered at the warehouse and spiritually cleansed my rotten soul before heading home to my Eden. My garden of paradise, who was on a fucking date with another man. If she let him taste her forbidden fruit, I'd kill him slowly and punish her for a month of Sundays.

She may not be religious now, but my girl would have a meet and greet with whatever god she believed in before I jerked her back to reality and fucked her until she worshipped my cock.

She was still at the restaurant when I pulled into my parking space. It took a monumental effort not to back out, drive down there, and drag her home. Something I had no right to do.

She might have gone out on a date with me tonight if I had just asked her like a normal person. But I was too comfortable in my current role of watching from the outside. I enjoyed the fantasy too much to make it a reality.

Besides, Eden was a sweet girl. Way too sweet for me. She deserved better than the likes of me. I'd be the serpent in her protected garden. Driving a wedge between her salvation and sanity. Fouling up a perfect soul.

Eden deserved an Adam, not a creep like me.

And yet, even after all that self-talk, I sat in my truck, waiting for her to come home. And when the headlights of her old car went dark, I opened my door and slid out.

"Isn't it a little late for a school night?"

She jerked around to face me, and I forced a smile, even though I knew my smile was more terrifying than my resting dick face.

Her gaze dropped to my mouth and lingered a full moment before she seemed to realize I asked her a question. "I'm allowed to have a night out."

"So, you asked permission?"

I loved the doubtful smile on her face. It told me she wasn't sure if I was teasing her or not. "I'm an adult. I don't need to ask permission."

I snorted and walked towards the building. "Barely legal, and she thinks she's seasoned."

The locks on her car sounded. "I do not think I'm seasoned." She rushed after me. "What does that even mean, anyway?"

I entered the code and held the door. "Ladies first."

Her fists lifted to her hips. "Age before beauty."

A genuine laugh left me as I entered the building. "At least she speaks the truth."

She pressed the elevator button. "Again, he speaks in riddles."

I opened the heavy door to the stairwell, and she scowled at me. "Too old to ride in the elevator with an unseasoned, barely legal woman?"

I faced her as the elevator door opened with a ding. "You forgot to add the word beautiful, Eden."

She put her hand on the open doors to keep them from closing as she attempted to come up with something else to say to me.

I didn't let her. "And you *are* beautiful. I hope whoever you graced with that beauty tonight appreciates it as much as I do."

Her frown was all the confirmation I needed that James did not, in fact, admire her the way she deserved.

I was going to kill that college kid if he didn't get his head out of his ass soon. I hated the thought of him touching Eden, but I loathed the thought of him not treating her like the precious thing she was.

Ah, who was I kidding?

I was going to kill James anyway just for looking at Eden.

Eden

Sweet Angel

My encounter with Logan had my stomach aflutter with nerves. That man oozed danger and darkness, but my panties were soaked because his gaze promised nothing but sweet agony. I didn't even like pain. I was smart enough to recognize a potentially abusive relationship when I saw one. Hell, I was still living in one.

James was a safer bet. A man looking for the mother of his children and a stable life. While I knew nothing about being a good mom, the idea was growing on me. But the more I tried to picture what our children would look like, the more they looked like Logan instead of James.

I picked up my phone and typed out a text.

Did you make it home alright?

He left me unread, and I sat there looking at my phone for way too long, waiting for him to look at my text. I put the phone on the charger in my kitchen with a dejected shake of my head.

"Desperation is a bad look on you, Eden," I parroted my mother's words from the past.

Was I desperate, though? What was so wrong about wanting to find love? I was lonely, but not desperate.

Really? You just pictured what your children would look like with a scarred, grumpy old man.

I was still throbbing at the prospect of Logan putting those babies inside me.

Because he called you beautiful?

My inner self was an asshole who made me feel like a fool who fell in love with the first man who showed interest.

And guess who immediately stopped throbbing and dried up?

And no, it wasn't because he said I was beautiful. It was the way he said it like he meant it. The feeling he put in the word had me almost believing him.

And that hurt more than James, leaving me unread because I knew I wasn't beautiful. Well, maybe on the inside most of the time, but I was not a traditional beauty. There were parts of me I liked. I had pretty eyes and unique hair. Sometimes I loved my freckles and other times, I hated how they dotted my face when I was an overheated hot mess. Which was nine months of the year in Florida.

Most of the time, I didn't look too closely at myself in the mirror. I was what I was, and even though I tried to watch what I ate and worked out regularly, ninety percent of the time, I avoided my body issues.

I stripped off my clothing and curled up in bed. The shower could wait until morning. I needed to sleep, but my brain wanted to hash out my imperfections instead. It pointed out the fact that I was dangerously close to allowing men to turn me into my mother by pulling up memories of my mom's depression after dad left.

While my mother was tall, slender, and gorgeous, I did not want to end up like her. She blamed all her problems on my father's cheating heart. It didn't help that it was her younger, prettier sister that filled the shoes she ripped off. Her resentment had only grown as their relationship had bloomed into something more than a fling. In fact, I didn't think my father ran around on my aunt, like he had on my mother.

I'd stay away from all men if they hadn't shown me that love could succeed. It was because of my father and aunt that I longed for the partnership they had. What was so wrong with me that I couldn't find true love?

Also, why was it feast or famine with me?

Every single time I felt like I was winning in life, suddenly men flocked to me. I swear it was like they knew I was doing great and swarmed in to fuck it all up. It was two in the morning when my phone dinged with a text notification from the kitchen. I had just drifted off, but that sound made my eyes pop wide. I shouldn't have gotten out of bed, but inquiring minds had to know.

I had a great time tonight.

He could see that I read the text, but I shouldn't answer him until morning. Right?

My fingers disagreed.

Me too.

The little three dots started dancing right away, and I held my breath, waiting for the message to come through.

Can't sleep.

I really shouldn't have responded. **Same.**

His next message took a while to arrive. **I'm naked. My roommate is snoring, and my dick is so hard it hurts.**

Right to the point. My lips stretched into a broad smile. I knew exactly where this was going, but instead of jumping into sexting with James, I wrote. **So snoring is a turn on?**

You turn me on, Eden.

This time, I didn't hesitate. **Do I, though? Tonight felt more like hanging out with a buddy, not a date.**

His message took forever. **I thought I was clear about my intentions. If I was looking to hook up, you'd be here with me right now and I'd be feasting on you. And while I regret not taking you home now, I want more than just a fun time.**

I put the phone down and took a step back. It was too early in the morning for this. I was standing in my underwear in my kitchen, hanging onto every word this man was typing into his phone. They were heavy words, meaningful even. I just couldn't believe he was a virgin with the way he kept pushing the risqué talk. Was he just ready to pop his cherry and thought I was an easy target who wouldn't complain if he was bad at it? Or did he truly think I was the right one?

This was exactly what I had just been pining about, and the rapid beat of my heart wasn't excitement. It felt more like dread.

I picked up the phone once more. **Thanks for clarifying. It's late and I have an early class tomorrow. Chat later?** I must be as nutty as my mother.

Wow... rejected... LOL. Sweet dreams, babe. I'll make our next "date" better. See you tomorrow.

I let him have the last word. Wasn't there a kid's movie about a pig called Babe? It was a good movie, but I wasn't sure how I felt about being called babe. And why did he put date in quotes?

I knew sleep wasn't in my future, so I sat down at my desk and opened my sketch pad when I should have caught up on assignments. My hand reached for the pencil, intending to draw James's sensual lips, but they took on more of a cruel twist than originally intended.

I flipped the page and started over drawing hands. James had pretty hands with manicured nails and proportionate fingers. The knuckles on the page were a patchwork of scars. The hand had pronounced veins and fingers so long they could be called elegant.

No matter how hard I tried to draw James, the sketch became Logan. This happened more frequently with my creative side lately. There was something beautiful about the different parts of an experienced man who had lived a hard life. The unobtainable grump consumed my art.

I spent the rest of the night deconstructing the beauty in all of Logan's broken parts.

Chapter Eight

Soul Sucker 6000

Logan

The college kid in the sketch book came to life on my monitors as he entered Eden's private space carrying grocery bags as she laughed at something he said.

He glanced around the condo like he was casing the place as he headed towards the kitchen. I zoomed in on his face, took a snapshot and moved the photo into the facial recognition program.

"Fuck, I knew he had a record."

James Holbrook's mugshot popped up almost immediately. He had been arrested for criminal trespassing and spent sixty days in jail. He was caught stealing shit from unlocked cars in his own damn neighborhood when he was nineteen.

"Idiot."

I looked for more charges, but that was it.

My gaze shifted to the live feed of this guy unpacking the groceries and rifling through Eden's kitchen cabinets.

"Shit, I pegged him for more criminal mischief than just teenage petty theft."

From the way she laughed and smiled at him as he taught her to cook, Eden was falling for this guy.

I desperately wanted to find some dirt so I could soil him for her. But he was just an average nobody who wasn't nearly the villain I was when I was his age.

They locked eyes, and he made his move on her. A slow and calculated head tilt as he leaned in. She received his lips, and he gave her a gentle, passionate, practiced kiss. This boy had enough game to realize that slow kisses had the opposite sex wondering how that mouth treated the downstairs area.

His pull-away was perfectly reluctant and Eden followed him, not wanting the kiss to end. She wanted slow, gentle passion between her legs, and I wanted to be the man who delivered it.

Part of me wanted to torture both of them for having the audacity to fall in love in front of me. The other part warmed at Eden's face as she looked at him. She deserved everything she was currently feeling... only she deserved it with me, not this chump.

But I was relegated to only a bird's eye view as they cooked, ate, and finally ended up on the couch, making out and feeling each other up.

When she cupped the bulge in his pants he quickly fumbled with the zipper and pulled his dick out. She immediately grabbed it with both hands, and he spread his legs and leaned back with a large grin on his fucking face.

He wasn't small. Maybe seven inches, but they had already texted about the size of his huge dick and how she may need to train for it, but Eden appeared unimpressed as she lowered her mouth to suck him off.

"Oh, come on, Eden!" I pushed away from the monitors as her head bobbed up and down on his lap. "He's barely touched your pussy over the top of your underwear and you're sucking him off?"

I stood up but turned back to the monitors. "Have some self-respect. That fucker should have had you spread out for dinner making you scream his name before he ever let you touch his dick."

I stomped back to the computer and sat down. "And where has that dick been?"

I pulled up James Holbrook's medical records. HIPPA doesn't apply to the BFR. We can access everything about anyone and often do.

"He's squeaky clean, but you don't know that." I felt dumb for chastising a video feed, but I couldn't stop myself.

I shoved my keyboard away.

"Am I going to have to tell your daddy to have the safe sex talk with you?"

She lifted off his dick and finished him with her hands. He lifted his shirt before he shot his load and Eden fixated on his strong abs as she slowly pumped his spent dick. She got up but he caught her hand and pulled her back to him. She went to kiss him, but he turned and kissed her cheek instead of her lips. A man who wouldn't kiss the mouth that just sucked him off was a pansy-assed boy, not a man.

I'd let her transfer my jizz to my mouth in a long sloppy kiss after she did for me what she just did for him. The only redeeming quality of the night was Eden's frown as she came back with the towel.

As they were wrapping up the night, I grabbed my cat food, locked up and headed downstairs.

As James came out of the elevators, Lurch was standing in his way.

He lifted his eyes to my menacing glare and his spine stiffened as they focused on my hideous scars.

"Oh man, excuse me," he said as he pushed past me.

My voice was ice. "Who the fuck are you?"

He froze and slowly turned back to face me, confused. "What?"

"You don't live here." I approached him slowly.

He shrunk back. "I was visiting a friend who lives here."

"A friend? Just a friend?" My temper got the better of me before I asked the right question.

"Who?" I walked him backwards.

"Eden... ah... McKenzie." The fucker had to think about her last name. He reached the side door and fumbled for the knob.

"You fucking her?"

His eyes widened dramatically. "No! I swear, I haven't done anything with her."

I reached out and fisted his shirt. "Anything? Really? Because the jizz on your shirt tells a different story."

The door behind him opened as he floundered for words, looking properly panicked.

I leaned in, enjoying the satisfaction I felt as I let Lurch out to play with the kid. My jaw tightened as I spoke through my teeth. "If you so much as cause one tear, I'll fucking cut your balls from your body and shove them up your ass while I skull-fuck your face. Understand?"

I shoved him backwards, and he tripped over the small hedge and dramatically sprawled on the ground before he scrambled to his feet and sprinted towards his car in the parking area. Gravel spun as he backed out like a maniac.

"Asshole!" he shouted from the safety of a rolling vehicle.

"Slow down, Sport. Don't want you to wreck on the way home," I called out.

"Fuck you!"

I smiled, rolled my shoulders with a satisfying crack, and headed towards the dumpster where my strays impatiently waited on me to arrive with dinner.

I was squatted in the center of the open cans and wary cats when her shadow from the streetlamp fell over me.

She thrust the heavy, plastic Publix bag at me. "For the cats."

I stood up and stalked forward. The cats scattered, and she took a step back as I towered over her, the bag of cat food between us.

"Do you think I can't afford cat food?" my gravelly voice growled defensively.

Her eyes popped wide. "No, I just think what you're doing is sweet, and I want to help."

My fingers captured her chin as I leaned down, putting my face right into hers.

"Don't mistake what I'm doing for sweet. I do this so they go into the traps the rescue sets for them."

My jaw tightened, and I spoke through clenched teeth. "I do this to be rid of them."

Her breath shuttered out of her, and while she was too stunned to think or move, I ran my nose along her temple, pulling her scent into my lungs with a loud inhale.

"Go with your first opinion of me, Eden. Do not mistake me for a good guy because I feed cats."

I let her chin go with a gentle push. She dropped the bag and scrambled back to the safety of her home, like she should.

James might break her heart, but I'd wreck her soul with what I'd do to her. My instincts told me not to be so damn invested in her. I should keep my distance and protect her from the stain that was me.

But then I watched the footage of her reaching her condo and leaning against the locked door, panting, as she touched the spot on her chin where I gripped her. I smiled as I observed how she turned that memory into a fantasy as she moved that touch lower and came all over her fingers.

Eden

I was so confused as I browsed the dildos at the sex shop I'd finally gotten the courage to visit. The abundant fake dicks were not the cause of my confusion. It was that I held a comparable dong to what I imagined was Logan's dick and not James.

Was I disappointed that James wasn't as big as he led me to believe? Not really. Men often imagined themselves bigger than they actually were, and James had that confidence about his body I could only dream of having. Plus, James was manageable, but the dildo in my hand was intimidating.

I hadn't expected to blow James last night. He told me we wouldn't have sex until he was sure I was the one. I still didn't believe his virgin claims, but I couldn't figure out the endgame. I really liked James and was happy to take things slow.

I picked up a dildo of comparable size to the one I tasted last night, trying to choose between the two. It was a broody, dangerous scarred man I had touched myself to. Did I really have to choose just one? I dropped it in the basket with the much longer one and went in search of the Soul Sucker 6000.

Penetration was nice, but I needed more to finish. I had seen some online reviews and was curious about the toy. They had a whole section of clit sucking devices, but when you had a stomach like mine, reaching the sweet spot could be difficult. So, I chose one with a small handle to give a bigger girl more reach. I added lube, toy wash, and some wishful thinking condoms to my basket before I gathered the courage to face the cashier and check out. I hoped nobody I knew was driving down Tyrone Blvd as I rushed to my car.

My nerves only settled when I got into the safety of my condo. I didn't open the boxes until I was behind my bedroom door. It was silly. I could have stuck the dongs to my kitchen counter, lit some candles, and held a dick seance, but shame drove me to the furthest corners of my home.

I don't know why I was embarrassed over buying sex toys. Maybe it was because Mom went religious after divorcing Dad. She'd dragged me to church three times a week, determined that I'd embrace Jesus with her. Maybe it was because they said God saw everything I did, and I'd be judged at the pearly gates later even though he knew a good orgasm chased the gloom away for me. I mean, why would He make humans so sexual if it was wrong?

But it had been the Sunday School teacher's son who took my virginity in a backroom of the church. He said as long as we asked for forgiveness, the slate would be wiped clean. I hadn't been looking for salvation. I had just wanted someone to love me. He had just wanted to get his dick wet. He had been the one who needed God's forgiveness, not me.

I still needed to forgive myself for letting that twerp use me. And I had let him use me, repeatedly, at church. We fucked, then prayed, and he'd ignore me the moment we left that little room. He said he wasn't allowed to date anyone, so we had to pretend we didn't know each other. I believed him, until Chrissy showed everyone the promise ring Charles gave her. I had been devastated. All my stupid dreams of being the wife of a future preacher had been completely shattered.

We were fourteen, and it was a miracle I hadn't gotten pregnant. Mom would have killed me if I had asked for birth control at that age. Hell, it wasn't until much later I learned about condoms.

I stuffed the package of condoms in my nightstand just in case things got heated between...

Who?

James or Logan?

Because my heart and ego wanted James, but my body and something twisted deep inside me wanted Logan. Of course, it was just wishful thinking on my part. Logan scared me too much to flirt with him.

My phone vibrated, and I dug it out of my bag and hit the accept call button the moment I saw James's name.

"Hey, I missed you at school today." His smile radiated through his voice.

"I didn't have class."

"So, you're home alone, thinking about me?"

I smiled. "Yeah, sure. What are you doing later? Wanna come over?"

"Ah, I can't. I made plans with the guys; they were getting pissed because I've been spending all my free time with you."

"Bummer."

"Yeah, bummer. Hey, who is the tall guy with the scars on his face?"

My brows drew together. "Logan?"

"Wears a hoodie and was carrying a bag of cat food?"

"Yeah, that's him. He lives here."

"He's a fucking dick, and if I see him again, I'm going to beat his ass."

I sat up at the anger in his voice. "Why? What happened?"

"The mother fucker questioned me and then pushed me out of the building. He's lucky I didn't beat his ass last night, but I didn't want you to get in trouble for something I did. I'm just giving you a heads up, if that dude fucks with me again, I'm going to kick his ass."

"Are you sure that was Logan? He's like a loner who lives upstairs. He feeds the stray cats at night. I don't think he'd assault a stranger." But even as I said those words my stomach dipped at the lie. Logan would assault strangers.

"Well, he did."

"Fuck, I'm sorry that happened to you. I'll make sure he doesn't do that again."

"No, I'll handle it. Don't you worry. I just wanted you to know. You should stay away from that man. He's unhinged. Probably a serial killer or something."

"Okay, I'll stay away from him. Thank you for letting me know." My stomach flip-flopped as I vowed to do the exact opposite of what I planned.

"No problem, babe, I'll call you later. Okay?"

Could Logan be a serial killer or was James just overreacting?

He said he fed the cats to get rid of them, but I knew that a lot of rescues trapped cats to spay and neuter them just to re-release. I'd seen several cats outside with their ears tipped which was a visual to indicate those felines had already been through a rescue program and weren't fit for adoption.

He said he was a bad man, but he just didn't fit the profile of a serial killer in my mind. No, a murderer would try to appear normal and non-threatening. Logan was menacing and unapproachable. I checked the time. If the scary asshole stuck to his normal schedule, he'd be in the gym working out right now.

I smoothed my short skirt in the mirror and fixed my hair. The laundry was right next to the gym, and I had a whole load to do. I grabbed the basket of dirty clothes and headed for the elevator. A quick check through the window of the gym confirmed he was there, lifting weights like always, but I needed to start the washers first. I needed time to think of what I was going to say to Logan. The dryers were tumbling someone else's clothing, but the small space was empty as I entered. I dropped my laundry basket and started sorting as I muttered my thoughts to myself. Everything I thought of just felt stupid and childish to me. The washers were already doing their job as I stood there, delaying the confrontation with a man I barely knew when the door opened.

I spun around as Logan stepped in, glistening and flushed from his workout. His hair was almost black with sweat as he pushed it out of his eyes. He went to check the dryers as I gaped at the male who made this room much smaller than it already was.

It was now or never.

"Did you attack my boyfriend last night?"

His back straightened as he closed the door to the dryer and fished out a couple more quarters to add more time to the drying process.

"Attack?" He didn't even give me the courtesy of looking at me.

"Yeah, did you assault my boyfriend last night as he was leaving?"

He blew out a long breath as he looked at the ceiling and rolled his shoulders. "I questioned a stranger lurking in the hallways." His voice was low and rumbly.

My fists clenched as I strode forward to close the distance between us. "He said you shoved him out of the building."

He spun around so fast I barely had time to stop my forward momentum. His hand gripped my throat, long fingers wrapping around my neck as his thumb pressed under my jaw. My heart stopped as he pushed me against a double load washer and loomed over me as I bent backwards against the machine. I sucked in a sharp breath of all male scent and almost lost my mind at the lust that unexpectedly shot through me. What the fuck was wrong with me?

Dark eyes sparkled with an anger that matched mine. "Funny, he didn't identify himself as your *boyfriend*."

He watched my anger dissolve into doubt and pain. "It's... new. We haven't had the talk yet," I confessed immediately.

He leaned in closer, and I turned my face to the side. "Get off me," but my voice lacked the bite needed to make him step back.

His mouth moved to my ear as his thumb caressed my cheek. "Ah, I'm sorry he hasn't made his intentions clear by asking you to go *steady* with him."

His fiery breath fanned my ear as his lips moved against the shell, causing gooseflesh to rise all over my body. I even forgot to remark on the absurdly old-fashioned words he used. Words I forgot as his erection pressed between us like the leg of a fucking sturdy chair was stuffed in those soft shorts.

"Eden, you deserve to know exactly where you stand with this chump."

He pulled his hips back and moved his lips across my jaw and over my pursed mouth. *Wait. Did I turn my head towards his just now?*

He kissed the side of my cheek as he moved to my other ear. "If you were mine, you'd have no doubts."

He inhaled and licked up my neck to my earlobe, and I swear my heart stopped its rapid rhythm for several agonizing seconds.

"I'd be shouting it from the rooftop... that you're mine."

I twisted my lips to his as I went from gripping the washer to his rugged and harsh face. I had no idea what I was thinking, feeling, or doing. I just needed to touch him. I smoothed his hood back and relished the feel of his soft hair as I angled my face and parted my lips.

There was no hesitation from him. His mouth opened, and he took it all in the most barely restrained, passionate kiss I'd ever received. His tongue immediately invaded my mouth, and he savored it in an almost forceful reverence. *How could a kiss possibly be both?* His fingers tightened on my neck as his other hand slipped to my back and clutched me to his front. His dick pressed into my stomach, harder than before.

This man was hot for me, and God knew I was melting. I whimpered into his mouth, and he took that, too. I wanted this, wanted him. No games. This was a man who wasn't afraid to take exactly what he craved.

When he pulled his hips back again, my hand slipped between us. My fingertips grazed his dick before his hand snatched my wrist. He pulled back from the kiss with a smirk that was equally frightening and sexy.

"If you were mine, you wouldn't get to touch this until you came three times." His voice was a deep rumble that had my skin feeling too tight.

He returned my hand back to the washing machine and grabbed my hips as I leaned forward and attempted to kiss him again. "I'd need your pussy drenched and begging for my cock."

He lifted me onto the machine in a show of brutal strength and brushed his lips over mine tenderly before moving his mouth down my neck to my cleavage. I was sure he felt my racing heart as he bit down on the flesh of my breast. My legs parted, and he filled the space, pressing himself against me in a way that had me clutching his shoulders as my blouse opened under his deft fingers.

My bra strap fell down my shoulder, and he pushed the cup off my breast as his mouth found my nipple. My breath shuttered out of me as he sucked the tight peak. His hips ground against me, rubbing his dick along my panties in a way that created a fog of lust in my head.

I leaned forward and kissed his scarred temple. "Logan..."

He shied away from my kiss, but moved lower until he squatted between my legs, mouth on the inside of my thigh.

Dark eyes lifted to mine in question.

I spread my legs in answer, but asked, "What if someone comes in?"

His mouth moved to the cotton of my crotch. "I'll fucking kill them."

Fingers pulled my panties aside and his breath fanned my aching and suddenly needy pussy. I'd never felt more exposed than I did at this moment. "You are more beautiful than I imagined, Eden."

He licked along my labia, sucking one side of my pussy before moving to the other side.

I leaned back with a gasp as his tongue grazed my clit. "Jesus, Logan."

His voice rumbled against me. "That god is not here right now. I am."

He worked his tongue deeper, curling it around my clit as he continued to kiss and suck and use his teeth in such a sensual manner that... "I'm going to cum."

He gave my clit a sucking kiss and agreed. "Yeah, you are. You're going to come so hard on my tongue that I'm going to taste this pretty pussy for the rest of the day."

He pulled my hips closer to the edge of the washer and pushed my legs wider as he dove back in like a man on a mission. Spreading me open, his mouth latched on to my clit and sucked me in. His tongue flicked without mercy as my legs started shaking.

Two fingers slipped inside me and curled, stroking a spot that had my back arching and my jaw dropped open. "Oh my God!"

He moaned against me as his tongue drove me to new heights.

Fucking hell, I didn't know someone could do those kinds of things with his mouth. My limited experience with cunnilingus lowered as a new, much higher standard took their place.

I lost my mind as I peaked and then fucking soared again. My pussy pulsed and clenched around his fingers as he eased me down the other side with his mouth. I was a panting, babbling mess as he put my panties back over my pussy. My hand cupped the still throbbing organ as my legs clamped closed. He stood up and my gaze fell to his heavy erection and wet spot on the front of his soft shorts.

"That was number one."

He had promised three orgasms before he'd let me touch his dick. This counted as only one? Cause I just came twice. I was still having mini aftershocks of residual pleasure as my clit pulsed with my slowing heart rate.

He put his two soaked fingers in his mouth and sucked them clean. "If you're still here when I come back, I won't be able to stop myself from having seconds."

He picked up his gym bag but halted at the door. "Now that you've had a man, I better not catch that boy back inside this building."

Chapter Nine

Douch Canoe

Logan

Her friend Tracy called after my girl made it into her bedroom. I put the call on speaker so I could handle other things as I listened.

"Hey girl, what's up with you?"

Eden still sounded breathless. "Dude, I just had the strangest encounter..."

"Hopefully not with the serial killer living in your building."

Serial killer? Seriously? I mean, I was a killer, but there were no bodies in my freezer.

"He's not a serial killer, Tracy."

At least Eden sounded confident even if I was questioning my past and if my actions would have put me on the FBI's most wanted list. Yeah, they would, if they knew about what I had done for the Blue-Frosted Rose Society. What I continued to do for my extended family.

Eden let out a long sigh. "I've never had a man look at me the way he does. It's like he *sees* me."

"Yeah, like you're some juicy meal or something. If you go missing, I'm checking his freezer."

Eden chuckled. "Well, I have other options besides the serial killer."

"Look, I don't know what is going on between you and James, but I'm not sure I like his friends."

"What do you mean?" Eden's voice was wary.

"He had some shady visitors today. They weren't college kids. When I asked him about them, he seemed nervous as he told me they were his older brother's friends."

"He does have an older brother."

"Whatever, it just felt off to me. Tell me all about this strange encounter."

Eden deflected the question. "It was just a weird laundry room moment. Has James said anything at all about me? I mean, we've been officially dating for over a week now." *Oh my little liar.*

"Dating? Like actual dates with dinner and such?" And the white lie worked because Tracy sounded suitably impressed.

"Yeah... and kisses and such..." Eden tried to keep the triumph out of her voice, but it was clear as a ringing church bell.

The silence made me shift uncomfortably, because I saw the pain bleed into her features as distinct as her taste on my tongue.

"Girl, I hate to break it to you, but I don't think James is ready to settle down. I don't know for sure, but he flirts with everyone."

Eden's face fell as she sat down on her couch. "Well, it's only been a couple weeks, but I really like him, and I thought he felt the same."

"Maybe he does, and he's just a friendly guy. I just don't want to see you get hurt, Eden. I know you, and you deserve a guy who appreciates your love."

After a pause she said, "I do. If James isn't shouting his love for me from the rooftops, then he doesn't deserve me." Eden sounded like she was trying to believe what came out of her mouth.

I smiled despite the crack in my heart.

"Yeah girl, fuck him. He's a douche canoe if he can't see how great you are."

Eden laughed and asked, "Douche canoe?"

A knock on the door had my girl jumping to her feet. "Someone's at my door. I gotta go."

Tracy said, "Don't get murdered, and call me later."

I almost jumped up with her but switched to the hallway surveillance camera. A tall, impeccably dressed woman stood in the hallway with Mrs. Bennett who appeared to be coming home after walking her dogs.

The woman knocked again right before Eden opened the door.

"Mom, what are you doing here?"

How did she get inside the building without a code? I quickly accessed the recording of the lobby downstairs. She met Mrs. Bennett as she came in with her small pack of tiny terrors. She held the door for the older woman and became fast friends as they rode the elevator.

The woman pushed past her surprised daughter but not before waving to Mrs. Bennett. She frowned as she surveyed the condo.

"I missed my daughter. Is that a crime?"

Eden closed the door and turned the lock. "Not at all. You could have called me, though." She accepted her mother's hug with light arms and a pinch of the brows.

"Next time." She looked over the living room with an upturned pert nose. "So, this is where Dan set you up. Did he buy this furniture too?"

"No, it came furnished."

Her mother flashed a grin of fake relief. "Oh good, I thought he'd lost his sense of taste."

Eden snorted but said, "I like it. It has a coastal, shabby chic feel."

The woman had moved into the kitchen. She opened the refrigerator and *tsk*ed her disapproval at all the leftover boxes. "I was hoping to see healthy choices in here."

Eden gently pushed the door closed. "I'm learning to cook, and there's a gym here, too."

Her mother, whose name was Karla Anne, straightened with a frown as she looked over her daughter. "You're not wearing makeup. I worry about you."

"I don't have class today," Eden responded quickly. "I wonder though, would you still be banging on my door if I did?"

"Don't be daft, I know your schedule."

Karla Anne started down the hall towards the bedroom and Eden followed.

"Where are you going?"

"To make sure you aren't hiding a boy in your bedroom."

Eden jerked to a stop. "Mom. We are alone."

Her mother opened the bedroom door but didn't go inside. She just peered at the pile of clean laundry Eden had dumped on her bed before turning back down the short hall.

"When was the last time you cleaned?"

Eden backed out of Karla's way and followed her back into the living room.

"What do you want? And don't tell me you were just in the area and decided to pop in."

Her mother stood in the middle of the living room after deciding not to sit down on the couch. "I *want* you to come back home."

"That's not going to happen." Eden's voice was low but firm.

"There's a hurricane in the Caribbean and they are predicting a category five to hit us next week."

Concern gripped me as I pulled up the Hurricane Center on the monitor to my left immediately. There was a disturbance they were watching but it was October and they were actually predicting it would peter out well before it reached the Gulf of Mexico. My scowl returned to the scene playing out in Eden's home.

Eden tilted her head. "They don't know where this tropical depression is going to be in three days, much less next week."

Good girl for not falling for your mother's lies.

"Well, your father hasn't deposited any money in my account this month, and I can't pay Larry to put up my storm shutters. I need your help getting the house ready just in case."

"I'm happy to help this weekend, but I have things to do today."

"Of course," her mother pouted. "I shouldn't have come over unannounced. I just don't know what I'm going to do."

Eden stepped forward as if to comfort her mother but stopped. "It's going to be fine, Mom. Tampa Bay hasn't had a direct hit from a strong hurricane in over a hundred years. Besides, it's too late in the season for a big one to blow in."

Barely controlled rage flashed in Karla Anne's face before she quickly regained control over her features. "Not the storm, silly girl. Your father. He moved you into this dump so he could cut me off financially without notice." She turned away from Eden. "I guess I could get a job, but who'd hire me? I've been a mom and housewife ever since I graduated college."

Understanding dawned on Eden's face. "Mom..."

Karla spun back to her daughter. "I know. I'll be fine. I might have to sell the house you grew up in, but I'll be just fine."

"You can't sell the house."

Rage briefly flashed on Karla's face again before she gave her daughter a sickly sweet smile. "Are you going to help me pay the four-hundred-dollar electric bill?"

"No, it's just the house is in dad's name."

Karla's hands curled into fists and the way Eden took a step back had me rising in my chair.

She advanced on Eden with menace in her voice. "Then he needs to pay for the fucking thing, because I can't."

"Mom, don't... We'll figure something out."

Instead of running downstairs and busting down Eden's door to throw the woman out, I picked up the phone and dialed Dan.

"Hello?"

"Your ex-wife is visiting Eden."

"And?"

"Has she always been abusive to her daughter?"

"What?" The man sounded shocked.

He was clueless about his own family. "Don't cut this bitch off. She's taking it out on Eden. Handle your shit, Dan, or I will handle it for you."

Eden dodged a well-aimed slap, but her mother landed a firm back hand. I was certain Dan heard the shouting through my speakers before he hung up on me. I stood up and gathered my keys before heading to the door. The last thing I heard was Eden telling her mother to get out.

The elevator stopped at Eden's floor, and Karla stood fixing her hair, outrage still plain on her face. I wasn't wearing my hoodie, but she didn't even look up as she charged in. If she'd been in a better state of mind, I was sure she wouldn't have gotten in the elevator with me. She finally looked at me when I hit the stop button before we reached the first floor.

"What are you doing?"

The panic in her voice soothed some of the inner turmoil inside me as I backed her into the corner of the elevator. I wanted to wrap my hands around her throat and squeeze the life out of her. But leaving her body in the dumpster would only hurt Eden more.

My upper lip curled as I made eye contact. "You know as well as I do, Ladies of the Rose do not simply get to walk away from the Society."

Understanding and recognition flashed in her eyes as she realized who and what I was. I leaned closer as her breathing increased. “You’re living on borrowed time, and instead of being grateful for every breath you take, you’re over here causing a scene over a home that does not belong to you.”

Her mouth opened with a response, and I caressed her lips with my finger. “Don’t...” I leaned closer to her ear, “say a fucking word. It’s called a secret for a reason, Karla Anne McKenzie.” I punctuated her full name slowly.

Angling my face to meet misty eyes, my voice was a low purr. “Don’t come back here. Understand?”

She nodded quickly, and a tear slid down her cheek. “Dan will hear about this.”

My lips pulled back in a breathy laugh. I had to give her credit for bravery.

“I’m higher on the food chain than your ex-husband, Karla. So, if you ever raise a hand to your daughter again, I’ll personally call in the debts of your borrowed life. Do you understand me?”

Her gaze latched on to mine. “Is she safe here?”

My thumb brushed across the trail her tear left on her cheek. “She’s in the cradle of safety, but you’re not, Karla Anne. The Society is always watching.”

Her lips pursed before she nodded again. “I understand.”

I smiled again as I reached over and started the elevator once more. I was back on the other side of the elevator when the doors opened, and she rushed out.

Eden

After shoving my mother out the door, I doctored the scrape left by her ring. Tears spilled down my cheeks making the band-aid I applied fall off. The uncooperative band-aid created more tears as I stared at myself in the bathroom mirror.

The backhand had been a new move I hadn't anticipated. I also didn't expect my fear to bleed into outrage.

I was no longer trapped in her depressive world, and I planned on talking to Mrs. Bennett about letting my mother inside the building as soon as my eyes dried up.

I loved my mother. When she was good, she was great, but when things went bad, she was a terror. My dad was always the catalyst to the dark side. There was a reason I had given the wrong door code to my mother.

The worst part was that my home felt violated and judged as inadequate, and everywhere I looked I saw dirt and flaws. I couldn't do anything about the mismatched furniture I called coastal chic earlier, but I did what I could about the filth. Once everything sparkled, I sat down with my sketch book and put my rage onto the paper, ignoring the homework and projects I needed to finish because I couldn't focus on anything else. It wasn't good enough. Why was I never enough for anyone?

At the end of the day, I had five missed calls from my dad. His ears must have been burning earlier when Mom visited, but I didn't have the emotional capacity to call him back tonight. There was no way I'd be able to pretend everything was wonderful.

Besides, I'd see him in a couple days anyway. That brought my thoughts to James, who hadn't called or texted. I obsessively went over every conversation and interaction we'd had up until last night. He had been the one who suggested we take things slow. That didn't sound like the flirtatious player Tracy made him out to be. If he just wanted sex, then why play games? He could have had me last night. Had I not been good enough for him either?

Then again, my dad was the perfect example of a man who lived multiple lives. All my childhood he was the perfectly doting husband and father to his little family, and yet, Mom's accusations of infidelity had been spot on.

I hadn't understood their arguments back then, but as much as I loved my parents, it had been clear, even to a child, that they both had problems. The thing was, Dad never denied his transgressions. Mom knew he had been a cheater from day one and still chose to marry him.

It wasn't until he cheated with her younger sister that she drew the line and asked for a divorce. At first, he denied her the paperwork even after she kicked him out of the house. It was only after years of negotiations and secret mediations before he granted my mother the freedom she desired.

But even after Dad signed the divorce papers, Mom still felt trapped by him. I remembered a long bout of paranoia where Mom constantly thought she was being followed before she settled into the depression that changed her completely.

They say it's never the child's fault that parents don't stay together.

She said I was the reason she'd never be free of *them*, as she exhausted her anger on my bare tender bottom. I never asked who *they* were. I just assumed it was my father, aunt, and the rest of the family, who also ghosted me after the divorce.

Well, now she *was* free of *me*.

Even though my dad was the cause of the abuse I suffered as a child, and my many trust issues when it came to love, I was grateful he had the foresight to get me out from under her control.

And what did I do with that freedom?

I let a scary man give me the best orgasm of my life on a washer in the laundry room. And I didn't even know if it counted as cheating on James. I mean, I thought we were moving toward exclusivity, but I wasn't so sure I even wanted him anymore.

As I undressed to shower before bed, my hand lingered between the choice of dildos I now had available to me. A choice between James and Logan.

A smile formed on my face for the first time today. Both of these dongs belonged to me. Maybe I was more like my dad than I thought, but damn it, this was my fantasy, and not anyone else's.

I stuck both dicks to the tile in the shower and turned on the water as I conjured a scenario that had both men vying for my attention. I imagined two sets of hands touching me as I wrapped my fists around both dildos and stroked. Two mouths kissed up and down my neck as I repositioned my dicks.

I moved the bigger one higher so I could nuzzle and suck it.

I nestled the smaller one between my lower lips, teasing my clit before slowly pressing inside. A moan left me as my body adjusted and took James inside.

In my head, Logan's hand snapped out and snatched James by the throat. His deep rumbling voice vibrated against me as he said, "Make her feel good, or I'll rip it off and you can watch me use it on her properly."

With that thought, I pulled the dildo that was James out of me and lubed up Logan's much bigger dick as his voice in my head snarled, "Or you can just watch as she screams around my cock."

I popped the dildo against the wall and backed up against it as my other hand used the tip of the second dick to swirl around my clit.

My vagina resisted Logan's dildo, but with some adjustment and determination I was able to take the tip before I came so hard I pulled the shower curtain down.

"Fuck!"

I shut off the water and put the tension bar back in place as my pussy throbbed and ached from being stretched. Just the tip, and I was sore. But the thought of both men taking me at the same time had made me come.

Maybe I wasn't built for monogamy.

There was no way either man would agree to share me like they just did in my fantasy, but that didn't mean a girl couldn't dream. Right?

And Logan had me daydreaming. He wasn't as conventionally hot as James was. He didn't give me daddy vibes even though he was at least ten years older than me. No, he gave off dark and dangerous vibes that thrilled me to the core.

The next day, I searched for what I knew I should stay away from as I left for class. I found him in my hallway looking uncertain, like he had been looking for me too.

In a moment of temporary insanity, I marched right up to him and wrapped my arms around his neck. When I pulled him down for a kiss, he resisted at the last minute.

"Those lips are searching for trouble, angel," he rumbled in a low breath that fanned my face.

I lifted to my toes, bringing us closer. "I know what I want."

His gaze roamed my face and lingered on the small scratch on my cheek. "I don't think you do."

His head dipped forward to allow our lips to graze, and just that gentle touch had my body blooming and my heart racing.

His lips twitched in a barely there smile as he spoke against my lips. "Careful what you wish for. You're flirting with the devil."

I leaned in, parted my lips, and kissed him. With a small growl, he attacked. The thrill that shot through me as powerful hands seized my waist had me panting. I gasped as he jerked me flush against him, bending me backwards. Then his mouth devoured mine, and I lost all thought.

This man could have slammed me against the wall and had his way with me. Instead, he pulled back. "I'm not a good man, Eden."

"I don't care," I said breathlessly.

"If you kiss me again..." He scowled and looked away.

I grabbed his face in both hands and slammed my lips against his.

His hands wrapped around my wrists, pulling my hands off his face as he lifted to his full height. "Such a dangerous game you play, little girl." His fingers dug into my flesh. "I play for keeps, and there can only be one winner, Eden. Think about that during classes today. Toy with me, and you'll lose more than you know."

He dropped my wrists and stormed to the stairs as I struggled with an immediate flood of dark daddy vibes to a maelstrom of emotions at war inside me. I didn't know what to latch on to. Fear? Hate? Desire?

Lose more than I know?

"I'm not a virgin, Logan."

His laugh was dry and humorless as the door slammed behind him.

"Or a little girl," I murmured too late for him to hear.

Chapter Ten

Dick Goblins

Logan

Eden looked for me when she got home from her classes, but I made a point to finish everything I had to do outside my home while she was gone. She found the unhappy gang of feral cats waiting for me to show up with dinner later that evening, but not me. The traps worked better if the strays skipped a few meals before I set them.

The disappointment on her face tempted me in ways I had never imagined. It made me want to rush down there and pin her against the building. I wanted to do unholy things to this girl, but she needed time to process the warning I'd give her earlier. I snorted at my attempt at chivalry. It amused me that I tried to give her the illusion of a choice in this matter. Eden was already mine.

It was two in the morning when I plucked my keys off the peg by the door and slipped out of my condo barefoot and silent. Entering her space could become a nightly habit if I let it.

I felt a small thrill as I opened her door and stepped into the quiet, dark entryway. There was always a chance she'd wake up in the time it took me to arrive inside her home. Even if I hadn't been watching the footage all day, I would know she had cleaned the place by the altered scent of her space. While I loved a clean scent in my own home, I grimaced at the intrusion of it here.

At least I didn't have to worry about tripping in the dark. Normally, my girl scattered her belongings like a tropical storm leaving branches and trash everywhere.

Her bedroom door was open, and her sweet scent grew stronger as I lowered myself next to her bed. Her breathing was heavy and even, telling me she was oblivious to my presence.

In fact, she had passed out after masturbating, and her toys were still in bed with her. I moved like a snail and picked up the dildo next to her pillow. All she had to do was open her eyes, and I'd be caught, fake dick in hand. But she was a sound sleeper, and I'd studied her sleep patterns enough to know the signs of wakefulness as I brought the large silicone dick to my nose.

My tongue darted out and her taste consumed me. My cock thickened with envy as my mind pulled the memories of watching her performance on camera earlier. I sat back on my heels as I gave into the urge to unleash myself.

She had chosen to fuck herself with the bigger of the two dildos tonight. The image of her eyes popping wide before her brows turned down with determination came to my mind. It took some time and work, but my girl had managed to take this cold, lifeless likeness of my dick.

I opened my mouth and sucked the tip as I worked my cock with my free hand. The taste was all her. She had been so wet after using the Soul Sucker 6000 on her clit; my good girl hadn't needed to use lube.

It was hard to remain silent as my hand jerked my dick faster, and my breathing kicked up. I had refused my dick earlier for a reason. I bolted towards the finish and lowered the fake dick to my tip. My balls tightened, and my body stiffened, but I marked her dildo with my spunk. I spread my cum all over the fake dick, painting it like I wanted to paint her ample breasts and juicy pussy.

She rolled onto her back and threw the covers off her. It was the first sign of her waking up, but I couldn't move. Her beautiful body was on full display, and my eyes refused to blink until she rolled to face me and pulled the covers back over her. I had mere seconds to drop the dildo and duck down before she flipped the covers back off and headed to the bathroom.

Staying low, I quickly moved to the foot of the bed, rounding the corner just as her feet hit the floor.

"What the..."

Lying flat, I peeked at her from under the bed.

A thrill shot through me as she lifted her foot and picked up the sticky dildo.

"Oh my God, gross."

Ouch.

Footsteps moved away, and the bathroom light flicked on. I tucked myself tight against the bed.

"This can't be all me," she murmured as she lowered to sit on the toilet.

The sound of her peeing reached my ears, and the flush followed. The water from the faucet had me carefully peeking to witness her washing my cum off the dildo. I lowered back down with a quiet snarl at the feeling of rage that churned inside me.

How dare she wash that toy after I claimed it so beautifully?

I recognized when my thoughts and feelings strayed from reasonable and normal and resisted the urge to confront her as she made her way back to bed. The consequences of past mistakes reminded me to play this cool. Eden was mine, but I needed her to want to be owned before I unleashed my particular kind of crazy on her.

Through the video feed I watched Dan visit my girl the following day. Eden's gaze shifted from her dad to the woman standing behind him.

"Aunt Mandy."

She clearly hadn't expected her dad to bring his girlfriend to their dinner date. But Eden had the grace to step back and invite them both inside.

"It's been a while," she murmured as Mandy passed her.

The blonde paused and took Eden's hands. "It's been too long, Eden. I'm sorry for that."

"Yeah, well, that wasn't your fault. Mom hasn't been right since."

Mandy let go of her hand and touched the tiny bruise on Eden's cheek. "Are you okay?"

Eden shrunk back from the touch. "Yes, I'm fine." Her gaze moved to her father. "Have you spoken to her lately?"

Her father embraced her. "Yes. We are renegotiating our original agreement now that you are out of the house."

"Renegotiating?"

They moved into the living room, and Eden seemed pleased that her aunt didn't frown with distaste at her home. Still, she let them have the couch and pulled up a chair from across the room.

"What are you renegotiating?"

He shrugged. "What else is there to negotiate other than money?"

Eden frowned and leaned forward. "Dad, it's not like she can go get a job. She has no skills or experience."

His jaw tightened as he regarded his daughter. "She's had years to prepare for this day, Eden."

Eden rubbed her face and tried again. "Mom hasn't been herself since you left."

Dan lifted a hand. "She kicked me out of my own home and demanded a divorce I didn't want."

Eden glanced at Mandy. "How would you feel if the roles were reversed?"

Mandy lifted both hands. "Let's not go into this right away. Your dad has been more than fair with Karla, and he won't abandon her completely now that you've moved out of the house."

Dan nodded at Mandy's words and added, "The house isn't going anywhere. I'm happy to keep paying the mortgage and utilities. I just don't see why I need to pay all the additional expenses that come with your mother's lifestyle, now that I'm also paying for your expenses outside the house. I mean, Karla really needs to take some responsibility for her own wellbeing."

Mandy put a hand on Dan's knee. "You promised you wouldn't drag Eden into this."

Dan covered Mandy's hand with his own. "I know. I'm sorry."

He turned back to Eden. "So how is school going?"

As I watched this small family maneuver through an awkward dinner, I wondered how each one would react to my presence at their table. Would Eden forgive me for the ritual I had just participated in? Would Dan shrink with the thought of Eden's mouth around a cock both he and Mandy had sucked?

This was why I was still just a stalker to my beautiful girl.

Eden

Sweet Angel

I thought Mandy's presence at dinner would make an already uncomfortable dinner unbearable, but it turned out my mom's younger, home-wrecking sister was the perfect buffer between me and my dad.

It had been the first time I'd seen her since my dad made their relationship official by buying her a new home and moving off the sailboat he had lived on after mom kicked him out. I had loved sailing with my dad on the weekends. I enjoyed boat life even when we merely stayed on the dock. But the moment mom found out about the house, my weekends with dad ended.

Mom had flown into a three-day rage that ended with a week in her bed crying uncontrollably. I had just turned fifteen, and I spent my birthday month caring for a depressed mother who was certain Dan wanted her dead.

Looking back, I should have called a doctor for her, but I was just a kid clinging to the only parent who hadn't left me.

My dad left his marriage, but he never wanted to leave me. It had been my mom who forced his absence in my life. He continued to support his previous family the only way he knew how, by throwing money at us. I should be grateful he did that much.

Mandy wasn't a husband-stealing slut. In fact, they seemed to be a great team. Their love for each other was evident in lingering touches and long stares. It made me wonder how my life might have been different if dad had fought for me. Did Mandy suffer from the same extreme mood swings as her older sister? I wasn't sure knowing the answer would make me feel better about my childhood.

I wasn't sure I wanted to get to know Mandy now. First off, my mom would have a fit if she knew this woman was in my home. I was bad at keeping secrets from her. A dinner with dad was doable but a whole relationship with Mandy was beyond my deception capabilities. I just didn't want to feel the pain of regret.

It was better for all of us if I kept my distance.

The moment I sent them on their way, I rushed to my phone, hoping to find a text from James, even though I was mad at him. My screen was empty. No new texts. Disappointment settled on my shoulders. He knew I was having dinner with my dad tonight. This was important to me. It had been important enough for him to teach me to cook this meal, but not enough to text me during the dinner.

Should I text him?

My thumb automatically opened his last message.

Sweet dreams.

Scrolling up, I reviewed our previous texts to make sure I didn't miss anything. I've been known to misunderstand people, especially in writing. There's no inflection or nuances in text.

But these text messages were all green lights... even spicy at times. Rereading his filthy words had me smiling.

I let my thumbs skim across the phone's keyboard.

Dinner went well. Thank you for teaching me to cook.

My fingers hesitated before I added: **Miss you.**

I hit send and stared down at my phone for a full five minutes like a lovesick fool.

He never responded.

I put my phone back on its charger and walked away from it with a vow of self-respect. This hot and cold shit was wearing on my nerves. Next time I saw James, I'd act uninterested. If he texted me back, I'd make him wait just as long as he had made me wait for my response. I straightened my shoulders. I wasn't desperate. He was the one who pursued me. I just couldn't help but obsess about the fact that he started drifting the day after I sucked him off. Had I moved too fast for someone looking for a wife? We had waited a stretch of time before I even saw his dick, but I had no idea what length of time was not slutty.

My brows drew together. *Was I bad at blow jobs?* My head did a small shake at that thought. I mean... he came. So, it couldn't have been that bad.

I've never really asked for better blowie techniques from anyone with a penis. Maybe I had been doing it wrong all along. Not that I've blown many dicks in my life. But the ones I have sucked on seemed happy with what I did. Charles had even coached me a bit, but his was the first penis I'd ever dared to taste.

Thinking of dicks. Shouldn't I be the one disappointed in James? He led me to believe that he had a big one. It had been nice, but not Logan big.

Why am I even thinking about Logan's dick?

I needed to focus on myself right now.

Why do men come around and fuck with my emotions the moment I feel like I'm finally getting my shit together?

I swore the dick goblins could smell when I felt self-confident and happy. They gathered in tiny hordes just to take a dip in lonely pussy and destroy hearts. *Let's knock her down a peg or two.* No, thank you dick goblins, I'm perfectly capable of knocking myself down a couple of pegs.

A weighted cloud settled over me as I sat down at my little desk to do my schoolwork. No matter how lonely I got, I didn't need dick goblins in my life.

Tracy turned dick goblins into lovestruck fools with just a bat of her eyes. Once she was finished with them, they were dancing to a completely different tune, while she was on to the next conquest. Did that make her a pussy monster? I wish I had the capacity to eat dick goblins for breakfast like she did. But then, she never really connected with anyone. Tracy was unable to function without several love interests. It was how she was able to bounce back after a breakup. I wanted true love and connection, not just an orgasm.

Though, that tongue lashing Logan gave me lingered for days. I still couldn't believe I let him do that to me in a public space. I shook my head and tried to focus on what I was doing.

But my mind refused to let Logan go. Was I that desperate for connection that I fell for a man with good oral?

I flipped my notebook to a blank page and tapped my pen on the paper. What was it about him that had me obsessing?

Besides his tongue skills?

He wasn't my type. Logan was rude and obviously had deep-rooted issues. His dark soul intrigued me. Drew me in like a child reaching for a hot stove. I knew it would hurt, but the wonder of a dangerous man had me hooked. Was that a negative? Maybe.

The man lived in the penthouse condo above me, which checked off the security part of my female desires.

Okay maybe it *was* the tongue.

My pen glided over the paper as I wrote the words, mature and secure. Was I really writing a pros and cons list right now? Yep.

Chapter Eleven

A Fluffy Gray Terrorist

Logan

A week had gone by, and my girl was sinking deeper into a lonely depression. The pansy college kid still hadn't responded to her last text, and Eden wasn't taking it well. Sadness had seeped into her daily life, and as a result, into mine.

She'd stopped going to the gym, so I wasn't able to reschedule my workouts to be with her. Laundry day was delayed because she came home and put on the same oversized t-shirt and shorts she'd worn the day before. And the last time she passed me by on the stairs, she didn't even look up.

I didn't realize chasing her new love away would be so easy. She hadn't looked for the man-child, but I had. He hadn't been staying at the dorm. Eden's friend Tracy verified that over the phone when Eden finally called and asked her about James. He wasn't in jail or the hospital. Curiosity forced me to check when he ghosted her last week. Not that I cared about the kid or wanted him back in her life. I should have made my move by now. Snatched her up and fucked her so hard it blew the clouds away.

What was stopping me?

Besides the fact that I had no clue how to date a beautiful woman almost half my age? I had no social skills outside the Blue-Frosted Rose Society. I had allowed my job to become my personality, and in turn ruined myself for anything good. Now, I was obsessed with stalking this girl, and it was so fucking wrong, but I was in too deep to turn back now.

Something brushed against my leg, and I stopped typing the report I was writing to pick up the scruffy gray kitten. I could feel his bones through the soft fur and winced at how light he was.

"Hey little terrorist, you hungry?"

The tiny bastard started his loud motor and curled up in my lap.

"Goddamn it." The words were harsh, but they carried a tender note.

All the years I've worked with the rescue, I never once had the desire to adopt one of my strays until I saw myself in Eden's sketchbook holding this thing. Now I was responsible for a tiny soul when all I knew was snuffing out lives. I let my index finger move over the base of its skull to scratch behind his ear, even though I had caught him climbing my blinds this morning. I was going soft and it was all because of Eden. The kitten needed toys, and I didn't possess the mental capacity to deal with the general public alone. So, like it or not, Eden was coming to the pet store with me.

A check of the monitors showed Eden finally getting out of the shower after sleeping all day. An impulse hit me, and I was locking my apartment door and pulling up the hood on my light shirt before I could change my mind.

Mrs. Bennett's dogs started yapping as I knocked on Eden's door. It felt weird to knock on a door I'd entered through countless times uninvited.

The lock turned, and Eden opened the door with the towel still wrapped around her wet hair. Her gaze hit my chest and widened as they lifted to my face. "Logan?"

I hadn't thought about what I'd say to her before we were face to face. "I need you to go to the pet store with me."

The door behind me cracked open, and the yapping got louder.

Eden tilted her ear towards me as her face scrunched up with confusion. "What did you say?"

I pushed my way inside Eden's home and pressed my back to the door. She looked alarmed but didn't scream so I said, "You're coming with me to the pet store."

"I am?"

"Grab your shit, and let's go." Because now I needed to get out of her house before I picked her up and carried her back to bed.

Her hand went to the towel on her head. "I can't just... Wait... didn't you say you didn't need me to buy cat food for you?"

My scowl had her eyes flying to the scars on my cheek and her other hand touching her neck. The thin skin of my old burns turned white when I scowled. Pulling my hood down, I strode forward and turned her towards her bedroom. "Go and get ready to leave Eden."

"Okay?" But she marched in the direction I pointed her like a good girl.

My knees bounced wildly as I waited on her couch. Her home was a complete wreck, and all I wanted to do was start picking it up. It was a literal internal fight to sit still.

Ten minutes later she came out, and I stood up. "I don't need you to buy cat food. I just need you to come with me."

She shouldered her purse and asked, "Why?"

I opened the door to the now quiet hallway. "Why not?" I whispered with a dark look towards Mrs. Bennett's closed door.

"You haven't been out in a week, so it's not like you're breaking plans to go with me."

She stepped through the door and put her key in the lock. "How do you know I haven't been out?"

I schooled my features to hide my slip. "Who do you think monitors the security systems in this place?"

She looked up at me as we walked down the hall. "You... watch me?"

I rolled my eyes and opened the elevator doors. It had stayed on the same floor. This building was only busy from November through May as my BFR brothers used it mostly as snowbirds.

I clenched my fists to keep my hands from reaching for her. She eyed them suspiciously. "Look, if you're just going to be mean, you can go to the pet store by yourself."

I grinned at her. "Way to stand up for yourself, Eden. But you're still coming with me."

The elevator reached the bottom floor as she lifted her chin defiantly and charged out the doors as soon as they opened. "You can't force me—"

I grabbed her wrist and spun her back to me. Her shocked face almost made me laugh. "Don't tempt me with a good time Eden. I'm happy to force you for hours."

Realization dawned on her face. "You're insane."

A silent laugh left me. "And you're wet." I leaned closer and whispered lightly,"Aren't you?"

She ducked away with a huge grin. "Oh my God! I am not." And instead of fleeing up the stairs and back to the safety of her home, she marched towards the side door to the parking lot. She glanced back at me and added, "I'm not driving."

I pulled my keys out of my pocket and gave them a cheeky flip. "Didn't ask you to."

She followed me to my truck. "You're not going to kill me. Are you?"

I snorted, "As long as you're a good girl, you've got nothing to worry about."

She climbed up into my truck without hesitation. "I'm worried."

I glanced over at her. "You don't look worried."

Her grin turned bashful as she put her seatbelt on. "It's a flaw."

I started the Dodge. "I know all about flaws, Eden, and when I look at you, I don't see any."

She was quiet as I headed to the closest pet store chain. But after a few moments, she spoke as she looked at her hands. "What happened to your face?"

"Asking blunt questions now?"

She glanced over at me, and I smiled at her. "My biological father was abusive."

"Are you being serious?" Her voice was chilling.

I glanced over at her again so she could see just how serious I was. "My mother died from an overdose when I was two, and my dad took it out on me. I ended up in the foster system until the state gave me back when I was twelve." I didn't know why I was so open with her about my childhood. Maybe it was because she had an abusive mother, and I knew she could relate.

We pulled up to a red light, and I continued as I watched her face. "He wasn't ready to raise a gerbil, much less an adolescent boy. I was fifteen when I forgot to wash a pot I'd used to cook ramen, so he grabbed me by the back of the neck and slammed my face on the old coil stovetop."

"Oh my God, Logan," She breathed in a voice that matched the horror on her pretty face.

I shrugged. "It could have been worse. I had the foresight to reach and grab a knife from the block by the stove. I could have stabbed him thirty-six times instead of just seven."

The pain she felt for younger me was evident in her voice. I was pretty sure she was evaluating her relationship with her mother and comparing it to mine with my father. "Good for you for fighting back."

"I ran to a neighbor, and they called the police. Dad ended up in jail, and since I was almost sixteen when it happened, and I'd stabbed him more than once, they put me in juvie until they could figure out where to place me until I turned eighteen."

She lifted a hand as the light turned green. "Wait, they put you in kid-jail because you defended yourself?"

"No sensible family would take in a teenager with my particularly violent history. Fights and petty theft are chump change compared to attempted murder."

She let the silence stretch between us several heartbeats before she asked, "Is that why you needed me to come with you to the pet store?"

"Because I'm scarred and violent?" I snorted a laugh. "Yeah."

She frowned and looked down at her hands. When I realized my attempt at humor didn't meet its mark, I said, "Your presence is soothing, Eden, and I'd like to explore this feeling a bit more."

She shifted in her seat before glancing at me. Her lips parted with words, but she bit her lip and hung her head again to hide the blush blooming on her cheeks.

So, I addressed the elephant in her mind. "I don't give orgasms to women I don't like, Eden."

Her head snapped in my direction, and I added the obligatory warning. "You deserve a good man who will make all your dreams come true."

Eden

I couldn't believe those words came out of Logan's mouth. It's the fat girl equivalent of "it's not you, it's me," rejection. He didn't get to do that.

I sneered. "Don't give me that shit. How dare you assume what I need? That's just a bullshit excuse as to why you won't have a real relationship with me."

He almost drove over a curb in the parking lot as he gaped at me. "You want a relationship with me?"

My stomach dropped, and my breath caught before I quickly said, "No, I hardly even know you."

"And yet you spread those pretty thighs for me in the laundry room like a dirty, little good girl."

I folded my arms. "I'm not a good girl, and I had a moment of weakness, Logan. It won't happen again."

He waited to park before he asked, "No? You didn't like it?"

I fumbled with the seatbelt. The damn thing wouldn't release me. "It's not that I didn't like it. I don't even know you."

He put his hand over mine. "You, dear Eden, know more about me than most."

He clicked open the seatbelt and lifted a brow. I almost swore under my breath at how sexy it was. I really shouldn't have wanted this man. He was frustratingly confusing, and way too old for me.

"How old are you, anyway?"

"Thirty-seven."

He lifted the hood on his lightweight shirt and hopped out of the truck. I rushed to catch up with his long stride. Jesus, he made me feel like a short person. "Slow down."

He growled, "Speed up."

But he slowed his roll anyway and held the door to the pet store open for me. I asked as I passed him, "What are we here for?"

A pink tinge stained his cheeks as he said, "I adopted a kitten, and he needs stuff before he destroys my entire house."

We passed a glass wall with cages and surly looking cats inside. I stopped walking. "I've heard that the best toy for a kitten is another cat."

He snatched my hand and jerked me away from the adoption area. "I already regret the one I've got." His prickly reply made me grin. It was obvious he was already head-over-heels in love with that kitten.

Instead of dropping my hand he laced his fingers through mine and held on as he led us to the cat aisle. It gave me butterflies in my stomach. *I swear.* One lift of an eyebrow, some bold and grumpy words and a minute holding my hand made me so wet, I was surprised I wasn't making squishing sounds as we walked.

"What do they play with?" His annoyed voice snapped me out of my feels.

"How should I know? My mom took our old cat to go live on a farm when I was just a kid. Haven't had pets since."

"Was it sick?" He was staring at me with a weird look on his face.

"No. He didn't like her anymore. Used to pee in her closet. Now he pees outside in a barnyard with chickens."

His face transformed with compassionate pity as he tucked a stray lock of red hair behind my ear. "No, he doesn't."

I felt foolish. "Well not anymore, probably. He was older when he left."

Logan shook his head slowly and turned back to the rows of cat toys and supplies. I chose a feather on a string, and he picked up a laser with a red dot, some treats, more wet food, a fancy litter box, and a wiggly ball with a tail attached to it.

It wasn't until we were in line when he spoke again. "You really should look up what it means when a parent takes a pet to 'go live on the farm.'"

I tugged my phone out of my back pocket. "Oh my God." It was all I could say.

The cashier took one look at Logan's face, and her smile went soft. She was super sweet and chatty with Logan even though his smile was too tense, and his eyes flashed with anger as he thanked her.

On the walk back to the truck he said, "Either they are too horrified to take a second look, or they are way too nice."

"I didn't know someone could be too nice."

He opened the truck and said, "It's not nice, it's fucking pity. Poor man with the fucked-up face."

"I think it's compassion for the pain you endured, and your self-pity is skewing your perspective."

He hit the brakes and stared at me for a moment. "You're sure you're twenty-two?"

My face heated, and I broke eye contact. "They've always said I was wise beyond my years."

"I'm still too old for you."

I met his gaze and held it. "Is that what you were saying to yourself when you ate me out?"

"Keep being a smartass and I may be forced to spank that juicy pussy on the balcony of your condo just so everyone can see what a naughty girl you truly are."

My lips twisted up. "Promise?"

The look he gave me made me want to touch myself, right here in his truck, just for his enjoyment. I didn't. But oh, God help me, I wanted to.

He grabbed all the bags and walked me to my door even though the way they twisted around his fingers must have hurt like nothing else.

I was so fixated on his pain that I let him step inside my condo after me. "What are you doing?"

He dropped the bags on my floor and locked the door behind him. "Making good on a promise."

"What?" Alarm rang through my voice even though my body blossomed. "You didn't promise, though."

"You're going to learn real quick that I don't make idle threats." His gaze roamed down my bare legs and his tongue darted out to lick across his bottom lip. "You have a three second head start."

I didn't think twice before darting down the hall towards my bedroom. It was only when I slammed the door on him that I realized my bedroom did not have interior locks.

Strong arms wrapped around my waist before I could make it to the bathroom. He lifted me, and I squealed a strangled scream.

Which was insane because... Why didn't I want nosey Mrs. Bennett to hear me and call the police? Did I actually want this man to spank me? The moment he nuzzled against the back of my neck; I knew the answer was a resounding yes.

His hand slipped under my shirt, and his voice was rough as he said, "Fight me."

I twisted around to meet his gaze and asked, "Do you get off on overpowering women?"

He grabbed the crotch of my jean shorts and slammed me back against his rock-hard erection. "Feel that? It's been hard since we left this place. I get off on *you*."

I threw an elbow and stomped his foot, and he laughed as he let me go. With my heart in my throat, I shot out of my bedroom, but he tackled me in the hallway. I found myself face down on the carpet with his weight on my back.

"Asshole," I growled as he pinned my wrists above my head.

His legs wrapped around my thighs as he flipped us. His chest heaved against my back as I stared up at the ceiling. He unbuttoned my shorts and slipped his hand inside. A finger dipped inside me, and he moaned in my ear. "I knew you'd be into this."

"I've been wet since you raised an eyebrow at me in your truck." I cringed at my words. *Why did I just confess that?*

He laughed lightly and nipped my ear. "And now you're even wetter than before."

Before I could confirm or deny anything, his soaked finger took several turns around my pulsing clit, sending zings of pleasure shooting through my body. My lips parted on a gasp, and I exhaled a long moan.

His voice shook with feeling as his hot breath fanned my hair. "Good girl."

If my wrists and thighs had been free, I would have kicked off my shorts and parted my legs wider.

His hand slipped out of my shorts, and his legs uncurled as he tugged down the denim taking my cotton panties with them. I was barely able to kick one leg out before his legs secured my thighs again and pulled me wide, exposing my naked pussy to the cool air.

His palm came down on my tender lower lips in a resoundingly wet smack. A shout left me as I struggled wildly against his hold. But this man under me was all corded muscle as he held me open and secure for his pleasure.

I shrieked, "What the fuck are you doing?"

His hips rolled against my ass, lifting me as his voice purred in my ear. “That was one of fifteen for behaving like a brat.”

His hand lifted and came down on my tender bits, and the percussion of his palm against my clit had my spine stiffening as white-hot pleasure coursed through me.

“Logan...”

Slaps three, four, and five came in quick succession as the familiar warmth of an impending orgasm curled low in my belly. My labia heated and swelled as he cupped me gently, holding me as my body bucked and twisted.

“Logan, please...”

His hips rolled, rubbing the front of his jeans against my ass. “I know, beautiful angel. It’s a lot.”

His hand lifted and the cool air met my inflamed flesh right before he smacked my pussy again in several claps.

My thoroughly confused body stretched as that fleeting orgasm shot forward and then rushed away. My hips thrust against the comforting palm cupping my pussy once more. His large hand held my wildly pulsing clit as if it was a hug. “Logan!”

Two fingers dipped inside me, pushing in and out slowly. “Sopping wet and practically sucking my fingers inside you.”

I didn’t know if I wanted to scream or cry or moan or beg. I went with the latter. “Please, oh please, Logan. I need to—”

He pulled his fingers out and delivered four more slaps before cupping my throbbing pussy once again. I jerked and gasped in his strong embrace. My body was positively feral with the need to be fucked hard and rough until release.

His fingers parted my pussy, pulling me wide so his palm could press against my erratically charged and overly full clit. My hips moved, but his hand moved with me, and I moaned loudly, twisting my face toward his.

The look on his face matched the lust I was feeling. I chased his lips, but he moved back. "How many?"

"Huh?"

His lips twisted into a cruel grin as he pushed three fingers inside me, pumping them in time with my hips. "How many spanks has this little pussy had?"

It took me a long minute to form coherent words as his fingers slowly fucking me continued to be an insane distraction. "Fifteen?"

His laugh was pure sin. "Ten."

"Fuck." My voice was drawn out between pants like I'd run a mile on the treadmill.

His lips pressed against my forehead, and my pussy slammed tight around his fingers as warmth ran through me. "But you've been a good girl through it. So brave and wonderful for me. If you want to stop at ten, I will."

My eyes popped wide. "No! Please, I need to come."

"If you come during punishment, then you don't get to stop coming until I say so."

"What does that even—"

He pulled my legs impossibly wide. His hand left my body and hovered over my parted labia.

"Logan?"

"Hold still."

Then his hand came down right on my aching clit. The clap reverberated through my brain like a gunshot in a tin building. It was hard and, "Oh fuck!"

My legs opened and then tried to clamp closed, but his hand lifted and hovered once more. My clit filled so much I swear it was reaching up to give him a high five before it was spanked once more for being so greedy. My body went wild with bucking as I blew out a loud and unsexy groan.

His hand slapped my exposed clit a third time, and that orgasm that had been playing games with me rushed forward. My body convulsed and tightened with the next slap. Then I stiffened and quit breathing all together as he smacked me again.

I was stuck on the edge of a precipice, dangling from the edge of a sharp cliff waiting for the rope to snap, and it was all-consuming. His soaked fingers parted me and gently, almost too gently soothed over my stalled-out clit. It was as if he'd taken a pair of scissors and snipped the rope.

My lips parted and I sucked in a huge breath as I came all over his slick fingers.

Chapter Twelve

Only Boys Could Be Knights

Logan

Eden practically vibrated with ecstasy as she finally came for me. "Good girl. Such a sweet, unbridled, beautiful girl."

My slick fingers continued their light, slow roll on her dripping cunt even as she stiffened and made a confused noise. She thought it was over as she came down, but I was far from through with her amazing body.

She wasn't supposed to enjoy this. I thought she'd scream bloody murder and claw my eyes out when I showed her the man I truly was. The Lurch that everyone feared. But her screams had more thrill and pleasure in them than they should have, and that was an undeniable, mother-fucking turn on.

Shit, my alter ego had me wanting to tie this woman open on my bed to savor an entire night of vile and sadistic shit.

"Logan?"

"You've got another for me. Don't you, sweet girl?"

"Yes..." she breathed, and I pressed my lips against her temple as I moved my fingers slightly faster.

Her body tightened, and her hips undulated against my neglected dick. I needed to be inside her like a heart attack needed a defibrillator. Fuck, I couldn't wait to see her stretched around me as I worked my length inside her. The thought had my own orgasm rushing front and center, but by some miracle of will, I was able to hold it off.

Not that it would ever happen after this encounter. I'd force a few more orgasms on her, tuck her in bed, and she'd come to her senses and run the next time she saw me.

I pushed three fingers inside her convulsing pussy. "Good girl. So wet, you'll be dehydrated after this."

Her hips met each thrust, and the sounds of my fingers fucking her made her cheeks go redder.

I withdrew from her and maneuvered her so I could pick her up as I stood.

"Logan!" Her eyes popped wide as she clung to me.

"Yep," I drawled as I carried her to her bedroom.

"You can't carry me."

"Seems like I am, though."

She buried her face in my neck as I entered her bedroom and placed her on the bed. She kicked her shoes off, and I pulled her shorts off that were dangling from her leg.

She sat up as I climbed onto the bed and shouldered my way between her thighs. "I... Logan... I can't."

I pulled in her scent with a long inhale. "You can, and you will. Now lie back."

She reached for the drawer of her nightstand. "I'm not on birth control."

I buried my face in her drenched cunt and spoke against her, "And I have no plans to fuck you today."

She flopped back but jolted as my nose grazed her well-used clit. "Logan!"

I laughed as I licked up her slit, sending her spine rigid. "I can't..."

I gave her sensitive little clit a sucking kiss, and she gasped and clamped her thighs down around my shoulders. I shoved three fingers inside her and spread them wide as I pulled out. Her legs opened, and my tongue found her clit.

Her hips wiggled, and the squeal she let out went straight to my dick. My hands secured her waist, and I pulled her closer as I worked her with my sharp tongue. She tried to climb up the bed to find relief, but I had hooked my knees on the edge of the mattress and forced her to stay where she was.

Her next series of orgasms were so sharp that she lost control of her voice and limbs. I slowed down, became gentler as I loved on this pussy like I was starstruck. She came again with a loud whimper.

Then she went completely limp, surrendering her body to me.

I moaned as my own pleasure focused at the tip of my cock.

Her entire pussy slowly pulsed under my lips. Each throb against my mouth had her clit jumping and her body jolting. The noises she was making were like nothing I'd ever heard... pure satisfaction and ecstasy.

My cock exploded, and I met her well-pleasured pussy with deep moans as my hips moved in time with my pleasure. "Fuck, Eden," I whispered like a prayer as I drained my balls inside my pants.

She lifted her head and met my gaze. Her eyes were full of tears, and a sheen of sweat glistened at her hairline. "Fuck me, Logan... Please."

I pushed off the bed, and her thighs pressed together as an aftershock ran the length of her spine. A surge of pride rose in me at the sight of her quivering on the messy sheets. "Remember what I told you in the laundry room?"

She lifted to her elbows as I stalked towards the door. "I've come like a million times already, and I still haven't seen your dick."

The jizz in my pants was starting to cool off, making me feel dirty and sticky. My discomfort reflected in my voice. "That was two, you've got one more left."

"Logan!" she called after me as I picked up the bags of cat stuff and left.

Later, after I had cleaned up and spent some time with the fluffy gray terror who had claimed my home as his personal playground, I turned on the video feed to her bedroom. I rewound and watched everything I had done to Eden.

For someone who had done some seriously fucked up shit in his life, my alter ego, Lurch, failed to put fear into Eden. While there were flashes of panic on her face throughout the experience, she was plainly thrilled most of the time. I wasn't mad about it.

Even after I left her, even as she cleaned up and sat on the edge of her bed weeping into her hands, the look on her face seemed cathartic. She spent an hour picking up her apartment and washing dishes, moving like she was still in a post-orgasmic haze.

Then she picked up her phone and dialed her friend, Tracy.

The girl picked up with a cheerful tone. "Hey, girl! What's up?"

Eden sounded troubled. "Hey, so I just had the weirdest encounter."

"Do tell."

"You know that older guy who lives in my building?"

"The serial killer?"

Eden snapped, "He's not a serial killer. At least, I don't think he is."

Tracy sounded doubtful. "Oh-kay." But then eagerly added, "What did he do this time?"

"He took me to the pet store. Just out of the blue. Knocked on my door and said, 'let's go.'"

"And you went with him? I would have slammed the door in his face."

Eden was silent as she weighed the option of telling her best friend about what happened next. But all the words and feelings tumbled out of her mouth in what felt like one breath. When she finished with her version of what happened, it was Tracy's turn to create a long silence. She finally said, "Girl... Eden... that sounds like sexual assault to me."

Eden rushed her words. "It wasn't like that. He would have stopped, but I never told him to."

"I'm not sure you believe that."

"It's true, and girl, I've never felt like that before. I came so hard, so many times, and even when I begged him to fuck me, he kept his dick in his pants."

Tracy sighed. "Just because he didn't rape you, doesn't mean he didn't assault you. This guy is a walking red flag."

Eden mimicked Tracy's sigh. "I know. I saw the red flags... I just didn't care. Now I wonder what is wrong with me. I enjoyed it, Trace. Like best not-sex I've ever had."

"Look, you need to get out of the house and hang around people your own age. We are going to a Halloween ball downtown Friday night. It's a private thing, but a friend is getting us tickets. I'll see if I can get an extra."

"A ball?"

"Yeah, like a masquerade thing."

"I don't have anything to wear."

"Neither do I, so I figured I'd wear my old prom dress and buy a mask."

"Who all is going?"

"If you're asking if James will be there, I don't know. He's back in the dorm, though. Said his grandma died."

Eden's face fell. "Why didn't he call me? I... Nevermind. I'm over his ass."

"Maybe you'll dance with a handsome young stranger at the ball and be swept off your feet."

Eden laughed. "He better be strong if he's going to sweep *me* off my feet."

"So long as he's not fifteen years older and a walking, talking red flag."

"Okay, I'll go. I need to go home to visit my mom, anyway. Gosh, I don't even know where my old prom dress is."

She hung up with Tracy and immediately called her mom.

"Hey, Mom. Do you know where my old prom dress is?"

"Your prom dress? Why do you need that?"

Eden's face lit up. "I've been invited to a ball."

Her mom went silent a moment before speaking again. "I put it in the hall closet after it came back from the cleaners. I'd assume it's still there."

"Cool, I'll come pick it up tomorrow." Her mother must have apologized to Eden for her outburst. If Eden was so good at spotting red flags, she wouldn't keep running back into the arms of her mother. But I get it. I had been desperate for my father's approval when I returned home. The few times he gave it and acted proud of me, I soaked it up and walked on cloud nine for weeks.

"When is the ball? You've lost a lot of weight since you were in high school, it may need some alterations."

"It's Friday at a theater downtown. Tracy invited me."

"That doesn't leave a lot of time to get it altered, but I think I know someone who might help. I'll call her tonight and see if she can come over."

"That would be great! I can try it on tomorrow, and she can take it with her."

Another awkward silence stretched between them. "Will James be there?"

Eden's face fell, and her voice reflected the disappointment she felt. "I don't know. He hasn't called me in a while."

"Boys that age can be fickle."

"Tracy said his grandma died, and he was away with family."

"Well, that explains it. I bet he didn't want to bother you with his grief."

Eden shrugged even though her mother couldn't see it. "Probably. Listen, I've got to go. See you tomorrow?"

"Sure, honey. See you tomorrow. I love you."

"Love you too, Mom."

Eden

Going home brought a flood of childhood memories as I pulled onto the street I used to ride my bike up and down during hot summer days. My bike, long outgrown and absent from the two-car garage, was named Trigger. To my younger self it wasn't a bike at all. It was my trusty steed, and we slayed dragons together daily, until a boy who lived two streets over told me only boys could be knights.

I parked and walked up to the front door because said garage door was now closed. It used to sit open all day long when I was a kid. Before Dad betrayed his family and went to live on a sailboat in St. Pete.

Should I knock? Ring the bell?

I tried the handle, and it clicked open. “Mom? I’m home.”

“I’m in the kitchen with Shelly.”

I moved through the foyer noting that everything was in its proper place. Mom was a minimalist who kept her home in perfectly pristine condition.

I really needed to declutter and deep clean my condo.

I found them sitting at the kitchen bar with my prom dress laid out between them. “Hey, Shelly.”

I greeted my mom’s friend with a smile. She had been an ally during my mom’s depression and was the one who led us to God. While church had been exactly what my mother needed, Shelly’s appearance brought another, darker memory to mind. She sat in the exact same spot as she had when she comforted my mother after I was caught kissing a boy behind the church.

“This is a beautiful dress, Eden.” Shelly picked at the off-the-shoulder satin sleeve as she spoke.

My mother answered her friend. “Thanks, I picked it out for her prom. Though she was a bit heavier than she is now, it looked amazing on her.”

My weight loss during senior year had been her greatest achievement. It had come with a healthy dose of fat shaming and snack deprivation.

“I’m going to put it on.” I picked up the dress and rushed to my old bedroom so they wouldn’t see my smile wane.

The reality was, I hadn’t lost that much weight. Thirty-five pounds was something to be proud of, but when you weighed a little over two hundred pounds, well the dress wouldn’t be falling off me anytime soon.

It was an elegant dress, though. A perfect dark purple that didn’t clash with my fire-red hair due to the black lace overlay. The high-low hem hit perfectly below my knee, which had been a miracle for a teenager who was taller than average. The black lace still covered my arm pudge but it was as loose as the bodice was.

Thirty-five pounds, straight out of my boobs and not where it mattered.

When I left the mirror and arrived in front of Mom and Shelly, my face heated at my mother's considering frown. Did she also notice where the dress remained tight around my middle? All that work she'd done to fix her fat kid, and it had the audacity to still have a belly.

Shelly stood up with a grin and started pinching fabric here and there. "A few simple darts and tucks and it will fit like a glove."

My mother lifted a finger to her lips and tapped it twice before asking me, "Are you wearing the girdle I bought for you underneath?"

I froze. "No."

"Well, it should still fit since it was let out as much as it could be the last time you wore this dress. Go put it on so Shelly can get an accurate measurement."

I turned back to my room keeping my heavy sigh to myself. That girdle had been the most uncomfortable contraption I had ever worn. So much so, that I knew the exact drawer it rested in, untouched and still sweat-stained from dancing all night.

The hooks and laces were still as sturdy as they had been years ago, but the bite wasn't as bad as my memory served. I slipped the dress back on and pulled the matching heels out of the back of my closet. I put a pair of black panty hose on my to-do list, since my old pair had long since been trashed.

My mother bit her bottom lip as she ran a critical eye over me once more. "Can't that go any tighter?"

Shelly thankfully said, "Her waist looks amazing as is. Plus, we don't want to take it in too much or it might not fit if she is bloated on Friday."

Mom conceded with a wave of her hand. "You're right. Knowing my daughter, she'll have a big salty lunch the day of and gain three pounds of water weight."

She turned to refill her glass of wine. "I used to attend the most extravagant balls with..." She made that face she always did when she didn't want to say Dan's name. "I'd limit my food the day before and drink exactly four glasses of water and nothing else the day of."

She brought the burgundy liquid to her lips and took a sip as she surveyed me. "I'll text you my diet, and if you are careful, you might be able to tighten that girdle another notch the night of your ball." Her gaze traveled from my head to my toes. "Do that, get a spray tan, let a salon do your hair, and wear pantyhose and you will be simply stunning."

I smiled through the pain in my heart. It was as close to a compliment my mother would ever give me. "Thanks, Mom."

Shelly got back to work, tucking, pinning and measuring as my mother asked for details about this ball. I had to text Tracy multiple times in order to answer her questions. Thank goodness Tracy confirmed that she did indeed get my ticket, and that ticket revealed most of the answers to satisfy my mother's curiosity.

My mother disappeared into her room and came out holding a pink hat box. The look on her face told me she'd debated long and hard about giving it to me as she presented it. "I used to attend the most elaborate galas and masquerades."

I opened the lid and gasped at the mask that lay on delicate, soft pink tissue paper. It was a black cat mask that had sparkling jewels lining the edge. "Mom..." I breathed.

"It's a panther, and the diamonds are real. I couldn't bring myself to sell it after *he* left me."

I met her gaze. "Did he fix what he did?"

I didn't want to bring up her finances in front of company, but she understood the meaning of my question. "He's being frugal." She pursed her lips but smiled reassuringly. "Don't worry, I have it figured out. We'll be just fine."

I lifted the box. "Thank you for this. I'll take such good care of it and return it on Monday."

Shelly packed my old prom dress back in its bag and said, "I have some ideas that would go wonderfully with that mask. Do you mind if I add a hint of elegant bling to the dress?"

I smiled at the woman who'd been more like an aunt than Mandy ever had been. "I love bling."

She picked up the dress with a broad grin. "I should have this finished by tomorrow afternoon. I'll call you when it's ready, and you can come pick it up."

I nodded eagerly. Shelly lived in Pinellas Park, which meant neither one of us had to drive to Tampa.

Mom seemed to realize that meeting wouldn't take place at her home and said, "Pictures. I'll need lots of pictures of the final product."

"I'll send you tons."

I gave her a kiss on the cheek and gathered my things. I needed to study some hair tutorials and decide what to do with my flaming hot mess of hair.

Chapter Thirteen

Halloween Ball

Logan

The moment Tracy confirmed Eden had a ticket to the masquerade ball, I secured my admission as well. There was no way in hell I'd miss this opportunity to play with her in my element.

My alter ego purred with satisfaction as I opened my closet full of costumes and masks. Lurch had all sorts of fantasies he wanted to play out with Eden. Had I lived a normal childhood, I might have been that drama kid who took his acting to the next level. We did enjoy dressing up and scaring the shit out of people on Halloween.

The BFR gave me a reason to be scary every day. But that was work. Friday would be pure pleasure as Lurch imagined bending Eden over in an alcove at the party. My hand paused on a vintage black tailcoat. The matching vest and pants hung beside it, and I gathered all three hangers in one hand.

I moved to the hand-carved oak dresser and pulled out a drawer that displayed my favorite masks. A feral werewolf mask glared up at me with vacant eye holes and pearly-white canines gleaming from the upper jaw. It was a custom-made, realistic piece made from vintage fur coats, and it sat over my head like the hoodies I wore on a daily basis. The snout covered my face even though the bottom jaw was missing to allow the wearer the freedom of food and drink.

I had the perfect gloves to pair with this ensemble. They were handmade, leather gauntlets with enamel claws jutting from above four of my fingers. It left my fingertips and thumbs free to handle whatever I needed to touch—Eden's smooth skin—but made an impressive image.

Would she be terrified by the werewolf in an expensive suit? Or turned on? My gut did an unfamiliar dip. It had been so long since I felt anything other than the thrill of doing bad things, that it took me a minute to associate that flip with a positive feeling.

My first instinct was to run. Love had never been for me. Even when Mr. Dalton officially adopted me into his family, I hadn't allowed myself to feel much for the old man. I forced a line between my new brothers who had embraced me wholeheartedly into their spectacular world. That universe had been high-falutin and upper class, but I had been living in survival mode.

I picked up my phone and clicked on one of my favored contacts. The phone rang twice before Theodoric answered. "Hey, Logan."

Unlike his brother Mickey who enjoyed drawling my alter ego name out like a frat boy, Todd preferred to use my given name.

"How did you know?"

Todd knew me better than most, so my bluntness never bothered him much. "Know what?"

"That you were in love with Lizzy."

He paused. "Okay? I just knew that my life would be dull and boring without her by my side."

Bless this man. Mickey might have jumped right into teasing me, but not Theodoric. He'd always been the emotionally stable one of the family. It wasn't Mickey's fault that he had been thrust into the role he played for BFR when our father died. He had been too young, and his boisterous attitude became a wall for him.

I shook my head to clear my rambling thoughts. "How did you get her to love you back?"

"Well, I knew her outside of BFR. We had this flirtatious banter where we worked together, but I was sure she wouldn't fit into the brotherhood, so I was prepared to walk away until Mickey found out about her."

"I don't think I can walk away." That wasn't supposed to come out of my mouth.

"Then don't."

I inhaled a deep breath and let it out slowly.

Todd took my silence as a cue to elaborate. "If anyone deserves someone to love them like Lizzy loves me, it's you."

I mumbled, "She deserves better than me."

"You don't have to be the bad guy of BFR anymore, Logan. There's a host of up-and-comings that can take over. Maybe it's time to retire Lurch and live your own life."

"I don't know..." Lurch was a huge part of my personality. It wasn't possible for me to drop him just like that. He'd manifest in less productive ways.

"Look, I'm just saying that if you need to adjust your role in the company to better fit with a committed home life, then BFR will accommodate you. Don't let anything stand in the way of your happiness, Logan."

Happiness was such a foreign word. "Thanks, Todd. I appreciate it."

We hung up, and I spent the rest of the day pondering my feelings. Eden liked me. She didn't shy away from my rough edges. Yeah, I was too old for her, but she enjoyed my experience where it counted. I didn't deserve her, but damn it all, I would have her.

It was time I made my move.

The problem was Carl's gang was rumbling loudly about the gift they received. Apparently, he had been a beloved piece of shit among his brothers, and the Death Adders' leader declared war the moment he received Carl's testicles in the gift box I sent him. They declared it loud and proud, which was not our desired outcome. BFR was a secret society.

I received a message from Bentley: **Something is going down on Friday. We are working to find out what it might be, but they have gone radio silent.**

Silence, while the ultimate goal, wasn't a good thing after all the rumbling the Death Adders had done recently. We might have underestimated this gang, and because of that, I might be called away to deal with their shit instead of romancing Eden.

My guys were playing defense when we should have been playing offense. I responded to Bent's message: **Pull in Monk.**

His message was immediate: **NO! Please, gods, no.**

When I didn't respond he sent: **Fuck.**

Yeah, fuck. I'd only met Monk twice and the man got the job done both times. He should have been called the Hellhound, but Tor and Gaul already had that call sign. Why Hellhound? Because he controlled the demons of Hell.

Monk had been around longer than I had, though he looked barely thirty. Blond hair so pale it was almost white and icy blue eyes that were completely dead. One didn't call in Monk for trivial shit. He controlled the power that gave the Blue-Frosted Rose their reason for existence.

Lots of legends surrounded the mysterious Monk. Rumors and speculation preceded him like mist, but if anyone could infiltrate the Death Adders without all-out war, it would be his demons.

The Death Adders would no longer be a problem for Central Florida. It would be a bomb of bad luck for them. Suicide, freak accidents, and probably a police sting followed by a string of confessions that wouldlead to jail time. The notorious gang would implode and disburse without any idea we were involved.

There would be a cost for their demonic services. I'd already put the order for more demonic rituals into our private pipeline. Monk would receive an influx of power as members lit candles and placed offerings on their altars, but a job of this size would require something special from me.

Dread twisted my stomach as I prepared myself for what was to come.

Eden

Sweet Angel

Tracy's text popped up on my phone, announcing that the limo was here. I stepped back and took one final look at myself in the mirror. Even without the girdle my mother had suggested, I smiled at the final image. Shelly did an amazing job with the fitting, and I loved the tasteful bling she added to the lace covering the dark purple gown.

I'd practiced braiding my unruly hair, and after many tutorials and a trip to Tyrone Mall for supplies, I'd mastered the look I wanted. My hair, when tamed, was my best feature, and the tutorial I followed was inspired by the show *Vikings*.

I grabbed my mother's beautiful mask and the clutch that matched my dress and rushed to the door. I straightened my spine and gracefully strutted down the hallway towards the camera outside the elevator. My lips quirked up as I gave the lens a tiny little wave, wondering if Logan was watching.

I hadn't seen him around since he'd barged into my home and pushed my body past its limits. I was still shook. He changed the way I loved myself. James's dick was a lonely inadequate tool sitting in my bathroom cabinet while the much larger dildo slept in the side table next to my bed. And my clit would never be the same. One orgasm would never be enough now that my body had awakened.

My face was flushed as I got to the awaiting limo. The door opened and music spilled out as Tracy exclaimed, "Damn bitch! You're hot!"

I performed a little spin for the crowd inside the limo before diving in. The colorful satin, chiffon and variety of perfumes felt like confetti to my senses.

Tracy said, "You guys remember Eden from the dorm party a few months back?" She waited for them to confirm before reintroducing me to Lisa, Dulci and Chandra.

Lisa passed me a glass of champagne. "Open bar courtesy of Chandra."

I took the flute carefully with a smile to Chandra who was stunning in her lavender gown. "Thanks."

Before Tracy could remind them I was an uptight party-pooper, I took a sip. It was a short drive, and I had three more sips before we arrived at the Coliseum. It was just enough to tame my nerves as I fixed my mask around my head.

Dulci exclaimed, "That's an amazing mask, Eden."

"It's my mother's."

Tracy said, "Her mother used to go to all sorts of soirées in her day." She set her jaw and spoke through her teeth as she drew out the next words in perfect snobbery. "Very classy indeed."

Chandra laughed so hard she snorted as the limo driver opened the door.

Tracy's grin widened. "Nice entrance, Chandra."

Dulci added, "You will forever be known as the snorter."

Lisa laughed, "Stop, I'm going to pee myself."

All I could do was smile at the antics of my four tipsy companions. *Should I have started drinking earlier, too?* While I liked a soft buzz, I hated being out of control drunk. And these four were rushing headlong into fall down, blackout drunk by the end of tonight.

The sunset was a spectacular backdrop of pinks and blues for our entrance into the building. I said, "Wait, let's take a picture."

Dulci pulled the others back towards the limo. "Oh, hells yeah."

Tracy fished out her phone and handed it to the driver. "Do you mind?"

His smile was quick. "Not at all."

He snapped several photos, and I said to Tracy, "Send those to me, so I can show my mom."

"I got you, girl." Tracy thanked the driver and promised to text him thirty minutes before it was time to leave.

My phone chimed, and I opened the string of photos, chose the best one, and whisked it away to my mother before silencing my phone and stuffing it away.

The decor inside was stunning and unexpectedly classy for a Halloween Ball. We passed tables filled with finger food, champagne fountains, and ice decorations as we found our table.

My stomach dipped. Right next to our table, sat James surrounded by a bunch of rowdy friends. He was wearing a button up black shirt and tie but no mask. Instead, he and his group had opted to paint their faces to look like skulls. He waved at Tracy but bit his knuckle as his gaze moved to me. The action smeared a bit of his makeup, but he stood up and said, "Damn, is that Eden under that kitty-cat mask?"

Tracy snorted. "Of course, it's Eden, dumbass. Regret much?"

"Very much," he said without taking his eyes off me.

I opted to ignore the thrilling butterflies that took flight inside me and sat down gracefully. He was too late to manage my chair for me, and his awkward jolt was icing on the cake.

James swapped seats with his buddy to sit closer. The hair on my arms stood up as he whispered in my ear from behind, "You look amazing tonight."

I moved away to keep him from smearing his makeup in my hair, or God forbid, my mother's mask. "Thanks."

He filled the space I made. "I'm sorry I ghosted you. My grandmother died, and I'm not taking it well."

I put my hand on his chest and pushed him back so I could look him directly in his dreamy blue eyes. "I'm sorry to hear about your grandmother. I'm also sorry you felt like you had to deal with your grief alone, but I don't think I'm ready for a committed relationship right now."

It took everything in me not to roll my eyes at the word committed. If James had truly thought I was wife material, he wouldn't have ignored my frantic messages for the past two weeks.

He blew out a harsh breath, and my nose scrunched at the stale alcohol I smelled. "It was a shit thing to do. I tend to withdraw when I'm hurting. I know I need to work on that. Again, I'm sorry."

I turned my back to him. "Apology accepted, but again, I'm good with just being friends."

He sighed, "Okay, friends it is."

He turned back to his table, but a short while later he turned back around. "I'm going up to the buffet. Want to go with me? As friends?"

"I think I'll wait to eat, but thanks."

He countered, "Want me to bring you a glass of champagne?"

I lifted the chilled glass of water in front of me. "I'm hydrating before drinking."

He got up and said, "Cool, let me know when you are ready to cut loose. I'll grab your first glass for you." I watched him join his friends as they prowled towards the food-laden tables.

My gaze lifted to the twinkling lights suspended high above us. Movement caught my eye, and I said to the girls around me, "Look, this place has a balcony."

The excited conversation stopped as the girls spotted the second story. Lisa gasped, "Oh my God, there's a werewolf up there."

Tracy said, "It's looking right at us."

Chandra added, "That costume is so cool."

Dulci turned to Tracy, "You should go up there and ask him to join us."

I glanced at Dulci and said, "What if he's really a she?"

Chandra countered, "That's a dude."

The werewolf was shadowed in darkness as it stared down on our table. Was it staring at *me*?

Lisa asked the question on my lips. "How can you tell from this far?"

Chandra grinned a feral smirk at her friend. "Oh, I can tell."

"Well then, go get him."

Brown eyes turned to me. "He'd have to take that mask off first. I don't play like that."

I laughed and revealed way too much information to a complete stranger. "I prefer the mask on."

Lisa barked a laugh. "Kinky."

Tracy shook her head. "She's really not."

I sobered but couldn't help the grin that tried to break through my serious look. "You don't know the type of smut I like to read."

Dulci slapped the table with her palm as she howled with laughter. "Monster fucker."

The voice behind me made me cringe. "Who's a monster fucker?" I had forgotten James was still sitting behind me.

Tracy covered her mouth as she laughed and pointed to me. My face heated as Chandra said dramatically, "Put the mask back on Were-Brad."

I shook my head and embraced being the butt of the joke. "Oh Were-Brad, you're so handsome when you wear the monster-mask. I can't resist all that fur." I busted out laughing but said, "Oh that's okay. Hairballs are sexy."

And that's how the rest of the night went. Me, the monster fucker, and them trying to hook me up with every demon, werewolf, and furry that seemed single. Everyone except the werewolf watching our table from the balcony.

Chapter Fourteen

Romantic Werewolf

Logan

Stunning. She was absolutely ravishing tonight in that beautiful dress and elegant mask. I'd watched the painstakingly tedious way she got ready and laughed softly at her tiny wave to the camera outside the elevator.

I relished the way that boy looked at her as she rejected him. The look that came across her face as she turned away from him had my chest expanding. Good for her. After all those ignored messages, he deserved her dismissal.

Then she looked up at the VIP balcony and spotted me immediately. My heart thundered wildly with the feeling of being caught stalking her. I almost ducked behind the railing as her eyes locked on me but then I remembered that I was wearing a mask.

The lighting dimmed, and the stage at the far end of the cavernous building lit up. The program had listed some risqué entertainment, but the best part of shibari was watching Eden discover her feelings about what was happening on stage. Her lips parted in a silent exhale as the rope bunny on stage was suspended.

I knew my way around knots and suspension, but the artist on stage checked in with her subjects, ensuring their safety and comfort as she tied them up in time with the blaring music. My experience with bondage centered around pain and torture. I'd never considered rope to be anything other than a tool, but this performance had me spellbound.

My phone vibrated, and I pulled it out of my pocket to view the screen. Bentley was calling. I hit the answer button, and my earbud activated. "Hold on."

I moved down the stairs and out the front door, nodding to the attendant. "What's up?"

"Are you at a party while I'm dealing with Monk?" Bentley sounded annoyed.

"It's an assignment. What's up?"

"About thirty gang members are moving in your direction. They are heavily armed, and Monk said they were coming for you."

"For me?"

"He said you have to fuck a virgin in the sea and steal sleeping beauty."

I jerked my mask off. "What?"

I heard the distinct clipped accent of Monk in the background. "That's not what I said, you dolt."

Bentley sighed with more annoyance as he repeated exactly what Monk dictated. "To survive the night, you must go west with what you most desire. And... in payment, you must betray sleeping beauty and shed the blood of an unsullied body."

My brain immediately attempted to sort the riddle as I asked, "How much time do I have?"

Bentley answered, "Two hours."

I put my mask back on and silenced the chaos in my head. "Buy me three."

"You got it." Bent ended the call.

I called Dan and didn't wait for pleasantries. "Do you still have your sailboat docked in St. Pete?"

"Yeah, why?"

"We have a security situation, and I may need to use it."

"The key is on a hook under the console. Is Eden safe?"

"Yes." I ended the call knowing Bentley would brief Dan later.

The show was over by the time I got back in. Music was playing softly, and several people were on the dance floor. Eden was still sitting at the table watching her friends dance and fending off that kid. I had three hours to woo my heart's desire enough to go sailing with me.

I beelined through the crowd and extended a clawed hand to her. "Care to dance?"

The kid half stood with a territorial glare. "No, she doesn't want to dance. If she did, she'd be out there with me."

My lips twisted up as I kept my gaze on Eden, my hand still extended. Recognition flared briefly at the sound of my voice as she scrutinized what was visible of my jaw and lips from her viewpoint.

James warned, "Eden," as she slipped her hand in mine.

I helped her up, and the kid asked her, "What are you doing? You just said you didn't want to dance."

Her beautiful smile fell, and I said, "Maybe she was waiting for the right partner to come along."

I didn't wait for her to placate the boy. Instead, I led her to a clearing on the dance floor. "You okay?"

"Logan?" Her voice held a note of doubt.

"You sure about that?"

She shook her head like she could straighten out her thoughts. "What are you doing here?"

I took her hand in mine and supported the small of her back with the other. "Follow my lead."

Mild surprise filled me as she started moving in perfect time with me. I shouldn't have been shocked she knew how to dance;

most BFR children were groomed for the lifestyle at an early age. Manners, running a big house, dancing, and etiquette were just as important as school. I had just assumed because of her broken home, that she hadn't been raised with the same values as those families who adhered to their vows and stayed together for the benefit of the society and children.

"I didn't know you could dance, Logan."

I pulled her closer. "There's a lot of things you don't know about me, Eden."

Her steps faltered, but she quickly got her body under control. "Same could be said of me."

My lips parted in a silent laugh, and her gaze trained to them under my mask. "You do surprise me sometimes." We spun around the dance floor, and I added, "You smell aroused, Eden. Did that show get you wet?"

"It was beautiful." I noted the wistfulness in her voice.

"I'm happy to tie you up anytime you need it."

Her steps faltered again as wide eyes peered up at me. I just kept moving. The music eventually stopped, and I held her hand as I led her towards the VIP area. She inspected the porcelain claws positioned over the top of my fingers. "Where are we going?"

"You'll see."

"But..." She gave my arm a little tug as she searched the crowd for her friends.

"Afraid I won't let you go back to them?"

"No, but I did arrive with them." Finding Tracy, she gave her a little wave, and her friend gave her a thumbs up as the others giggled.

We climbed the stairs together. "What would they say if you left with me?"

She glanced over at me. "That you'd probably murder me."

I snorted and changed the subject. I knew she liked to speculate on my serial killer status. The thought that I might murder her turned her on and that titillated Lurch.

"Why weren't you dancing?"

"I..." She shrugged and shook her head.

"Is it because your heels make you taller than everyone else?"

Her gaze snapped to mine as I led her to the private buffet table. "What?"

"I watched you sit there sipping your water as everyone else ate."

She stopped walking. "I wasn't ready to—"

"If you'd just shed the weight of other people's opinion, you'd free yourself for happiness."

Her steel blue eyes blinked behind that elaborate mask she wore. Her lips parted slightly before they tugged upward. "Oh my God. You're right."

She glanced at the long table laden with food. "I *am* hungry."

I tucked a finger under her chin, capturing her attention once more. Leaning closer I whispered, "This is a judgment-free zone, Eden. Nothing you do, say, or eat can ever change my opinion of you."

"Which is?"

My lips twisted up. "That you are absolutely perfect, as you are."

She leaned forward as if to kiss me, but I moved back. "Eat."

She jerked back with a frown. "You're not one of those weird guys who gets off on watching fat girls eat, are you?"

I laughed, enjoying the feeling that accompanied that sound. "You have no idea how many times I've gotten off watching you, Eden. *You* get me off. Eating, swimming, working out, reading, singing to yourself... My dick loves everything you do."

She laughed, and I noted how much my body enjoyed that sound too. "So, you *have* been stalking me."

I didn't respond, and she put her fingers to her chin as her lips twisted to the side. "I've never had a stalker before." She smiled as she surveyed the food once more. "I think I like it."

I handed her a plate. "Give it some time, and you'll learn to hate it."

She turned away and began putting food on her plate. "Who would hate being the center of someone's universe?"

"The grass isn't always greener..." I said casually but found pleasure that she felt comfortable enough with me to put what she truly desired first.

"What if you lived in a sandlot? Wouldn't grass be an upgrade?"

I couldn't help the chuckle I let out as I picked up my own plate and scooped some pasta salad onto it.

Eden

Sweet Angel

Those eyes behind the wolf mask were so attentive as I ate, I swear he was counting every chew and swallow. Beneath the snarling wolf, his shadowed lips were tilted up in a satisfied smile the entire time.

"Are you sure you don't have a feeding kink?"

I loved the sound of his tiny laugh. The way his lips parted slightly reminded me what he could do with them. "I'm sure."

"I like your costume. I want to reach up and scratch you behind the ears. Is the fur real?"

"I had it custom made from vintage fur coats. Animals were harmed, but not by my hand."

He moved to take it off, but I stopped him. "Leave it."

His hands slowly lowered, "You sure you don't have a mask fetish?"

A smile bloomed on my face as heat crept up my neck. I hedged, "I might have a tiny werewolf kink."

"Well, you already know this werewolf likes to feed kitties."

"And how is the adoptee doing? Did you name him yet?"

He shook his head slowly. "Terrorist."

I laughed. "That's a terrible name for a kitten."

"You don't know this kitten."

The lights dimmed, and the stage lit up for another show. The music changed in an attempt to compete for my attention, but my gaze remained on Logan.

He sat back in his chair and held out a hand. "Here, kitty, kitty. Come sit in your werewolf's lap. It's the best seat in the house."

"My werewolf?"

He patted his thigh, and my stomach did a little tumble. "Cat's rule."

I chewed my lip as I glanced around, but his fingers closed around my hand. "Don't... Fuck what anyone else thinks, Eden. If you want to sit in my lap and let me hold you while you enjoy the show, then do it."

This was nuts, but I felt an impulsive tug. I stood up, and he parted his thighs, arranging my back to his front before pulling me down onto his... "Is that a baby's arm in your pocket or?"

"You make me hard, Eden," he growled against my neck. He put my legs on the outside of his thighs, wrapped his arms around me and spread our legs. My dress rode up my thighs.

"What are you doing? Someone might—"

"See? Let them look."

I gasped as his fingers dug into my thighs to keep me spread open. "I was going to say, see up my dress."

He let out a small laugh and gave the tablecloth a light tug. "Good thing this is here, otherwise I'd have to rip the eyes out of everyone on the floor below for getting a peek at your cute, little undies."

I turned my face towards him, and he angled his head to meet my gaze under that snarling wolf snout. I asked, "Who said I was wearing panties?"

His fingers splayed on the inside of my thigh sending a shock-wave of anticipation up my leg as he growled. Seriously, fucking growled into my ear. "Naughty little liar."

I turned away as he spread his legs wider. His teeth scraped down the side of my neck as his hand inched upwards. "Do you lie so I'll punish you again? Liked it so much you want me to spank your wet pussy again?"

His finger traced the edge of my panties ever so slowly, and I about went into convulsions on his lap.

"Watch the show and stay silent, Eden."

My attention moved to the stage down below. People were performing some sort of BDSM show that involved bondage and whips. A man in leather flogged a woman in a G-string cuffed to a cross, and the visual alone was enough to send me over the edge.

Logan's fingers lightly teased my panties. He purred against my ear, sending shivers down my spine. "You like watching her? Does it make you wetter thinking of us... doing that?"

I twisted my neck, and he nipped my jaw, before moving his lips to mine for a brief kiss. My voice shook as I admitted hoarsely, "Yes. I want you to spank my pussy again."

His finger slipped under my panties but stayed slow and light as he traced my seam.

"Gods, Eden, I'm going to own this pussy. It will weep on command, and you will give it up and come for me as I see fit. Understand me?"

"Yes, Sir."

His fingers dove deeper, parting me before they clamped down on my clit, gently trapping and holding me hostage. The pressure was almost too much. I squirmed as my clit pulsed erratically. "That's it, Eden. Fuck, you feel so good writhing on my cock."

"Please, Logan... Fuck me."

"Soon. I'm going to fuck you until you beg me to stop. You will be so full of me, I'll leak out of you for days after."

He tugged gently, and I bucked against the trap his fingers created. I was right on the edge, but the pressure choked out the pleasure. "You can't. I'm not on..."

He squeezed my clit, and I gasped and stiffened. "It won't matter once you're pregnant."

His free hand moved to my throat and gently squeezed, holding me to his chest as his lips caressed my temple.

My brain couldn't formulate any objection. It just fuzzed out as his fingers loosened and he started stroking my clit, up and down, like a tiny dick, sending sparks of pleasure shooting through me. "Oh fuck, oh fuck, oh fuck." My legs tightened and my back arched as I shot over the edge.

He cupped my pulsing, pounding pussy, and it felt like a loving hug as I lay boneless on his body.

He wrapped his arms around me and squeezed my limp body. "You're going to go downstairs and tell your friends you are leaving with me."

It took me a minute to gather myself. Reality slowly pushed its way back into my brain. Because I was the idiot who had canceled my doctor's appointment after James ghosted me.

"Uh, no?" I sat up.

His arms left me. "No?"

I moved back to my chair and faced him. "We can't have sex yet."

"Because you're not on birth control." Like he already knew this small fact long before I mentioned it.

"Exactly and because we hardly know each other."

Those sexy lips twisted up. "I think I know you well enough."

My pussy agreed wholeheartedly with that statement. I clamped my thighs together to shut her up. "Yeah well, this is how it's going to go down. I'm going to rejoin my friends before they realize I've been gone for an hour and call the police. I'm going to dance and maybe have a glass of champagne or two. You're welcome to join me."

He snorted his disapproval, so I stood up and smoothed my dress down. "Tomorrow, you're going to take me out on a real date. You're going to answer all my questions, and we are going to get to know one another. You're going to show me the real Logan."

He barked a laugh. "I've already told you–"

"That you're not a nice guy. I get that, but you're going to prove to me that I'm not lying when I tell people you don't have bodies hidden in your freezer."

"I don't have bodies in my freezer cause I'm smarter than that."

I did a double take, and he grinned. "Go play with your friends, Eden. I'll be right here, watching over you."

"Just like that? After all that talk about how you own this pussy?"

A muscle ticked in his jaw. "No need for caveman dramatics. You're not an impulsive girl, and I'm not an insecure boy." He jerked his chin down towards where James sat, staring up at us. Had he been watching this entire time? My brain reminded me that it was too dark to see much past the railing. Besides, there was a tablecloth draped low enough to cover any indecent exposure. Even though I wanted to let Logan drag me home and continue this debauchery he started, I wanted to celebrate my independence tonight.

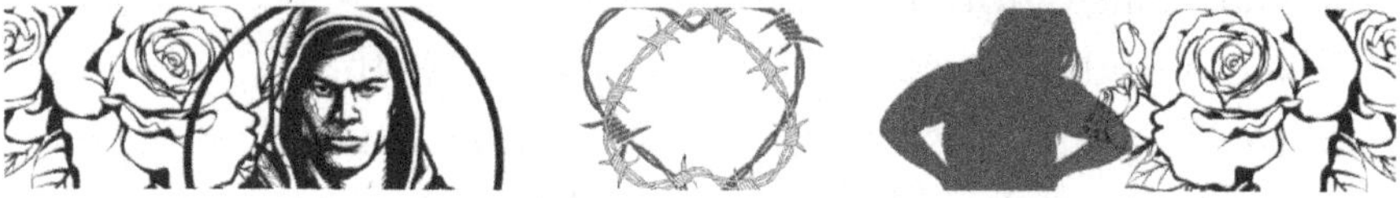

Chapter Fifteen

Special Fucking K

Logan

No, I didn't want her going back down there to yuck-it-up with her so-called friends. Not when danger was on the way. Not when I had the feeling they were coming for Eden, not just me.

I could go down there, toss her over my shoulder and carry her off screaming and kicking, but that would cause an unnecessary scene. Normally, I wouldn't mind causing a scene, but involving the police would eat up time I didn't have.

Eden had shed her shoes and was dancing with her friends when that kid, James, approached. He hovered, pretending to be a part of the dance group, waiting for the music to slow down. His opportunity came, and I watched him coerce her into a slow dance with him. I swear he mouthed the words, just friends.

Eden glanced up towards the balcony, but I remained stoic. Her attention returned to James, and I knew she said yes before he pulled her close. My girl, who had been beautifully trained to dance, was trapped into a middle school sidestep. Way too close and way too confined. If he won her heart, he'd cage her when she needed to spread her wings.

My alter ego wanted to do bad things to make sure that never happened. It reminded me that we weren't a good choice for Eden either. I wasn't a good person even without Lurch whispering terrible things in my head. I'd often wondered who or what Lurch was. An imaginary friend? Another personality? A demon? Or was he just me? Even after all the therapy my adopted father provided in my teens, I'd never spoken about him.

Either way, he would be a part of any relationship I had, and Eden didn't deserve that.

The dance ended, and James handed her a flute of champagne. If he was trying to get her drunk so he could take advantage of her, he'd die tonight. This was her second glass, and she had hydrated after the first. I doubted she would allow herself to get that drunk.

My brain wandered as I observed the small group at the table. 'Collect the blood of an unsullied body' was cryptic priest-speak for 'kill a virgin.' Or maybe just take some blood. A bit of research from a blood bank, and I could possibly get my hands on a child's donation. It didn't guarantee they'd be unsullied, but it was a good gamble.

Take what you love and flee to the sea. Did I love Eden? What else could he mean? Maybe the terrorist kitten destroying my home right now? I liked the feline, but love? That's not what he'd said though. What was it? What you most desire. That was Eden.

So, who the fuck was Sleeping Beauty?

I pulled out my phone and read Bentley's last text. **Maybe one hour.**

Fuck. **On it. Brief Dan and send someone to the condo to take care of my cat.**

You have a cat? Since when?

Does it matter? Just don't let the beast starve.

Eden was sitting next to James at his table. She was frowning and pale. James was hovering way too closely. Something was wrong.

Was she sick? I swear if that food she'd eaten earlier was bad, I'd burn the caterer alive.

I stood up and leaned against the rail as James waved Tracy over. Tracy sat down on Eden's other side and leaned in close to speak with her. James glanced around nervously as Eden nodded her head to whatever Tracy asked.

Tracy stood up looking for her other friends, but James caught her attention. They spoke briefly before Tracy turned back to Eden. Eden nodded slowly, head in her hands and James picked up Eden's purse, mask, and shoes. Eden swayed as she stood up, but James slipped his arm around her to steady her.

None of this checked out. Two flutes of champagne, even for a non-drinker, wouldn't get you this drunk. I pulled out my phone and started recording as I rushed down the stairs and followed them out to his car.

Eden stumbled and James managed to keep them both on their feet. "For fuck's sake, Eden. Try a little." His tone made my hackles rise.

"I'm sorry." Her words were slurred. "I think that last glass of champagne turned bad."

"Champagne doesn't go bad," he managed to say with a grunt as her knees buckled again.

"It tasted off."

"Yeah, Special K is bitter. Come on, Eden. Just a few more feet, and then you can rest."

Eden jerked to a stop. "You drugged me!" Panic laced her voice. "You asshole."

The kid fished out his keys and hit the unlock button. "Get in the fucking car."

"What the fuck, James?" She tried to jerk away from him.

"Don't make a scene. Just get in the car."

He jerked her arm so hard she fell to her knees. I moved closer, ready to strike this fucker down and save the day, but Eden asked a question I wanted to know the answer to.

"Why would you drug me? Are you going to rape me?"

He jerked her up. "Rape you? That is the most disgusting thing you've said all night. First off, you've been throwing yourself at me for over a month now."

She managed to stumble forward enough to lean on his car. He jerked the door open and said, "I'm the one who wanted to take it slow, not you."

He pushed her towards the opening. "I have standards, bitch."

As she fell into the seat, she had enough presence of mind to snatch his keys and jerk the door closed. The locks clicked shut as I launched forward.

The kid was too preoccupied with shouting at Eden to notice me.

My hand closed on his skull and shoved his face into the window as my mass collided with him. Eden's scream was muffled, but I was focused on the young body before me. The claws strapped to the back of my hand cut skin as I drove my fist into his side. The pain only drove me deeper into my rage.

I fisted his hair and tossed him off the car. He sprawled on the parking lot briefly before getting to his feet. "What the fuck?"

His lip was bleeding where his tooth punctured it from where he had impacted the window. He wiped it with his fist and said, "You fucked up wolf boy."

I grinned savagely. "Oh? Please show me." It was at this point I noticed the temperature drop. A nearby streetlamp went dark, and the shadows seemed to press in from all sides.

James was purely focused on me until a wisp of smoke caressed his swollen lip. He jerked his head back and swatted at the dissipating cloud like it was a gnat.

Realization dawned on me. "You really are a virgin." He'd been claiming it to Eden, but I hadn't believed a word he'd said to woo my girl.

His face twisted with outrage. "What the fuck? No!"

I laughed as I circled him. "Liar."

He twisted and swung wide, so I bopped him in the mouth. Claws parted the skin of his cheek as his mouth gushed more blood. The shadows grew darker, taking shape as they pressed closer. I hit him again, slicing open the other side of his face.

The car door opened, and Eden called out. "Stop! Fighting."

She couldn't see the demons and James didn't see them until they were on top of him. He fell back with a scream that was muffled by darkness.

I turned to Eden. "Come on. Let's get you out of here."

Her eyes rolled into the back of her head as I tucked my arms under her and lifted her out of the car.

James was on his back in the middle of the parking lot, legs and arms flailing through dense demon-shaped smoke. He wasn't going anywhere, and my truck was merely two lanes over.

I placed her in the front passenger seat and buckled her in. "Rest. I'll be right back."

She didn't answer me as she lolled to the side.

I snatched up my phone and dialed Bentley. "Tell Monk to call off his demons. I need the kid to live a little while longer. Also have Visuals disrupt all cameras in the parking area and at the marina."

I heard the clipped accent of Monk complaining about his payment and said, "I'll make his death spectacularly bloody, but he needs to answer some questions first."

"You tell him fine, but I'll be monitoring, so he better make good on promises."

There was a rustle like he turned away from the nosey man. Bentley's voice shook as he whispered. "Dude. Don't fuck this guy over. He's creepy."

I picked up Eden's things and returned to my truck as Monk's demons slowly dissipated off the now quiet and still body sprawled on the ground. I said to Bentley, "I know, brother. It will all be over soon."

Opening the back passenger door of my Dodge, I grabbed a pair of handcuffs out of my go-bag even though I was sure James didn't have the energy to continue the fight he started. His face paint was smudged, and his clothing was torn and bloody. I rolled him onto his stomach and bent his arms behind his back. "You poor, stupid kid."

He moaned as I hoisted him over my shoulder, carried him back to my truck, and dumped him in the back seat. "You're making a terrible mess of my truck."

It took some adjusting to get all of him wedged in enough to close the door. I pulled my mask off and ran my forearm across my sweaty brow. Once I was sure the scene was ready for the cleaners, I got into the driver's side and checked on Eden. Her breathing wasn't too labored, and she opened her eyes when I tried to wake her up.

She said, "Logan." Then grinned wildly as her eyes rolled back and closed once more.

I had a choice to do the right thing. Did she need a hospital? Maybe, but we needed to get out of here and I had a bloody, painted up prisoner that needed interrogating. A quick stop at home provided all I needed to treat both my guests while at sea.

Eden

My racing heart slowed to a crawl as I fought the drugs in my system. I couldn't believe James had drugged me. Why?

His handsome face contorted from annoyance to rage when I asked if he had planned on raping me. What was I supposed to think after what he'd done?

Then Logan appeared like a beast in full alpha mode. My brain struggled to stay online because he was fucking hot as he threw James around like he was nothing. I didn't want them fighting, but damn, nobody had ever fought over me before.

Darkness became a void until a maskless Logan got into the truck I was in. He must have won the fight. Did that mean I was safe now? I managed to open my eyes and take in his tight profile as he drove us away. Would he take me to the hospital where they would treat me? Would I become addicted now? Would James go to jail? I was unable to voice the questions tumbling around in my disembodied mind.

He was carrying me again. I inhaled against his neck trying to take in his scent, but it was mixed with the smell of low tide at... "Where...?"

"Shh. You're safe," he said against my head.

I couldn't trust what I was seeing, hearing, and smelling. My brain must have been hallucinating because I was sure we were on my dad's sailboat.

No, I was at a hospital. I was undressed, put in a bed and an IV was inserted in my arm.

"Rest now." Had that been Logan or a male nurse?

Muffled screams and pleas for help cut through the stillness, verifying that I was indeed at the hospital, and the sound of waves lapping against a boat must have been the drugs.

Logan had said to rest. So, I let sleep take over.

Chapter Sixteen

Keelhauling

Logan

Dan's sailing vessel was as nice as I expected. It was the kind of sailboat one could live on as they navigated the open ocean. Her name was painted in bold lettering on her hull: *Divinity.*

"They paid you ten grand to drug and deliver her to them?"

The attempt to keep my voice calm must have alarmed the kid because he said, "You can have the money. Please, man. I'll get it if you just take me to the dorms."

It had taken the kid hours and a bag of fluids to finally stir enough to realize he wasn't still sprawled in the parking lot. The handcuffs had startled him, but I convinced him that if he wasn't here, he'd be in jail.

"I don't need your chump change, and if you walk into those dorms after what you did, it won't end well."

"The cops don't know yet, right? I mean that cow should still be out like a light."

The last time I checked on her to swap out the intravenous fluids, she didn't stir, and his calling her a cow after drugging her almost to the point of overdose...

It took several deep breaths to restrain Lurch from pushing this kid off the back of the sailboat. I swallowed hard before I said, "The cops don't know, but whoever gave you ten grand to deliver the girl won't be happy with you by now."

For the first time, panic and fear flashed across his face. "Shit. I didn't even think about that."

"Who hired you?"

James took a long moment before speaking. "Can you loosen these cuffs?"

"I can take them off if you promise not to start swinging again." I lifted my jacket to show him the firearm holstered at my side. "I really don't want to clean your brains out of this cockpit."

He sat up straight. "Dude, I'm good."

Fishing the key out of my pocket, I asked again as I motioned him to stand up and turn around. "Who hired you?"

"Somebody my brother knows. Said his buddy got a call from some woman who said Eden's dad was rich. He would pay a lot of money to get her back." He rubbed his wrists as he sat back down, eyeing where my gun lay hidden at my side.

I moved back to the captain's seat. The boat was on autopilot heading for the deeper parts of the Gulf of Mexico. "Your brother's buddy, is he a Death Adder?"

The kid stiffened the moment I said the gang's name. "Yeah, so is my brother. How do you know about them?"

I leaned back in the captain's chair, and studied the instruments before looking out at the dark ocean. "I've seen what they do to people who double cross them."

Apparently, James also knew what they did because he jumped up, realized there was nowhere to run on a sailboat in the middle of the Gulf of Mexico, and then sat back down. "You gotta help me."

I grinned. "Well, we are headed West. I could drop you off in Mexico." I laced my hands behind my neck. "I would, but I need names."

"Names?" his voice shook.

"You're already on their shit list. What's a few names going to do?"

He thought about this longer than he should have. "You're right."

James gave me everything he knew. No torture needed. Trust given freely with a false promise to help him escape certain death. I relayed the information to Bentley so he could pick up the fuckers who had arranged to kidnap Eden.

I tossed the kid a towel. "Clean your face."

He caught it and winced as he wiped the grease paint off his brow. "Man, you really did a number on me."

How much of that encounter did he remember? Most people don't see the things I've been trained to see. Their mind just doesn't have the bandwidth to process such horrors. I envied that about them.

"Don't fuck around if you don't want to find out."

"Bet. Where did you get those claws you were wearing?"

At least he wasn't holding a grudge. I kind of felt bad because what I had planned for him was far worse than anything the Death Adders could fathom. I had promised someone else to make his death spectacular.

It was time to test his trust. "The boat is on autopilot. I need you to keep watch while I check on our guest downstairs. Can you do that for me?"

"Sure," his answer came casually, like he thought we were fast friends.

I'd be ready for his attack when it came.

Eden didn't stir as I removed her IV and disposed of the empty bag and needle. I traced her brow and temple with my fingers as

I focused on her breathing. It was steady and even now. She was so peaceful, she tempted me to crawl in bed with her. Instead, I gently kissed her warm cheek. I hoped what I was about to do didn't wake her, because I really wanted to spend some time holding her. My chest tightened at the thought of exploring her without any preconceived thoughts or self-consciousness on her part. She'd be totally relaxed and open for me.

Fuck, I had work to do. I needed to focus on that, not her.

"I'll be back. Sleep well."

Was she my Sleeping Beauty? The Monk's riddle came together in my head in such a tantalizing way I had to adjust my cock.

I dug several lengths of rope and two heavy-duty carabiners out of my go-bag and went to deal with James.

He was still sitting in the captain's seat. "Everything okay?"

My eyes went to the gauge that told me how deep the water was. It was plenty deep enough for my endgame. I scanned the radar. Nothing around. Far enough into the deep sea that nobody would hear or see anything.

"I need some help with the mast."

His eyes narrowed in the glow of the instrument panel lights as he noticed the rope in my hands. "Why? What's wrong with the mast?"

"I was told it needs to be restrung or something, and we need to conserve fuel if we plan to make it to Mexico."

Hell, I wasn't a seasoned sailor, but I knew my way around a boat. It must have made complete sense to the kid. He got up and patted his pockets before frowning. "I lost my phone."

He didn't lose the phone. I'd tossed it out the window on our way to the marina. We didn't need that shit pinging a cell tower, though I doubted there were any towers reaching out here. My phone connected to a satellite; no towers needed.

"Shit man, sorry. Here, I think there are lights..." I flipped a switch, and a floodlight came on to illuminate the mast and deck before I put the engine in neutral.

"Cool," he sounded impressed as he made his way towards the bow of the large sailing vessel. The seas were calm, but the boat still pitched slowly.

A wave of guilt hit me as I followed him. The kid wasn't completely evil. A dumbass? Yes. An asshole for what he did to Eden? Absolutely.

I tied one end to a cleat at the bow, dropped the middle over the bow pulpit, and into the water. It would catch on the keel as I tied the other end to the halyard with a shorter rope and a climbing knot. Guessing the distance needed, I made a loop in the longer rope and secured it using the carabiner.

"Hey, crank the winch to raise the sail."

James hurried back into the cockpit and began turning the winch, lifting my makeshift rig high up the mast.

I made my way back to the cleat where the other end of the rope was tied and walked it around to do the same climber's knot and loop. "Lower it..." I eyeballed the distance I needed. "Right there."

I stood up and scratched my head. My gut twisted with more guilt. Last chance to change my plans and spare the kid. But at what cost? I'd made a deal with a devil who demanded blood. If it wasn't this blood, then who's blood would he demand?

"Shit. I need your help up here."

"Dude, why is the rope in the water?"

"Why did you call her a cow?"

His gaze jerked from the dark water to me. "What?"

I shook my head. "We gotta fix this. Here grab the rope with both hands."

Before he could react, I started wrapping his wrists, tying him to the rope attached to the mainsail halyard.

It took him a couple of seconds to resist. "What the fuck are you doing?" He jerked back as far as the halyard would allow. "Dude!"

"You had to be rude, didn't you?"

His voice rose a few octaves. "Rude? I've been nothing but nice."

I finished my knot and stepped back as he struggled to free himself. "Nice? You threw her down and called her a cow. That's nice in your book?"

I made my way to the winch in the cockpit as he said, "Have you seen her? She was being an idiot."

He struggled harder as the winch turned, taking the slack. "Because you drugged her." I kept turning the winch until his feet left the deck.

"Please, man. Don't do this. Help!"

Had he just realized what was in store for him?

He kicked out with his legs twisting as he hung over the deck. I made a lasso out of the remaining length of rope. "I'm a good person. I didn't mean to—"

"Abuse Eden?"

"What? No!" He stilled enough for me to slip the rope around his ankles and tighten it down. His knees came up in defense, but I dodged the blow and flung the rope around the line, securing his legs.

I snarled up at his horrified face. "You betrayed her trust in you. For what? A little bit of money? Good people don't do that shit, James."

"So you're going to kill me?"

I stepped back and surveyed my handywork. It should hold for as long as I needed it to. "I have never pretended to be a good person, James."

"You're just as bad as they are."

I moved back to the cockpit and grabbed the handle of the winch. "No, I'm worse."

Each turn moved James lower and lower until his body scraped across the rail. He started screaming the moment he realized why the rope went under the boat.

"Somebody help me!"

I cranked faster, wishing I had the foresight to gag the shithead. He was loud enough to wake the damn dead. Sleeping Beauty needed her rest before the Beast joined her.

The blood-curdling screaming was silenced by the dark waves, and I continued to crank the winch until feet appeared on the other side of the boat. James hung upside down, head just above the highest waves, hurling buckets of sea water. His cheap costume was shredded and even in the darkness over the side, I could see where flesh had been torn away.

The temperature around the *Divinity* dropped, and I felt the darkness pressed close. Demons drawn in by the unsullied blood of their sacrifice. No stretch of water would keep them from their feast tonight.

Barnacle cuts were the absolute worst. I thought Dan would have kept up with the maintenance of the *Divinity* and had her bottom cleaned regularly. Lucky for me, he'd waited, and she was due for a good cleaning. James made choking noises as I turned the winch again. This time in the opposite direction. I could hear him struggling against the hull as he was slowly pulled under and over, headfirst. As he came up, the side of his scalp, face, and arms were mincemeat. His shirt and pants were in tatters, and it was hard to look at his once young and powerful body. The shadows dimmed the floodlights as I raised the ruined kid higher. Blood and saltwater rained onto the pristine deck as James puked, choked, and moaned.

"Again? Or is this good enough?" I asked the shadows. I wasn't sure the kid would survive another bout with the hull and sea, but I'd do what was necessary to keep Eden safe.

James screamed a choked sound as the entities descended on him, great shadows, so dark and dense I could no longer see the kid.

I fished my phone out of my pocket and typed a message to Bentley.

It's done.

Logan

Logan Lurch

I gave the demons some privacy with James and went to check on Eden. The snarl that left me as I entered the bedroom was pure Lurch.

"She is not for you," I said to the shadow hovering over my Sleeping Beauty.

It jerked back and sped past me, escaping into the darkness as I focused on Eden. She whimpered and tossed in her sleep but didn't wake. The covers had been pulled down her naked body but there wasn't any evidence of injury or violation. I was still tempted to charge after that shadow. What I might do if I caught it, I had no idea. One simply didn't snatch a shadow demon from the darkness and beat its ass for touching what doesn't belong to it.

James let out a horrific scream above. Eden rolled to her side with a tiny noise of distress. I jerked forward but paused. As much as I wanted to comfort her, I was filthy. My fingers went to the buttons of my vest as I toed off my shoes. My vest, dress shirt, and pants landed in a pile next to her discarded dress. James screamed again as I eased into bed with her in the dim light of the cabin. Her skin was icy as she turned towards my warmth.

"Fucking asshole demon," I murmured with enough venom to down a horse.

I tugged the covers over both of us, wrapped my arms around her, and pulled her close.

She inhaled against my bare neck, and I could have sworn she whispered my name.

"It's okay. You're safe now."

She sighed and her lips turned up in a peaceful smile.

I leaned in and kissed that smile. She moaned softly, and my hand moved up and down her spine. My free hand traced the curves of her soft breasts. Eden gave me another soft sigh as the back of my hand grazed her hard nipple. I peeled the covers back just enough to expose her. Just enough so I could watch her body react to my touch.

Steal something from Sleeping Beauty. A betrayal. I knew what I had to do. No, what I *wanted* to do. More than anything else in the entire world. Gods, the things I wanted to do to this incapacitated woman were wrong on so many levels. I kissed her ear and whispered, "Please forgive me." I knew she wouldn't, even though she'd begged me to fuck her earlier.

My hand left her breast and gripped her thigh, pulling it wide across me. A simple twist of my hips and she was straddling me. The pressure of her pubic bone on my cock was maddening. With a leg on either side of my thighs, I pulled her wide and started rocking my cock back and forth, sliding it between our bodies and through her open pussy. The weight of her relaxed body on top of mine felt amazing, and the moan she let out behind barely parted lips almost sent me over the edge.

I turned my face into her neck. "Damn Eden, you are so fucking beautiful. I want to spread you open and explore every inch of you with my mouth."

My fingers tightened on her thighs, and I swore a ripple went down her spine as I continued to stroke through her labia, rubbing the underside of my cock along her thick clit.

"Did you just come for me?"

She moaned again, and I nipped her collar bone as I adjusted myself lower down her body. Once my cock was freed, I lowered her leg and rolled us, so I was on top. The covers fell off the bed as I rose to my knees between her open legs. Her arm was bent, and her fist was laying on her fiery hair. I came over her, tasting every inch of her skin, pausing to suck each nipple before flicking on the reading lamp attached to the headboard. The soft glow illuminated my girl, casting shadows that accentuated her beautiful curves. I arranged her other arm next to her head, so she lay in complete abandon. I leaned back to admire the view. Her hair fanned out around her. A wealth of curls she had painstakingly put in earlier this evening before braiding it like a Viking princess. Her breasts were perfect. Big nipples no longer peaked into tiny points. That simply wouldn't do. I bent over her and licked around the areola until it was as erect as I was before moving to the other one.

She moaned, and the muscles in her legs spasmed.

"Greedy girl. Okay, I'll get to the good part."

I snatched a pillow from the floor and lifted her hips, tucking it under. A pillow her father probably laid his head on. Well, now it would smell of his daughter's pleasure.

Pushing her thighs wide, I ignored my throbbing cock and settled lower. My fingers toyed with her, tugging on her lower lips gently and pulling her wide. The muscles in her legs trembled again as I blew on her needy clit.

"I'm going to need you sopping wet, my love."

I lowered my mouth to her and gently sucked on her thick little clit like it was a tiny dick. She jerked when I let my teeth gently scrape against her. I loved that she enjoyed a shock of pain with her pleasure. Her breathing went ragged. I sucked hard, and she let out the most delicious noise as her clit jerked and pulsed wildly.

I let her go with a few sloppy kisses and reluctantly lifted away. "Later, I'm going to make you come for hours."

On my knees, I angled my tip to her entrance. "I can't wait anymore." The squeeze of her body around my tip made my eyes roll into the back of my head. "Ah fucking hell, you are utter Heaven, Eden."

I inched back and pushed deeper. Her body not only accepted me, but it opened and sucked me in. She was so hot and wet, the sound of me entering her felt loud in this cabin. The temperature was warmer too. James had gone silent, and that dark, twisted part of me wanted to carry Eden out on deck so he could watch me fuck her as he took his dying breath. I couldn't bring myself to leave her luscious body. So, I pushed deeper, inching in and out until I hit bottom. I stilled, and she moaned again. I was taking advantage of her. I knew exactly what this was, and as much as I was enjoying it, I hated myself for it. I started moving, giving her long, slow strokes. I sank deep, and she accommodated my length without a whimper. I pulled out to the tip and pushed back inside. Pleasure washed through me.

I leaned over her and nuzzled her ear. "You were made for me, Eden."

My hips found an easy rhythm as I slipped an arm under her lower back. "Made for my cock." My arm tightened around her as my breathing increased to match hers. I sank deeper and deeper until my hips were flush against hers. My legs spread wide as I worked to get even closer, pumping faster, harder.

Her back arched, and her eyes popped open. They found mine as her pussy clenched around me. Her lips parted, and her face turned to me. Her hand lifted and clumsily wrapped around my neck, pulling my lips to hers. Or maybe she was trying to fight me off, I wasn't entirely sure, but I kissed her anyway.

The moment my lips met hers, I came, moaning my pleasure into her mouth, my hips pushing, pushing, my arms holding her steady as I spilled and spilled inside her.

"Do you feel that?"

My hips thrust and held.

"I'm filling you up."

I pushed deep again with a gasp at the explosion of sensation at the tip of my dick. "I'm going to get you pregnant, Eden."

Her eyes rolled back in her head as I stilled inside her.

"You'll be a wonderful mother."

Her eyes opened and tried to focus on me before closing again.

I withdrew from her body and rolled to the side of her pulling her into my arms for a tight hug. "You just wait and see."

Honestly? I didn't think either one of us would be stellar parents, especially me. Poor Eden hadn't had the best childhood or mother role model. My dad had tried to kill me twice.

"Maybe we'd be the best parents because we know what it's like to have horrible ones."

If she heard me, she never showed it. The drugs had thrust her back into deep sleep. She was as boneless as I felt after such a beautiful moment. I wanted to hold her, make love to her and cuddle with her for the rest of the night.

But there was a dead body hanging above deck, lit up and flying like a flag for anyone to come along and witness. I needed to deal with James before I had to get rid of nosey Good Samaritans, too. I gently withdrew from the bed and padded naked out of the room.

The scene was straight out of a horror flick. James wasn't dead yet. He was standing at death's door, but the kid was hanging on for dear life. He let out a wheezing sound as I lowered him to the bloody deck. I could try to save him. The Monk hadn't demanded his death, just his blood. But the kid would never be the same, and he'd always be a liability.

Did he even deserve a chance after what he did to Eden?

Will she ever forgive me for what I just did to her?

I'd hate to have to force her forgiveness.

I shook my head at that thought. No, I'd love to force that. I was twisted and fucked up enough to tie her to my bed and keep that pussy swollen and raw until she loved me back.

My bare feet left dark, sticky footprints as I searched for what I needed. I definitely needed a shower before going below deck again. Good thing Dan had a spare anchor for his dinghy tucked in storage above deck. I wondered what absent daddy would say if he saw what I just did to his daughter, on his sailboat, in his bed.

I untied the stained rope from the halyard line and wrapped it around James's body. His breathing was slow and raspy, but he was still alive. I leaned close to the ear that hadn't been damaged by the barnacles.

"Now is the time to get right with whatever god you believe in, James."

I finished tying the anchor to James and tested my knots before going back to the cockpit and firing up the engines. We'd drifted quite a bit from where I wanted to drop the body. It was deep out here, but not deep enough for my comfort. There were several recreational dive spots I needed to steer clear of, and I needed to take the currents into consideration to make sure James didn't inadvertently make his way to a popular wreck.

So, I pointed the *Divinity* towards deeper and less interesting water. No fishing holes, no cool dive sites, just the barren underwater desert.

The sun was just starting to brighten the sky when the bottom started dropping off deeper and deeper until my gut said it was time. James had stopped breathing at some point in the dark. He slipped away like a quiet mouse without any fanfare or farewell. There was nothing else to do but drop him and his anchor over the side and clean up the rest of his mess. Coagulated blood was easy enough to pick up and toss overboard, but the stains required a bristle brush and strong detergent. Even the side of the sailboat needed a good scrub and hose down.

By the time I finished, the sun was making its journey high in the sky. It was time to check on Sleeping Beauty. There'd be hell to pay when she finally woke.

Chapter Seventeen

Stolen Firsts

Eden

For a moment I thought I'd gone back in time. Waves lapped against the hull of the *Divinity*. The sound was as warm as my childhood memories. But I was in my father's bed, not the cabin at the bow which had been my space. My brain was so cloudy, it hurt to think as I sat up. *How did I get here?* Naked.

I parted my thighs and lifted my belly as my pussy complained happily from down below. She'd definitely had a wild night without me.

My dress and mask from the party were discarded in a pile next to a werewolf mask and a man's tailored vintage suit. Except, the suit was caked with dark stains.

I made the few steps to the bathroom. The movement made my head throb and my stomach churn, but the urge to pee took priority.

Yeah, I definitely had sex last night.

On the vanity was a bottle of water, some pain relievers, and a note.

Hydrate and take three of these. When you are ready, come on deck.

L.

How in the hell did I end up on my dad's boat with Logan?

I remembered meeting him at the masquerade ball. He made me feel so good about myself. Comfortable even, as he made me come while I sat on his lap. But I was sure I had returned to my friends after that. *When did we leave and why would we be on my dad's sailboat?*

I leaned over to where I could see our hastily shed clothing from the toilet. *When did we do... that?*

"Come on deck wearing what exactly?"

Instead of following orders, I turned on the shower, hoping the water would clear my head. But I only had bits and pieces when I got out. Something had happened, and I remembered that James had been there.

Maybe James and Logan?

Good God, who did I have sex with? And why can't I remember it? And, who else was up there? How did we get on my father's boat without my father being present?

My stomach had settled enough to brave the water and pain relievers, and I moved back into the small cabin to find something more appropriate to wear before meeting whoever was above deck. I really didn't want to greet my father in a towel or my old prom dress.

There was an unfamiliar duffle bag next to the bed. It was already unzipped, and I parted the edges and jumped back when I saw the contents. Sure, there was clothing inside it, but there was also coiled rope, handcuffs, zip ties, duct tape, a rather large knife in a leather sheath, and a holster with a high caliber handgun nestled inside.

"What are you doing?" Logan's voice was casual from the doorway he filled.

I choked on a startled shout before pointing at the bag. "Is that yours?" My other hand secured the towel that barely covered my breasts.

He leaned against the doorjamb and crossed his tattooed arms as he tracked my towel struggles. "Of course, that's mine."

I wasn't sure if he was talking about my towel or the duffle.

"There's a gun in there."

He leaned forward with a crinkle at the corner of his eyes. "Actually, there's three."

Who needs three guns? "So you *are* a serial killer."

He pushed off the doorjamb but didn't advance. "So this is how it's going to go."

"What am I supposed to think?"

He strode forward, and I backed up until I was against the dresser. I brought my fist up between us, and his hand closed around my wrist before I was jerked forward against his body as his other arm came behind me. My towel popped open but stayed trapped between us. He leaned down and spoke against my ear. "What does your gut tell you, Eden?"

I inhaled as I took a moment to check in with said gut. He smelled so good I wanted to turn my nose into his chest and huff all of him. I couldn't trust my gut. I jerked to the side trying to resecure my towel. "I don't know."

"You do know," he countered quickly.

I met his tender gaze with a scowl. "Where's my father?"

He shrugged. "How should I know?"

I finally got a handle on the edges of my towel. "Look, I don't remember how we got here. I'm not comfortable standing here half naked with you towering over me as I attempt to figure things out."

To my surprise he stepped back. I stiffened as he bent and reached into the duffle bag. Instead of a gun, he pulled out a black t-shirt and tossed it to me. "Put this on and come up when you are ready. We'll talk when you are dressed."

He picked up the duffle and left as I chewed on my thanks. I wasn't sure it was the appropriate word to use just yet. I quickly pulled the shirt on. I loved how the hem came down to my thighs. His shirt smelled like him, and my body reacted in a way that created more questions in my muddled brain. Was he the hero or villain of last night's story? I searched through my father's clothing until I found a pair of soft, stretchy shorts that made it over my hips and thighs. I didn't bother checking my old room for clothing since I hadn't stayed here since I was twelve. Nothing in there would fit the adult me.

The next search came up empty: my phone was missing from my purse.

Taking the bottle of water with me, I moved through the *Divinity* and up the companionway. The sun was bright, causing me to blink away tears. Logan had stripped off his shirt and was sitting where I expected my father to be. My gaze lingered on his tattoos, sucking me in like a mesmerizing web of sex, lies, and murder.

I sat down as far as the cockpit would allow. I had spent many a night laying on these bench seats looking at the stars as a kid. It was my favorite thing to do when we did overnight sails. Today, it was sunny, and land was nowhere in sight. The engine was silent, and we were drifting.

I ran my fingers through my damp hair. "What happened last night?"

"You hungry?"

I folded my arms. "Right now, I'm hungry for answers."

"What do you remember?"

I leaned back as my eyes narrowed on his. "Let's assume I remember nothing."

"That's because James drugged and attempted to kidnap you."

I shifted in my seat and glanced down at my bare legs. My knees were skinned. I remembered James manhandling me to his car. Remembered the betrayal I'd felt when he shoved me down in the parking lot. "Why?"

"Because he was paid to do so."

I rubbed at the scabs that had formed. "Who paid him?"

"We are trying to find out who the source is, but a notorious gang was hired to collect and hold you for ransom."

"Did they? How did you and I get here?"

"I took you from James."

An image of a werewolf came to me. James being slammed against the window of his door and tossed like a rag doll. "Where is James now?"

"Gone."

My gaze lifted to Logan. "Did you shoot him with your gun?"

His brows lifted on a surprised laugh. "No."

"You said, 'we.' Does my dad know we are out here?"

He sat back and crossed his arms. "How much do you know about your dad's business and personal life?"

My world felt unsteady. "Honestly? Not much, but I know he doesn't own a duffle bag full of nefarious things like you do."

Logan ran a tattooed hand through his hair. His grimace tightened the scars on his cheek into thin white lines. "I'm about to tell you things you can never repeat to another living being."

My heart raced as I leaned forward, eager to finally hear the secrets Logan knew about my family.

"I need your verbal vow because I'm the one who enforces the secrecy."

"With your guns?"

He nodded. "I am loyal to a fault. Please don't put me in a situation where you are no longer on my side of things. Promise you will never reveal anything I'm about to tell you."

"Okay?"

He lifted a brow, and it took me a second to realize he wanted an actual vow from me.

"I promise I won't say anything."

His lips tugged at the corners of his mouth. "That's a lie. I have a feeling you're about to say a lot. Be more specific please."

I lifted my right hand. "I solemnly swear, I won't reveal anything you're about to tell me."

His smile bloomed with approval, and my chest warmed as he said, "Now that's a vow." That bit of praise shouldn't have felt so good coming from him and considering the subject.

He scanned the horizon before he said, "Your father and I belong to a secret society called The Blue-Frosted Rose."

He let that sentence sink in, and my lips quirked up at how serious and ominous he looked. It just didn't match. "Like you're a Mason or something?"

He shook his head but then lifted his shoulder. "Or something. BFR could be considered a darker version—"

I shot up at the acronym. "BFR? That's the people Mom said wanted her dead."

He shrugged fully. "Karla was lucky because Dan did everything he could to protect her, well, you. He didn't want you to lose another parent."

"Lose another parent? Wait. You're telling me she wasn't delusional? This club you belong to would have actually killed her?"

He pressed his lips together. "*I* would have eliminated her if she proved a threat to our secrecy."

"You?"

He nodded slowly. "I'm head of enforcement. I'm not a serial killer, but I have killed to protect my family."

"Family?"

"Our members are a family of brothers and sisters. You won't find our rules and rituals in a handbook or on any website."

"What kind of rituals do you do?"

He quirked an eyebrow, and I sighed. "Secret ones. I get it. So my dad does these rituals too?"

Logan nodded and added, "Your mother did too, and so does your aunt."

"So, you knew my dad before I moved into the condo?"

"The building is owned by BFR. The condos are for brothers and sisters. Your dad asked me to keep an eye on you."

I shifted in my seat before leaning forward and pinning Logan with a direct glare. "But you did more than just watch out for me. I'm guessing that what is currently leaking out of me, came from you?"

He stood up, eyes pinned on the space between my legs as he knelt before my tightly pinned knees. Large hands covered the tops of my thighs as he dragged his teeth across his lower lip. As his heated gaze lifted to mine, my brain supplied a memory of what those teeth felt like on my neck. I sucked in a breath as my body tightened in response.

"Do I need to fill you up again, Eden?" His voice had dropped into a low purr.

"No. You can't."

His brows rose. "Can't I?" The twinkle in his dark eyes as he looked up at me made me squirm.

"I can't."

He gave a self-satisfied smirk. "Sore?"

"No." I blamed that smirk for the lie.

He huffed a breathy laugh. "You're a pretty little liar. Almost as beguiling as when you came all over my cock last night."

I sat back and crossed my arms. "I'm sure it wasn't that great because I don't remember it at all."

He rubbed my thighs slowly. "Well, I remember every second. I'm happy to do a replay."

I pushed him with my foot, but he didn't move. "You see, that's the problem. I was drugged, and you took advantage of the situation. I feel," I swallowed as emotions circled inside me, "betrayed. You took something from me I'll never get back."

His hands stopped their reassuring movements. "I know. I had my reasons for doing what I did. It had to do with those rituals we can't talk about. I'm not saying I didn't enjoy every second, because I did. Your fucking body was absolute Heaven, and I'm starving for more." He nodded and stood up. "But I did betray your trust. You have every reason to be upset." He turned away. "But I hope you'll find your way to forgiveness."

My gaze narrowed. "And more sex with you?"

He ducked into the companionway but paused to meet my gaze. "Your emotions are not what is stopping me right now. I hope you'll forgive me, but if not," he shrugged, "I'm not above taking what I want."

The thrill that shot through my body had my heart skipping beats. *Did I want him to take me against my will?* I shouldn't want that. I scanned the silvery blue waves. There was no one to hear me scream in the middle of the ocean.

"You coming?" he asked from the darkness inside the parlor.

Logan

Logan Lurch

She stood up but halted in the companionway. "That depends on what you plan on doing."

I grinned up at her as I moved towards the galley kitchen to her left. "Right now? I plan on seeing what Dan has to eat on this sailboat. You need to regain your strength and hydrate."

She came down the steps slowly. "For what?"

I started rummaging through the cabinets and found pancake mix. "Did Dan ever teach you how to actually sail?"

Eden slipped into the tight space with me and pulled out a mixing bowl. "Yeah, why? What's wrong with the *Divinity*? Why are we drifting right now?"

"She didn't have a full tank of gas when we left. I had to motor all the way out here."

"All the way out here? Why?"

I shrugged. "Had something to get rid of." I lifted a hand and added, "And no, it's safer for you if you don't know."

She started mixing the pancakes in the bowl as I put a pan on the stove. "Is this how it's going to be between us? Making breakfast every morning together while we dance around secrets?"

I turned towards her. "No." Her face dropped, and I added, "I'll make breakfast, and I'll always share the important stuff. I'll never lie to you, Eden."

She shoved the batter at me. "No, you'll just drug me and fuck my unconscious body."

The moment I took the mixing bowl, she spun away and ran back to the master cabin. The door slammed shut, and I heard a sob leave her before the lock turned.

A heavy sigh left me. Her tears created a storm of emotions within me. They both excited and made me feel like total shit. I rubbed the ache in my chest before finishing the pancakes.

I carried her plate to the door. "Breakfast is ready." The silence stretched so long I shifted on my feet and leaned against the wall. "You need to eat something."

"How do I know it's not drugged."

"I didn't drug you the first time, Eden. I know you feel—"

"You have no idea how I feel, Logan," she snapped from the other side.

"Well, you said you felt betrayed, and you were just crying in there, so I do have an idea of how you feel. Those feelings are valid, and I hate that you believe you must suffer them alone."

"Why do you care? You got what you wanted."

My fingers clenched on the plate. "What I want, is for you to eat these goddamned pancakes before they get too cold and soggy."

"Why?"

"Because that moron valued money over your wellbeing and almost overdosed you with animal sedatives. You need to eat and hydrate."

The door unlocked and parted slowly. I was struck in the chest as she peered up at me with those wide, glassy blue eyes. She was devastatingly beautiful.

I lifted the plate. "Please?"

She reached for the plate, and I moved back. "Come sit and eat with me."

The door opened further, and Eden put her hands on hips. "Why do you like watching me eat so much?"

I stepped back, and she came into the cramped hall with me. I leaned in and put one hand on the wall beside her head. Her eyes widened.

"It's not that I want to watch you eat. It's because I want to sit down and have a meal with you." I shook my head and continued, "I've spent most of my life eating alone. Even after Mr. Dalton adopted me, I was alone most of the time. Mickey, my older brother, was in college. Todd was in high school like me, but he had his own set of friends, and I was still adjusting to normal life. The only time we all sat down to a meal was on special occasions."

Her chin trembled slightly. "That's so sad."

I pushed off the wall. "It was an immense blessing, Eden. I don't know who or what I'd be without Mr. Dalton's guidance and support."

She followed me the short distance to the table in the parlor and sat down across from me. "I don't like eating in front of other people."

I nodded as I poured maple syrup on my room temperature pancakes. "I've noticed."

"And that's what makes me feel weird. Nobody else cares to notice me until I do something stupid, like eat too fast or too much..."

She took an awkward bite, and I lowered my fork. "I notice everything about you because you are a ray of sunshine in the depths for me. How can I not look at the only light in my life?"

A blush crept up her neck and bloomed on her cheeks. "You don't even know me."

I broke eye contact as uncertainty filled my voice. "I do. I've been stalking you for over a month now." My body shifted as I toyed with my food. I needed to be honest with her if we had any chance to move forward as a team. "I've listened to your conversations and watched you daily."

"What?"

"I told you I wasn't a good man, but you make me want to do better, Eden. I won't lie to you."

"You really stalked me? Listened to my conversations? Like a tracker? Where is my phone?"

"I left it on shore. I didn't want anyone to find us."

She leaned back from the table. "This feels more like a kidnapping than anything James did."

"It's for your own good."

Before I could react, she picked up her plate and sprinted back into the cabin. I sighed as the door slammed and locked. I finished another meal in solitude and made my way back to the locked door cursing the low ceilings of this sailboat.

My knees bent and my ass hit the teak floors. "I knew I'd fuck this up."

"I want to go home." It sounded like she was sitting against the door.

"As soon as my team gets the right people in custody, we will go home."

"How long is that going to take?"

I shrugged even though she couldn't see me. "It could be a couple of days."

"Do my parents know I'm here?"

"Who do you think told me where the key was?"

After a moment of silence she asked, "How did you watch me?"

Fuck. "Cameras."

"Inside my condo?"

"Yes."

"I can't trust you."

"You can trust that I have your best interest at heart."

She barked a laugh. "My best interest? You put cameras in my home and a tracker on my phone before you kidnapped me and proceeded to fuck me while I was drugged."

"When you put it like that, I can understand how you might feel unsafe."

She didn't respond, and I hoped she was finishing her stack of pancakes. "Can I explain my perspective?"

"If you want." That didn't sound very encouraging. My heart felt heavy as I explained how her dad asked me to watch her. "My program monitors every member and their immediate family. Nothing is private in BFR."

She snorted and I smiled. "I don't know why Dan didn't indoctrinate you as a Blue Rose Lady when you turned eighteen, but he decided to keep you separate."

"What do you mean 'indoctrinate?'"

"It's a benign ritual that brings children into the fold of BFR. They dwell in the outer rings of membership until they graduate from college. We educate them about the society, the requirements, rituals, and benefits before they can make the decision about full membership."

"I'm sure only pretty people are inducted."

I laughed. "Yeah, only the most beautiful, like me."

"I didn't mean that. Women are held to a different standard than men."

I reminded her, "Mrs. Bennet is an honored BFR Lady. Most of the women living with us are. That doesn't mean you are wrong about different standards; it just means we take care of our members."

At her silence, I sighed again and attempted to explain my perspective. "So, I did put cameras in your condo and a tracker on your phone. The footage, texts, and audio go into a secure folder which is only held for three days before it's automatically deleted."

"Where are the cameras, Logan?"

Seconds ticked by. "I have full coverage of your entire home. Before you ask, yes, I've seen it all. And yes, I know I took my duties too far concerning you. I don't know why, I just became fascinated with you. My days felt darker when I didn't watch the footage. The way you sing the songs stuck in your head had me singing on the inside with you. The way you poke your tongue out when you are drawing or the way your face changes when you read one of your books became addictive."

"I should feel violated."

"I did violate you. I couldn't stop myself. Finally holding you in my arms, so vulnerable and relaxed. I took advantage of you."

"I wanted to have sex with you, Logan, but I wanted to be present and participate in our first time."

I wanted to tell her the next time we had sex I'd make sure it was a spectacular first time for her. It didn't matter that it was the second time for me. It didn't matter because every time would be a discovery. Instead, I said, "I'm sorry. I don't say that often, Eden. I pray we can get past this, because I want more than just a stolen orgasm from you."

The lock clicked and the door swung open. Eden sat down in the hall across from me with a guarded expression. "Like what?"

It amazed me how beautiful she was even when suspicious and mad. "That depends on how fast you want to go."

"Where are we going, Logan? Give me your roadmap."

I didn't want to scare her, but I also didn't want her to minimize what I needed. "I want you to be my lady, eventually my wife, and the mother of my children."

"I'm still in college. I can't be a mom, too."

"You'd be a wonderful mother because—"

She jerked and wide eyes met mine. "We know what it's like to have terrible parents."

I smiled. "You heard that."

"I remember more and more. Where is James?"

I frowned. "He got what he deserved for disrespecting you."

"You killed him?"

My gaze dropped to my folded knees as I nodded slowly.

Her voice was soft. "He didn't deserve to die."

Anger flashed through me. "That's where you are wrong. The people he would have turned you over to are bad news. They would have done terrible things to you, much worse than I did. Anyone who'd put you in that situation deserves to die. He traded you for a measly ten thousand dollars."

Her hand went to her chin as she stared at the wood panel wall in front of her. "That's a lot of money."

"No amount of money is worth your suffering."

Her eyes flicked to mine. "I could do a lot with ten grand."

The matter-of-factness in her voice surprised me into silence until she smirked.

My lips twitched in response. "Want to host your own kidnapping then? I bet daddy would pay a lot more than ten grand to get you back."

"Would you be my kidnapper? Make the ransom note?"

The sparkle in her gaze spoke to Lurch. I expected her to freak out after learning James was dead, but instead she wanted to play a game. "It would be a ransom demand, and if you want me to make this legit, I'd have to tie you up."

Interest lit her face. "What would you do once you got me tied up?"

"Careful, little angel. You already know how impulsive I am when it comes to you. I'd hate to start playing a game that would wreck you."

She tapped her lip with her index finger, and my gaze followed the motion. "Maybe being wrecked is what I need right now."

I pushed up from the floor. "Did you eat your breakfast?"

"That was lunch, and yes, I did."

"Then you better run."

Chapter Eighteen

Boat Bondage

Eden

My heart skipped as his gaze darkened. The way his voice lowered at the word 'run' had my stomach twisting in anticipation. I stood up slowly. "But we are on a boat..." Granted, the *Divinity* was just over fifty feet long, but still way too small to run from a psychopath.

The sadistic twist of his lips made my knees tremble.

He finished for me. "In the middle of the ocean," he said, leaning close enough to put his face inches from mine. "There's no one to hear you scream."

After he so casually admitted to killing James, the fear that had my legs moving was almost real. Deep down, I didn't think he'd actually hurt me, but he was an admitted murderer.

He let me slip past him because, honestly, unless I jumped ship, I had nowhere to go. I made it up the companionway steps and into the cockpit as my brain pointed out that I could have just gone back into the cabin and locked the door. I wondered briefly about my mental state because I felt more alive in that moment than I ever had. That day in my hallway was a close second, but this location was freeing. I made my way towards the bow as Logan came into the cockpit.

His gate was relaxed, and he merely glanced at me before searching the cockpit for his duffle bag. The zipper felt louder than the waves lapping against the hull. He was so focused on what was inside that I inched towards him.

My brain offered up a plan as he set a bundle of rope on the bench. I could push him overboard and drive away. He said we were low on gas, but he didn't know about the extra tank my dad had installed when he purchased the *Divinity*. This blue water sailing vessel was outfitted to sail the world.

Logan was also making a plan. One that included bondage and knives from the looks of it. He glanced my way, and I retreated towards the bow once more.

"Ah, the thrill of the chase would be better on land."

I surveyed the water.

He warned, "Don't even think about it."

I hadn't been. Being separated from your boat in the middle of the ocean was a solid fear for most sailors. But Logan didn't need to know this. "I'll jump if you come any closer."

He paused his approach immediately. "Don't jump." His voice was casual and soothing.

"I don't really want to ransom my dad."

His lips quirked. "I know you don't."

"How?"

"Because you're a good person, Eden."

I shook my head. "I'm really not. I have dark thoughts."

His lips parted on a silent laugh, and I was struck by how beautiful he was. "You're human, Eden. We all have dark thoughts occasionally."

My chin lifted. "I once watched a kid almost drown at sleepaway camp. I could have tried to save her, or call for help, but I didn't."

The amusement in his eyes had my face heating. "Why not?"

I shrugged, feeling like an idiot. "She was a bully who was trying to sabotage the kayaks so she'd win the paddle race. But she fell in and I did nothing to help her."

He inched closer, and I put the main sail between us as he said, "How diabolical of you."

"Are you making fun of me?"

He dodged left, like he was going towards the bow. I rushed towards the stern on the other side of the mast. He hesitated but then shot right and ducked under the beam. I screamed as his hand closed on my arm. He let me jump down into the cockpit before spinning me to face him, pinning my arm behind my back with a grip that was on the edge of pain.

"I would never make fun of you."

The scars on his face thinned with his grin, and I was again reminded of how difficult his childhood had been. I was an ass to bring up sleepaway camp when he probably never had vacations.

"Is that pity I see as you look at my flaws?"

"No, I'm just a self-absorbed dumbass. I'm sorry."

He jerked me closer and lowered his mouth within inches of mine. "Not sorry enough. Not yet."

His kiss started tender and soft. The passion in it shot through me like lightning. I sucked in a sharp breath, and he dove deeper. Nobody had ever kissed me like he did. His hand tightened on my wrist as his arm locked my body to his like a vice.

Before I realized what I was doing, I kissed him back. I lifted my unpinned arm, and threaded my fingers through his soft dark hair. He moaned at the touch. Moaned a ragged starved sound into my mouth as he devoured me. That sound traveled down my spine and pulsed behind my clit. I felt heavy down there. Heavy and full and suddenly needy.

I was so focused on my body and his kiss that I didn't notice his free hand until I felt the soft rope looping where his hand had been. It pulled snug and I jerked back from his lips.

His grin was unhinged. "I caught an angel."

He let me put my captured hand between us. The coils were perfectly straight, and the knot at the tail was tight. He had done all that behind my back as he distracted me.

My gaze lifted to his. "Maybe you merely have a tiger by the tail."

"Promise to scratch and bite, little tiger?"

I fisted his hair and jerked his neck back.

Laughter burst out of him, causing my lips to twist up into a smile until his gaze met mine. "I'm about to wreck an angel who thinks she's a diabolical tiger."

I let go and twisted away to put some distance between us. He let me get to the other side of the cockpit before he clamped down on the tail of the rope, jerking my arm towards him.

"Fuck!"

He reeled me in slowly. "I think I like you leashed."

"Leashed?" I tugged against the pull.

"Yeah, I bet you want to be tamed by me. I bet you're soaked for me. Aren't you? Are those shorts wet?"

"No." I dropped down to my ass in the middle of the cockpit. It really wasn't a vast space, but if he wanted to prove my lie, I wouldn't make it easy for him.

"Such a pretty little liar."

He was on me in a heartbeat. I shrieked as his weight settled on my legs. His knees clamped my thighs together as he straddled me. I tried to twist away but he captured my other wrist and started coiling another length of rope around it. Like the rope on my left wrist, this one was also thick and snug, yet comfortable.

He grinned at me like he knew all my secrets before lifting off my legs to survey the canopy over the cockpit. He pulled me to my feet and backed me up in front of the companionway. I thought he might back me down the steps and tie me to the bed but instead he tossed the tail of the rope holding my left hand through the bars of the canopy. My arm was pulled high, and the knot fit perfectly into my palm. It felt secure as my hand curled around it, holding on to it as he did the same with my right hand.

He stepped back holding both ropes in one hand. "You're going to have to climb, angel."

I blinked and his gaze shifted to the cushioned seat to my right. "Hop up."

I put a bare foot on the cushion, and he pulled both ropes until I straddled the companionway like the Colossus of Rhodes, the ancient statue that straddled a harbor. Except, my body swayed precariously with the waves gently pushing at the *Divinity's* hull. After securing the ropes, Logan pulled a bone-handled blade from his duffle bag and unsheathed it from its leather case. The Damascus blade gleamed in the sunlight, causing me to wince.

"What is that for?" My voice sounded less nervous than I felt. He wouldn't hurt me. At least, I didn't think he would. But maybe I put too much trust in a confessed murderer. Maybe, I truly was a gullible dumbass.

He eyed me for a long moment. "You are entirely over dressed, little angel."

He sliced the hem of the black shirt and tore it open with both hands. An impressed gasp left me at the sudden violence of the movement. As strong as he was, the collar remained intact. The tip of the blade rose towards my face. "Look up. I don't want to nick that pretty chin."

I closed my eyes and lifted my face as he slipped the blade under the collar and tugged. Cool air hit my torso, and I felt my nipples tighten. I squeezed my lids and held my breath, waiting for the comment everyone makes when they see my tits for the first time.

Well, it wasn't his first time. Someone had to get me out of my prom dress last night. If he took the time to fuck me, he surely took the time to inspect my lopsided tits.

At his continued silence, I dared a peek.

Dark stormy eyes were watching mine with curiosity. His lips tipped up in approval before his gaze lowered to my breasts. His mouth parted slightly before he whispered, "Beautiful."

He flipped the knife in his palm before his gaze dropped to my shorts. The knife came forward. "Hold very still."

I held my breath as the back of the blade pressed into my skin at the waistband. The elastic parted with an ease that spoke of experience, like he often cut clothing off people. He opted to rip the rest of the fabric like he had with the shirt. That shouldn't have made my body come alive like it did. I should have been begging him to stop, in fear for my life.

I scanned the horizon as he worked on the rest of the shorts. "What if..." I paused because the sound of my father's shorts being shredded stole my thoughts. "What if someone comes along and sees me like this?" That thought had my throat closing.

Heated dark eyes slowly raised up my body. "Let's pray that doesn't happen. I'd hate to send another body to the bottom of the ocean."

I closed my eyes again as air caressed my pussy and ass. I was completely naked and spread eagle for anyone to see. I inhaled slowly, focused on breathing through the tightness in my throat. All my rolls and fat lumps were exposed to the ocean breeze. If he wanted to shame me, he knew exactly what to do. I felt like a whale hung out to dry.

He was so quiet I thought he might have walked away. I opened my eyes and sucked in a breath when I found him. I was forced to look over my asymmetrical floppy tits and past my belly to where he knelt. His head was craned back as he stared up at me with soft awe.

I winced as I imagined what his view looked like. "What are you doing?" I questioned with as much courage I could muster.

"Enjoying the view of a fucking goddess in the flesh."

His grin was contagious. "You're insane."

He laughed. "You're just figuring that out?"

My smile grew as he stood up and said, "Doesn't change reality, though. I do believe you are the most beautiful creature I've ever seen."

"Bullshit."

He lunged forward and pressed the blade against my collarbone as he clutched the back of my neck. "Are you calling me a liar, Eden McKenzie?"

Hair fell across my eyes as I dipped my chin to look at the knife. He held the backside of the blade to my skin. I met his unhinged gaze as he said, "I promised myself we'd start this relationship off in truth. I confessed to murder and stalking. You believed me then, but when I tell you how I see you, you don't believe me."

"I own a mirror, Logan."

He brushed my hair back with his thumb. "Then your eyes tell ugly lies, angel. The fact that you trust those eyes tells me we need to fix this."

He stepped back and let his gaze move casually over my bare body. "You're naked from here on out."

Shock at his statement had me pulling on the binds. "What?"

He moved the blade between my breasts, dragging it slowly across my skin. "And when I tell you what I see, you'll say yes sir, or merely, thank you."

Logan

Logan Lurch

"Or?" Her voice was breathless even though her chest rose and fell rapidly with excitement. Her breasts heaved and swayed with the movement.

I lifted my face to hers. "I'm going to work this body into a frenzy of lust. You're already a tight ball of hot need. You'll accept my compliments like a good girl, or I'll deny your body the pleasure it already craves."

Blue eyes widened. "You wouldn't."

I flipped the knife so the flared end of the handle was against her stomach. Tracing a heart there, I said, "Oh, I would, and don't think for a minute that I'll deny myself release."

I leaned in and captured her breast in my fist. My fingers dug into soft flesh as my tongue darted out to lash the tight tip. Her gasp was delicious as I captured the bud between my teeth and gave it a gentle tug. Her hair fell across her eyes as she nuzzled my temple. Hot breath fanned my cheek as I gently sucked the pain away. It was an unexpectedly tender moment.

But I was a deviant man.

I traced the end of the bone handle lower. Down her stomach and over her pubic bone until it pressed between her parted pussy. She hissed at the pressure on her clit but tried her best to get closer to me.

Her hips moved, undulating slowly in a sly attempt to gain friction. I let the handle move with her.

"Logan."

Gods help me. The way she said my name like a prayer had my body tightening.

"I'm going to fuck you with my favorite knife, Eden."

I moved the handle back and pressed it against her vulva.

She threw her head back with a moan. "Please..."

Her slick body resisted the wide knob, but with gentle pressure it swallowed the tip. "Begging so soon? Do you know how many people I've taken apart with this blade?" I pulled the end out of her, only to reintroduce it deeper. "Will you beg for my cock the way you beg for my blade?"

"Yes," she hissed as I adjusted my hold lower on the handle.

I let the weight of the knife inch the handle out of her as I angled my face to hers. Red hair created a veiled halo around us as our breath mingled.

I pushed the handle so deep my hand touched her pussy before moving to pinch the blade between my fingers. "Do you want to come all over my blade?"

Plump, kissable lips parted on an inhale as the finger guard at the hilt pressed against her clit. "Yes."

I smiled against the corner of her mouth as I gently fucked in and out of her with the bone handle that I had once killed with. "Then what do you say?"

"I'm a goddess." It was barely a whisper.

I pulled out to the bulbous tip and held it still. "Not good enough."

Her eyes opened and found mine. "I'm a beautiful goddess?"

The knife left her, and her brows drew together as she frowned. The slick handle appeared between our faces. "Show me how much you love yourself."

"What?"

I put the handle against her bottom lip, running it back and forth slowly. "Show me how much you love yourself, Eden."

She eyed the slick handle before parting those lips. She met my gaze once more as the tip of her tongue darted out to taste herself.

I took a long inhale, smelling that scent I craved. "You're going to have to do better than that."

It took her a Texas minute. So long, I got to witness her figure out the puzzle of what I wanted. It all played out on her face. She went from disgust to curiosity and finally determination. Her lips parted and her jaw opened wide as she leaned forward and sucked the bulb that had just been inside her.

"Good girl," I purred approvingly as I pulled the hard handle out of her mouth to kiss those tasty lips. They trembled as I licked into her mouth, stealing back what belonged to me.

This time, I lowered myself with the knife. The hair growth on my chin made her gasp and jerk until I was once again on my knees before my parted goddess. I drew the back of the blade up her inner thigh until the handle was once again pressed against her pussy. Her body opened and took the fat tip with slick ease this time. "Oh fuck, yes, Eden."

Pinching the blade once more, I took my time and enjoyed the view as I pushed it in and out of her, teasing her clit with gentle nudges of the steel finger guard.

"More." Her voice was deep and hoarse as her knees bent and her hips jerked.

"Do I own this pussy yet?"

"Logan, please..."

She didn't want to say it. I pushed the blade deeper and swiveled the steel across her clit before pulling out. Her body opened readily as I pushed it back inside her. This pussy knew who her master was. It was weeping with the knowledge. "I need to hear you say it."

I gave *my pussy* a few quick, short strokes. Her legs shook wildly. I wrapped my arm around her thighs, just under the crease of her ass and pushed the handle in and out of her. Fast and shallow, stimulating the nerves of her swollen clitoris.

"Logan! Yes. Oh God! I'm yours."

The bone handle left her, and I stayed still. She panted above me. I inhaled her sweet scent again. The words she spoke were forced and begrudging. "You own my pussy."

I pushed the handle all the way inside her, grinding the finger guard against her clit. Her legs stiffened on a scream. She rose to her toes, but I followed her movement, pressing hard for a count of five. I leaned forward as I pulled the knife out and gently kissed her trembling clit.

Her body jerked but relaxed at the feel of my lips. "I'm so sorry sweet baby," I rumbled against her pussy. "I had to punish you so your owner would understand why you react the way you do for me."

I gently fucked her with the handle as I coaxed her clit with my lips and tongue. It slowly filled with desire as it grew heavy once more. Eden groaned and ground her hips above me, trying her damnedest to gain the friction she needed to come.

But I moved with her, barely teasing her pussy until she made a frustrated noise. "Okay! Okay, Logan, you've made your point. I'm dying up here. Please... your pussy needs you. I need you. Please fuck me."

Oh thank fuck! My cock was weeping with the need to be inside her again.

I clasped my mouth around her clit and sucked hard as I pulled the bone handle out of her body. She stiffened and shouted but then lowered as much as she could, giving herself over to me. "Please, Logan. I need you."

My teeth captured her labia and tugged as I moved back.

She whimpered and said, "It's yours. You own it. Please!"

I pulled the quick release knot on the rope that held her arms high and wide. Holding tension, I said, "Step down."

Her legs shook as she lowered herself to the deck under the canopy. I threw an arm around her waist as I gathered the tails of the rope once more. Moving her to the cushioned bench on the starboard side, I gently encouraged her to her knees before stepping out of the cockpit and finding a cleat to tie her hands to. I unbuttoned my jeans and fisted my erection, resisting the urge to stroke it. Moving to my knees in front of her, I clutched her hair and tilted her face up.

"This belongs to you now. Anytime you need it, it's yours. Do you understand?"

She eyed my cock with a hunger I'd never seen on her face. Inching closer she licked her bottom lip before placing a tender kiss to the tip of my dick.

"Fuck, Eden. You're going to make me come before I'm ready."

There was a feral look in her gaze as she grinned up at me, drunk on the power she had over me in this moment. All resolve to drag this out left me. "Open that pretty little mouth, angel, and greet your cock like a good girl."

She opened wide and I inched inside. "Get it nice and wet for your pussy."

Her mouth closed around my head, and I saw stars as she suckled me. When her tongue flicked along the underside of my tip, my hips pushed forward, driving me deeper into her sweet mouth.

"I knew your mouth would be heaven."

I pulled out to the tip, and she did that little tongue thing again, eliciting a tight groan from me. "Sinfully sweet."

I pushed deep, hitting the back of her throat. She relaxed around me and then swallowed my tip. *Good gods, she didn't have a gag reflex*. My hips found a slow rhythm.

"You were made for me, Eden. Destined to be mine from the moment I saw you exit the elevator." I met her gaze. "This mouth is mine. Gods, I want to come down your throat so bad."

Her lips were sealed around my root, and I held myself deep, counting the seconds, stealing her breath. "And I will, eventually. I'm going to mark every part of you and brand myself into your skin."

Her eyes bulged with the need for air. Tick tock. Time seemed to slow as I sensually fucked her throat. One minute. Tears poured out of her eyes, but they held a note of trust. Ninety seconds. It was the same length she'd stayed underwater as she lapped the pool at the condo. I gently pulled out. Drool flooded down her chin as she sucked in a huge breath.

Her triumphant smile made my chest ache. "Such a talented girl."

I moved into the cockpit behind her and adjusted her to her feet on the cushions, widening her legs until her pussy was the perfect height. I took a hold of myself and pressed just inside her, stretching her open before reaching around her and fingering her. Parting her gently, I pinched her clit between two fingers and held her captive. She groaned and jerked, her back arching as she attempted to impale herself fully on my dick.

"Shh. Steady. I'm going to make you come around the tip of my cock. The same tip you teased with that sinful tongue. And you're going to give me the names of the men you learned that technique from."

"What? No!"

I gave her clit a gentle tug as I rocked my hips in shallow strokes. "You're going to tell me their names and where they live. Describe them in detail, so I know that I have the right dicks when I cut them off and present them to you as a trophy."

She made a noise of alarm, but I started circling her clit as I pulled my head just barely outside of her heat only to push back in. Whatever she was about to say morphed into a whimper.

"His name was Charles. He was the son of the pastor of the church we went to." She paused to pant as I worked her body just enough to take her to the edge. "Dark hair and chocolate eyes. I had the biggest crush on him." I pinched her clit, and she let out a shuddering breath that radiated down her spine. I held on, crushing her orgasm with a hint of pain.

She flexed on my dick, and I groaned. "What else?"

When she merely panted, I fisted her hair and pulled her head up. Her eyes popped wide. "He used me. Took my virginity and then dumped me for Chrissy. She knew what he'd done and rubbed it in my face."

I stroked her clit and thrust a little deeper. "Chrissy's dead, too."

"Oh God!" Her pussy vibrated as her body tightened and bucked under me. Her orgasm shocked her. "Fuck, fuck, FUCK!"

I let go of her clit and grabbed her hips, holding her steady for the ride she was about to endure.

Chapter Nineteen

A Whispered Promise

Eden

I never knew the meaning of rearranging your insides until Logan. He had the ability to punish and pleasure with only his cock. This man fucked like a demon. All I could do was hold on, brace myself, and scream.

I had never been a screamer. I always thought those women who made a lot of noise were acting, but I was on a rollercoaster ride of dick, and Logan knew just how hard and deep to go to keep me on edge. I felt every inch of him dragging in and out of me. Slow, fast, slow, and then deep and fast. It was like a ride in the dark. I couldn't see where the dips and twists were, but boy did I feel them.

Just when I thought that ride would never end, he reached around and started rubbing my clit again. He pushed deep, held still, and whispered roughly, "I'll kill everyone who ever hurt you, Eden. I'll make anyone bleed and suffer for you. Come for me, my angel, my queen, my fucking goddess."

And I did. I came so hard as he emptied himself so deep in me, he might have been inside my womb.

Seconds ticked into minutes. He softened inside me, but I was still impaled on a killer and had just come undone with a whispered promise of death.

What did that say about me?

I could already be pregnant, and all I cared about was how tightly he held me. How secure I felt in his arms. His chest was on my back, and his scruffy cheek was at my sweaty neck, but there was no weight on me. In fact, he was holding me up with one arm, and his pelvis pressed me against the back of the bench. Trapping me, holding his come inside me with his dick, and I loved it.

Eventually and reluctantly he finally slipped free. He untied my hands from the cleat at the edge of the boat and pulled me around by them so that I settled across his lap.

Sperm leaked from me and onto him as he cradled me. "Relax."

He adjusted my torso so I leaned against the bend in the bench. "Open those thighs, angel. Let me see how I ruined you."

I stiffened but let my legs fall open. His gaze dropped down my body to the mess he made. He parted my pussy with two fingers and scooped up what lay on his thigh with his free hand. "This belongs in here." Two fingers pushed inside me.

"And if I get pregnant?"

Dark eyes met my half-closed ones. "Oh, you *will* get pregnant. I'm going to breed you until you're heavy with child. Then I'm going to keep breeding you until I deliver our child and promptly put another inside you."

"You're crazy." His fingers moved inside me, and I jolted at how sensitive I was. "Fuck that felt good."

He smiled as he moved his fingers again, and it transformed his normally harsh face into something stunningly beautiful. "Of course it feels good, angel. *My* pussy knows what it needs." I watched his profile as he pleasured me. My throat closed with emotion as his fingers gently caressed the walls of my vagina.

He said, “I need to get you cleaned up before you get a UTI”

I shifted. “I need to pee anyway.”

His fingers left me and went right to his mouth.

My nose wrinkled. “You know that’s probably mostly you by now.”

His gaze slid to me with a twinkle as he pulled his fingers from his mouth. “Mostly me but tastes like you.”

He patted my thigh and said, “I’d carry you, but the companionway is a little tight.”

A small laugh left me as I swung my feet to the floor. “What? You think you fucked the legs out of me?”

“I’m going to make you eat those words later.” He slapped my ass as I got up, and I squealed and darted for the steps.

He followed close. “First we need to figure out how far we’ve drifted and how much gas we have left.”

I sighed. “We have plenty of gas to make it back. Just have to switch tanks. I just wish we had more time together.” I turned around at the bathroom and almost ran into his chest. “What are you doing?”

The corner of his mouth tipped up as he put his palms on the low ceiling and leaned forward. “Spending time with you?”

I craned my neck to meet his gaze. “I have to pee.”

He quirked a brow. “So?”

My hand went to my hip and his gaze dipped to my breasts reminding me that I was still buck-naked. “I’m requesting a little privacy.”

He grabbed my wrists as I crossed my arms over my chest and directed them around his neck. He leaned down and his hair fell across his scarred cheek and temple. “You haven’t had privacy from me for over a month, but I’m willing to give this to you, for now.” His lips pressed to my forehead and warmth bubbled up inside me. “I’ll be right here.”

I stepped back with a shy smile. "Thank you."

He dipped his chin in acknowledgement and pulled the door shut.

I sat down on the toilet, and my bladder immediately had stage fright. I was arguing with my body, trying to reason that the door was shut and there was no damn stage. "Just pee already," I whispered to myself.

It was almost there when a strange voice from outside the cabin hollered, "Ahoy *Divinity*!"

Logan swore before he spoke through the door. "Stay below."

"Don't kill anyone."

I thought I heard him snort before he said, "No promises."

Logan's footsteps retreated as the stranger called out again. "Anyone onboard?"

Logan's voice was deep and gruff. "Yeah. What's up?"

I quickly finished peeing and washed up, noting that I was slightly tender and well-used. It felt nice to be wanted the way Logan wanted me.

I rummaged through some more drawers and found a string bikini that had to belong to Mandy. My heart did a tiny jealous jerk as I realized Dad had brought her sailing too. It was a stupid reaction. Of course, he took Mandy sailing.

The bikini barely fit and only because it was secured by long strings that I loosened all the way. One wrong move though and my boobs would pop right out. I looked ridiculous in the too-tiny stringy bikini, but it was all I had at the time, and I didn't want to be naked if it was the Coast Guard or something.

The voices above came clear as I approached the companionway steps.

The stranger said, "Like I said, it looked like you guys were drifting. You're getting close to the shipping lane. We just wanted to make sure everything was okay."

I climbed the steps just enough to see the fisherman in the powerboat. He immediately looked at me and I said, "We're good. Thanks for checking on us though."

Logan cut his glare to me and gave an exasperated sigh as he gripped his shirt from across his body and pulled it off in one swift movement. He straightened the black t-shirt and then pulled it over my head. "I told you to stay below."

I poked my arms through the sleeves. "Why? Embarrassed to be seen with me?"

His face darkened. "You'll pay for that comment later."

I rolled my eyes and pushed my way past Logan.

He growled. "And for that, too."

I waved at the fisherman as he started his engine. He waved back as he left.

I sat down in the captain's chair as Logan asked, "Why do you think I'd be embarrassed to be seen with you?"

I took a moment to refamiliarize myself with *Divinity's* controls before starting the engine. Then I let my gaze travel over Logan's tattooed chest and arms. "Why did you tear off your shirt and put it on me the moment I popped my head up?" He was so corded and fit, it was ridiculous.

His finger curled under my chin and lifted my gaze to his face. "Because your body is for my eyes only. Mine. No one else, especially not some random, nosey fisherman.

"You know it's maritime law for other boaters to render aid. What if we had both fallen off the boat earlier? We might have stood a chance at rescue because of that 'nosey fisherman.'"

"Point taken." He leaned closer and gripped the hem of my shirt and pulled it off me.

"Hey!" Well, it was his, but since he put it on me first... I immediately straightened the tiny cups of the bikini, but he tugged the string at the base of my neck and the cups fell over my hands. "What are you doing?"

He pulled the string tied behind my back and tugged my top off. "When I said naked, I meant naked."

When he reached for the bottom string, I said, "I don't think that's entirely sanitary."

His lip lifted in a mock sneer. "You can sit on a towel."

"Gee, thanks." I lifted slightly so he could pull the bottoms off me. He grabbed the towel I'd brought up with me earlier and placed it on the captain's chair. "Such a gentleman."

"Keep it up, angel."

I rolled my eyes, and he lifted a brow. *Why do I find that so hot?* I shook my head and fired up *Divinity*. We had a quarter tank of gas left in tank one. I reached under the console and flipped the switch. The gauge moved to full, and I put her in gear.

"I'm going downstairs to look at the charts. We need to find a place to moor for the night."

I grinned. "I'll just be up here, tits blowing in the wind, waving to all the ships we pass."

He was already halfway down the steps as he said, "And what fine tits they are."

I considered using the radio to call for help just to be spiteful. The reasoning part of my brain knew Logan was a walking, talking, blood-red flag. I knew all this could go south in seconds. He was a murderer. But honestly, I'd never felt more alive than I did at that moment. Even though there were no other boaters in the area, I wanted to cover my body. Except, I also wanted to show Logan that I could be just as reckless and wild as him.

When he returned, he was stark naked too.

My jaw dropped as my gaze soaked up the view. He had tattoos stretching up his thighs as well as those on his chest, back, and arms. *How in the heck did I bag this guy?* Like, there might be something wrong with his brain, but his body was banging.

His cock, even in repose, was intimidatingly thick and long. *How the fuck did all that fit inside me?*

"Like what you see?"

My gaze shot to his, but my mouth said, "Yeah."

His satisfied smirk had me biting my bottom lip. "Good, cause all of this belongs to you."

I let go of my lip. "I'm not sure how I feel about that."

He sat down on the bench and put his arms on the back, stretching them wide. "Why is that?"

Logan

Logan Lurch

She was watching my junk like she'd never seen a naked man before. Or maybe she was worried it would leap up and bite her. I wasn't entirely sure as she answered my questions slowly.

"This all feels fast." She glanced at my face and said, "Maybe not for you since you've been watching me for, since before we actually met, I guess?"

I lifted an eyebrow but remained silent. This looked like it was hard for her, and I didn't want to ruin her courage.

"I mean, like you're ready to get married, and have kids and I don't even know much about you."

I leaned forward and put my elbows on my thighs. "You know more about me than most. My brothers don't even know how I got my facial scars."

"They're not as horrifying as you make them out to be. In fact, they look like three crescent moons, stacked side by side."

I ran my hand through my hair. "They may not look horrifying anymore, but I can assure you it was a literal hell growing up."

"I'm sorry. That was callous of me. I'm sure it was painful. Kids were probably mean about it. I just, I find your face attractive, maybe the way you find my body attractive?"

"You say that like I'm secretly disgusted by your body."

She scanned the horizon before admitting, "Like I said, this is all new to me."

I sat back and opened my arms. "What do you want to know about me?"

She pursed her lips but then smiled. "I don't know. What's your favorite color?"

"Red-orange."

"That's specific. Why?"

I grinned, "It reminds me of your hair, but before I saw you, it was my favorite crayon to color with."

"Did you color a lot when you were younger?"

I nodded slowly and she asked, "Did you go through my stuff when I wasn't home?"

My gaze dropped to the floor. "I did. I also entered your home when you were sleeping."

She jerked. "How?"

I met her gaze. "I own the building. Well, my family does. I have keys to all the condos."

"You watched me sleep?"

I held her gaze. "Yes."

She looked away. "Have you done that with anyone else?"

"Just you."

It took her a long time to ask another question. When it came my heart sank. "What would happen to me if I left you? Like calling the police and getting witness protection or something."

I stared at her in disbelief. After everything we'd done together, after all I'd confessed... Did she really want to escape me? I inhaled and blew it out slowly. "You can't run from me. Not now, not ever. I'm yours, Eden. I will always be there, watching, protecting, and loving you, even from a distance. If you truly don't want me to be in your life, by your side, I'll fade into the background. But I'm never completely going away."

She scratched her head. "I don't know if that's what I want. I just want to know there's an out - that isn't death - if I feel like I need it."

"You're worried I'll kill you." It wasn't a question.

She shrugged but then nodded. "Will you?"

"I can't imagine a world without you in it, even if we are not together."

"Do you enjoy killing people?"

The change in subject threw me a little, but I responded immediately. "I enjoy killing people who deserve it."

"Like James?"

"James left me..." I searched for the word. "The kid made a stupid mistake that I couldn't let slide. He undervalued and disrespected you. I murdered him. How I feel about it doesn't matter. Most of the time I feel nothing, but sometimes, yes, I enjoy killing very much."

Her gaze dropped to my junk, and I answered the question forming on her face. "Yes. I have been known to get an erection as I killed someone. It doesn't happen often, but it *has* happened. Sometimes I get aroused about it days afterward. Do you really want to hear about all this? What happened to my favorite color?"

"I'm just trying to understand."

I shook my head. "You can't understand because you aren't a killer, Eden. I've done some fucked up shit. I'll continue to do fucked up shit to protect my extended family. I'm the enforcer. It's who I am, but it doesn't have to be who *we* are."

"So, you kill to protect the secret society my dad is in."

I nodded, holding eye contact. "All my kills, including James, were for the Blue-Frosted Rose. I'll kill the two we have in custody once we get the information we need from them, and then I'll go after whoever hired them to kidnap you."

Eventually she nodded, hopefully accepting that what I did for a living was part of me. "Why did you take all your clothes off?"

I grinned at the change of subject. "What's good for the goose," I shrugged. "Besides, I was hoping to be your towel."

She grinned. "What? How?" A little laugh escaped her as she said those words.

I crossed the tiny space between us. "Stand up."

I slipped into the chair behind her, my cock already thickening in anticipation as I pulled her down on my lap. We'd done this before, and she spread her legs over my thighs as I wrapped my arm around her middle to secure her to me on the moving vessel.

"Just relax." I said as I reached past her and put the coordinates into *Divinity's* autopilot. The boat would take it from there; we just needed to be on the lookout for other boats or floating obstacles.

I let my hands smooth over her body, enjoying the feel of her in my arms. "You are my queen, Eden. Let me be your throne. Your request is my command."

My hand circled her breasts before moving to trace the lines of her face.

"I think I told you last night Mickey is a little older and Todd is younger. I was held back in school and needed a lot of tutoring to catch up. That made me closer to Todd than Mickey. Well, as close as I could have gotten to anyone at the time. Honestly, I craved Mr. Dalton's attention and company over everything else."

Her body relaxed even more as I spoke. My hands continued the slow exploration of her body, memorizing her and noting her reaction to where I touched.

She began petting me back. Touching me with light curiosity. Tracing the tattoos on my arms as she studied them.

I pressed a kiss to her temple and continued talking. "He seemed pleased that I took an interest in the Blue-Frosted Rose Society. I wasn't a businessman. Those jobs belonged to Mickey and Todd. I was interested in the rituals and magic."

She turned her face to mine. "Magic?"

I kissed her nose. "Yes."

She smiled. "Do you have a wand?"

"This isn't Harry Potter."

"More like devil worshiping and witchcraft?"

I sighed heavily. "I'm going to punch your father right in the nose the next time I see him."

She laughed but trailed her hand down her body and cupped my jutting cock, pressing it against her parted pussy. Warmth rose in my chest at the cradling feel of her hand on my dick. It was like she was holding my heart against her core. "Explain why you feel like that, Logan."

Fuck. The way she rubbed her pussy against my length fuzzed my thoughts. When I finally spoke, my voice had dropped lower. "Because you should have a better understanding of what BFR is by now. It was his job to educate you and your choice to accept or reject the society. Whether it was his decision or your mothers doesn't matter. Someone decided not to educate you in even the basic rituals that promote prosperity and wellness."

She rolled her hips, rubbing her clit on my dick. Her gaze went to the rune tattooed on my forearm around her waist. "So, it's like paganism."

"That's the closest religion to ours. We use what works for us. Sometimes we work with gods, and sometimes demons are necessary."

She leaned forward and rose up on my thighs, giving me a spectacular view of her ass and pussy as she lined me up and slowly stretched herself around me. Both my hands gripped her ass and spread her cheeks. Her body was fiery as it encased me. Her back tensed. "Fuck, you're big."

I lifted her ass and she rose. My head glistened as it popped out of her, only to press against those swollen lower lips of hers. She lowered again with a hiss. "I'm a little sore," she admitted over her shoulder.

I pulled her back against my chest and wrapped my arms around her as my cock seated itself deep inside her. Her moan was luxurious. "Just relax, Eden. Let me soak in your heated glory. Let your body adjust. You were made for me. You'll see."

She took a deep breath and let it out slowly as my hands resumed their lazy laps over her torso and thighs. "I feel so full."

"I'll keep you full in every way I can, angel."

"Why do you call me angel?"

My fingers trailed up her inner thigh and skipped over her stretched and full pussy before doing a lap around her clit. "You have brought a ray of heaven into my life. You're *my* angel."

She moaned. "And you're my beast."

"How so?" My circles grew smaller but stayed light and slow.

A tremor went through her, and her breath hitched as I nudged her clit. "You make me feel dangerous things, Logan."

"Are you going to come on my beastly cock nestled deep inside you?"

She shuddered again and whispered, "Yes."

I nudged her clit again. "Does it thrill you that a bad man, who bathed in blood for you, is making you feel this good?"

"Fuck. Yes."

"Then I am your beast. I'll kill anyone you point this scary dog towards. Anyone, angel. I'm yours to wield, and yours to tame. Whatever you command."

Her pussy throbbed under my fingers and bucked around my cock. My finger continued its slow roll around her clit as it pulsed. I said, "The darkness in you reaches for the darkness in me, but your light fills me with purpose."

She gripped my bicep with a deep groan as her body stiffened and bucked through her orgasm. I leaned closer to her neck and pinched her skin through my teeth. Her back arched on a gasp. I snarled against her flesh and squeezed my arm around her middle. My finger kept working her clit. "Keep coming on your beast, angel." I bit her again, and her mouth fell open on a cry. "Good girl. Soak your beast in your pleasure so he can rut inside you." Her legs clamped around my thighs as she shook wildly. I forced them wider by parting my legs.

"Logan!"

I focused on her clit, rubbing it lightly as she fought her reaction to the sensitive, jerking flesh. "Stay open, Eden. Fuck, you feel amazing, coming all over me..."

She screamed. I leaned up and pushed her body down, sinking deeper. Her scream cut off into a choke as my free hand wrapped around her throat. Her pussy was still throbbing as I secured her waist and lifted both of us off the seat. I turned us and bent her over. Her hands slammed onto the seat as I adjusted her legs wider. My hands gripped her hips as I pulled my dick out slowly and began fucking her like a crazed animal.

She whimpered loudly, but I was beyond control. She wanted a beast to fuck her. A bad man to find redemption inside her body.

"You're doing so good, angel."

My hips slapped against her ass.

"Taking me so well."

Her groan was deep and guttural as I pumped faster. "Oh God! Logan... Fuck me."

"That's right. I'm fucking you. I'll keep fucking you, Eden. By the time we get off this sailboat, you'll be so fucked you'll submit to all the filthy, messed up things I want to do to you."

My fingers found her clit again, and she shot upright. I adjusted and fucked her harder. "You gave this to me, Eden. It does what I say, and right now, it needs to take what I give it."

"Logan! Oh fuck!" She fell forward against the seat, her hair falling around her face.

"And you're doing so good. So fucking good, letting your beast rut you."

I kicked her legs wider and pushed her face into the seat. Her fingers dug into the vinyl. Her legs trembled. "I'm going to come again."

"Yeah, you are. Come all over this dangerous dick, angel."

She stiffened, rising to her toes as her orgasm tore another shattering scream from her.

I pushed deep and spilled my own pleasure, holding my hips against her upturned ass as my own voice rose with hers. "Fuck!"

Her arms hung limp off the sides of the seat. Flaming locks of hair spread wild over the stark white vinyl as she panted. I held myself deep as I said, "Such a good girl for letting her beast breed her pussy. Stay still. Let my seed do its work." I pulled back an inch and groaned as I pushed against her cervix again.

She whimpered, and I crooned, "I know. It must be deep in order to work. But you're doing so well."

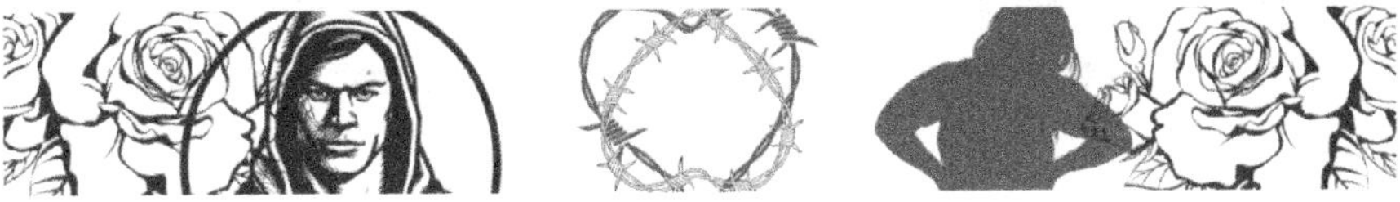

Chapter Twenty

I need Therapy?

Eden

Fifteen minutes later I was still face planted on the captain's seat, ass high, and Logan still semi-hard and deep inside me. Occasionally he'd pull out an inch or two only to push back inside. He seemed to savor the idea of pushing his cum deeper inside me.

"Holy fucking shit, Logan," I panted.

"Oh, I haven't even started planning fucking your ass yet." He traced a finger over my asshole.

I stiffened and turned red at the realization that he'd been staring at my butthole this entire time. "I don't do anal."

"Good to know. It takes some extra time and work to prepare a virgin ass for penetration."

"Um, I just said, no anal."

His finger circled my puckered ring. "No, you said you don't do anal. Don't limit your pleasure. I'm actually very good in that hole."

"You've fucked assholes before?" I sounded jealous.

"Angel..." he drew the word out. "Don't ask questions you don't want to know the answers to."

My gut twisted, and I looked back over my shoulder at him. "Men or women?"

He grimaced as he slowly pulled his cock from my body. "Both." His voice was heavy.

I picked up the towel that had fallen to the floor and sat down on it. "You're attracted to both?"

He sat down on the couch mere feet away. "I'm attracted to you."

"Don't dance around my question." I hated how jealous I sounded.

He lifted his hands and stared at them. "I've done lots of terrible things with these hands." He let them drop to his lap and spread his thighs. "And with the rest of my body. Just because I've fucked both men and women in the past doesn't mean I had the emotional attachment I have for you."

"I don't even know what that means. These rituals you do... Are they orgies?"

"Sometimes they do involve sex. I haven't performed in any of those rituals since I started having feelings for you, though."

My gaze narrowed on him. I had to physically relax my lips and jaw. "Why not? It's not like we're together."

He glanced down at his junk and back up to me. "We are together, Eden. Once you are inducted, you'll have a better understanding of our rituals. Then we can have a conversation about what we are comfortable with."

"So I should be comfortable with sharing your body with others?"

He shook his head and pushed his hair off his forehead. "I'm not telling you anything. I'm saying we can discover together what we are comfortable with. What I *am* telling you is I belong to you. You're my queen, and I won't do anything to make you upset or uncomfortable. There are plenty of dicks waiting in line to do the job I once did."

"So we'll cross that bridge when we get there, and you'll do whatever I want?"

He nodded.

I chewed my lips for a moment. "What if I want to participate in an orgy?"

His smile was tight and didn't reach his eyes. "Then we'll participate in an orgy."

I tensed with surprise. "Really? You'd let other men fuck me?"

His gaze went frosty. "We'd have to find a work-around for that; I'd slaughter any man who dared to put his dick inside you."

My jaw tightened again. "I feel the same way about your dick."

He grinned wildly. "Good. Because it belongs to you."

He stood up and went to the hose at the back of the boat. Holding on to a guideline, he turned the water on his body, cooling himself off and cleaning his junk. He shook his wet hair, spraying me with chilly droplets, making me squeal. "Your turn, angel."

The water was shockingly cold, but it felt amazing on my swollen lady bits. Logan watched me with a serene smile on his face. "It will get better with more use."

I turned the hose off and snatched up the towel to dry myself. "You think I'll get loose?"

He snorted. "No. I think your vagina is a muscle that needs regular work to become stronger."

I faced him. "I know you're a workout fiend, but I refuse to be bullied into going to the gym several times a day."

He wrapped his arms around me and kissed the top of my head with a laugh. "You don't have to step another foot in the gym if you don't want to, my fiery angel. The only muscle I will ever dictate a workout for is the one between your legs." He kissed my head again. "I workout twice a day because I've had body dysmorphia my entire life. I have to work on the things I hate about myself in order to function like a regular person."

"There is nothing regular about your person, and you've got a perfect body."

He let me go and stepped back. "Thanks? But it's perfect because I'm obsessed with making it so. It's something I need to work on."

"Just something?" I pressed my lips together to keep from grinning as I took over the captain's seat once more.

"You're the one who used the word perfect. Do I need to turn you over my knee?"

I laughed. "Like a child?"

His grin made my breath catch. "Like a royal brat who needs a quick adjustment to her cheeky mouth."

"Maybe later I'll show you exactly what this bratty mouth can do. But first we need to find a place to anchor for the night."

He nodded and said, "I'll go down and see what I can scrounge up foodwise."

"I like that you cook."

He chuckled. "It's a good thing I like to feed you, because I've seen you in the kitchen."

My whole being jolted with realization. "Did you see me with James?"

His spine stiffened before he looked over his shoulder at me. "Another reason he deserved what he got, the ungrateful bastard."

I shouldn't have found that as hot as I did. James was dead. His body lay at the bottom of the Gulf of Mexico. I had just had the best sex of my life with the murderer. Logan didn't care that James had family who loved him. People who'd be looking for and missing him. What if the body washed up? Would they track me down as the last person who saw him alive?

I moved to the bench seat closest to the companionway. The galley kitchen was just to the left. Logan was at the stove frying hamburgers. He glanced up, saw me, and said, "Your dad doesn't have lettuce or tomatoes onboard, but there's cheese and hamburger buns."

"I'm surprised any of the food here is still good."

"Yeah, well the meat was dated, but the buns are slightly stale."

I sat there for a while, splitting my attention between the surrounding waters and watching a naked man cook. Logan was much more interesting than the scenery. It helped that Logan didn't seem to mind that I was kind of creeping on him. I just really liked looking at his naked body.

"People are going to be looking for James."

He shrugged a tattooed shoulder. "So?"

"I was the last person who saw him alive."

Logan stilled. "I had the cleaners scrub the site. Before we return, they'll let you know the story they came up with. The evidence will back your story. Just don't say anything to anyone until the attorneys get there. Then they'll do all the talking."

"I'm guessing my dad knows what happened, but what do I tell my mom? She's probably freaking out by now."

"I'm sure your dad will handle your mom."

I was silent long enough that he looked up from cooking. He sighed and nodded. "I'll call your dad and tell him to handle your mom."

"Thanks. I just..." I glanced down at my hands. "I know she's going to grill me, and I can't lie to her."

"It will be fine, Eden. Your mother was a BFR Lady for years. She understands."

I wasn't sure Logan understood my mother. I shook my head. *I* didn't even understand. She had been in this secret society, and I had no clue. Granted, I had been a kid at the time. I remember my parents going on trips and leaving me with my nanny for long weekends, but I felt betrayed by them for never telling me what they were doing.

"Did my mother know Dad put me in a condo owned by his club?"

He stopped plating the burgers he'd cooked and looked up at me. "I met your mother in the elevator after she slapped you in your condo just to make sure she knew whose protection you were under."

He brought the plates up the steps and handed me one as he added, "If she's freaking out, it's because she knows who is wrecking you."

"You know my mother?"

Taking the space next to me he nodded. "Not personally, but yeah, we've been in the same room many times."

I set the plate on my lap and met his gaze. "Same orgies?"

He laughed, "No orgies that I remember. I'm the enforcer. During the divorce there were many meetings with your parents and aunt for security reasons. You know your mother was raised in BFR, right?"

I shook my head slowly. "I know nothing about my mother's parents. They disowned her after the divorce."

"They had to separate themselves from her. Everyone did after she left the Society."

I picked up the burger and took a bite. Mayonnaise and ketchup. Of course, he knew how I liked my burgers. I glanced at his plate. He'd put the same condiments on his. I wasn't sure if that was because it was all my father had available on the boat or if he also enjoyed the flavors.

My mouth was dry which made swallowing difficult. "So, BFR destroys families when someone wants out."

He shrugged. "It was better than the alternative."

I gave him a sharp look, and he lifted his shoulder and explained, "The vow for the final indoctrination is for life. She could have gone back home to her family, remained a BFR Lady and remarried within the Society. But she wanted out. I don't know why, but she did, and Dan and the rest of your extended family supported her decision. They worked on her behalf to break her vows to the Society and let her go free. It was unprecedented, which was why I was involved in those meetings."

"Because you are the adopted son of the man who started BFR?"

His smile was indulgent. "One of the founding families. The society began in the 1800s. If you are born into a founding family, you are groomed from day one to run the organization and its companies. The Dalton line is Blue-Frosted Rose royalty. I'm not blood, like Mickey and Todd are, but I've had a privileged life. And my vow is unwavering, unlike your mother's."

"Am I going to have to become a BFR Lady?"

"I'd love it if you did, but the choice is yours. We can start your education the moment you return."

I took another bite of the burger and swallowed before I met his gaze again. "If I don't want to be a BFR Lady? Where does that leave us?"

He smiled. "I like hearing that word from you. Us." He set his plate aside and twisted to face me. "*We* do not change. You're mine no matter what. If you opt out of joining the Society, it will just mean that I won't be able to share my secrets with you. My work life would be completely separated from you. Even if you do join, there will be times I won't be able to tell you what I'm doing, but the rituals, the wealth of true magic and blessings will extend to you. You will be a part of those things."

"And you want me to be a part of those things?"

"I do. I want you to be a Dalton, Eden. I want you to be my wife and partner in almost every way."

I know my face revealed the confusion at the word *almost* because he tucked my hair behind my ears and added, "I don't see you getting bloody to enforce the laws of BFR."

I focused on our meal, and when we finished, Logan took the empty plates down and washed them as I kept a lookout for other boats.

When he came back up, he wore his jeans. Over his bare arm was the shirt he'd worn earlier. "Put this on."

The soft fabric smelled of him as I slid it over my head.

He retreated below again but returned quickly with a bottle of water and two small pills. "For pain," he said, as he dropped them in my palm.

I frowned at them for a long minute before finally popping them into my mouth. My pussy was too sore to refuse help and if these pills were something more sinister, I'd rather not be conscious for it.

Logan

Logan Lurch

We settled into a routine on the sailboat. Someone had to keep watch as we neared shore and the sun set. It was late before we arrived at the anchorage I had picked out earlier.

With an artist's eye, she had grilled me on all my tattoos. It had been a long time since I spoke about the meanings of each one. I worried she'd think me shallow as a lot of the art on my body didn't have deep reasons behind them. Mr. Dalton had a memorial space on my spine between my shoulder blades where angel wings dripped with blood and roses.

Our conversation made the time fly.

"What is a blue-frosted rose anyway? I thought all blue roses were man-made."

I smiled at her curiosity. I too asked the same questions about our rose. "You're right, blue roses do not occur naturally. Man had to put his finger in the mix. One of our founding fathers loved his white roses so much, he painted and even bejeweled their petals. His roses had a unique scent that his friends seemed to enjoy. As they solidified their bonds and friendships, organizing into a group, they commissioned the gardener member to create a symbol for the secret society."

We were silent as we navigated the anchorage, monitoring depth and obstacles. We found a spot set away from the three other sailboats that all looked vacant tonight. Eden dropped the anchor and set it by putting the engine in reverse and backing down on it. A wave of pride drifted through me. She was a better sailor than most men I knew.

When we were settled, she asked, "So what's the big secret if it was originally just a bunch of nature lovers getting together?"

I snorted. "It's a secret, Eden. We are good at keeping them."

"It just seems silly to me."

"It might from the outside, but once you start initiation, you'll see."

"Initiation? Like some sorority?"

"Yeah, just like a sorority."

Her brows lifted. "Oh?"

My lips tugged upwards. "You have to peel off that shirt and get on your knees."

She caught on quick as her grin matched mine. "Then what?"

"Open wide and savor everything I give you."

She folded her arms across that dark shirt with a pout. "And what if I don't?"

My grin widened. "Please don't."

Her pout morphed into an excited grin before she darted towards the companionway steps. I was hot on her heels by the time she rounded the corner towards the master cabin. The cramped space and low ceiling made me more cautious than normal, so she got the door closed but not locked before I shoved it open.

She squealed and put the bed between us as I stepped inside. "You keep trying to lock yourself away, and I'm going to remove the door."

Her gaze shifted to said door as she said, "I don't think you're skilled enough to take that door off."

I made my move before she finished her sentence. Lunging forward, I grabbed her ankle as she leaped onto the bed in an attempt to dodge me. She shrieked as she fell onto the mattress, and I dragged her towards me. Her fingernails raked my chest as she sat up to face me. I let out a painful hiss even though the welts exhilarated me. My soul was alive, and my dick was at full attention inside my jeans.

Getting hold of her wrists, I pushed her to her back and straddled her. Careful not to put pressure on her heaving chest, I leaned close and whispered in her ear. "Before we take this game any further, we need to have a conversation about consent and safe words."

Her face twisted to mine. "That kind of takes the fun out of it."

I couldn't help my grin. "I also like to live dangerously. However, once I truly get started, I won't stop until you call out the safe word."

She wet her lips before she smiled, and I just about lost it.

"And what's the safe word?"

"Traffic light. Red means stop. Yellow for slow down, and green is go."

She bit her lip before asking, "And how does consent factor into you holding me down on a bed?"

"It doesn't, because either way you are sucking my dick." I kissed her shocked face and added, "Let's call this communication."

Her voice became husky. "So communicate, Logan Dalton, enforcer of secrets and owner of the sexiest body I've ever enjoyed." Her face flushed as she finished. She was terrible at dirty talk but damned if I wasn't enthralled by her husky voice and those bedroom eyes.

"You said it yourself. I'm your beast, and beasts sometimes get so excited they take things too far. Fuck, I'm about to test your limits, Eden, and I need you to tell me you'll use the power you have over me if I take things too far."

"Power?" She glanced at where I gripped her wrists beside her head.

I leaned in and captured her bottom lip with my teeth before gently sucking it. When I pulled back, I said, "Traffic light. Tell me what it means."

"Red is stop. Yellow is caution. Green is go."

"What color are we right now?"

"Green."

I rocked back on my knees and pulled her up with me. Grabbing the hem of the shirt she wore, I pulled it over her head, leaving her naked before easing off her to stand beside the bed. Pointing to the wood floor, I quietly said, "Kneel."

She glanced from my face to my finger and then the floor. "No."

She made to bolt to the door, but my arm shot out, and my fingers curled into a mass of red locks at the base of her neck. Her head pulled back as I tugged her to me. Curling my arm around her, I pulled her flush against my chest. Having her breasts against me, skin on skin, is what I lived for. "It's time you learned some new words, brat."

I sat down on the bed and used the fist in her hair to pull her down across my knees. She screeched as she caught herself with her hands on the floor, and my right hand smacked her ass. I widened my thighs to better support her and let my hand fall repeatedly.

She fought me. Screaming my name with some creative cuss words as her legs fell open. An invitation to spank her exactly where she needed, where she loved to be spanked.

My hand was stinging. Her ass was almost the shade of her bright red hair, and she was grinding herself against my knee. I smoothed my palm over the hot globes, giving her a temporary break. "Close those legs, angel. This doesn't turn into fun until you stop saying 'no' and start saying 'yes, Sir.'"

Her head dropped forward as she repositioned herself on my lap, pressing her inflamed ass into my palm.

"Yes, Sir." Her voice broke on a tiny sob. "Oh fuck, yellow."

I let my hand travel down the backs of her thighs. "When was the last time you were turned over someone's knee and spanked bare bottom?"

The question triggered an emotional response, and it took her several minutes to win the battle she fought for control. "I was fourteen."

"Who was it?"

Another, stronger emotional response, but she refused to let it control her. "My mother."

"For?"

She spoke through a clenched jaw. "For being a brat."

My fingers trailed up her thighs to her pussy. "You sound angry."

"I *am* angry."

"Part your legs."

She did as I asked but seemed shocked as I gently pet her. Stroking her labia lovingly I said, "Your feelings are valid, Eden. You can be angry at anyone, including me. You are allowed to demonstrate your emotions, even the bad ones. I am a safe place to express them."

She lifted her ass and widened her legs to give my fingers more room to play with her. "I can't."

My hand stopped. "Why not?"

"Because I just can't."

Frustration laced her voice, and all my plans for her tonight went out the window. "Get up."

She lifted her head, twisting to look at me through her hair. "What?"

I reached for her arm. "Come sit with me."

She got to her feet and sat gingerly as I moved to my knees in front of her. Her lips quirked. "Shouldn't I be the one kneeling?"

I dragged my thumb across her bottom lip. "I love this snarky mouth. I enjoy it when you challenge me. That you feel comfortable saying dangerous things to me. That's so fucking brave, Eden. Especially because you know what I'm capable of."

My hand dropped to her thighs, and I parted them. My gaze lowered to soak up her body as I grabbed the back of her hips and pulled her to the edge of the bed, closer to my watering mouth. "It shows me you feel safe with me."

I gently pressed her back until she supported herself with her elbows. My fingers splayed as I dragged my hand down between her breasts. I leaned forward and pressed a kiss just above her clit as I inhaled her scent. "But you have buried these emotions for so long, you've forgotten how to deal with them in a healthy way."

Her legs parted further. "Nobody taught me how to deal with them at all."

My gaze flicked up to hers. "I understand, and we're going to learn together. I know a great therapist—"

She stiffened. "I need therapy? Me? I'm not the one who hides my face and murders people."

I pushed my tongue through her wetness, and she just about choked on her words. "I didn't just say *you* needed therapy." My voice rumbled against her flesh. "You jumped to conclusions." My tongue swirled around her clit. "I know my flaws, Eden." I gave her a sucking kiss. "I'm certainly not coming from a place of holier than thou." I dragged my teeth across the outside of her right labia. "I've neglected my own mental health lately." I licked into her, and her head fell back with a sigh.

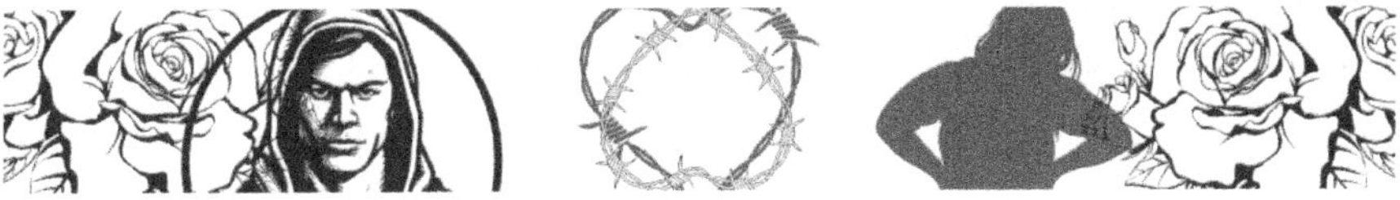

Chapter Twenty-One

On Your Knees, Angel

Eden

"Oh my God, Logan..." His tongue moved in languid strokes. Licking, tasting, kissing, and teasing me just enough to bring me to the edge of climax before denying my body the release it desperately needed.

Somehow my foot ended up on his shoulder, and my leg fell open, giving him all the access he desired, and yet he merely teased me without mercy. I writhed with luxurious moans, wanting this to last forever and craving completion at the same time. Lost in stasis of the in-between, the slack tide of passion, I wanted to fist his hair and force him to focus his sinful mouth where I frantically needed. Yet, I also wanted to give my body over to his whims. I needed to submit to him as the beastly god of my bliss. It was his choice if and when I climaxed. The thought of fully submitting to Logan thrilled me to my core.

How long had he been on his knees between my legs feasting on me? I lost track of time.

His large hand smoothed up my stomach to cup my breast. The way he held me brought unexpected emotions forward. I threw the back of my hand over my eyes to hide the moisture collecting there. "Logan, please..."

His mouth slowed to a crawl before cool air kissed my open, splayed pussy. I opened my eyes and lifted my head to look down my body at him.

"Please. What?"

The fire in his gaze made me swallow hard for saying, "Fuck me."

He dragged the back of his hand across his mouth and grinned. "On your knees, angel."

I rose to my elbows. "What?"

He stood. "You heard me."

I sat up and slowly moved to the floor on my knees.

He frowned down at me. "Widen your knees. I want that slick pussy nice and open as you remove my pants."

I slid my knees open. "Like this?"

"That will do for now." He stepped closer, and I reached for his button and fly. He let me open his pants slowly, my fingers grazing the soft skin of his tip as I worked. His pants lowered, and I held them as he stepped out. Without thinking about it, I folded them and set them aside. In the lights of the cabin, I lifted my eyes, dragging them over his thighs to pause at his jutting erection from underneath.

He looked intimidating from this angle as he stared down at me, head inclined, dark hair falling over his forehead and temple, shadowing his face.

My hands slid up his powerful thighs, enjoying the feel of the hair on his legs. The muscles under my palms flexed as he sat on the edge of the bed. I moved between his thighs and let my hands slide towards his dick.

He leaned back as I trailed the backs of my fingers over his balls. One lifted slightly and then relaxed. I met his gaze, and he smiled at me. It wasn't a full grin, just a half smile, but I got the feeling he was giving me full permission to explore his body, the way he had just explored mine.

I leaned closer and tasted the spot I just caressed. That same ball lifted slightly. I opened my mouth and drew it in, gently sucking it.

The groan he made sent a hot thrill that pooled deep inside me. I slid my fingers around his shaft, gripping him firmly, holding him steady as I tongued the ball in my mouth. He hissed, and his fingers gripped the sheets.

"Gods, Eden." His voice was breathless.

I let his testicle go and licked up his shaft, adjusting myself so when I reached the tip, I could swirl around it before licking back down. I repeated the process slowly until he was soaked by my tongue.

My knees were aching, so I rose to my feet and pushed him further up the bed before settling between his long legs and resuming my slow exploration of him. I fit his head into my mouth and fondled him slowly with my tongue as my palm smoothed over his abs. As they tightened, I let his dick go only to stroke up and down with my hand just as languidly as he had toyed with me.

I savored the way he responded to me. So vulnerable and almost putty in my hands and mouth. He was vocal, too. Moaning and sighing even though he still fisted the sheets with a powerful grip. I slid him deep into my mouth, and his hips lifted. His knees bent, legs trembled and then relaxed.

This man was doing everything he could to keep from losing control. But I wanted him to. I sucked as I pulled back and then pushed him against the back of my throat, swallowing as his legs writhed helplessly around me.

One hand held his base and the other cupped his balls. They both were high against his body. I coaxed them lower until they both rested in my palm. It was at this moment that I realized I had no idea what to do with them. I could suck a dick, but balls were completely foreign territory to me. I closed my hand around them, holding firm, and he stiffened.

My gaze met his as I bobbed up and down on his dick.

His Adam's apple bobbed on a swallow. "Harder."

I squeezed, and his face lifted as his legs stiffened. "I'm going to come."

The pleasure I felt at his outburst had me refocusing on his dick.

His back arched. "Holy shit. Don't let go of my balls, Eden."

They rose towards his body, tightening in my hand before they pulsed and bobbed.

"I'm coming, angel." He sounded desperate.

I pushed his tip deep and swallowed repeatedly as I lost hold of his balls.

His hand threaded through my hair as his hips rocked. "Oh gods. Fuck. That's a good girl." I could tell he wanted to fist my hair and hold my head to his pelvis as he came, but his hand stayed gentle and soft.

I was in control. So, I slowed my pace and drew out every ounce of pleasure from this man. By the time he relaxed, he was sprawled on his back, legs splayed and both hands were holding the headboard above him. I released his spent dick and kissed my way up his body to find a spot on the pillow next to him.

Once he realized where I was going, he wrapped his arms around me and pulled me close with a smile. "Here I thought *I'd* wreck you, but you just *ruined* me."

He leaned close and I moved back. His eyes flew open, and calculating dark eyes studied my face. "You don't want to kiss me?"

I wanted nothing more than to be kissed by him. "Most men don't want to after—"

He cupped my cheeks. "They are not men." He moved in, angling his head, and kissed my lips. I thought he'd roll over and go to sleep after proving his point, but this man had more to prove. He licked across my lips with such a passion I kissed him back. The moment my mouth opened for him, he licked deep.

I inhaled sharply through my nose as he rolled on top of me, settling between my legs, and continued to kiss me like he had all night to do so. Any hangup I had about kissing a man with his taste on my lips dropped away. My hands went to his hair, and my legs wrapped around his thighs as I fell into his kiss.

After a few minutes, I felt his erection pressing against me. I moaned into his mouth as my body became aware of how empty I'd been. He'd teased me for so long without release, and I was desperate to be full of him. He broke the kiss and leaned up on his arms. My hands left his hair and smoothed down his firm biceps. His thighs widened, splitting me open to his poised erection. He looked like a supernatural god as he looked down on me. His silky hair had fallen forward and the shadows enhanced the angle of his face as he pushed inside me.

He watched my face intently as he moved his hips, rocking in and out and deeper. Filling every inch of me and requesting more space with every gentle pull and push. My body acquiesced to his dick, to him, and I had the sudden urge to pull him closer, deeper.

I pulled at his arms. "More."

He lowered to his elbows and put his arms around me as he slowly fucked into me. The weight of his solid form, along with the heat of skin on skin contact, had me squeezing him to me. I wanted to feel Logan's soul snuggle with mine as he fucked me ragged.

I nosed into the base of his neck and kissed him with a soft sigh. "Logan..."

He angled his face to mine. "Do you like this, angel? Do you like it when I'm inside you?"

"Yes..."

He brushed his lips over my temple. "I'm going to be inside you all night, even when you are sleeping."

There would be no sleeping while he was doing this. It felt too good to sleep through.

"It's going to take me a while, but I'm going to come inside you again."

This time, instead of the twist of fear that ransacked my gut the last time he started talking about impregnating me, I whispered, "Please."

"That's right, beg for it," he said in the small space between us.

"Come inside me, Logan. Come deeper than you've ever come before."

His dick instantly felt harder as he curled his hips into me. I gasped and groaned as he pushed against my cervix.

He kissed my temple. "I know, baby, but you are doing so good for me. You're going to take every inch I have to give."

He adjusted his knees wider, bringing him closer. He took one of the many pillows on my dad's bed and leaned back. The movement had his cock pressing up inside me with such force I put my feet down and lifted my ass. His hand cupped my butt and lifted as he slipped the pillow under me.

"Open up those legs, angel. Offer your pussy and womb up for breeding." My knees fell open as he got closer. "That's my good girl."

Holding my hips secure, he started moving again, giving me slow and deliberate strokes. His gaze lowered to watch himself slide in and out of me. The look on his face was intense, focused and controlled. My back arched on a wave of pleasure at being gently stretched and filled by him. His gaze shot up my body, lips parted on a gasp as a tremble coursed through me. I reached for him, and he lowered his upper body on an inward thrust.

The angle of his dick with him caging me ground his shaft and pelvis against my aching needy clit. My nails dug into his lower back. "Oh fuck, Logan."

He hissed, hips moving faster. "What do you need, angel?"

I wrapped my legs around his thighs once more and squeezed. "More."

And Logan provided what I asked for. He gave all of himself to me. Moving inside me. Holding me tightly. Kissing and biting as I clung to him, scratching and clawing. He ground deep, creating the friction I needed to slowly make my way to climax before he spilled into me.

Logan

Logan Lurch

I untangled myself from my worn out woman as the sky lightened, and I got in the cramped shower. Most buildings and homes were not designed for people of my height, but boats were downright uncomfortable and dangerous.

I dried off and padded to the companionway. Once on deck I was able to straighten fully and stretch my back.

The anchorage had been calm and quiet all night aside from the occasional lusty moan from Eden. Okay, so she had screamed a few times, and I think I might have shouted my pleasure to the world once or twice.

After a good stretch I fished my BFR phone out of my duffle. I should have secured the bag below last night. Anyone could have came aboard and had their pick of weapons to assault us with as we fucked.

I turned the phone on and waited for it to connect to the secure satellite.

The few vessels anchored in this small bay looked uninhabited. I could see no houses, but that didn't mean there wasn't a whole ass neighborhood just on the other side of the mangroves.

It was time to check in with my crew, time to return to reality when all I wanted to do was stay on this cramped sailboat with her for the rest of my life. Numerous notifications filtered into the phone soundlessly, reminding me that dream was a fantasy that wouldn't actualize anytime in the near future. Well, that would just give me time to have someone build me a sailboat with size-appropriate ceilings.

I dialed Bentley.

"Dude, where have you been? Have you checked your messages?"

My brows lifted at the urgency in his voice. "It's only been twenty-four hours since I last checked in. You were the first person I called."

"So, that's a no. Listen, this was an inside job. Like inside, inside. Whoever ordered this kidnapping had serious internal information. They worked with a talented hacker. We almost missed his trail, Logan."

"We don't miss shit, Bentley."

He quickly agreed, "I know."

"Do we know who he is?"

"She."

"Find her and either put her on the BFR payroll or end her."

"Already on it."

"Good. Are the bad birdies we trapped singing?"

"Yeah, but the big bird seems to have caught wind and is in clean up mode. Where are you?"

"Safe, but we'll be back tonight. Will you let Dan know and call a staff meeting?"

"Yeah. Eden should probably call her friend Tracy to let her know she's okay. We intercepted her call to the police to report her friend missing, but I don't think this girl will let this go."

"She's a better friend than I thought she was."

"Yep, but the kid's friends are starting to worry about him, and once they put two and two together, they'll ring the four alarm bells."

My mind had been working on an explanation. "Kid dropped Eden off at home where she met with me, and we went on a date that ended with us sailing."

"Got it. We'll support that story." By support he meant digital evidence supporting our alibi.

"The boat will need a cleaning crew."

"On it." He knew I didn't mean a regular maid's service. "She knows to keep her mouth shut, right?"

I hoped she trusted me enough to follow my advice. "She does."

"Good. I hope this works out for you, man."

I finally let myself smile. "It already has, Bent. She's perfect. Everything I never knew I craved."

"I'm happy for you."

I believed him. He was one of the few in my life that had my best in his heart. "Thanks, man. I'll touch base when I get her settled at home."

The sound of the shower below reached me as I hung up the phone. Eden was awake, and as much as I wanted to greet her in the shower with a kiss and some dick, I merely pocketed my phone and set out to brew some coffee. There'd be plenty of time for morning showers when she was settled in my home where we'd have more than enough room for kissing and dicking.

I turned off the BFR phone and fished out my regular mobile. Once powered on, I checked to make sure it had enough battery power to make a phone call and pocketed it.

The coffee had finished, and I found the cream and sugar by the time she padded barefoot into the parlor where I sat. She was wearing only my shirt, and that was the sexiest thing I'd ever seen. I passed the mug to her. "Good morning, beautiful angel."

She took the mug in both hands. "I feel more like a beast today."

"Am I rubbing off on you?"

She sat down on the couch across the table from me. "More like you rubbed off *in* me, all night."

I knew my smile was smug, and I didn't even try to hide it. "That I did."

I put my cell phone on the table and changed the subject. "You need to call your friend Tracy before she reports you as a missing person."

Eden sat up straight and eyed the phone. "Really?"

"Yes, and we're going to get your story straight before you make that call. It has to be flawless before you tell it to anyone. Understand?"

Her gaze narrowed on me. "But you said I shouldn't say anything to anyone other than the lawyers my dad hires."

"They are BFR attorneys. They are brothers and understand the inner workings of the Society. You will do and say exactly what they want you to."

"And what is that?"

A heavy sigh left me. "Right now, the story is that James dropped you off at home where we met and went on a date that ended up as a sailing trip on your dad's boat. You left your phone in my truck at the marina so you couldn't call anyone."

"But I'm making a call now."

I nodded. "On my phone using a cell tower that will verify our location."

She picked up the phone, and the screen lit. Her face screwed up as she typed. "I only know two numbers by heart."

She got up and went topside as the phone rang. I followed, grabbing our coffee mugs.

"Hey, Trace." There was a long pause as Tracy immediately went into full protective friend mode.

"It's Logan's phone." Another pause. "We met up at the condo and went sailing." She paused for Tracy to continue her tirade. "Yeah, I was pretty drunk. I forgot my phone in his truck. I'm sorry. I would have called sooner, but Logan didn't have service until now."

Eden's eyes flew to mine as she said, "I haven't seen him since he dropped me off. He was pretty drunk, too. He shouldn't have been driving."

I nodded slightly and handed her coffee over.

She said, "I hope nothing happened to him, but remember he also ghosted everyone for like two weeks recently. It might be that he's still struggling with the death of his grandma."

Eden's eyes popped wide at whatever Tracy was telling her. "No way. You spoke with his grandma? Is she not dead? I can't believe he lied about that."

Apparently, that's not all James lied about because Tracy was serving some family tea. The call was being monitored, and my team would weave that tea into the final story.

"No, I'm good. Logan is..." she blushed and turned away, "Really great." She was quiet for a moment and then said, "Yeah." She glanced over her shoulder at me. "I can't really give you the details right now." I grinned at her, and she turned back around.

"He's right here. Like, we are on a sailboat Trace. You know how cramped it is. I'll tell you later. Promise."

Her back stiffened. "My mom called you?"

She ran her hand through her hair with a sigh. "I told my dad we were going sailing. He should have told her. Jesus, Tracy, I can't keep being the middleman between them. They have to start communicating at least a little. No, I'll call her. Thanks for letting me know."

She hung up and faced me. "My mom called the cops and reported me as a missing person."

I took the phone from her. "That's a problem."

I dialed Dan's number. "You need to contact your wife, and tell her that her daughter is fine and on a sailing trip with a friend. Eden asked your permission, and you granted it, but forgot to tell her."

"Eden didn't call her mom and tell her?"

"No, she was drugged and passed out when we left. How could she? I assumed you'd let your ex-wife know. She filed a missing person on Eden."

"Can't Eden call her now?"

"She could, but you are going to weather that storm like you should have in the first place. Stop putting your daughter in the middle of your business."

Eden pressed closer, and I wrapped an arm around her. "It's not fair to her. She's an adult now, and it's time she starts her own life."

"I agree. I'll call Karla right away."

I hung up on him, but Eden heard his response and smiled at me. "I can't believe he was so agreeable with you."

"I can't believe he didn't ask if you were okay."

She frowned, and a deep sadness crept into her gaze.

I said, "It would have been the first thing I would have asked."

She looked out over the bay. "You were right."

"About?"

"Us being better parents cause we know shitty ones first hand."

I moved to her back and pulled her into my front. "We've got each other now."

Her chest rose and fell under my arms. "What if you change your mind?"

I nuzzled her neck as I spoke. "What if *you* change your mind about me?"

She twisted enough to look into my eyes. "I might. I don't really know you all that well."

I kissed her nose. "It takes time to really know someone, but I'm willing to invest in us."

She turned around in my arms. "Do you mean that? Cause, I've been lied to a lot before."

"Recently, it seems. But, I won't ever lie to you, Eden. I'll face the hard stuff with direct honesty."

Relief played over her face. "That's all I ask."

My lips twitched. "I hope you ask for more than that." At her confusion I said, "I hope you ask for a partner who loves and respects the shit out of you, even when he makes you kneel."

"Is that what you are offering?"

I nodded. "Yes. That and more when you are ready for it."

She put her cheek to my chest and I hugged her.

"This feels nice."

It felt better than nice to me. Warmth bubbled up inside my chest as she wrapped her arms around my waist and hugged me back.

She murmured against my chest. "For once, I feel like someone has my back."

"Angel, I've got all of you."

"Thank you."

Chapter Twenty-Two

Not Going Home

Eden

We worked well together. I'd never experienced a person who was so attuned to me. By the time we pulled anchor and raised the sails, we were communicating with little words. The wind was perfect, and the breeze was cool as we headed home.

"Who is taking care of your kitten?"

"Bentley. He was just as shocked as you that I adopted the little terrorist." His smile was relaxed and warm as he continued, "I saw the drawing you did of me holding him and was forced to add him to my life."

"I still feel violated that you came into my home while I was sleeping."

"Angel, you don't know the meaning of being violated. Come on over here and straddle my lap for a bit."

I might have refused if he hadn't given me a few more of those little pills earlier. Man, they worked like a charm to fix my swollen pussy. I asked what they were when I took them last, but he merely smiled and said they were a special mix of vitamins and herbs. It was a BFR secret ingredient, and I'd have to join the society if I wanted to know.

He opened his fly and lowered his pants as I put a knee on either side of his thighs. His cock wasn't fully erect as he pulled me flush to him and kissed me slowly. I pulled up my shirt between us so I could feel his chest on my breasts. He moaned into my mouth as his hand slipped up and down my spine. I adjusted my body until my pussy touched his shaft. His other hand cupped my ass and I rolled my hips, rubbing myself on him.

Eventually he pulled back and cupped my breast with both hands. His mouth on my nipples made me squirm. "Oh God, Logan."

"Stay alert and keep watch." My gaze snapped around the horizon at his reminder. It would be devastating to run into another boat or buoy right now.

He patted my ass. "Lift up."

Confused, I did as he said and he slid down until his entire body was off the couch and his mouth was directly below me.

His hands went to my hips as he urged me to lower myself onto his face. "Ugh, I don't think you want me to do this."

He patted my ass and pulled me down. My knees went wide, and I gripped the cushions on the back of the bench seat at the first swipe of his tongue. My spine jolted as pleasure raced up my body. I reached down and fisted his hair as I rode his face. Undulating and gasping as I ground myself onto his frenzied tongue. His moans shot through my clit and radiated throughout my body. It was sloppy and messy and empowering. I came with a guttural yell, and he drew the pleasure out, holding me steady as he licked and licked me until I begged him to fuck me.

But he had no plans on fucking me when I released him.

He wiggled back into a sitting position and held his dick for me to fuck *him*. And fuck him I did. I took his cock deep like a pornstar and pinched my nipples as I bounced on him.

His face softened as he watched me use his dick for my own pleasure. He let me set my own pace as his cock stretched and filled me repeatedly. He was so big, and yet my body yielded to him. I was so wet and excited it felt like electricity against my innermost walls. Penetration had never felt so amazing.

When he reached between us and pressed down on my clit, it took my pleasure to a whole new level. My nails dug into his shoulders and I rode him harder. Driving recklessly towards the cliff. I careened over it without slowing and let the fall shake my entire being knowing Logan would catch me at the bottom.

He would always catch me. He could handle me, empower me, protect me. He was what I had longed for my entire life. Someone who held my best interest at heart. Someone who would ask if I was okay before worrying about anything else.

I stopped moving and wrapped myself around him, resting my head on his shoulder as his dick pulsed deep inside me. Tears poured out of my eyes and over my temple, pooling on the bare skin of his shoulder.

He hugged me tighter as my chest heaved and sobs escaped. "Let it out, angel."

Not, *don't cry* or *be happy*, just *let it out*. He didn't ask why I was sobbing after fucking him the way I had. He just held me as I cracked open and bawled like a baby. I don't think I had ever sobbed like this in the company of another human being. At least not since I was a little kid. Even then, I wasn't allowed to show any emotion other than happiness.

When I had calmed down, I whispered, "I'm sorry I'm not your ray of sunshine all the time."

His silent laugh bounced me. "Never apologize for being human, Eden." He kissed my shoulder and said, "We are allowed to feel strong emotions. I just want you to express them with me and never lock them behind a door."

He handed me a fresh towel he'd brought up earlier, and I wiped my tear-stained face. I asked, "What about you? Will you trust me enough to express your emotions in front of me?"

When I tried to lift off his soft cock he grabbed my hips. "I don't have a problem acting out. I usually break shit before I can cry, but I promise I won't break you."

He urged me up slowly, and the feel of him leaving my body stirred a hint of pleasure right before the loss. He took the towel from my hand and gently cleaned up the mess we made.

The neglected sails flapped in the breeze, so I sat down at the captain's seat and adjusted everything until they popped full once more. The sailboat leaned slightly and moved forward again.

I said to no one in particular, "I forgot how much I love sailing."

He sat down on the bench closest to me. "If the ceilings below had a little more height to them, I'd say we should just keep heading south."

"I don't think sailboats are made for people your height."

He laughed. "I'm not average, that's for sure."

I grinned at him. "I like that about you. I can wear heels and still look up at you."

"Even though I'm taller, I feel like I'm always looking up at *you*, angel."

I didn't know how to respond to that, so I just smiled and returned my attention back to *Divinity*.

Logan let me do the sailing. He supported me by helping when I needed him to turn a crank or keep watch when I needed to go below. He brought me snacks as he raided my dad's under-seat storage in the main parlor. But mostly we both just enjoyed being on the water in each other's company.

The sun had set by the time we motored into the St. Petersburg marina. He'd made a few calls an hour or so ago, letting everyone know when we'd be at the dock. He had some meetings to attend with his team after he got me settled. I wasn't sure where we'd go from here. Would he invite me into his home or leave me at mine? Would my dad want me to stay with him?

When we finished securing *Divinity* and headed down the docks, I wasn't prepared to see my mother standing apart from Dan. Logan didn't miss a step when I jerked to a stop. He just put his hand on my back and whispered, "It will be fine."

I tugged at the hem of my shirt, even though it fell mid thigh on me. "I should have put my dress back on."

"It will be cleaned and returned to you."

My mother stood by her car in the parking lot as my father met us half way. He gave me a cursory glance before he said to Logan, "I don't know why she is here."

My mother stepped forward. "Eden! Come here sweetheart."

I addressed my father. "I'll find out what she wants." Glancing at Logan, I added, "I'll be right back."

The moment I took three steps away from them chaos erupted. Bright lights flipped on, and men started yelling.

"Get on the ground!"

"Show us your hands!"

"Don't reach for anything!"

"Get on the ground!"

It was such a slew of confusing commands that I turned back to Logan and Dan who looked as startled as I was. Someone slammed into me from behind, and I was dragged backwards away from them. Logan's face transformed into something feral as the commands grew more urgent and forceful. I was deposited by my mother, and from this angle it all clicked into place. Logan and my father were surrounded by highly armed and agitated police officers all dressed in armor and pointing assault rifles at them. They seemed to realize this as well because Logan and Dan raised their hands and slowly lowered themselves to the ground.

The police rushed them. Knees on backs and necks as they hurried to cuff them. They were shouting, "Don't resist!"

But neither man was resisting.

I turned to my mother who was staring at my bare legs with distaste. "What is happening?"

Cold eyes met mine. "They are being arrested for kidnapping and murder."

"What?" I shook my head.

Triumph lit her face. "You don't think I knew exactly what happened to that boy? That I provided proof for the police to be here tonight?" Her red lips twisted into a frightening grin. "I've been preparing for this my entire life."

A deputy walked up to us as Logan and Dan were escorted to a police cruiser. My dad looked stunned but Logan looked determined as he said to my mother, "You won't get away with this."

The officer behind him shoved him so hard he stumbled forward. "Don't talk to her."

Logan's gaze moved to me. "Exactly." I knew what he meant and nodded.

He regained his stride and added, "Bentley will get in touch with you."

I opened my mouth to respond, but my mother said, "Bentley is being arrested, too."

The way he glared at my mother put ice through my veins. "You are dead to me, Karla."

The cop shoved him again. "Did you just threaten her?"

Logan was prepared for the shove this time, and he faced the eager man. "Did that sound like a threat to you?"

My mom grabbed my arm and pulled me towards her car as the police swarmed Logan. The deputy or detective that had approached us earlier followed. "The protective custody agents will be stationed outside your home all night."

"Thank you. We really appreciate it, and Eden will give her statement as soon as she can."

"Tomorrow morning," he said firmly.

My mother's smile sparkled. "Of course." She opened the passenger door and gave me a little push. "See you tomorrow morning."

The moment she got in the driver's side I asked, "Why did you lie to him?"

The sparkle was gone but she seemed clear headed. "To save your life." She turned the car on and backed out of her parking spot. "Since I'm the only one who seems to give a shit about you."

I studied her for a moment as she pulled away from the marina. She didn't seem to be having an episode. "That's not true."

"Oh? You think Logan Dalton actually cares about anyone besides himself and his society? Dan?" She glanced over at me as she spoke. "You do? Idiot girl. Those men, that society, are as dangerous as they come. He played you like a fool." She sighed. "It's my fault. I should have told you everything before you moved out. It just happened so damn quickly, and suddenly Dan was back in your life and sucking you into that devil's club of his." She glanced over at me again as she headed south on I275 instead of north. "Do you know that Logan threatened my life when I visited you?"

"You hit me."

She shook her head. "How many times do I have to apologize for that, Eden? Will you never forgive me? I was scared, and that man made it worse. He trapped me in the elevator and threatened to end my life if I came back to *his* condo. I should have known Dan would put you in a society building."

When I didn't answer, she said, "I should have warned you. Why do you think I tried to get you to move back home? I knew that monster was watching you. Hell, I am sure he has cameras installed in our home." She jerked to attention. "You don't have your phone on you, do you?"

"No."

"Good, cause he has a tracker on it."

She glanced at my bare legs again and asked, "Did he insert anything besides his dick into you? Think about your answer. They are very tricky. Dan had a microchip installed in my arm while I was under for a medical procedure. Made me think I was crazy when I complained about a bump there."

I shook my head. "James drugged me. I was out for a while, but I'd think I'd know if someone inserted a tracker in me."

"We'll have to check, but I'm sure Logan hadn't planned this out when he *rescued* you." She made a face when she said the word *rescue*.

"How do you know all this?"

"Honey, I was raised in that secret society. Born to be a Blue Lady and married off to a prominent member to breed more BFR men. Hell, when we found out Dan's balls weren't working, he offered me up on the private message board for an elite breeding party."

My jaw dropped. "What?"

"This was after you were born. You are legit, and Dan had no clue that I had my tubes tied during my C-section with you. He had a low sperm count, but I made sure I'd never get pregnant again."

"What is an elite breeding party?"

"It's exactly as it sounds. Have a poor Blue Lady who can't get pregnant? Well there's a line of well-bred men willing to run a train on her until she gives you an heir."

"Did you consent?"

She snorted. "They didn't need my consent, but I rode the train willingly. They fucked me silly, and Dan watched me get off on dick after royal dick. It was the best night of my life. Especially since I had just found out he'd fucked my little sister."

"Jesus, Mom," I breathed out as I wondered what Logan would do if I couldn't get pregnant.

She was speeding but wasn't driving recklessly as we headed over the Skyway Bridge. "Where are we going?"

"Somewhere not even the BFR heir can find us." She glanced at my legs again. "But first we need to get you some clothes." She said it like she couldn't believe I'd let Logan fuck me, much less enjoy it.

"Do we need to get you a morning after pill too?"

My entire face went hot. "What? No."

"At least you were smart about one thing." Actually, I wasn't even smart about that. But there was no way I'd admit it to *her*.

"I didn't know you'd be practically naked. I only brought your passport with me."

"Are we leaving the country?"

"I know you think I'm crazy. I'm not. There's so much I need to tell you. Trust me. You'll understand soon enough."

Logan

Logan Lurch

The stark light of the interrogation room never brought out my best features. "I don't know why you are still trying to talk to me, I requested to call my lawyer hours ago."

The detective leaned in. "We just want to know where James is."

I leaned as close as the handcuffs allowed and glared at the man. "Who?"

He slipped a photo of the kid I tortured and killed in front of me. "James. We know you had a fight with him, and you carried him to your truck. Where did you take him, Logan?"

"I have no idea what you are talking about."

The detective tapped the photo. "We have proof you do."

I shrugged. "Then charge me, and let me call my *team* of attorneys."

The detective stood up and opened the door. "Take him back to the holding cell."

Another cop came in to unchain me from the wall. "Bob must be new."

He huffed a half laugh and asked, "How can you tell?"

"Somebody upstairs doesn't like Bob if they are letting him cut his teeth on me."

The cop moved me into the hallway but stayed real close. "They've got real evidence on you, Mr. Dalton. They're letting a rookie get his first win."

Over the next hour, they systematically filed prisoners in and out of the holding cell I was in. They were attempting to wear me down by keeping me awake and on my toes. It wouldn't work, but they didn't know that.

So at the end of an hour of drunks, druggies, and downright criminals, they pulled me out and brought me back into the interrogation room.

I immediately started in on the rookie. "I still haven't been able to make that call to my lawyer. Are you intentionally trying to shit all over my rights?"

He smirked. "You clearly know your rights. Daddy also knew them but look where he is today."

I ran my fingers through my hair, pulling it back from my scarred temple. "My sperm donor tried to kill me, not once, but twice. He's exactly where he deserves to be."

"And where do you deserve to be?"

I leaned forward. "Talking with my attorneys."

"Yeah well, you'll get your phone call in the morning."

I let out a long sigh. "My attorneys would take my call *now*, but if you won't give me access to a phone, then take me back to the holding cell. You won't break me down with these detective games."

The door opened and a female officer called the detective out to have a word with her. He was gone so long that I closed my eyes and leaned my head back.

I was drifting on the edge of sleep when the door opened and he came back in. "Wake up, Mr. Dalton. Your attorneys are here."

I slowly sat up and glanced at the clock. It was three in the morning. I was sure the detective thought their prompt attention was due to a high retainer but the detective said, "Are they in your little club too? The blue rose club?"

It was hard to keep my reaction calm with the way my heart dropped. "I have no idea what you are talking about."

His laugh made the hair on my neck prick. "We are learning more by the minute. At this point, I don't think your *team* of attorneys will be able to do much for you."

I just gave him a tight-lipped smile as he moved me. My attorneys would do whatever was necessary to get me out of here and then, heads were going to roll.

Chapter Twenty-Three

Locked Down

Eden

She exited the interstate, and I asked, “Where are we going?”

“There’s a Walmart open twenty-four-seven here.”

I shook my head. “No, where is our final destination?”

“It’s best if you don’t know.”

I watched her closely as I asked, “Why?”

She didn’t answer until she pulled into a parking spot. “Look, Eden, you were an accomplice to that murderer. The cops don’t know that now, but they will find out soon enough. They will be looking for you, so don’t get any brilliant ideas about running for help. I know you don’t believe me, but help is here, right in this car with you.”

“I don’t know what to believe right now, Mom,” I whispered as I looked around the nearly deserted parking lot.

She gathered her purse and dropped the keys into it. “I know sweetie. I’m truly sorry you got caught up in this. I tried so hard to make sure we both were free of them without disrupting your life too much.”

“It’s just a lot to process.”

She opened the door. "I know. You'll have plenty of time to understand both sides when we get to where we are going. It's all going to be fine, Eden. Give me a chance, and if you want to go back to them, we'll return."

She got out and said, "Of course, they'll kill me, but if that's what you truly want, I'm willing to sacrifice myself for you."

A mother's guilt was delivered with precise aim, right to my gut. I swallowed loudly in the silence of the car. She wasn't just tossing meaningless words at me. They would kill her for what she'd done. Logan would probably be the one who did it, too.

There had been times when I wanted to strangle my mom to death, but the thought of Logan killing her... I shifted and pulled the t-shirt I wore over my bare knees. Would he strangle her? Or just shoot her?

The thought that she might not be as crazy as I assumed had me wanting to hear her out, to give her a chance to explain her side. Once we reached our destination, wherever that might be, I might be able to leave her and come back.

How could I be with someone who would kill my mother?

Mom thought he'd be convicted of murder or something. How she knew about James, I had no clue, but if he went to prison where would that leave me? Did I want to be the wife of a death row murderer? What did I truly know about Logan anyway? Sure we had connected on our little sailing excursion, but I had connected with men before and every single one of them had let me down.

By the time she returned with several bags of stuff, I'd decided to give my mother a chance. Sure, she had her issues, but she had been the one constant in my life that truly cared about me. She was all I had in this life.

I dug through the bags and pulled out a pair of panties and soft shorts. "How did you know about James?"

She backed out of the parking spot. "Dan told me." Glancing over at me she added, "Grab that phone and put it on the charger."

"You bought a burner phone?"

She checked her rearview mirror before saying. "Are you sure you don't have your phone on you?"

I shook my head wondering exactly where she thought I would hide a phone. I didn't even have shoes on. I opened the package and powered the phone on. "It's fully charged."

She gave me a number to call and reached for the phone the moment I hit send. Whoever I dialed didn't answer. My mother left a voicemail that had me cocking my head at her. "Scout, it's Rabbit. I have the bunny, and we are en route to the airport."

She hung up and put the phone on the console between us.

"Who is Scout?"

The secretive smile she gave me made my eyes narrow. "Well, I guess it's safe to tell you everything now that you didn't bolt the moment you had a chance."

"Mom, Logan told me a lot of shit that felt authentic."

"About what? The Blue-Frosted Rose and what he does for them?"

I swallowed. "That and about you and dad. I knew this man for maybe a sum total of three days, but I don't think he lied to me."

"I may not have told you everything about us, but I never lied to you."

I folded my arms across my chest and faced her. "So don't start now."

"Right. You're an adult now. So, I guess you can handle it."

Sometimes silence was the best response when she made statements meant to diminish me. It worked because she sighed and said, "Scout is the hacker I used to get the evidence I needed to put Logan away for the rest of his life and expose the rest of them."

I stayed quiet and she said, "They all think they are so untouchable. Well, not anymore. They are going to fall so far off that high horse they won't recognize themselves."

"They?"

The glance she shot at me filled my stomach with dread. "Logan was an easy target. He should have never threatened me in that elevator. That man thought he had all the power, but he left some tiny cracks in his program." She made a sassy face at the word program. "Scout slipped in three months ago and started gathering evidence. Shit his team neglected to get rid of in a timely manner. Logan won't be a problem anymore."

"So just Logan? Why did they arrest Dad, too?"

She gave a vindictive grin. "Dan is an accomplice in James's murder." She glanced at me with triumph. "I wonder how long Mandy will stick around after she finds out he's broke."

My stomach sank. "You stole his money?"

Her eyes popped wide. "Do you think all this is free? We are starting a whole new life in a different country. I thought you were an adult now. I didn't take it all for myself. Technically, we are also broke. I used the money to pay Scout to keep us safe. We'll have a small nest egg once we reach our destination, but money will become an issue for us, too, very soon."

"I'm happy to get a job," I offered as the sinking feeling turned to lead.

"We both will have to work, but I have a plan. How's your Spanish?"

I took Spanish in high school, but I hadn't used it since. "Are we going to Mexico?"

She made a face. "Oh no. We are going to Costa Rica."

"Are there no Blue-Frosted Rose members in Costa Rica?"

She frowned. "There are BFR members everywhere, especially where we are going, but they won't be looking for us there. We just have to be careful and never let our guard down."

Logan

Logan Lurch

"Are you fucking serious right now?"

My team of lawyers sat across from me with grave faces. I had just sat through my arraignment hearing, and it had gone horribly. The state had enough evidence to charge me, not only for James, but several other murders, too. There would be no bail. At least this hadn't turned into a media circus yet.

I pinned my brother, Mickey, with a dark scowl. "Tell me Bentley is close to revealing the hacker who set me up."

"He is, and we'll get her to confess, but in the meantime, you'll have to play by the rules."

My lead attorney leaned forward putting his hands together on the table. "Tell me they won't find DNA evidence that James was on that sailboat."

My gaze swung to him. "They might find a hair or two, but I scrubbed the shit out of the deck and hosed it off."

"A hair or two can be explained since Eden danced with James at the ball."

My gaze swung to the man who spoke. "She tell you that?"

Everyone went still and dread dropped my gut. "What is it?" My voice was as cold as this room had become.

Mickey cleared his throat. "She's gone."

My hands tightened on the edge of the table. "Gone? How?"

"Best guess is her mom took her." Attorney Number One's voice shook as I swung my icy gaze to him. "It was," he flipped through some paperwork, "Karla who made the original missing person's report on Eden. She had arranged protective custody for some undisclosed reason, but never showed up at the rendezvous point."

Attorney Number Two added, "Eden was supposed to come in the next morning to give a statement, but never showed up either."

"Where is Dan?" My jaw ached with the force of clenching my teeth.

Attorney One looked surprised. "He's still incarcerated. You haven't seen him?"

My lip curled. "They've had me in isolation."

"Why?" Attorney Number Three asked. Darla Waters was a smartly dressed woman with a cool confidence the other two did not possess.

She met my gaze and held it as I said, "Because they can."

Her pen started moving like rapid fire. "That's abhorrent treatment. I'll make some calls when I get back to the office."

"Don't."

Her pen froze and her eyes lifted to mine. I gave her a grim smile. "I am happy where I am. Take that fury and use it to get me the fuck out of here so I can find my girl."

Attorney Number One sat up straight. "We are already working on getting the case dismissed."

"Good." I found my sadistic bastard of a brother staring at me with renewed interest. "Find her, Mick."

His head bobbed as if confirming the thoughts in his head. "She won't escape us."

Did he believe she willingly ran with her mother? *Fuck, she ran from me?* The shock of this realization hit me so hard I bent forward to rub my chest because the handcuffs on my wrists were chained to the floor at my feet.

My brother cleared his throat and said, "Can I have a moment alone with my brother?"

Once the room cleared he pinned me with a serious look. "The elders have called a tribunal."

My head snapped up so quickly I might have cracked my neck. "This is all on me. Eden is innocent of any wrong doing."

He nodded gravely. "Is she worth it?"

I held his gaze. "I'll take the punishment. Whatever they decide, even if it means they cut me loose and let me rot in jail, as long as she is safe."

"The BFR won't turn its back on you. You're a fucking Dalton."

A muscle in my jaw ticked. "Not really."

My brother's face darkened with barely concealed rage. "Bullshit. You are *legally* my brother and I *refuse* to let you go. You deserve to be happy, Logan."

I let my head hang once more. This was all my fault. I stalked her, took advantage of her, and then tried to entrap her by filling her with my kid. It shouldn't surprise me; I gave her every reason to bolt the moment she had a chance. But fuck, the pain in my chest felt like betrayal. My brain replayed every moment we spent together, searching for the signs of shady behavior from her. Clues that she had deceived me into thinking things were fine when they weren't. I found nothing but an authentic angel. That didn't mean much, though. She might have been a master manipulator. It might have been her only defense, stuck on a boat in the middle of the ocean with a psycho like me.

Maybe, just maybe, this was *exactly* where I belonged because I had lied to her when I told her she had a choice. I breathed through the pain as my fists clenched on the table. The voices in my head only grew louder. *Find her, catch her, punish her.* This whole situation felt wrong. The voices in my head were never right.

And even though my chest ached worse with each minute spent away from her, maybe she needed this time to cool off and think. I should have taken my own advice, but I knew the moment I was free, I'd collect my little angel and haul her beautiful ass home.

Chapter Twenty-Four

New Life

Eden

I was officially Grace Brown, and my mom was Mazy, my older sister. I laughed when she told me, but everyone bought the lie. Who was I to question her?

The moment we arrived, Mom took us to a hair salon for "a change." It took a week to recognize myself in the mirror every morning. I had chosen a short bob and to lighten my bright red hair to strawberry blonde. Mom took it even further. I'd never forget how her long brown locks lay on the floor of the salon like fallen leaves.

She sported a platinum pixie cut she called liberating, and I had to agree. Freedom looked amazing on her. After growing up in the society we shall not name, all she wanted was to be free. She had been groomed since birth to be the wife of a high rose. Her parents tried to arrange a marriage between her and Logan's brother Mickey even though he was younger than her.

He was horrible to her. He raped and raped her. Tied her up and performed twisted kinky medical acts on her that he called "play," but she thought he wanted to make sure she'd be a good breeder for him. And though the thought of Logan performing those same acts on me was titillating, I could see where my mom would consider it abusive and demeaning.

When she ran into Dan's arms, her parents were less than pleased with her choice. He had been a real charmer, and Mom fell for every sweet lie he told her. She pinned me with a knowing look from under her wide brim hat. "Dan married up, you know." Leaning back in her poolside chair with a sigh, she said, "My family was practically royalty in that society. You come from old stock my dear. A Dalton-Brownstone union would have been a celebration to behold. But I chose a McKenzie."

It had been a month since we'd settled into a quaint cabina of a seaside home in Costa Rica. A young, muscled man strutted by on the beach access lane next to our rental, and she dropped her sunglasses down her nose to stare at him. He waved at some friends down by the water and we both enjoyed the view of him jogging towards the sea to meet up with them. While I thought Florida was hot, December in Costa Rica was like a furnace, that was, unless it was raining.

"I thought marrying down would provide me the freedom to live life on my own terms. That Dan would be grateful enough to follow my lead." She huffed a laugh. "I was young and dumb." She glanced at me again. "So, listen to me when I tell you that you dodged a bullet. I'm going to find someone who will give you the freedom I never had, and you are going to put in the work to capture that man."

"What if I don't want to get married?" I turned my attention to the water in the distance. "What if I opened a little art gallery in town to sell my paintings in?"

"That would be adorable, and you can have that dream once you are free of your husband."

I put my paperback down in my lap. "What do you mean?"

"I mean, we all must make sacrifices, but I will assure you that yours won't be for long. We'll find you a nice wealthy man on his deathbed."

"Wait... you're looking for an old man for me to marry? Isn't that a little cliche and a lot gross?"

She removed her sunglasses completely and sat upright. "Not any more gross than what you probably did with that Dalton man. At least an old man won't be able to perform in bed, so you won't have to work that hard to keep him happy."

A laugh left me. "Okay. If you can find a single, rich, old man on his deathbed looking to marry the likes of me, I'm game."

"Good, but you'll have to play by my rules and go on a date with every man I set you up with."

I opened my mouth, but she said, "No complaints."

My mouth shut and her tone lightened. "In the meantime, let's get some painting supplies so you can work on stocking up that little art gallery."

My gut tightened and dropped at the mention of spending more. When would the money she stole from dad run out? She rented a two-bedroom cabina, which was Spanish for cabin or house, adjacent to the main house with a pool near a public beach, called a playa. The entire property was over an acre with a main house and two cabinas, and Mom said she got a deal from the investor-owner by cleaning and getting the houses ready for short-term vacation rentals.

Besides the expensive salon visit, she had purchased both of us a whole new wardrobe. And Scout never called her back. Never got payment for the work she did either. I worried that Mom was blowing through Scout's payday. I didn't know who this Scout was, but I knew there would be consequences for what my mother was doing.

Someone back home was feeding Mom information about the case though, so maybe Mom did get ahold of Scout, and maybe I just wasn't there when she talked to her. I didn't ask and she didn't offer. Money had always been a touchy subject with Mom. It was the source of her stress, and it brought out her angry side. Things had been great between us since we settled in Costa Rica. But it was easy to slip back into old habits when it came to our relationship. Even though it felt like I had betrayed myself, if I wanted to keep the peace, I would have to trust that she had things under control. She was all I had to cling to in a foreign world.

"Any news about Dad and the trial?" Logan was a taboo subject between us after she saw my mess of emotions when I'd gotten my period a few days ago. I was happy but also devastated that I wasn't pregnant with a tiny Logan. And I didn't even know why. I didn't want to be a death row baby momma, as Mom so eloquently put it.

"They are holding him without bond until his trial, which is set for late February."

"Wow, next year?"

Mom shrugged. "It's only a few months away."

Thanksgiving had come and gone without acknowledgement. "Are we going to do something for Christmas?"

She sighed a tired sound. "Maybe we'll try out that new restaurant across town, but I really would like to sit this holiday season out. I've been the host of every holiday since you were born. Maybe next year you'll be hosting a grand Christmas party from your husband's estate."

I understood my mother more now than ever before. She was tired of all the restraints living under the BFR rules. She wanted to toss tradition into the ocean and be feral for a time.

"If he has an estate, you'll have your own cottage."

She smiled. "That would be nice. Now, why don't you go down there and join that game of volleyball? Make some new friends."

"Why bother? They are all tourists who'll leave in a few days anyway."

She dropped her sunglasses down her nose and gave me a once over. "That doesn't mean you can't have fun while they are here. Besides, you need the exercise."

I gave her a tight smile and a terse nod before I closed my book and got up. Why her exercise comments still hurt so bad was beyond me. It was true. I hadn't been working out since we arrived in Costa Rica. The sand was hot on my bare feet as I walked down the beach. I did feel better about myself when I worked out, and some fun never hurt anyone.

Eden

We tried out that new restaurant the week before Christmas. Mom often complained that everything here was rice and beans, but I liked rice and beans. I also liked seafood, and the fish was phenomenal. We lived in a touristy area, but I enjoyed visiting the food vendors that lined the streets.

"Don't forget your date tonight." My mom's voice stopped me at the door.

"I really don't feel up to it. My period is due again, and I have cramps."

I could feel the tension ramping up from the other room. "Take a pill for pain and go for a run. I'm sure you'll feel better later."

I didn't have a choice. I never won a fight with her, and this was my first date since agreeing to her plan. Ricardo wasn't her first choice; he wasn't old enough, dead enough, or rich enough, but he would be useful to "get back on the horse," as she called it. Like I had ever been on the dating horse in the first place.

"Okay! See you in a few." Keeping my voice cheerful all the time was a downright chore. Sometimes I just wanted to scream and throw shit. The thing was, my mom could scream louder and throw shit harder than me. If I started, she'd finish, and I'd lose. So, I took my frustrations out on my legs, thighs, and knees as I jogged down the beach until the house was out of sight before slowing to a walk.

I would have to go on this date tonight no matter what, so I might as well make the best of it. Mom had been busy making friends and met Ricardo through a neighbor. They both owned vacation homes near us, and she was using them to gain access to their internet. She refused to have electronics in our home since she still worried about BFR digitally tracking us down. Apparently, she wasn't worried about the neighbor's safety.

Ricardo was in his fifties and lived here a few months out of the year. The rest of the time he rented his home to vacationers and mom somehow got the job of managing his rentals. I went with her to greet the guests, take care of anything they needed, and then clean up the property after they left. Her little business was growing by word of mouth.

Ricardo had seen me on his surveillance footage and asked my mother about me. Funny how twice now a man has been interested in me after watching me on video. The camera was supposed to add ten pounds. Well, myth busted. It made me, an already fat girl, suddenly attractive, and now I have a date.

How I felt about that, I couldn't answer. I hadn't settled on a feeling. My reasoning brain agreed with moving on from Logan. The dude was toxic as fuck. So why did I feel like no other man would ever measure up?

Later on that evening, I had come to the conclusion that Ricardo wouldn't be the one to snatch the bar Logan had set. He was sweet, almost too sweet. I felt as if I told him to heel and bark like a dog, he'd rush to obey. While it might be fun to play some kinky games, eventually Ricardo would bore me to tears.

Dominating Logan, on the other hand, would be challenging and stimulating. I wondered if he'd let me tie him up and spank him like in that show we'd watched at the ball. I shook my head to clear my thoughts from Logan and focus on the man sitting across from me.

"Are you alright, Grace?" Ricardo had the warmest eyes I'd ever seen on a man.

"Yes, I just..." *Should I tell him?* "started my period today, and I'm not feeling the greatest." It was a lie. I hadn't started my period yet, it wasn't due for another week, but this time I had no reason to wonder about who my baby would look like because I hadn't had sex at all. I'd been having as much fun as an introverted twenty-something could have, but not that much fun. Of course, Mom didn't know that either, because my whole life had become one big lie.

"Grace?"

I jerk my attention back to Ricardo. "Sorry."

"It's okay if you want to call it a night after this." This guy was too kind. He was the type I should want even though "Grace" had just turned eighteen a couple months ago. Did that make him a pedophile? Wanting to date a freshly turned adult? Would he have said no to a date if Grace had been sixteen? Mom would have aged me younger if she'd thought she could pull it off. She had always been obsessed with youth. For as long as I could remember, her vanity had been filled with anti-aging creams and oils.

"Thank you."

He looked disappointed but waved to the server to get a check.

She was waiting in the living room when I opened the front door and waved to Ricardo. "You're back early. Everything go okay?"

I sat down on the couch across from her. "He was very sweet."

Her brows lifted. "Sweet?"

"Nice."

She frowned. "And that's not attractive to you?"

I shrugged and looked towards my bedroom. "I'm not feeling very well, and he understood so he dropped me off after dinner."

"You didn't tell him you were on your period, did you?"

My gaze swung back to her. "What did you want me to do? Let him fuck me while bloody?"

"There's no need to get dramatic."

"I'm not being dramatic, Mom. I just wasn't attracted to Ricardo. Besides, he doesn't even know my real name or age."

"And he'll never know the real you," she affirmed.

"I'm tired of lying."

She laughed. "Well, you better get used to it, *Grace*." She sneered at my fake name. "You'll be lying for the rest of your life if you want to keep us alive."

Speaking of being alive, what do you think happened to the hacker?"

My mother's brows bunched at my off-the-wall question. "Scout? I'm sure she's just laying low for now. She's fine. She knows how to hide."

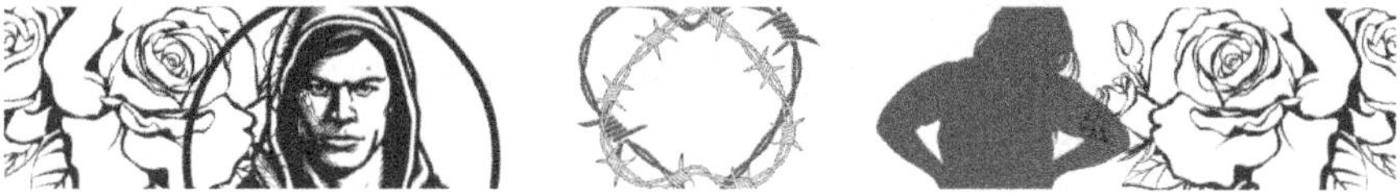

Chapter Twenty-Five

Hacker Caged

Scout

My eyes opened, but all I saw was dense darkness. It was so thick that I instinctively attempted to touch my lids to make sure they were indeed open. Except my hands wouldn't move. Metal bit into my back and feet as I struggled against the panic rising in my chest. I was in a small cage, and every movement shifted the thing like it was suspended in pitch black.

My first thought was he had survived, and it had taken him this long to get me back. But my brain supplied the unseeing eyes of my *daddy* before pulling back and showing me his lifeless body riddled with bullet holes and laying in a pool of blood. He hadn't been my dad, and he hadn't survived me.

"So how the fuck did I end up here?"

A deep rumble sounded from the darkness below me. My brain conjured monstrous images of mythical beasts and creatures, which was ridiculous. Shoving the fear aside, I remembered leaving my solitary office. I had been at my car when a solid force slammed me against the door. There had been a pinch in my neck followed by a cool burn in my veins.

Now, I was naked, secured in a tight cage, hung in some dark space, protected by a dog, not some mythical monster. And yet, my brain continued to provide unreasonable answers to the growling below. My chest heaved in the cool air as my senses stretched around me, hoping to find facts not fantasy.

"Hello?"

A deep bark was my only answer.

"Hey, puppy. You're a good boy. Doing your job like the guard dog you are." *Dog... brain, not a werewolf.*

Nails clicked on concrete until they were below me. How high was this cage anyway?

"Who do you belong to? Hmm?"

The dog started barking, and this time he didn't stop. Deep, low, and menacing, like he meant business. He would bite me if given the chance.

I put him on the long list of my enemies. There was no shortage of people who wanted me dead. But none of them hurt my feelings like Old Barko down there. Couldn't he tell I was an animal lover?

Hell, animals were the only thing I allowed myself *to* love. That, and taking down the piece of shit humans who stain the innocent with their wants and needs. *Isn't it always about that? The abuser's wants and needs.*

Whoever took me would be in for a surprise, because whatever they wanted to do to me, I'd already been there and done that. Unfortunately for them, I learned from past mistakes and was prepared to endure, survive, and eventually destroy.

The dog was so noisy that I didn't realize we weren't alone until the lights caused me to wince and the dog stopped barking at a foreign command. Had that word been German or maybe Russian? I blinked down at the man the Rottweiler greeted with a wiggly butt. He was as thick as his dog. A solid mass next to the trimmer blond man in glasses next to him. He craned his neck back and let out a low whistle. "Look at the birdie in the cage."

Birdie? The heat in my face was an inferno. "Fuck you! Get me out of here!"

The dog followed the big man to a crank on the wall. It clicked as he turned the handle, and my cage lowered. It would jerk occasionally, sending terror through the rage I was holding onto. Luckily, it didn't crash to the floor. Unluckily, he stopped lowering it at eye level with Blondie.

"Divina Collins. We just want to talk."

He reached through the bars to caress my cheek. Even though I had no one left to protect, the knife of terror at my full name still cut through me. I did the only thing I could. I turned and bit the hand that attempted to pet me. I got a piece of the meaty part right under his thumb and bit down as hard as I could with a snarl.

He jerked away with a shout, and my teeth clacked together the moment my mouth was empty.

"Fuck! She's a biter," he informed Dog Man as he held his wrist tight inspecting the teeth marks I left behind.

I spat at him. "And you taste like shit, you child-molesting monster!"

"A what?" His eyes were stunningly blue as he matched my glare. "No honey, you got me all wrong. I'm a hacker, just like you."

"You are *nothing* like me."

Dog Man grabbed the cage and pulled it close. "No, pet, he doesn't bite back. But I do." His voice was deep and full of threat.

I met his dark brown eyes with a curl of my lip. "I'm twenty-six, Fido. Way too old for the likes of you."

His face scrunched up before he glanced at Bleeding Blondie. "What the fuck is she talking about?"

Blondie grinned at Fido. "Now do you believe me when I say you are looking more like Gaul everyday? Fido?"

"Hey, Gaul is a sexy dog."

"Ewe. Please tell me you don't molest animals, too."

Fido looked at me with open disgust. "You are some twisted little bitch. Who hurt you?"

Blondie answered. "Men hurt her. From the moment she was born until she was eight years old, sick and nasty men used Divina for their sexual pleasure." He met my scowl. "Didn't they?"

"Fuck you."

His lips curved into a cruel smile. "Only if you're a good girl."

I sputtered at him, and my rage took control of my mouth. "A good girl? You made a mistake by taking me. I'm going to enjoy killing you."

The mother fucker had the audacity to laugh. "Are you talking about your little failsafe program that checks in on you every day because you have no one who actually cares about you?"

Wow. That actually hurt. Tears burned my eyes. "The moment I don't check in with my team, they'll come crashing down on your heads. You both will die, and I'll take that dog home and turn him into a couch potato."

Fido laughed a hearty sound. "He already has his own couch, little lover."

"I am not your lover."

His gaze roamed my naked squatting body and settled between my legs. I closed my thighs the best I could, and he pulled his bottom lip between his teeth. "The more you threaten me with violence, the harder my dick gets. And once it's stretching that tiny little pussy, I think you just might fall in love with me."

I rolled my eyes. "Oh please. Spare me. Every man thinks their dick is God's gift to women when in reality they are always less than impressing. That's why you fuck kids. Right? It makes you feel like a big man to hurt children. Am I right?"

Fido scowled at Blondie. "What the fuck is she talking about?"

"She thinks we are from some pedophile ring. That's what she does." He pinned me with a knowing look. "You hack and gather information on evil men, and then sick independent mercenary groups on them."

I smirked at him. "And they get justice immediately. You fuckers die in the most horrible ways, and the kids are rescued."

He let his gaze drop to my tits. "Like you were?"

"Fuck you. You know nothing about me."

"But you know something I want to know. I need to find someone you helped escape."

It was my turn to laugh. "I'd rather die than help you recapture kids."

He shook his head. "Not kids. These two were adults. You set my boss up and helped two women escape. I'll double what they paid you if you help us find them."

The puzzle pieces fell into place. "Oh, you are with the Blue Fucked-up Boy's Club. I don't know what world you live in, but fifteen isn't an adult in the real world."

He looked confused for a moment but shook his blond head and turned away. "Do you research your clients at all?"

"Why would I need to research the victims?"

He opened a briefcase and pulled out a photo taken from what looked like surveillance. He slapped the grainy image against the flat metal bars of the cage I was in. "Does she look fifteen to you? No? That's because Eden is turning twenty-three. Karla played you."

"Bullshit," I spit back immediately.

He leaned in and glared harshly at me. "We don't fuck with kids. In fact, anyone in our society caught messing with children gets to *fuck* with our enforcer. Unfortunately, you put our enforcer in jail."

"Your enforcer is a psychopath."

Fido piped up. "That he is, but a psychopath is exactly what is needed to keep a community of this magnitude in line."

"A community of men who kidnap women, undress them, and hang them in a cage?"

Blondie turned the cage so that I faced him. "We don't have time to fuck around. We need to clear Logan and find Eden."

I grinned at him. "I have all the time in the world to fuck around. So sorry for your loss."

"Yeah, you're about to find out how sorry."

Bentley

Bentley Hacker

The smash and grab had been textbook. Torrid had grabbed the girl, and I'd snatched her purse before she hit the ground. He had put her in the truck as I let my team into her office with the keys I took from her.

It turned out that she was a better hacker than I imagined, and her shit was on lockdown. My team could crack her security, but it would take time we didn't have. So here I was with an injured hand and a pissed off naked girl in a cage.

"I have to pee."

Torrid grunted, "So pee."

She turned her defiant face to him. "You gonna pick up my shit too?"

Torrid's lip curled. "I'd rather make you eat it."

"Stop. If I let you go to the bathroom, will you be a good girl and help me out?"

She glared at me. "Fuck you."

Torrid grinned at me. "I'm going to assume that's a no."

I shrugged. "Then let her shit herself. We can hose her down later." Turning away I said, "She chose her path. Do what you do best Tor. I've got some phone calls to make."

Gaul followed me out as Torrid said to Scout, "You chose the hard way, Sugar Tits. Should have just told Bent what he wanted to know. Time to face the music, Snapper."

Snapper? More like Piranha. I'll have permanent scars on my hand from that rabid beast.

I got why she bit me, and I took complete blame for putting my hand in the cage, but I hadn't expected the pretty girl to draw blood.

Twenty minutes later, I stepped back into the warehouse and paused to take in the scene. Scout was still in the cage, but it was lower, and her body, still squatting in the confined space, was secured to the bars. Torrid had braved the teeth and somehow got an O ring gag in her mouth. The way it jacked her jaw wide had my cock paying close attention. He had put her mouth at the perfect level for a good face fucking.

Her thighs were tied to the sides, spreading her wide. Gods, she was beautiful with her delicious little pussy on full display. Her arms were secured to the bar behind her back, pushing her perfect tits out for Torrid to pinch as he attached the nipple clamps to them.

"Estim... Nice."

Torrid smiled and gave the cage a little spin. Scout screamed her rage as he laughed. I have to admit, the tears streaming down her face hit me far deeper than any tears before. That was unexpected. Was it because she was a hacker, too? That I respected this chick's brain and what she did for a living? *I might have a hard time killing this one.*

I slipped two fingers through the rubber ring and over her tongue. "I think you owe me an apology, Divina."

Furious eyes bore holes into mine as I slowly took off my belt and draped it around her neck. She leaned back as my fingers went to my dress pants, but she only managed to choke herself. Instead of lunging forward, she leaned into the choke.

Torrid fisted her hair and pushed her face against the bars. "We'll have none of that, pet." He took a moment to adjust the belt around her neck so that she couldn't kill herself with it. "There we go. Much better."

She screamed as she glared at him. Then she fought the restraints with all she had, channeling all that rage into her struggle, shaking the cage and the wires dangling from her nipples. The restraints held, and she focused on my erection in front of her as she huffed and puffed her fury.

"Don't worry, I'll start gentle."

Her brows shot together, and she started yelling at my dick as I stroked it against her cheek. Torrid chuckled as he tied some cord around a curved pink sex toy.

"That's new."

He grinned in response and clicked a button. The insertable end began rotating and the other end... "Well, that looks fun." I turned the cage so she could get a better look at the clear cup with a lashing tongue. Her beautiful green eyes popped wide.

Torrid laughed. "Yeah, for like a minute, maybe two, and then she'll be squealing on your cock like nothing else."

I squatted in front of her and watched her face as Tor inserted the toy into her. The many expressions that flashed through her as he used the cord to tie the toy in place were simply fascinating. Anger was always there as she met my gaze, but surprise, shock, discomfort, and denial of bliss as that cup suctioned against her labia and that little tongue started moving around.

Her breath shuddered out of her as she closed her eyes. Fresh tears ran down her cheek, and I couldn't help but to lean in for a taste. Her breathing grew erratic as I whispered in her ear. "Good girl. Just relax and let it happen. Come for me."

An open-mouthed sob was her only response.

"See? This won't be all bad. To tell you the truth, I'm a little jealous of that toy. Licking your fat little clit as it fucks you."

I kissed her bright red cheek gently, and she let out a shout of frustration as I moved my tongue over her bottom lip. "Don't deny it, Divina. Just let it happen. Come for me." I licked into her mouth, caressing her tongue with mine as she did her best to bite down. Her spine stiffened, and her body quivered with intense pleasure. I pulled back and cupped her open jaw. "There you go. That's my good girl. You just keep coming as I take my apology from you."

Her muscles jerked and strained, but her body didn't move as I stood up and traced the tip of my dick around the O ring behind her lips. She was vibrating with the noises coming out of her mouth, and fuck if it didn't feel amazing.

Torrid went to the door. "Take your time. I'm going to take Gaul for a walk and maybe feed him brunch, watch a movie... I'll be back later."

She screamed as I pressed past her tongue, dipping into absolute Heaven. She gagged as my dick kissed the back of her throat. I held myself there, letting her struggle a minute before easing back to her lips. She coughed and started yelling something unintelligible, so I pulled the bars of the cage forward and repeated the action until she stopped yelling at me.

"That's it. Good girl. Can you take more? Hmm? Let's see."

I pushed deeper, testing the waters, and when she swallowed on my tip, I caressed her hair back from her face. "I'm sorry about your past."

Wet eyes flashed up to mine.

"Yeah, I know all about you, Divina. How your selfish mother gave you to a rich man."

Tears poured as she sobbed around my cock.

"Did he promise her a better life for you?"

I slid in and out of her mouth. "Or did she know what kind of monster she'd given her baby to?"

My hips moved slowly as I gently fucked her mouth deeper and deeper, until finally, I held her lips flush to my pelvis. "I knew you'd take my entire cock. Such a talented girl, aren't you?"

I pulled back and she let out a shuddering breath. Drool slipped down her chin and long strands attached us before I pushed back in. "Is that why you are such a recluse now? Hmm? I get that it's a lot of trauma, but you had... What? Eighteen years to heal?"

I fucked in and out, gaining speed slowly. "You've been killing pedos for about ten years now. Well, not you personally, but you've caused many deaths since you started this career of yours."

I held deep in her throat as she came from overstimulation again. Her muffled screams vibrated around me, and they shook me to my core. "Oh, Divina. You are a fucking goddess."

Her glare returned to me as I fucked in and out of her sloppy mouth.

"A vengeful, angry goddess who is going to make me come before I'm ready."

I pulled all the way out and knelt so we were face to face. The cool air chilled my raging hard-on as I cupped her slick cheeks and asked, "You still coming?"

She shuddered and closed her eyes.

"Fuck, you are. You deserve all this pleasure, Scout. You deserve to be worshiped."

Sweat coated her brow, and I wiped it away, combing her dark hair back with my fingers. "You ready to apologize yet?"

She nodded, breathing hard through her nose.

I smiled at her when she opened her eyes. "You gonna talk to me like a civilized person?"

Her eyes squeezed shut as she nodded again.

I stood up and gripped the cage with both hands. She glared up at me as I fit my cock back in her mouth. "I'm going to feed you first. You'll swallow every drop, and I'll think about turning that toy off while we chat."

That had been a lie. She'd endure a few more forced orgasms before I left her to Torrid's amusement.

Torrid

Torrid Gaul

I monitored the warehouse feed as I piddled around in the kitchen making Gaul's breakfast. He ate a fresh raw diet, and today was my day to prep our meals for the week. He followed me around the kitchen, supervising while the monitor blared Divina's screams, moans, and sobs.

The sounds she made had my cock uncharacteristically straining against my pants. I had watched Bentley work on many captives before without feeling an ounce of passion. Bent swung both ways. I did not, but the way he praised this girl as he abused her throat had me paying attention to him, too.

He took his time with her. Revealed how much he knew of her tragic past. Aimed his dagger right at her heart before spilling down her throat. She almost drowned on his cum, coughing and sputtering until it leaked out her nose and down her chin.

He knelt in front of her and used a shop cloth to gently clean her face as he used tender praise as a weapon against her psyche. She came every time he asked her to as he worked like he was moving through molasses.

The moment he unbuckled the O ring gag he paused and asked, “No more biting?”

Her eyes squeezed shut, but she shook her head no. He eased the rubber circle out of her mouth, and she let out a sharp breath. “Please...” Her voice was hoarse.

He angled his face right in front of hers. “Thank you, Bentley for removing my gag.” He swiped a tear with his thumb. “And for not going for round two.”

She glared at him but said roughly, “Thank you.”

He cupped her cheek and cocked his head. “Are you going to come again, Divina?”

“Please, it hurts.” But her body shook with intense pleasure. “Fuck!”

He chuckled as he unbuckled the strap securing her head to the bars and then untied her thighs. The moment they were free she snapped them closed with a squeal. “Oh my God!” She struggled to free her hands cuffed behind her. “Fuck!” It was a hoarse scream as she kicked her hips in an attempt to dislodge the toy.

Bent merely reached into the cage and gently removed her nipple clamps.

“Please, Bentley. I’ll tell you anything. Please turn it off.”

He gave her a tender smile. “Don’t you have one more orgasm for me?”

“No, please!”

His hands ran up and down her thighs. “Open up and let me watch, sweet Scout. Let me see you come for me.”

The muscles under his palms trembled violently as she opened her legs and arched against the cage. “Please, Bentley, please...” Her raw voice shook.

The click of Gaul's nails on the tile grabbed my attention. "Gaul. Place."

He trotted out of the kitchen as I opened my pants and pulled my dick out. Fisting myself, I jerked roughly as she screamed her orgasm, thrashing and bucking as Bentley leaned down and watched the toy jerk and roll. "Keep going, Scout."

Her toes curled and she lifted her hips, thighs wide, displaying the toy to Bentley as she rode out her never-ending orgasm. "Please, please, please."

Finally, he reached through the bars and turned the toy off. The lashing tongue stopped stimulating and the rotating bit inside ceased moving.

"Good girl."

Panting, she collapsed against the floor of the cage in relief. "I hate those words."

"Is it because they said those words when you finally stopped crying and let them use your little body?"

She opened her eyes and glared at him. "How do you even know that? I worked hard to erase every image and video they put on the dark web."

"It took me a month to find one recently shared by an old man who says he was the man in the video."

She leaned forward with intense interest, her arms catching on the bars behind her.

Bentley smiled at her response. "You give me what I want, and I'll bring that old man here and let you do whatever the hell you want to him. When you are finished, I'll clean up the evidence and get rid of the body."

"Whose body? His or mine? I'm not stupid."

He dipped his chin. "Oh, I know you aren't stupid, Scout. In fact, you are one of the smartest human beings I've ever met. Can I ask you a personal question?"

"Seriously?" You've seen footage of me being raped by an old man, and you came in my mouth. Why bother asking permission?"

"I forced myself not to turn away from the terror you survived. And I came down your throat because you bit me."

I jacked my dick faster, feeling the finish line coming and worried that what I'd hear next would ruin my orgasm.

Bentley leaned into the bars. "Why keep the name? You could have been anyone after you were rescued, but you held on to the name Scout. Why?"

A smile formed on her lips. "I wanted them to know who caused their deaths."

My palm slammed down on the counter as I lifted to my toes.

"Bring me the old man first, and then I'll help you clear your boss's name."

My cock thickened, the head bulged, and finally my orgasm left me.

Chapter Twenty-Six

Adventurous Little Slut

Logan

Straightening the lapels of my suit, I lifted my face to the sun and inhaled deeply. It wasn't fresh air that greeted my lungs, but the smell of a parking lot and the sound of nearby traffic was better than the past three fucking months.

The state's case was rapidly crumbling before their eyes. Evidence collected from the sailboat was mysteriously corrupted, and with a missing witness, they really didn't have a case at all. A judge granted me bail as a result of their incompetence and today I was a free man, sort of.

Mickey passed me a new phone with a grin. "Bentley and Torrid have an address for a Grace and Mazy Brown."

I cocked my head and he asked, "How do you feel about Costa Rica?"

"The hacker confirmed this?"

Mickey's grin broadened. "She's been a special project for the guys. Not quite on board, but our team broke into her system, and they found some shit."

I dialed Tor. "Yeah?"

"I'm out. We are going to Costa Rica to collect Eden and her mother."

Tor's pause gave me concern. "Yeah, um okay. What about the hacker?"

"Get rid of her."

Another pause. "What if we are enjoying her a little too much?"

I stopped walking and looked at the phone number showing on the screen just to make sure I'd dialed right. "You? Enjoying something?"

"What? Is that worse than imagining me in a tutu?"

"Fuck Tor. I've been sitting in jail for three months, and that image is not the first thing I need right now. I don't care what you do with your new toy. Just make sure she doesn't become a threat again. And who the fuck is *we*?"

Torrid's chuckle was low. "Bent and me. So, can we keep her?"

I sighed. "Fuck, I don't care what you do with her. Use her, abuse her, chew her up, but her fate will be up to the tribunal. Understand?"

"I don't think she's gonna like that."

I turned my scowl towards my brother since he was the only thing I could glare at. "I don't give a fuck what that bitch likes. She set me up with fake evidence that almost had me getting a life sentence. Handle your shit and prepare to travel."

I hung up, and Mickey busted out laughing. "They got it bad."

I rolled my eyes and resumed walking to Mickey's SUV. "*I've* got it bad."

Mick jumped into the driver's seat. "Yeah, about that. She's dating."

Lead weight settled on my shoulders and into the pit of my stomach. "Why?"

His face was grave. "Like getting paid to date, dating."

I shook my head. That didn't make a lick of sense. Escorting wasn't something she'd ever considered before me. After me? "If that's true, she's about to learn a hard lesson."

He headed towards St. Pete and admitted, "My asshole just puckered a little."

Eden

Sweet Angel

I had another date tonight. Mom had been setting me up more frequently, and these guys seemed to expect more and more from me.

My mother hovered behind me as I put on my makeup. "Where did you find this one?"

"Not Tinder," she quipped, quickly referring to our conversation after my last date that went haywire. That man had been very handsy, and it had taken everything shy of punching his nose to get away from him. Even Logan hadn't grabbed my tits as much as that guy did.

Mom sniffed. "I used a new, upper-class app. This guy sounds perfect. He's got a yacht and is taking you out for dinner on it."

"He knows I don't have sex on the first date. Right?"

"Of course, he does. You're a classy girl, Eden. No high value man would expect you to put out on the first date."

I stood up and faced her. I was wearing a new gown that was midnight blue and had a long split in the hem. I was a whole size smaller than I had been when I first got to Costa Rica, and I felt beautiful.

"How do I look?"

Her smile of approval warmed my insides. "Gorgeous." It was the smile I had dreamed of receiving as a kid. I wished I could go back in time and tell that child to hold on. There were things about her mother that she didn't understand, and life would get better.

The only thing was, I wished Logan was the one taking me to dinner tonight. I didn't think I'd ever get over that man. I was trying, though, and vowed to give this guy my full attention.

His name was Connor, and he lived in London for part of the year. Mom showed me his photo, and I had to admit he was attractive for his age. He certainly didn't have one foot in the grave like we had planned, but he was filthy rich and Mom had vetted him well. He had a wild gleam in his brown eyes that intrigued me.

"Your car should be here any minute." She went to the front door.

I grabbed my clutch and followed. The car was already here, and it was a nice SUV. Limos weren't necessarily a thing in Costa Rica. The roads weren't always the best here.

The driver took me to the marina where Connor was waiting for me. He was wearing a casual suit that looked like it was made just for his body.

"Grace." His voice was warm and welcoming as he greeted me with a hug. He stepped back and let his gaze roam. "You look stunning. More beautiful than your photos."

"Thank you." He was more handsome in person, too, but I couldn't bring myself to voice that. It just felt inappropriate.

"You said you loved the ocean and sailing. I thought you'd enjoy an evening meal on my yacht." He opened an arm to show me his beautiful boat down the dock. "It's not a sailboat, but it is a beauty. Wouldn't you agree?"

He slipped my arm in his and took me towards the massive boat. "She's a big girl. Needs a staff of six to keep her shipshape, but I gave most of the crew the night off. It will just be the cook and my captain tonight."

"Oh?"

He helped me across the gangway. "Don't worry. They are very discreet. Earmuffs, blinders, no photos, or videos. It's all safe here."

My face pinched as he retracted the platform and waived to a man on the dock who untied the yacht. "Should I be worried about safety?"

He straightened and guided me towards the interior of the boat. "Not at all, but I know a lot of women would. Just trying to put you at ease." His touch was light, and his voice was casual.

"Do you bring lots of dates on your yacht?" The parlor was lit up with a sparkling chandelier that bathed the elegant furniture in tans and whites. It was spacious, with a fully stocked bar, a leather couch, and an intimate dining table.

He shrugged. "Only a few."

He went to the bar and poured some chilled champagne. I waved him off when he presented it to me. "I'm not a drinker."

His mouth formed a silent oh. "That's right, but you said you sometimes drink champagne on your profile."

I smiled kindly. "Maybe after dinner?"

"Of course. Would you like to go up top for a bit while we wait?"

While we enjoyed the fresh air, we had meaningful conversations. Connor was a divorced father of two almost grown children. The boy was about my age, well Grace's age, and the girl was fourteen. His accent was charming, and I felt like he was truly paying attention when I spoke.

He asked me about my goals for the future during dinner and what I wanted in a husband. We even spoke about politics and religion with common ground. The food was delicious, and the chef was pleasant as he served the meal. Connor treated him like a friend, not an employee.

By the time dinner was over, I was feeling comfortable and agreed to go up to the top deck for an after-dinner cocktail. I watched Connor pour the Appletini for me and the Scotch for himself. I'd never drink champagne again, or trust a glass passed to me at a party. I shuddered to think what would have happened to me had Logan not been there to stop James.

"Are you okay?"

We were sitting on a couch under the stars. "I'm fine."

"You sure?"

I didn't know what to do or say. So, I kissed him. He seemed shocked at first, but then he returned my kiss with a low moan. When I pulled back, he smiled and said, "Finally."

His smile was infectious, and a lopsided grin formed on my face. "What's that supposed to mean?"

"Just that, you are so beautiful and fresh. I was worried that you weren't into me like I was you."

"I like you."

His smile bloomed right before he kissed me again. This time he controlled the kiss, and it was intense. My nipples hardened in my lacy black bra as he pulled me closer. His tongue invaded my mouth, and he tasted like Scotch and dessert. It wasn't a bad combination, and I gave myself over to his passion.

His hand slid up my spine to the back of my head as he adjusted me closer to his lap. I resisted straddling him, but the bite of his other hand on my hip forced me to retreat. I stiffened, putting both hands on his chest with a squeak as he pushed me down on his thighs. The slit in my dress pulled and stitching popped. I pulled back but he held firm. Twisting my face to the side I said, "My dress..."

He let go of me with a feral grin and grabbed the neckline of my bodice. "Needs to go."

Before I could respond he tore the fabric down to my belly button.

"Oh no!"

It was all I could say as he pulled my bra straps down and bared my breasts.

"Grind against me, princess."

His face buried between my breasts as his hands gripped my hips and forced them to move.

I pushed against him but he was unmovable until I fisted the back of his hair and pulled his face off my boobs. "Stop."

He looked confused for a split second. "Nobody is going to see—"

"Can't we slow down a bit?"

The way he frowned had my heart racing. "I didn't pay top dollar to go slow."

I jerked back with surprise. "What?"

He fit his hand around my throat and pushed me to my back on the couch as he crawled over the top of me. "You heard what I said. I paid top dollar, and I intend to get every penny's worth."

He grabbed my wrists and pinned them above my head as he fumbled with his pants. The skirt of my dress twisted around my legs as I attempted to kick him off me. His gaze lifted to mine and the way he looked at me had a whimper escaping my lips. "I love it when they fight."

His fist slammed into my face and head as I screamed and tried to get my hands free. Pain exploded in my cheek and head. I pleaded with him to stop. When he let my wrists go, I covered my face and head as he tore my legs open and shoved my panties aside. His hands grabbed my breasts as he poked and stabbed my pussy without finding the hole. I wasn't even sure that was his intent as he kneaded my breasts, muttering something about how great they were over the ringing in my ears.

"Please, please, please don't hurt me anymore." My lips were swollen. Two teeth were loose, and I'd bitten my tongue. All contributed to the slur in my words, but somehow, he understood me.

"Will you be a good girl from here on out?"

I reached between my legs and fisted his dick with a trembling hand. "Yes. I'll be a good girl." My voice shook as hard as my hand.

His grin returned. "Are you going to let me take you downstairs and tie you up like a good little princess?"

My heart sank and all I could think of was I couldn't let him take me to a second location. "Of course, I will."

He lifted off me and pulled me to my feet. There was no way I was going downstairs with this man. I'd rather die first. I wiped my mouth against my shoulder and said, "But first, will you do me a favor?"

"Anything."

My mind raced to find something, anything to say to avoid what waited for me downstairs. "I've always wanted to be fucked over the railing of a beautiful yacht."

His direction changed towards the aft of the boat. "Adventurous little slut."

I tried to close the bodice and cover myself, but he slapped my hands away. "Don't you dare."

I let my hands fall to my sides as I backed up against the railing. The wake streamed out behind me as he lifted me onto the bar and stepped between my legs. I spread them wide as he fumbled with my dress and panties. Glancing behind me, all I saw was dark water. I took a few deep breaths and put my foot on his chest while he was distracted with his pants. One swift kick and a second of falling was all it took before I hit the water. I was engulfed in darkness and the sound of the ocean. I might drown out here, but at least I wouldn't be tortured up there. Holding my breath, I floated to the surface. I gulped air and wiped sea water from my eyes as I looked around me for the yacht.

Sure enough, Connor had alerted the captain, and the yacht was making a slow turn. My heart skipped a beat as I huffed some deep breaths, located the direction of land by the tiny lights of shore and went under again.

There was no way to know if I was swimming in the right direction in the darkness, no time to think of what could be lurking underneath me, I just needed to evade the eyes on that boat long enough for them to give up the search. My dress was hindering me in the water, so I pulled it off.

The air in my lungs brought me back to the surface. Relief flooded me when I found the yacht searching in the wrong area. Keeping an eye on the boat, I stayed on the surface, riding the waves as I swam backwards towards shore. I had no idea how far I'd have to swim or even if there'd be a beach where I was swimming, but I had no other choice but to try.

After thirty minutes of searching, the yacht drove away. My body relaxed as the tension and fear left my body. I went under the water and screamed so hard it wracked my soul. On the surface, my eyes burned from the saltwater and tears as waves splashed me in the face repeatedly, reminding me that I needed to beat another challenge if I was to survive the night.

Chapter Twenty-Seven

Ain't No Sunshine

Eden

I woke up in a hospital bed two days later. My body was incredibly sore. The remnants of salty hair greeted my fingers as I pushed my hair off my puffy face. Tubes and wires ran from me to machines that created a melody of beeps and boops. I tried to swallow, to speak, but my mouth was so dry my tongue was thick and hard.

I blinked my crusty burning eyes until I could focus enough to find the little red call button. It didn't take long for a nurse to rush in but it took me a full minute to realize she was speaking Spanish. My Spanish had gotten much better since moving here, but my brain was slow and muddled.

"English?" My voice was raw and crackly.

She said, "I'll get the doctor."

The doctor was a blonde woman with a French accent who checked my vitals and let me take a few sips of fresh water.

"Can you tell me what happened to you?"

"I fell off a yacht Friday evening."

She looked at her chart before eyeing me suspiciously. "The injuries to your face and bruising on your throat tell me there might be more to this story."

My fingertips touched my fat lip briefly before moving to my swollen and tender eye. "I don't really remember everything. Just hitting the water and darkness."

"You've been here for two days. Whatever happened had been traumatic enough that you slept that long."

I remembered everything. I just hadn't decided what to do about Connor. There were things he said during his assault that made me question that dating app my mother used. Things that made me want to question my mother.

The doctor stood up and said, "I'm sure you'll remember more as you heal. The nurse will get your information and contact your next of kin."

"Thank you."

Her departing smile was warm.

Four hours later, my mother rushed in. Her first words to me had nothing to do with my wellbeing. "You didn't give them your real name, did you?"

I was so stunned and overwhelmed with emotion, I just said, "I want to go home."

She rushed over like she was going to hug me, but one look at my face, and she decided to pat my shoulder instead. "Of course. I already told them to release you immediately. I'll take you home as soon as they do so. Just tell me you didn't use your real name."

"I didn't use my real name, and I want to go home, home. I don't want to be here anymore."

I knew the calculated disappointment in her eyes well as she sat back to stare at me. A fight was brewing, but at this point, I just wanted to go back to where I felt safe. "You don't have to come. I won't tell anyone where you are."

"What about the police?"

I was silent for a long minute. "How much did Connor pay you to rape me?"

"He didn't rape you," she whispered harshly.

My gaze narrowed. "How do you know?"

The nurse came in and jerked to a stop when she saw my mother leaning over my hospital bed. "The doctor said Grace is to remain in the hospital until she clears her to go home."

"And how long will that be?" my mother asked in a clipped voice.

"You'll have to ask her."

A smile formed on my lips, causing them to crack. I tasted blood as I ran my tongue over them. "Can I get some more water please?"

The nurse smiled at me. "I'll also get you some balm for your chapped lips."

My mother made a frustrated sound as the nurse left, but my voice was icy as I asked again. "How did you know he didn't rape me?"

"He called and told me what happened."

Pain lanced through my chest. Did she not care at all about me? My teeth hurt from the way I was clenching my jaw. "Did he tell you about all this?" I waved a finger toward my face. "Were you expecting to see how hard he hit me? Or was this a surprise?"

"He said you hit your head when you fell."

I laughed, a hollow broken sound. "Right. That was after he beat the shit out of me, choked me, and ripped my dress in half."

Shame guttered her gaze as I asked, "Did you give him his money back? How much did he pay for me anyway?"

"This is not the place to have this conversation."

"How much was I worth, Mom?"

"Just stop it, Eden."

"Two days, Mom. Where have you fucking been?"

Her eyes snapped to me and the look in them chilled me to the bone. "Cleaning up your mess. I can't believe how ungrateful you are."

"Ungrateful? As far as you knew, I was floating face down in the sea. Was that the plan all along? Did he pay you to rape and kill me? Is that what he paid for?"

"No!" She glanced at the door and lowered her voice, "No."

She looked at me as if I was the crazy one spewing nonsense. Maybe I was reading too much into what she wasn't saying. "So, what did he pay for?"

"We can continue this at home."

I shook my head. "I'm not going back to that house with you."

"And how do you plan on paying for a flight home? Do you think customs will let Grace Brown, who was born in Denmark, enter the States from Costa Rica just like that? No questions?"

When I didn't respond she said, "No? We will continue this conversation when we get home. Don't even think about getting the police involved. Connor may have taken things too far, but if I go to jail, who will take care of you? Have the doctor call me for an update."

She spun on her heels and stalked out.

I refused to let one more tear spill over her. She was a shitty mother. I'd find a way back home where I felt safe. Had no clue what I'd tell the police or my dad, or Logan. I only knew that neither of them would have sold me to an evil man in an expensive suit.

Logan

Logan Lurch

The sunset was spectacular as our small plane landed on a remote airstrip in Costa Rica. We couldn't enter the country legally to do shady shit because I wasn't supposed to leave St. Petersburg at all. But I had a fantastic tech team who corralled my digital footprint to my condo and unless we ran into trouble here, the police would be none the wiser.

If all went well, we'd be back in Florida with my naughty little prize by morning. Eden was in for a world of darkness with my alter ego, Lurch. He'd prepared her room down to the smallest of details while we waited for the perfect time to start our journey.

Lurch made plans of painful bliss and sexual torture until our fallen angel repented and begged for mercy. I had a hard time disagreeing with him after setting up our date. I created a plausible online profile and opened communication with Grace on the app she was using to gain clientele. Grace didn't sound like the girl I once knew.

With time on my hands and my mind racing, I opened the app and obsessed over our messages from last week. No matter how many times I read them, something just didn't sit right.

Anything?

She responded: **Give me a week, the last one got a little too excited by the concept of anything.**

Excited?

It took her a few minutes to respond: **Look. I like it rough, just don't leave permanent marks or touch my face.**

So for five grand you'll pretend you don't want it and make me force you.

She responded: **Just don't get too violent.**

Can I tie you up?

Her reply: **For five G you can tie and gag me and have your way.**

Can I spank your pussy?

The answer came immediately: **No.**

Have you ever done it before?

No. My gut twisted and even Lurch thought something was off with that response. Maybe she drew that line because it belonged wholly to me.

You might find you enjoy it.

Liar said: **I don't enjoy it.** *Who the fuck am I chatting with?*

She'd lost her sunshine, and after what I planned to do to her, she'd never find it again. My fallen angel agreed to let me do anything I wanted for the sum of five grand. I transferred the money, and my team went to work on hacking the bank. She should know by now; I don't pay for sex.

Mickey got out of the pilot's seat, and Bentley exited from the copilot door before I was able to unfold myself enough to leave the Cessna. Torrid convinced me that he had to stay to babysit the hacker. Not that we needed the bitch anymore, but Bent and Tor seemed keen on keeping her.

I stretched as they tied down the plane and chalked the tires so it would still be here when we returned later with our fourth passenger.

It took an hour and a half to arrive at our destination because she changed the location at the last minute.

Come to my house instead of meeting me at the hotel.

The SUV Bentley rented bounced over a pothole in the road as I responded with a sense of unease slithering through me.

Everything still okay?

It took a full minute for her to respond: **Yes, I just feel more comfortable here. We are remote enough that no one will hear me scream.**

She provided the address, and we killed the headlights as we rolled up a long driveway towards an oversized home.

"It will be a smaller separate residence to the right of the main house."

Bentley parked the car, and we walked the rest of the way. We froze the moment we heard the shouting.

"He will be here any minute, so knock it off."

"Knock it off?! Mom, you promised me no more and then spring this on me last minute?"

I put my finger to my lip and crept closer. Mick and Bent followed my lead.

"Stop being so damn ungrateful."

"Ungrateful? I should be grateful that you almost got me killed? Do you not give a single fuck about me?"

The pride that bubbled up in me at witnessing Eden stand up to her mother dissolved into fury.

Karla said, "Oh here we go again with the dramatics. He didn't push you. You chose to jump. The worst he would have done was rough fuck you. Yet you had to turn that situation into a huge ordeal."

"Why not let him rip *your* dress off and beat the shit out of *you*? Why sell *me*?"

Karla shot back. "Because I'm not young enough for those men."

We were close enough to see through the window where they stood arguing but too far to make out details. Eden crossed her arms and jutted her chin out. "Well, I'm not doing this, so message that man back and tell him not to come."

Karla stomped forward. "You will do this because it's your ticket home. Do you think money grows on trees, child? Grace can't enter the states legally, so Eden has to, which means I have to get your paperwork here. That takes time. Then I have to pay for travel…" She twirled a finger in the air. "Unless you plan to swim home."

"Fuck this, and fuck you. *You* meet that man, I'm leaving."

"You aren't going anywhere."

"I am, and I won't be back."

"What are you going to do to live? Are you going to paint your way to the states?" she mocked. "No. You'll sell your pussy for forty dollars on the street until you die of some sort of tropical sex disease. That man paid five grand for one date. You'll do this for me, for you, so you can get what you want. You owe me this."

I pulled out my phone and messaged Grace: **Pulling up now.**

Karla went to the laptop to answer the notification, confirming my suspicions. "He's here. Go put something nice on and get ready. I'll stall him."

Mickey stepped in front of me as we approached the door. He shot a smirk over his shoulder. "I've got this."

Bentley and I stepped to either side of the door just in case Karla checked the peephole before she opened it. The scream she let out as Mickey grabbed her led me to believe she wished she'd peeked at who stood at her front door.

I pushed past the struggling woman and found Eden standing in the hall looking panicked. Recognition flashed briefly, and she took a step towards me before fear bled into her features. I would have given anything to be a fly on the wall of her mind in that moment.

"Run from me, and I'll catch you."

Her gaze flashed to her mother struggling with Mickey and Bentley before she did exactly what I wanted. She spun on her heels and bolted out the back door.

I flashed my brother a grin over my shoulder. "I'll be right back."

"Take your time."

I stalked out the back door and caught a glimpse of Eden's lightened hair in the moonlight as she disappeared down the path that led towards the private beach. My alter ego pressed forward as my senses stretched out before me. I scanned the empty beach and remained still until I heard a leaf crackle in the woods behind me. I'd walked right past her as she hid.

Without turning around, I said, "Eden. The longer you make me search for you, the worse it will be."

She bolted out of the wood and onto the trail behind me. I spun, noting that she had been closer than my ears led me to believe. Three strides were all it took before my hand closed on her arm.

She screamed as I hauled her against me. "Let me go!"

Her hands clawed and beat at my face and chest in panic. It took some effort to get her under control. "Naughty little angel."

Tears glistened in the moonlight as she turned her head away, refusing to look at me.

"There was a time you couldn't keep your eyes off me. What happened?"

She stiffened and finally met my gaze. "If you're going to kill me, just do it already." There was something off about her. I couldn't quite put my finger on it.

I let go of her waist to move a short strand of hair off her cheek. She flinched. She fucking cringed away from my touch. "What the fuck is wrong with you?" This time when I asked the question it was a demand. She sputtered over her words, making zero sense.

I spun her around, took her by the arm and marched her back towards the house where I could look her in the eye.

"Why run from me?"

"I, I, don't..."

"I thought we were planning a future together, and yet, you ran the moment you could. Not only did you run to another country, but you changed your name, cut your hair, and became a whore."

Her hand lifted to her hair before she winced at the word whore. I regretted the words the moment I said them. "Did a fuck you up that bad, Eden?"

In the light of the back porch, she tried to wiggle free of my hold. When she was unsuccessful, she jutted her chin and shoved her face in mine.

"You know what? Fuck you! You don't deserve an explanation for anything I might have done since you went to jail."

There's my feisty little angel. This time when she pulled back, I let her go. It wasn't just the venom in her voice or the look of murder on her face, it was the faded bruising and swelling I finally saw in the light.

I tried like hell to keep the fury out of my voice, "You said you liked it rough, but damn, Eden. You needed more than a week for your next trick."

Anger morphed into pure confusion. "What?" She shook her head and reached for the door. "Nevermind, the fact that you believe I'm out here fucking every man with a dollar—"

I caught her arm. "Not a dollar. Your mother *sold* you for five thousand dollars to do what I wanted to you."

She froze for a heartbeat, and then slammed the door open so hard I had to catch it to keep it from bouncing back and hitting her. She didn't notice as she beelined back into the living room where her mother sat weeping.

Mickey's brows hit his hairline as Eden stormed up to her mom, and my proud grin widened at the rage Eden was about to unleash on that woman.

"Five thousand dollars?"

Eden's voice became a harpy's shrill as she said, "You sold me for five grand to that man?" She snapped her fingers and pointed at me without looking away from her mother. "For... What was it? Anything he wanted? You promised me it would *never* happen again."

Mickey quickly read the room, and slowly eased away from the couch. Karla shook her head and sobbed into her hands. Eden grabbed her wrists and pulled her hands away from her face. "Did you tell Connor that, too? Did you know that man was going to try and rape me?"

Eden tried to get eye contact with her mother, but the woman kept turning her face away. "Look at me! Did you?" I guessed she saw the answer in her mother's eyes. "You fucking bitch. You prostituted your own daughter, and sent her on dates without her knowledge and pocketed the money." Her jaw clenched. "I fucking hate you, and I hope they kill you first so I can watch you bleed."

Chapter Twenty-Eight

Leave No Trace

Eden

"Eden."

He was right behind me. I broke eye contact with the heartless woman who called herself a mother.

His hand came forward. "Don't you touch me."

He jerked back, wary confusion on his damned handsome face. How dare he look so much like safety and home to me and yet believe the worst of me?

Shame flooded my eyes. Guilt took root in the form of tears. Logan figured out what had happened to me in minutes, but I was so stupid, it had taken me months. Going out on date after date, dodging grabby hands and eager kisses. Making excuse after excuse as to why I needed to go home instead of back to their hotel room. Blaming cheap hookup apps for their behavior. Thinking that this is what the adult dating scene was like, all while my mother was stuffing her purse with cash at my expense.

I couldn't take a normal breath, and the urge to run again had me looking for my bedroom door. "I need a moment."

He followed me until I said, "Alone."

"Eden..."

I lifted a hand as I reached my door, but his hand held it open. "Don't shut me out."

Facing him in the doorway I asked, "How could you think that of me?" My face crumpled with pain and fury. "You said you knew me." He pulled me against him, and the solid warmth of his body against mine broke the dam. I wailed, "I thought you had my back."

His deep voice rumbled against my cheek. "I do have your back, Eden. It's why I'm here. I came to take you home."

I lifted my eyes to his. "By buying me?"

His gaze warmed as his lips twitched. "Well, I had to find you somehow."

I broke eye contact as tears flooded them again. "I'm so stupid."

"No, you're not. You trusted someone who should have protected you."

"That's what I thought she was doing at first. She said you'd be convicted of murder. Encouraged me to move on with my new life. I thought these were just first dates. I didn't know until..."

He hooked a finger under my chin and lifted my gaze back to his. "Until?"

"I almost died."

We moved to sit on the bed as I told him what happened on my date with Connor and how I jumped overboard. Finally, I said, "I know you won't believe me, but you were the last person I had sex with."

I finally stole a look at him. His face was stoic. "It wouldn't matter to me if you fucked everyone in Costa Rica." He pursed his lips and lifted his eyes to the ceiling. "I mean, I'd have to kill everyone who lived here, but..." He shrugged. "It's doable." He stood up and took my hand. "Come out to the living room."

My mother was asleep on the couch with a dark-haired man taking up space on the chair I usually sat in. "Is she...?"

His lips twisted into a smirk. "Sleeping."

A stylish looking light-haired man with glasses approached us. As he passed Logan my mother's laptop, he unplugged a black box from the USB port. "It's unlocked."

Logan asked him, "Did you get what you needed?"

"Yeah."

Friendly blue eyes slid to me, and Logan said, "Eden this is Bentley. He's my right-hand man."

Bentley's smile was warm. "It's nice to finally meet you, Eden."

Logan jerked his chin at the man in the chair. "That's my brother, Mickey."

My eyes popped and Mickey's grin grew. "Heard about me, have ya?"

I wet my lips and nodded as my gaze returned to my mother. "How can she fall asleep with you here?"

Mickey's gaze narrowed with suspicion, but he seemed to shake it off. "I helped her." He pulled an empty syringe from his pocket. "It's much better than all the screaming, pleading, and crying."

Logan took my mother's laptop to the bar by the kitchen. "Connor Brien Walker." I stiffened, but he glanced up at Bentley briefly before scrolling again. "I'd like to meet him."

"Why?" I couldn't keep the nervousness out of my voice as I looked over his shoulder at the laptop screen.

Logan merely turned the screen towards me. Messages between Connor and my mother, posing as me, were displayed. My jaw clenched as I read through them. She basically agreed to let him rape me, encouraged it even. My scowl briefly lifted to her prone form before returning to the messages. They confirmed that she never loved me. I might have started crying again, but at that point I was numb.

In my state, my gaze had slipped to Mickey. He boldly held my stare before he said, "I haven't seen your mom in a long ass time, but even back then, I knew she was heartless."

I blinked a few times before I answered him. "And she said you were sadistic."

He broke out in a belly laugh. "She wasn't wrong."

"I don't want her to wake up... ever." My voice was as flat as I felt at that moment.

Logan handed the laptop back to Bentley and said, "Let's wrap it up then." Bentley donned a pair of gloves and wiped the electronic down with a cloth.

He turned to me. "Is there anything you want to take back home with you?"

I glanced at Logan, and he dipped his head. "I'll help you."

Bentley tossed him a pair of gloves. "Leave no trace."

"What about me?"

I met Logan's gaze as he said, "Grace will become a missing person. Your prints are expected here. We just need to be careful in case they trace those prints back to you in the States and the FBI gets involved."

"What happens then?"

His smile was tight. "We say nothing and let our lawyers handle it."

Mickey said, "This is still a third world country. I don't think they are going to dig deep enough to get the feds involved. Your mother will be ruled a suicide and you a missing person."

The casual way he said it made me ask, "You do this often?"

He leaned back in my chair and opened his arms wide. "Not as often as your future husband does."

My head whipped around to see Logan glaring at his brother. "You're not telling her anything she didn't already know, Mick."

I blurted, "Future husband?"

That dark look moved to me. "Don't act so shocked, angel. I told you from the very beginning where this was going to end."

He took my arm and led me back to the bedroom. “We can’t take it all. There’s a weight limit for the plane.”

I stiffened as he let me go in front of the closet. “I’ve dropped an entire size since I’ve been here.”

He squinted at me in confusion before running a hand over his face and through his hair. “I didn’t mean you, angel. It’s airspeed and gas and four grown adults...” He shook his head. “You look amazing, by the way.” He took a lock of my much shorter hair and rubbed it between two fingers. “I like what you did here.”

A muffled splash had my heart jerking to a stop. Those men dumped my mother into the pool. He put his arm out as I lurched toward the sound. “You don’t want to witness that.”

I let him pull me into a full embrace. “I don’t know how I feel about this. Everything is so numb right now. What if I regret this later?”

He tipped my face up to his. “This was not your choice. Karla knew exactly what the consequences of her actions were when she made the decision to betray the Society. She’s lucky we aren’t near a den.”

“A what?”

“A safe house for the Society.”

My gut tightened. “Why?”

Rage quickly flashed over his features. “Cause I’d spend weeks killing her for what she did to you.”

My gaze returned to the direction of the pool like I could magically see through walls. His arms tightened around me. “The last time you saw your mother, she was passed out on the couch. That’s the memory you need to keep.”

“I loved her.”

“She should have loved and protected *you*. That’s not your fault either, Eden. Some people can’t love anyone but themselves.” He turned me towards my closet again. "Come on, let's pack up and go home."

Logan

Logan Lurch

When we got in the car, Bentley called the guy we got the SUV from to let him know we were headed back to the airstrip. Then he glanced back at Eden before moving his gaze to me. "Something you both should know. Karla took out a life insurance policy on Grace. It was sizable."

My lips tightened. "That's what she meant by *anything*."

Eden whispered, "Of course she was trying to get me murdered. I was leaving her." Her wide eyes met mine in the darkness of the car. "Who the fuck does that to her own child?"

I gathered her against me as she fought fresh tears yet again. I knew the pain of a parent's betrayal keenly. All I could do was hold space as she grieved, not for a dead mother, but for the loss of hope.

Once at the quiet airstrip, Mickey encouraged her to sit in the copilot's seat on the flight home. He saw her trepidation about getting in the small plane and took it upon himself to give her an important job to focus on. "You'll be my copilot."

She shook her head and back peddled. "I'm not qualified for this."

Mickey grinned at her as Bentley untied the wings.

I said, "Sure you are, angel."

Her gaze moved to Bentley, who was practicing his dance moves as he waited for us to finish talking. "Why was the plane tied down?"

Mick answered, "To keep her from flying away."

Eden rolled her eyes but then glanced at me. Hooking her thumb towards Bentley she asked, "What's his deal?"

"ADHD."

Apparently, Bentley's music wasn't too loud because he said, "Medicated, unlike the psychopath and sadist we are sharing a plane with."

Mick snorted. "Get in the seat behind mine, Bent."

"Great." Bentley glanced at Eden. "Enjoy being smushed all the way forward with daddy long legs sitting behind you."

Mickey said, "It had to be the old Cessna for this mission."

I grunted. "It's fine, let's just go home."

Take off was a little hairy because this airstrip was essentially a dirt road without runway lights, and it was pitch black. Mickey had some sort of sixth sense though and kept the Cessna in the middle until she lifted.

Eden was astonished at how easy flying was.

"It's like the plane *wants* to fly."

Mickey's answering laugh was pure joy. "She wants to do what she was born to do."

He encouraged her to take the controls and taught her what all the gauges meant. She went from sending my brother suspicious glances to curious grins.

I wondered what her mother told her about him. I knew he'd dated Karla for a short time back in college. It had been more of an obligation rather than infatuation. Our father was a stickler for tradition, and Mickey was the oldest heir after all. The thing was, you couldn't control the living once you were dead. The royal son of the Blue-Frosted Rose never married.

After we landed, Mickey offered to take her flying again and she eagerly agreed. Bentley said his goodbyes and rushed off, presumably back to Lakeland to be with his new toy, the hacker. That girl should have been dead already, but Bent and Tor were determined to keep her. I didn't have the bandwidth to stick my nose into their business just yet.

Eden was surely traumatized by all that had happened to her, and she needed my sole focus for a while. I glanced over at her as Pilot, our driver, took us home. "You okay?"

"Yeah, I'm fine." She flashed me a grin that didn't feel sincere. "It's good to be home."

"You'll want to call your father to let him know you're safe, but I think we should wait until after you talk to our attorneys."

Her grin faded. "Attorneys?"

"The police will want to interview you regarding your disappearance. They will keep you out of trouble."

"Oh." Her sigh felt heavy, like the weight she had thrown off during the flight home had resettled on her shoulders.

"You know I won't let anything happen to you. Right?"

Her eyes misted before she broke eye contact. "How is it that an emotionally damaged stalker ended up being the one who protected me?" Her gaze returned to mine. "Why didn't my father come get me instead?"

"Ah, I see."

"What do you see?"

I wanted to pull her into me and kiss those tears away. Instead, I lifted my pant leg and showed her my ankle monitor. "Your father was not able to bypass this little piece of government technology. He wasn't capable of doing what needed to be done in Costa Rica. I could have sent him with a team, but his morality would weigh on his soul."

"So you protected him, too?"

I lifted a shoulder. "It's my job."

"What about *your* soul?"

"You are my soul, Eden."

Her gaze returned to the window as she absorbed what I said. I knew she didn't believe me, yet. It would take time for her to understand my truth when it came to us. Words meant little to her, but I had our entire lives to prove my devotion.

Pilot dropped us off at the front entrance and grabbed Eden's bag as I helped her out of the limo. I glanced at the camera, knowing Josh had looped the system to hide our arrival.

"Thanks, Pilot."

"No worries, boss. Hope everything works out for you and your lady."

I clasped his hand. "See you soon, my friend."

We entered the building, and I watched Eden stiffen as I pressed the button to the top floor. I guessed she thought we'd go directly to her condo. Except, I had her things moved the moment I was released from jail.

Even at such a late hour, Josh greeted us the moment I opened my front door. He was closer to Eden's age, fresh out of college, and newly inducted into the Society.

"Hey, boss. Welcome home." His eager grin gave me flashbacks to when I first started doing tech for the Society.

"Update?" I asked him as I watched Eden's gaze roam my home.

"Your ankle monitor is active. The spare is on your desk. Nobody came by while you were gone. The surveillance loop is still live." He lifted his hand to show that it was bandaged. "And your cat is a demon from hell."

"Attacked you, did he?"

"More than once, sir."

Eden's head whipped around. "You still have your kitten?"

"Of course, I still have the cat. I keep my commitments, even if I must share my home with a feline terrorist."

She gave a low chuckle, and the humor in her eyes stole my breath. It was the first hint that my girl was still inside this bruised shell. "Awe, he can't be that bad."

My lips twisted up. "He can and he is."

Josh gathered his bag and said, "Just don't try to pick it up like I did, and you'll be fine. Damn thing holds a grudge."

A chuckle left me. "That he does. Talk to you tomorrow, Josh."

With that, the kid dipped his head at Eden and slipped out the door.

I sighed as my gaze landed on every tiny mess Josh had left in my condo. A normal person might not notice the rumpled pillow where he sat on my couch or the smudged remote control, but my skin itched to do a deep clean on every surface he'd touched.

Eden's voice brought me back to reality. "Nice place."

"It was."

She opened her mouth to ask why I said that, but a yawn slipped out. "Sorry about that." She grinned sheepishly. "Where do you want me?"

Those five little words had my alter ego clamoring to the forefront of my brain. He wanted her naked and chained spread eagle to our bed. He craved her screams of pleasure turned into painful forced orgasms.

Her grin was replaced with heat as she studied the look on my face. "I mean, I'll probably fall asleep the moment my head hits the pillow, but that never stopped you before."

I blinked at her. She told me what Connor did to her that caused her to literally jump overboard and brave the sea. I figured she wouldn't want to play naked games for a while because of that soon-to-be-dead piece of trash. "Are you serious?"

Her face went red, and her gaze bounced around the room, looking anywhere but at me. "I'm sorry. I just assumed. You're right to want to wait to resume our... whatever we had."

"Stop."

Her spine straightened, mouth snapped shut, and those damned beautiful eyes misted yet again.

Maybe I should let Lurch speak his excitement out loud. "The *Master's* bedroom is at the end of the hall."

She studied my face a heartbeat before asking, "And where does the slave sleep?"

My heart melted. "Oh, angel, there are no slaves here. Only a Mistress. She sleeps next to the Master, naked, legs spread wide and ready at all times."

"So you won't be tying me up in there?"

My laugh was low and full of promise. "I have an entire room for tying my angel up and sullying her wings until they are just as black as my heart."

Her grin was slow to come, but it was lightning to my soul when it finally bloomed. "Show me."

"Not tonight."

She stifled a yawn, further solidifying my decision to wait one more day before I wore out her pussy. "Lead the way, oh dear Master." Until she mocked me with those words.

My hand shot out and gripped her by the throat. Her pupils blew wide as I leaned closer and growled. "Didn't anyone ever tell you that angels shouldn't taunt demons?"

The way her breath sucked in had me grinning like one of those feral demons. At her silence I tilted my head and inhaled her scent. "What? No snarky comeback?" Her lips parted as my fingers tightened. "Unbutton your blouse, little angel. Show me what I've been missing."

Her fingers shook as she worked the buttons that covered those amazing tits. It caused me to study her face. She maintained steady eye contact, and it was desire, not fear, that shone in them. "Bold little angel. Are you really this excited to be my little sex toy for the foreseeable future?"

Her tongue darted out to wet her bottom lip before she nodded slowly. Her shirt parted, and my gaze dropped to her bra as she reached behind her and unclasped it. The moment her torso was bare, I pinned her to the wall as I drank in her beautiful body. A tiny gasp left her lips as I plucked at her tight nipple. One of her hands gripped my wrist where I pinned her to the wall, and the other grabbed the waist of my pants and tugged me closer.

Electricity ran up my spine as my brain just about fried from that little movement. "Oh, you shouldn't have done that, little angel."

Chapter Twenty-Nine

You Said It Was Mine

Eden

I was desperate for Logan's affection, and he seemed oblivious to it. From the moment I saw him bust through the front door in Costa Rica, I craved his touch. Even through the emotional turmoil of my mother's death, I had expected him to rip my clothing off and take me. I wanted him to throw me down and claim me like a bull in a rut, but he treated me like glass. While it was sweet, it made me wonder about things I didn't want to confront. What if he didn't believe me? Was he rethinking our relationship? Did he think I was spoiled fruit now?

As exhausted as I was, I needed him to validate our relationship. Whatever that was. I didn't miss the fact that he had me in his home and told me I was the mistress of this place. But men often do and say things because they feel obligated.

So, I made a desperate move and tried seducing the king.

"Oh, you shouldn't have done that, little angel."

Or devil in this case. Maybe that was why my voice shook as I croaked out. "Why not?"

He leaned in and whispered in my ear. "That little move? Just sealed your fate."

He nipped my ear lobe as his hand slipped under the stretch waistband of my oversized linen beach pants. His fingers nimbly moved under my panties to cup my pussy. "Who does this belong to?"

My lips trembled. "You."

His lips moved down the side of my jaw as his fingers flexed on my neck. "What does this little pussy want?"

My breath left me as his hand tightened on my pussy. "You."

A finger pushed inside me. "Dripping with greed," he murmured as his lips found mine. I'd been dying to kiss him like this since we'd been separated. One hand around my throat and the other down my pants as he devoured me lit a flame and fanned it so much I almost orgasmed from just this kiss.

His finger twitched, and I broke the kiss to breathe through the spasms in my body. Maybe I did orgasm. Maybe that was just a different kind of orgasm than I was used to. A mind-originated orgasm? Because he only had one finger inside me. Was this a kiss-gasm?

His hand withdrew and before I could recover from the loss, he bent and picked me up like a child. Part of me wanted to protest but he was already carrying me down the tall, wide hall, past closed doors and into the master bedroom. The lights flicked on without so much as a word from Logan. This room recognized its owner's presence.

His bed was a massive centerpiece of clean lines and comfort. The walk-in had double glass doors tinted blue. It was bigger than all my closets combined, but he didn't head for the closet or the bed.

The lights to the bathroom also glowed warmly the moment he graced the threshold. If his closet was huge, this bathroom was, well, it was as big as my bedroom downstairs. Along the right was a double sink vanity in charcoal and blue. The middle of the space was taken up by a raised infinity tub the size of a small lap pool. You couldn't swim in it, but both of us could float comfortably.

He headed for the shower just beyond. My jaw dropped as he spoke to the console. "Temperature, eighty. Rain."

The light on the ceiling turned blue around the rain machine, making the mermaid-scale tile glimmer.

The rustle of clothing behind me had me slipping out of my favorite linen pants before Logan did something crazy like rip them off me.

His strong body pressed against my back as he walked me closer to the shower. One of the glass panels slid open allowing us to step inside. It closed the moment we were clear of it. "What do you do when the power goes out?"

His chuckle was low. "The power never goes out here."

I tried to face him, but he urged me up on the low step that led to a long bench seat along the back. "How is that even possible? Wait, don't tell me, Blue-Frosted Rose magic?"

Instead of letting me sit down, he placed my hands against the tiny shimmering tiles and used his foot to spread my legs. Water rained on my shoulder blades and tracked down my spine. He reached around and palmed both my breasts as his teeth grazed my neck. "Generators, silly."

He bit me, and I yelped at the sudden crush of his teeth. He immediately pinched both nipples and rolled them between the pads of his fingertips, sending sparks of pleasure coursing through me.

"Oh." The moan slipped from my lips, and my hips pushed backwards against his stomach.

He licked the spot he bit with another low chuckle before kissing the pain away. "Handheld, pulse."

My eyes flew open at the odd words that... "Oh."

He moved the jet of pulsing water between my legs, and I exclaimed, "My god!"

"Be still."

It was a lot of sudden sensation. I pressed my forehead against the tile with a shudder. "It's too much."

He dipped down, and I felt the press of his cock against me. "You asked for too much. Now, wet my tip, angel, and take me home."

His free hand parted my pussy, allowing the jet to pound against my clit. My body jerked back, driving myself onto his cock, squeezing his tip inside me. His hand went to my throat as he pressed the jet against my pussy, shooting the stream between my lower lips and against my clit. "Be still, Eden," he spoke through clenched teeth. "It's been months since I've come, and you will not make me spill before I'm ready."

His hips rolled slightly as he adjusted the jet of water until I stiffened, forcing myself to stay still.

"There we go," he whispered roughly, "right on that naughty little clit."

"Naughty?" My voice was a high-pitched squeal.

He nipped my shoulder as I vibrated under his mouth and that unforgiving jet of water. "Don't tell me you never once touched it in all these months we've been apart? Touched my clit as you thought about me?"

"Oh, fuck." The orgasm was sharp and punishing. The jet of water pounding, pulsing and unending. My entire body quaked with the sensation.

He rolled his hips and pushed deep, his thick cock stretching my inner walls as they convulsed wildly. Filling me with deep pressure as I jerked and wiggled in an attempt to evade the jet. His free arm slipped around my waist as he pushed up with his legs, impaling me on his cock, suspending me on my toes.

He moved the jet of water in small circles as he pulled out and slammed back inside with a groan. Each thrust hit deep inside me, pushed past bottom and seemed to drill deeper even as I levitated on my toes. I was impossibly full, and everytime that jet hit my clit, I squealed and my knees buckled. Dropping the jet, he groaned his release so deep it surprised me when I didn't taste it.

"Open up that womb, angel."

The jet sprayed my feet, pulsing as his hand secured my hips. Fingers bit into my skin as he gave a few short thrusts and slammed his hips against my ass.

"Logan!"

"That's right. I'm coming inside you."

His hips rolled several more times. "And it feels so fucking good." He ground his tip against my cervix. "You're going to make me a daddy, Eden. Half demon, half angel."

I gritted my teeth against the words, but they came out anyway. "I'm on birth control."

He didn't skip a beat. No sharp intake of breath and no anger in his voice as he said, "Not anymore, angel."

Logan

Logan Lurch

With gentle hands I washed and dried my tarnished angel. The yawns were coming more frequently as I put her in my bed. She snuggled under the heavy duvet with a satisfied smile. My bed was a big squishy marshmallow. After spending my childhood sleeping on floors, couches, and hard beds with scratchy sheets, I had an affinity for luxurious comfort when it came to bedtime. I slipped into bed next to her and hit the power off button on the remote control. Darkness swallowed us, and she scooted closer. I opened my arm and let her press against me.

"Five hours ago, you thought I was selling my body to random men on the internet."

I stayed silent waiting for the other shoe to drop.

"Yet, you seem to have moved me in with you."

I inhaled. "Is there a question coming soon?"

"I don't know. I guess I just want to know your thought process."

"About?"

"Us?"

I turned towards her, and pulled her close. "What happened before doesn't matter, Eden. You're mine. You were mine then. You're mine now and forever."

"Do you think I was stupid for not figuring it out sooner?"

It was my turn to yawn. "No. You see the best in the people you love. That's a wonderful trait, angel. It's what I love most about you."

"You love me?"

I sighed heavily before rolling her onto her back. "I guess I need to prove it to you."

Truth was, I was addicted to this woman the moment I tasted her pleasure. I could never get enough of her moans, gasps, and sighs. That night, I played her like a symphony for hours before she passed out.

My erection woke me up in the morning. The sun was just beginning to illuminate my window. My hand stretched across the bed looking for her before her breath fanned my engorged cock. I lifted the covers off my chest as I felt her cheek brush my tip.

"Angel..." I warned sleepily.

"No peeking," she quipped.

I dropped the duvet and let my gaze lift to the ceiling. If my little angel wanted some alone time with the object that defiled her, so be it. It only took five minutes before I realized my girl wasn't racing towards a finish line. She was sauntering down a lazy, winding trail as she nuzzled and licked my shaft only to lay her head on my thigh and slowly stroke me with her hand. Then she lifted her head and encased my tip in her fiery mouth so her tongue could torment me further.

My hands fisted the sheet to keep them from fisting her hair and forcing my cock down her throat. My knees locked to keep them from writhing wildly with pleasure. "Fuck, Eden, you're driving an already crazy man insane."

Her laugh was pure happiness. "You said it was my dick."

"It is, but we have a meeting with the attorneys in..." She stole my words as she sucked my cock deep. The heat and pressure alone were enough to send me over the edge, but when she flicked her tongue over my frenulum my toes curled. "Keep doing that, and I'm going to come."

She sucked harder and let me go with a pop. "I'm hungry, Logan. Will you feed me?" Her voice was small, like a spoiled little princess, and that made me want to punish her.

But she was back on my cock, greedily bobbing up and down. Tenting the duvet like a damned under-the-bed monster climbing between the sheets to murder someone. My legs parted to make room for her to settle between them.

I groaned when she let me go yet again. I throbbed with need. Would she ever let me come? The under-the-bed monster was moving again. My cock was in her fist as the duvet lifted higher and higher. I felt her thighs around mine right as the blanket lifted just enough to give me a peek. Her pussy hovered over my cock, poised for penetration.

She lifted more, and my gaze went up her body as her head emerged from the duvet. She widened her legs enough so that my tip touched her parted pussy. Then she slowly circled her clit with it as my precum painted her lower lips. She threw her head back with a moan as she masturbated using the mouth of my cock. Fuck the sight had me wishing my penis had a tongue and some suction to make her squeal like she had last night.

"I thought you said you were hungry."

Those stunning eyes opened and met mine. "I am." The tension in her voice had me lifting my hips. She gasped, rotating my cock faster.

I blindly reached for the nightstand until I found my phone. Tugging it closer I unlocked it and hit the call button.

"Yes, sir?"

"Pilot, would you please pick up breakfast for two at that place I like?" My voice was tight and breathy, but I got the words out.

"Yes, sir. Anything special?"

I met her gaze. She was so fucking close. "Anything in particular?"

She frowned. "Bacon, eggs?"

"You heard her?"

"Yes, sir. I'll be there in exactly forty-five minutes."

I hung up and put the phone back on the nightstand just in time to watch Eden's blissful orgasm bloom across her face. I would never get tired of watching her come. But what I craved most was feeling her come from the inside.

My hands moved to her hips. I adjusted her trembling body and pulled her down on me. The wet heat encasing me had my legs stiffening and my spine tingling. "Fuck, angel. You feel amazing."

She gasped. "So do you. So full of you."

I bent my knees and started thrusting from underneath.

"Oh God." She panted.

My thumb dropped lower and found the top of her clit. I put steady pressure on it, pinching it between my thumb and thrusting cock. The tremble that rocked her made me wish I had tentacles, so I could hold her body steady, pluck those nipples, tickle her ass, and choke her all at the same time.

My one free hand slid up her body to toy with her breasts as I fucked her harder from underneath. She gasped and fell forward as orgasm number two washed through her.

I planted my feet deep into the mattress, knees bent as I wrapped both arms around her, holding her steady as I thrust faster, chasing my own release. "I'm so addicted to you, Eden."

"Come inside me, Logan."

I had planned on it, but her voice in my ear had my cock kicking with consensual delight. I pushed deep, holding her tight. My face buried in her neck, groaning against her skin as pure intense pleasure washed over me.

Before my balls quit pumping, I rolled us over and lifted onto my hands. My legs widened and my ass clenched as I started moving again. I pushed past the intense sensations, forcing my body to submit to my will as I continued fucking into her.

Her legs stiffened as I ground deep. "Logan!" Her nails bit into my flesh as she thrashed under me, somewhere in between wanting to pull me closer while also fighting for her life to get free of me. I captured her wrists and pinned them above her head with one hand and rode her until my balls exploded.

I kissed her wet cheeks tenderly and whispered, "Don't move." A hiss exploded out of me as I slowly withdrew my waning cock from her succulent heat.

She whispered hoarsely. "You're going to be the death of me."

I headed for the playroom down the hall. "Probably, but not for some time."

I had converted a guest room into a dungeon just for my fallen angel before I left. It was far from finished, but instead of chaining her to the bed as I had originally intended, now I could take my time and really give in to my alter ego's plans. I found what I was looking for in a box on the dresser and returned to my little angel obediently waiting for me as I left her.

I knelt between her knees and opened the box.

She lifted onto her elbows and looked down her body at me. "What is that?"

I gave her a devilish smirk as I moved the plug to her leaking vagina. "You will wear this until we get back from our meeting."

I watched the device stretch her as the bulbous part was inserted. Her body closed around the thin neck, and I adjusted the flat base to line up with her labia. With two fingers I parted them and pressed the base firmly in place.

"That's not going to stay in there."

My attention went back to the box. "Oh, ye of little faith."

The remote was primed and ready. One push of the plus button and Eden's eyes bulged wide. "Oh my God! What the heck?"

"The knot is inflatable. It will stay put for as long as I want it to."

She shifted uncomfortably, and I let off the inflate button to give the vaginal plug a gentle tug. I rocked it a bit and she groaned. "That feels weird."

I gave her a tight smile as I downloaded the app onto my phone so I could continue to play with her remotely. "Come on, angel. Let's get you ready."

Chapter Thirty

Gaul Is The Bestest Boy

Scout

The days might have bled into weeks for all I knew. The blond man said he had to go on a quick trip, but that Tor would take care of me while he was gone. At first, I had no idea what he meant by take care of me. Nor did I care.

My greatest fear had come true, and it wasn't being kidnapped. A vibration hummed inside my body making my hands tremble and my body ache. Even the simple task of wiping my own ass was sometimes impossible. I was physically sick.

He peered through the bars of my new cage with narrow eyes. "How long have you been using?"

I glared up from the floor where I cradled my knees to my chest. "I'm sick." I was shaking so badly my voice wavered.

His cool demeanor didn't shift. "You're obviously going through withdrawal."

I put my head back on my knees. "Maybe I'm just cold from being naked and exhausted from the sexual torture you've put me through. How many days ago?"

Torrid didn't react. This guy's mask was unshakable. "Doubtful. How much do you drink? Or do you use something else?"

I stared at his shadow along the wall to my right. "I drink just enough wine to keep the horrors of my past at bay, but never too much."

The shadow's head tilted slightly. "What else?"

I twisted to glare at the man again. "What do you mean, what else? Isn't it enough to be born into the skin trade with your only destiny being an organ donor?"

"You were rescued as a child."

"And now I'm back in captivity."

"You should have stuck with chasing child predators if you didn't want to end up in a cage."

I fingered the collar he'd put around my neck before moving me to this oversized pet crate. "I thought you were, but maybe you just enjoy buggering your dog which is just as bad."

He frowned. "Look, I'm just trying to figure out what you need."

"I need to go home."

His head shook slowly. "That's not going to happen, pet."

"Then I'm not going to help you guys find that girl."

He barked a laugh. "You have no idea who you betrayed for a bit of cash. Where do you think Bentley is right now?"

I put my head down and turned my face away from the man to address the shadow. "Don't care."

The shadow said, "He didn't need you after all."

"So, what now? You gonna kill me?" Death would bring peace at this point.

His deep voice was flat. "We all die eventually."

"Wonderful, a philosopher," I deadpanned with a roll of my eyes.

"Until I get the order to kill you, I'm responsible for your well-being. But since you are unwilling to help, I'll order your medical records from tech and have someone toss your apartment."

My spine stiffened as I shot him yet another worthless glare. "Don't toss my apartment. I have some expensive electronics in there. I drink wine, smoke weed, and take a prescribed sleep aid."

He pulled his phone out of his back pocket, and it lit up his face as he shot off a quick text to someone. The lines on his face were sharper in the glow, but his eyes were still cold as both thumbs skimmed over the glass. This man lifted weights religiously; even his hands were thick, and the fact that he was texting so nimbly was stunning.

He returned the phone to his back pocket and put a key to the padlock of my cage. I stood up on shaky legs and put my back to the thick bars as he took the leash from a hook on the wall next to the door.

"What are you doing?"

He opened the door and stepped inside my cell. "It's time for your walk. The doctor will be here in an hour."

The snap to the leash came at me, and I threw my hands between us. "No."

His massive hand engulfed both of my wrists, and I lunged to the side with a scream, but the snap found the ring on my collar. "Let me go! You bastard! I am not your stupid dog."

He let my wrists go and gave the collar a sharp tug. My hands wrapped around the thick leash as I shifted my weight and dug my heels into the floor.

He turned his back on me and just pulled me along with him. "Gaul is smarter than you."

My fingers found the clip at my throat, and he growled a sound that made the hair on my arms stand. "You don't want to do that."

I tried to put enough slack on the leash to unclip it from the collar. "Fuck you."

He faced me with a feral grin. "Fuck around and find out." He tossed the leash at me.

I unclipped it, threw it to the ground and ran for the door as he just stood there. Over my beating heart and ragged breath, I heard a low whistle and the click of claws on polished concrete.

The sun blinded me as I stumbled into the light and into an empty parking lot surrounded by palmetto bushes and pines. Tears streamed down my cheeks, but I found the driveway and took off towards the exit. The pavement burned the soles of my feet, and at first, I was grateful for the dirt road.

But as I rounded the corner of the driveway my heart sank so deep my legs quit moving. We were surrounded by miles of Florida wilderness. I turned around, looking for any trails or a place to hide and froze when I saw Torrid holding Gaul's leash. The silent dog's ears were trained on me. He wore a large muzzle, but I swore the dog was grinning as wide as his master was.

Torrid leaned down and unleashed the rottweiler. "Bring her back."

A scream caught in my throat as the huge dog immediately barreled towards me. There was nowhere to go. Nothing to climb. Nowhere to hide. I was naked and vulnerable and not fast enough to flee, not healthy enough to fight. And that dog would be on me in mere seconds.

My hands flew up and I braced myself for his attack.

But instead of body slamming me, the dog ducked left and circled behind me, barking like a fiend. I faced him and he charged forward acting like he'd bite me. I didn't want to find out if he could get those teeth through that muzzle, so I backed up. "No! Bad dog! I thought we were friends."

He kept pushing me back toward his master.

"Go home! Bad dog."

Before I knew it the dog's leash was being clipped to my collar. "He is home, and he's the bestest boy." He patted Gaul's side and praised him. "Aren't you? What a good boy."

He stood up and faced me, his serious eyes boring holes into me, and I felt more exposed than ever. "You, on the other hand, naughty girl. Now you need a bath."

"Oh goody, I like baths."

He led me back to the warehouse like a farm animal. "I thought you realized by now there are consequences to your actions. Especially after nipping Bentley."

"I'm already fucking sick. Don't hurt me."

"Should have thought about that before you misbehaved."

I folded my arms around my naked body as I followed him. "Don't start with the good girl, bad girl, bullshit."

"You are in no position to make demands, pet."

"Fuck you."

"Careful what you wish for. I don't think you can handle fucking me."

He glanced over his shoulder as we stepped onto the hot pavement. I could hear my poor soles sizzling as I picked up the pace.

Torrid sighed before grabbing me by the arm and dipping to pick me up. "I should let you deal with the consequences of your stupid decisions."

I pursed my lips and looked away. Torrid's scent was annoyingly pleasant, and there was no escape while he carried me.

"Bentley will be back today."

Keeping my face turned away I quipped, "That was quick. Did he find the girl?"

"Like I said: didn't need your help after all."

Instead of carrying me to the front of the warehouse, he walked to the side of it. He sat me down and opened a door to a bathroom. It was a bare-bones campground style with one toilet, sink, and a shower without privacy. Torrid stepped in, closed the door and unclipped the leash.

I faced him with a frown. He folded his arms across the expanse of his stubborn chest and lifted an eyebrow.

Torrid

Torrid Gaul

She huffed, puffed, and even stomped her bare foot, but eventually she used the toilet and the shower. I stayed silent until she threw her towel on the floor.

"Pick it up."

She folded her arms across her breasts and set her jaw.

I kept my face and voice neutral. "Pick it up and hang it on the hook or leave it on the dirty floor. Either way, you'll use that towel three more times before you get a fresh one."

She huffed but picked the towel up and shook it out before hanging it up on the wall.

With the leash in hand, I crooked my finger.

Her gaze fell to the clip. "I'm not going to run again. Not when you'll just sick your dog on me. Normal dogs play fetch with balls, ya know."

I crooked my finger again and when she followed my silent command, I gave her a smile and said, "Nothing about Gaul is normal."

She ducked my hand when I went to caress her cheek. "Whatever."

I wrapped the leash around my hand and gave it a tug, bringing her closer to me. She closed her eyes and turned her face as I brushed the back of my forefinger across the freckles on her olive tan cheek. "Your defiance is highly arousing, pretty little pet."

Green eyes lined with coal lashes flashed with anger. "Fuck. You."

"Not until you beg for my touch."

A hollow laugh barked from her. "That will never happen."

My smart watch lit up with a notification from the entrance. I reached behind me and opened the door. "Come on. The doctor will be here shortly."

I led her back into the warehouse and into the medical wing. Her feet slowed as she passed the operation theater. "For organ harvesting?"

How she knew what that room was for was beyond me. The door was open, but the lights were out. "Sometimes. If there's a need and we have a match."

She grabbed the leash and dug her heels into the tile floor, stopping me. She waited until I faced her to ask, "Children?"

"Kids aren't allowed at the warehouse."

Her eyes thinned. "Then who?"

I shrugged and admitted, "You, if the order comes down to make you disappear."

Her throat bobbed on a swallow before she nodded once and let go of the leash. Her feet didn't slow until I flicked on the lights of the gyno room.

"Why are we in here?" She eyed the table suspiciously.

"Full physical. Get on the table."

She crossed her arms and frowned as her gaze bounced around the room. I agreed the table with all its straps, stirrups, and tools looked ominous. The room wasn't created to be cozy.

Dr. Griffen shuffled in. "Good afternoon, Tor."

His bushy gray brows lifted as he watched Divina get on the table. "What do we have here?"

I waved my arm towards the woman. "Dr. Griffen, this is Divina Collins."

Dr. Griffen jotted the name on the clipboard I gave him. All our medical records were old school. No copies and easy to destroy when needed. "And how old is Miss Divina?"

I opened my mouth, but she said, "I am twenty-six."

The old doctor lifted his gaze to her and made a slow perusal of her body. "Pretty."

Her glare slid towards me, and I flashed my teeth. "I agree."

He shuffled up to her and put his stethoscope in his ears. "Breathe normally."

He did all the usual stuff before he said, "Time to lay down and put those pretty little feet in the stirrups."

Divina's face pinched before sliding her glower to me. "I do not consent to this."

I stepped forward as the doctor said, "They rarely do, sweetheart."

Cradling her head, I helped her lay back on the table. Her body was shaking but not from the temperature. Green eyes pleaded with me for help. Somewhere deep I knew that she was asking for more than just escape, but for a way to deal with this situation in a way she didn't have to control herself.

Nodding slightly, I reached over her trembling tits to grab the first of many straps. The moment I buckled her in she whispered, "Tighter."

After tightening the straps around her torso, I lifted and secured each leg to the stirrups before moving to her arms. She was laid out like she was on a sacrificial cross as the doctor adjusted the stirrups and table to his liking. High and wide open.

I put a blanket over her in an effort to ease her shaking before stepping behind the doctor to watch over his shoulder.

His gloved hand parted her labia before he swiped a thumb over her clit. Her thighs tensed against the restraints, but the doctor merely lifted the hood and tested her again. She jumped and blew out a breath. "Has she come for you yet?"

"Multiples."

"Very nice." He parted her wider to expose her urethra. "Hand me the catheter."

It was already lubricated and set up to receive a urine sample. He deftly slid the tube inside her, and urine trickled out into the collection bag attached to the end as Scout whimpered. I put my hand on her calf and said, "Just relax."

"Easy for you to say. You're not the one with a tube in your bladder."

The doctor removed the catheter and sealed the bag. He put it on the metal tray and lubed the clear plastic speculum. It slipped inside her easily and he cranked her vagina wide.

His headlamp illuminated her lovely little cervix. It jumped as he swabbed it for her PAP.

"How long have you had the IUD in?"

"Uh, a year?"

Dr. Griffen glanced at me. "Leave it or remove?"

Scout gave a panicked, "What?"

I said, "Leave it for now."

The doctor nodded and removed the speculum. He lubed a finger and pushed it into her anus. She choked on a swallow and struggled not to cough. He finished his exam, snapped off his rubber gloves and said, "I'll need to take some blood to run a full battery of tests. I'd suggest using a condom until they come back."

I took a soft, wet cloth and gently cleaned the lube off her glistening pussy and ass as he moved to her arm and started collecting said blood from our patient. Her legs shook wildly as I took my time. Her clit slowly swelled as I intentionally cleaned around it. My fingers opened her labia ever so gently as I cleaned every nook and cranny she had down there.

"Make sure Bentley gets a copy of the results. The fool already had his dick in her mouth."

Scout snapped, "If I have an STD, it will be because Bentley gave it to me."

Dr. Griffen chuckled. "Bentley is clean. He tests more than the rest of them."

When I was finished, I let the backs of my fingers caress her pussy as Dr. Griffen collected his vials of blood and said, "I'll go process these in the lab."

"Thank you, doctor."

The old man collected his urine sample and shuffled down the hall towards the onsite lab.

Scout lifted her head. "What are you doing?"

My lips pulled tight, but I didn't answer her, I just continued petting her pussy.

Her head dropped to the pillow with a groan. "I'm not begging."

"Yet."

She took a deep breath, and her legs relaxed for the first time since I'd strapped her into the stirrups. I rewarded her by letting my knuckle nudge her clit. She let that deep breath out before she said, "Please stop."

I stepped back and patted her leg before unstrapping it. "See what happens when you stop spitting fire at me and say please?"

She waited to respond until she sat up. My little pet looked me straight in the eyes and said, "I do not have to be polite to my kidnapper. I don't have to pretend to be nice to anyone."

I grinned. "Keeping it real. That's what I like about you, pet."

I clipped the leash on her and on the way back to her kennel, I asked, "You got a boyfriend looking for you out there?"

"Not really. Why do you ask?"

"The IUD. It suggests things about you."

Her back went ramrod straight. "What things? Like I'm a slut because I'm responsible about birth control? Because I have an IUD I must sleep around? Is that why the doctor is testing me for STDs?"

I lifted both hands. "Whoa, slow down, pet. I didn't say those things, you did."

Her fists went to her hips. "But you were thinking it."

"Actually, I asked what I was thinking. One thing you'll learn about me is that I'm direct and blunt. Another thing, I don't give a shit how many dicks have been inside you. The tests are preliminary for all captives we may need to harvest. Somebody might need that pretty little womb of yours."

Her face screwed up. "That is just creepy and disgusting."

I reached around her to open the door to her cage. "Yeah." That was an accurate description of what I did for my Society. "We can't all be businessmen."

She walked in, and I unclipped the leash and locked the door. She hugged herself as she stared at me through the bars. "Why do you do this? This is America. You could be a businessman if you wanted to."

My hand curled around the bar as I leaned in. My lips twisted up in a feral grin. "When it comes to protecting my Society, I prefer to get my hands bloody."

Her eyes narrowed and she tilted her head curiously. "But I'm no threat to your stupid boy's club, unless you really are trafficking children."

"I know for a fact we do not hurt children." My grin widened. "Our members are constantly monitored, and the predators are culled on a regular basis. It is the primary reason we have a harvesting room." I pushed off the bars. "And, my dear little pet, you became an enemy when you helped put Logan Dalton in jail." I strode away from her.

"Karla told me—"

"Lies that you believed without verifying. That's on you, pet. Not me."

Bentley

Bentley Hacker

The night we abducted Divina Collins, my team broke into her office and home to take every electronic she owned. Once it was set up in our command center, they worked around the clock to break her security and reveal all her secrets.

I leaned over to peer at the list of over seven thousand usernames she'd gathered from one hacking session on the dark web.

"None of those better be Society members."

Jeanie glanced over her shoulder at me. "We are going through them now."

I refused to turn away from the absolute ick I found in Scout's work. The horrified looks from my team matched my own. I understood Scout's passion for bringing justice to this part of the web. She was once one of those children, living in misery and destined to become spare parts to someone wealthy enough to buy them.

A fucking commodity.

Liberated by chance.

And from the information I could find, she clawed her way through her education and rehabilitation just to jump right back into that world for revenge and justice. She used her trauma to help the helpless, and her golden heart landed her right back into captivity.

Is it a full circle of life and death?

I didn't know, but it didn't sit well with me.

While Logan had given her a temporary stay of execution, I knew it truly wasn't his decision alone. Even if she agreed to her situation, a communal of uninvolved men would ultimately determine her fate. If it went badly, a date would be set and Torrid would do his job.

I inhaled deeply and blew my breath out slowly, causing Jeanie to glance at my face once again. As if reading my mind, she said, "This hacker is brilliant."

"Yeah," I said heavily, "keep working on that list."

I picked up my laptop and started my own hunt. I'd give Scout the man who put an old video of her on the dark web no matter how short her life would be. His life would be shorter, and his death would be hers to command.

An hour later I had a name. Winston Adam Tallon. The sixty-two-year-old man lived in Oklahoma with his wife and adult son. I sent the information I had to our midwestern division for pick up and extrication to Lakeland before turning my attention to nailing down Connor Walker.

While Winston would be a quick smash and grab, Connor had a little more protection than the aged pedophile. I needed to get inside Connor's financial life before grabbing the rapist.

I sent what I had on Connor to Jasper. When I heard his email ping a notification I said, "That's from me. Get inside his secretary's system."

Jasp nodded quickly and picked up the phone to start his scam, where he convinced Connor's secretary that he was hired by the company to remotely install antivirus on her computer. She'd give him access, and he'd install our virus that gave us everything we would ever need from the network she used. And that would take time.

I left BFR tech command with Divina haunting my soul, and she wasn't even dead yet. My injured hand raked through my blond curls, and I shook my head. The image of her green eyes holding mine as I fucked her mouth kept returning. Amidst the fire and venom, there were flashes of something else. Maybe I was just imagining the desire and pleasure. I wanted her to take enjoyment from me, and my brain formed that experience. Memories aren't always reliable, but damned if her face, those freckles, that long dark hair, and her eyes felt honest.

How did this woman become as embedded in me as the teeth marks in my hand?

Instead of turning towards home, the place that called to me all day, I headed east towards Lakeland.

A tap to my smart watch and a few short rings through my car's speakers, and Torrid answered the phone. "Yo."

"How is she?"

His baritone laugh was dry and full of knowing. "Relieved to find out you did not give her an STD."

"Explain."

"Didn't check your personal email, did ya?"

"Too busy sorting through her messy life and doing damage control."

"Dr. Grif sent the results of her physical. According to him, she already has a few matches. She'll save more than a few lives."

"She already has saved more than a few lives."

"Spill."

"I'll be there in forty minutes."

"Just in time for her punishment."

I smirked. "Did she bite Gaul?"

His laugh was louder. "She had a brief bout of freedom."

"So, Gaul bit her."

"No, the damn dog likes her more than he should."

I sighed and admitted, "Same."

I hung up the phone, turned up my music, and drove to the warehouse. My fingers drummed the steering wheel in time with the beat as I sang along, getting lost in sound until I turned my vehicle off.

Her scent enveloped me the moment I stepped into the large space. A cell had been set up in the corner, but it was empty. A muffled sound of terror had me moving towards the back. I jerked to a halt as I rounded the corner. My eyes slowly savored what was displayed before me.

Torrid was sitting in a recliner, Gaul at his side, but instead of watching a game like usual, he was watching... "Fuck, Tor." My voice rumbled with envy.

His gaze remained locked on the woman suspended against the wall. "Pull up a chair."

I also couldn't look away as I moved to the wet bar and poured myself a squat glass of Scotch.

Torrid had mounted the Sybian about four feet up the wall. Scout was gagged and mounted on the rounded saddle, ankles and arms chained to the wall as the textured pad and custom dildo hummed relentlessly against her bare pussy. Tears poured from her eyes as they rolled back in her head. Her tits shook as she came, and clearly not for the first time.

"How long has she been there?"

"Five minutes."

"Double penetration?"

He turned to look at me. "Nah, her ass needs some training."

My gaze thinned with doubt. Torrid had never been one to give a single fuck about tearing up an ass before. Especially one that was attached to an organ donor. "Training huh?"

"She's damaged there. Anal is going to take some work before she'll enjoy it."

His dark eyes were almost black with blown pupils as his attention returned to Scout who was still in mid-orgasm. The Sybian did that to some women: prolonged their orgasms until they almost passed out.

Torrid turned the machine off, and Scout screamed in frustration and jerked on the binds. She tried her best to ride the sex saddle, but suspended as she was, she couldn't get purchase to grind on the pad or cock inside her.

I sneered at my old friend's smirking face. "You are one sinister son of a bitch."

"Don't talk about my mama like that."

At Tor's tone, Gaul lifted his head and met my gaze. I lifted my hands. "Sorry."

Torrid snorted but started the dick inside Scout once more. The gorgeous woman whimpered behind her ball gag and gave Torrid a pleading look. A look I'd not soon forget.

The dildo was probably the thickest we had but it was on the slowest setting. Not enough thrust or vibration to send her over the edge, yet just enough to make her crazy to come.

He glanced at my glass and said, "She's going through withdrawals. Doc gave her a benzo."

"Yeah, I noticed the cases of wine on the footage we took from her apartment."

He turned the knob up and she moaned a high-pitched sound. "I'll get her addicted to something else while she's here."

I glanced down at the tent in his joggers. Tor's cock wasn't the biggest I'd seen. Lord knew Logan had him in length, but he was girthy and long enough to make a girl squeal in pain.

"So, you've had a taste?"

He snorted as he shut off the sex machine and watched her jerk and struggle through another denied orgasm. "Nope." He popped the *p* and my brows lifted. I'd never known Torrid not to take what he wanted, and clearly his cock knew what it wanted.

"Why not?"

"She needs to beg harder."

"I think she's begging now."

Scout nodded emphatically, eyes trained on Torrid.

"Besides, I'd like to ride that machine while I watch you put that big, black—"

"Don't go there, asshole."

Gaul sat up to eye me again. I ignored the hell hound this time and apologized to my friend. "Sorry."

"But you can ride the machine when she's done getting it wet for you."

He clicked on the vibrator along with the dildo function, and Scout's eyes rolled up as her back arched. Her legs shook wildly right before he clicked both functions off. The way she struggled to deal with her waning orgasm had me slipping my hand down my slacks to fist my erection.

"I swear to all the gods, if you pull that out while I'm sitting next to you, I'm going to let my dog bite it off and use it as a chew toy. There will be no reattaching it."

I said dryly. "And here I was kind of hoping you'd suck it."

"If anyone is sucking anything, it will be *my* dick."

I glanced down at his erection. "Is that an invitation?"

He scowled at me but slipped his joggers down exposing himself. His cock was so fucking hard it looked painful. The electricity of hyper awareness jolted through me. We'd never done anything to each other before, but we'd done plenty to others together. Occasionally we'd shared a woman while staring at each other, but...

I slipped onto the floor between his legs and lifted his cock to my mouth. I waited for him to stop me, but he merely adjusted to give me more room to take care of him. I didn't know what was going on with our friendship, but I wasn't about to question my luck.

Scout said something like, "Oh my fucking god," but it was too muffled to hear clearly. I silently agreed with Scout as I cupped his tight balls. I was sure Torrid hadn't touched himself in days, even though she'd tormented him with her naked presence. His thick tip was salty with precum as I swirled my tongue around it. I moaned a low sound, just for his ears as I bobbed on him. His stomach muscles fluttered right before his hand threaded through my hair gently. His touch shifted things in my chest.

The sex machine rumbled behind me, and Scout squealed again, but I was so focused on making my brother come I paid no attention to her. His gaze moved from what I was doing to the entertainment hanging on the wall. Right as she started to come, he shut off the machine.

Her scream of frustration was the catalyst he needed, and I swallowed every ounce of pleasure he gave me. He grabbed the back of my head and pushed me down on his pumping cock. "Fuck, Bent," he hissed and lifted my head, opening his eyes to watch me lick his semen from the tip.

I grinned up at him through the smudges on my glasses. "That good, huh?"

He gave me a scowl before glaring at Scout. "That was your fault, pet."

She made a questioning noise of alarm.

"Something else you'll pay for later."

He tucked himself away and pressed a button that lowered the arm the Sybian was attached to. I returned to my seat slowly as he unchained Scout and pulled her off the sex machine. The cock glistened with her juices as I removed my clothing. He hadn't used the thickest dildo we had on her, which said way too much about how he felt about Scout.

He had her on her knees, fixing a spreader bar between them to keep her legs wide before cuffing her hands together and suspending them high above her head in front of the device.

"Touch her all you want, but she doesn't get to come until she begs me for it."

I hiked a leg over the much lower sex machine and slowly worked the tip of the dildo inside me.

Scout maintained eye contact with me as I smiled at her. "What? Are you judging me right now?"

Her eyes popped wide as I wrapped an arm around her middle and tugged her towards me.

"He's straight, I'm bi, and you drive both of us crazy."

I turned on the machine as I chose a nipple to torment. The vibration in my balls and the thrust of the dong in my ass had my cock jerking with each movement as I closed my mouth around the peak of her tit.

She undulated and moaned as I nipped and sucked her. My free hand moved between her legs, and she shook violently as I toyed with her clit.

I pulled my mouth off her breast and put my cheek between them.

"I know, I'm a piece of shit for playing with you like this. Especially after what you've been through, but I'm so fucking enamored with you right now."

I slipped two fingers inside her and said, "And Torrid gets to spend all his downtime with you. I can't believe he hasn't tasted you yet."

I pulled my fingers free and moved them to her back door, spreading her slickness on her anus slowly. Her eyes popped wider as my middle finger gently pressed inside her. I took her nipple in my mouth again and sucked as I finger fucked her ass.

"I'm going to do everything I can to save your life." I met her gaze once again. "But it will ultimately be your choice. Us or falling into a peaceful everlasting sleep."

She swallowed hard as a fresh set of tears fell down her cheeks. I hugged her tight as my hand left her pussy to stroke my jerking cock. She needed to see that I was just as much a deviant scum as the men she hunted for a living.

Chapter Thirty-One

Depraved Angel

Eden

I was surprised when I found I could walk normally with the plug inside me. It was by far not a normal feeling to be this full while doing mundane things like showering and dressing. I opted for a blue A-line skirt that landed just below my knees and a cream button-up blouse for our meeting at the attorney's office.

The driver, Pilot, was polite and kind as we got into the limo. "Your breakfast is in the cooler to keep it warm."

Logan laid out the foam plates and cutlery between us, and we ate our breakfast like my pussy wasn't stuffed full of inflated silicone and his morning cum. When we finished, he cleaned up and sat back to enjoy the ride to Tampa.

My gaze kept returning to Logan like a magnet. I would pull my eyes away, but they just wanted to look at him. His sexy body was completely relaxed, and yet he held a commanding presence over and above what his tailored suit projected.

"You alright, Eden?"

I glanced at the driver and swallowed. "Yes. I ugh..."

He leaned forward and hit a button that raised a tinted divider between the front and back of the expansive limo. "Spit it out."

I took a sip of my sweet tea to wet my dry mouth. "Are you going to remove this thing from me before we get there?"

The corner of his lip twitched. "Remove your panties and come here." He patted his thigh and ripped off my cotton briefs. They caught on my heels, but I straddled Logan's lap anyway.

He pulled out his phone with one hand and was gently caressing my clit with the other. The sensation had my fingers digging into the back of the seat on either side of Logan. Then the plug started vibrating and my head dropped back. "Jesus, Logan." My hips undulated of their own accord as he toyed with me, dark eyes watching my face closely.

"Still want me to take it out?"

This was an entirely new sensation that felt amazing, but I wasn't sure where the finish line was or how it would resolve. "No... Yes... I, ugh, don't know."

His finger moved to his phone and the vibration deep inside me increased. My breath caught and I panted, "I might pee myself."

"Can't get that pretty skirt all wet." He gripped me with both hands and moved me to all fours before pulling one knee to the back-facing seat in front of us. He knelt on the floorboard behind me, head cocked to the side to keep from hitting the roof.

The buzzing gently lowered until my vagina went still. Then the plug gently deflated. Logan flipped my skirt over my hips, and the car slowed to a stop. I lifted my head to see we were at a stop light. "They can't see us, can they?"

"No." He pulled the much thinner plug out of me and set the slick thing face up on the seat next to me.

I blew out a long breath. "Thanks."

He rose behind me, and I felt his blunt tip slide in, filling me to the brim. He groaned as he leaned forward, cupping my pussy with one hand and covering my throat with the other.

"Logan!"

"All they see is the limo rocking."

The light turned green, and Pilot eased on. "What about the driver?"

"He'll be careful so I can breed my angel properly."

Then he proceeded to fuck me like a man on a mission. His voice was tight and threatening. "You will wear my cum, plugged inside you, without complaint, until I'm ready to make another deposit."

He pinched my clit between two fingers, sending a jolt of intense pleasure through my body.

"You will keep your face neutral and stay present even when the plug is pleasuring my pussy, no matter where we are or what is said."

He gave my clit a tug, and I gasped.

"I am going to play with my pussy as much as I want, before, during, and after this meeting. Understand?"

His hips slammed into me as his fingers jerked my clit with every thrust. "Yes, Sir."

"Fuck! Fuck!" His hand moved faster, practically vibrating my trapped clit. "Come with me, angel."

I was practically climbing the door of the limo as he shoved me over the edge with him. My heart raced wildly as he pulled me back and pushed my chest low. My arms strained on either side of me as he held me down with one hand on my back.

He pulled his length out of me and reinserted the plug before expanding the inner bladder until I whimpered. I felt him grab a dish towel off the bar and clean me up as I panted. Logan hooked my panties over my heels and wrapped an arm around my waist as

I stood hunched over and pulled them up. After straightening my skirt, he placed me on his lap and wrapped both arms around me. I turned my face into his neck, unsure if I wanted to cry, laugh, or let out a lusty sigh. My body chose the latter.

"What have I gotten myself into?"

He kissed my temple. "My sweet fallen angel, you live with the devil now. Depravity will mark those pretty little wings for the rest of your life."

"And what if I like wearing your depravity like a badge of honor?"

"Don't taunt me with a good time, angel. I might lose what little self control I have over my dark side."

I leaned back and met his almost black eyes. "I'm not scared of you."

He smoothed his thumb over my bottom lip. "You're one of very few."

And as we pulled up in front of the towering law firm, the people who crowded by the door of the limo confirmed those five little words.

The door opened and we were greeted with eager voices. "Mr. Dalton, thank you for coming."

A hand was thrust at me. "Ms. McKenzie, nice to meet you."

Logan's hand found mine as another said, "Follow us, we are set up on the fourth floor."

They led us into a large conference room and put a massive oak table between us and the five of them. One man poured ice water into two glasses as Logan pulled me down to straddle his thigh. "She'll sit with me."

A chorus of voices said that was just fine with them, but Logan lifted a finger and silenced them. "I wasn't asking permission."

An older gentleman in a tailored suit cleared his throat. "Of course. Shall we begin?"

Logan put his phone on the table face up with the app that controlled the plug inside me open. He tapped a button and a low vibration started deep inside my vagina. My legs tensed around his thighs, but he ignored my plight and told them everything that happened. As he spoke, his hand pushed my skirt up my legs and started a lazy ascent higher and higher until he was stroking my pussy through the material of my panties.

Logan asked me to fill in the blanks as he got to my parts, but his hand and the low vibration had me almost panting the words. Questions were asked and eventually repeated because of the distraction Logan was causing. Unfortunately for me, each time I asked them to repeat the question he tapped the app and turned up the vibrations.

One attorney kept glancing at my chest until I glanced down at my pointed nipples pressing through the cups of my bra and imprinting themselves on my blouse. I crossed my arms.

The chest behind me rumbled with malice. "If you keep staring at her nipples, Grady, you'll have to learn braille."

The man's eyes snapped to Logan, and he swallowed. "My apologies, Mr. Dalton."

One of the senior attorneys gave Grady a reproachful glare. "Out."

"Yes, sir." The man collected his legal pad and laptop and scurried out.

The senior man's eyes trained on Logan. "Is there anything else we need to know?"

"Yeah, we have the hacker who set us up in custody. My team is working on gaining evidence to prove her involvement."

The attorney took a deep breath. "I assume this hacker won't be available to testify?"

"No. She's unavailable."

"Okay, we'll have your team send me any evidence they dig up about the case the DA is working against you."

He turned to me and said, "We will prepare your statement to the police and have you sign it before you leave. They may want to interview you, but I will accompany you if they demand your presence."

I nodded quickly.

The man stood up which cued his team to rise and file out. "We'll give you the room for as long as you need, Mr. Dalton."

The door clicked shut, and I stood up only to feel Logan's fingers unbutton and unzip my skirt. He tugged my panties down before turning me around to face him.

"What are you doing?" My whisper was harsh as I glanced at the wooden door.

He urged me onto the conference table and rolled his chair between my legs. "Lay back and let me enjoy my snack."

The moment his mouth touched my clit I fell back and said, "Oh, my God."

My fingers went to the buttons of my blouse, opening it so I could free my aching nipples. "Logan..."

"Shh, angel. They will hear you scream," he taunted against my buzzing and needy flesh.

I slapped one hand over my mouth and the other over my right breast. His hand covered my left breast as he feasted on me.

Once again, he forcefully shot me over the edge. It was quick and sharp, and my legs flailed trying to gain purchase until my left heel hit the chair he had been sitting in and sent it careening against the wall.

He pulled away and stood between my legs with a savage grin as the plug deflated and he dropped his dress pants. His dick stood ready, and he wasted no time pushing inside my soaked vagina.

"You just get wetter and wetter for me."

My legs closed around his hips and pushed him deep. "The devil needs to fuck his depraved angel."

He smirked deliciously as he put one hand over my mouth and lowered his lips to my breast. His hips delivered long, deep strokes, and the sloppy sounds were barely heard over my muffled screams.

Logan used his teeth and cock like lightning. Striking hard and fast before the rain cooled the ground to dampen the fire. Leaving charred marks on a lush environment ready to bloom. My sensitive vagina was overwhelmed, from the tingling feel of his cock driving in and out to the sheer size of him as he rocked his tip against my cervix, grinding into me without mercy until I whimpered with discomfort.

"Shh. It's okay. You are doing so good, angel. My beautiful girl." He moved his mouth to the side of my breast and struck again, pinching flesh between teeth and sucking hard as he ground his hips against me.

I writhed under him, digging my nails into his back as I wrapped myself around him. "That's my girl. Take all of me and beg for more."

"Logan!"

He secured my hips against his strokes. "Tell them who serves you, Eden. Who makes your nipples hard, and your pussy soaked."

"Oh Logan. Fuck, Logan. I need..."

"I know what you need, angel."

He lifted, peeling my hands off him and tugging me back to the edge of the table. "And I'm going to give it to you."

His arms tucked under my knees as he lifted and secured me to him. Then his hips started pistoning like a fucking machine. My hands slapped down on the table as my back bowed, and my voice rose. He rocked my world as he watched me unravel with a devilish smirk on his scarred face.

Needless to say, I was beet red as he paraded me through the law offices to read and sign the statement they had prepared for me. I still might have to appear at the police station to speak with detectives, but it wouldn't be alone.

Logan

Logan Lurch

It had been three days since Eden officially moved in with me and I was still fighting my basic instincts to keep her tied up and spread open for me to pleasure when I felt the need. She was more than accommodating, and I'd had her in just about every space in this condo. Every room except the one I set up for her before leaving. I'm not sure I trusted my dark side enough to unlock that door just yet. She may never leave it.

She had even charmed the tiny terrorist living in my home. She named him Rori because Terrorist wasn't a proper name for a kitten. When I pointed out that he was a young adult and not a baby anymore, she scoffed and scooped the thing into her arms. He let her plant a dozen kisses on his stupid face before she put him down so he could scratch my furniture. So, I ordered a scratching post after I fucked her on my ruined couch.

My obsession with my angel wasn't easing, and I'd all but neglected my BFR duties. This morning I let Eden sleep in, cuddling the cat, while I sat down at my computer for the first time in days. The moment my programs powered up, red alerts popped up left and right.

One stood out over the rest. An urgent message from our Oklahoma team leader, Jason. I fit my Bluetooth in my ear and climbed the spiral staircase that led to my rooftop deck.

"Where the fuck have you been?"

My spine stiffened at Jason's tone. "Busy. What's going on."

"We went to do that smash and grab you guys ordered, and it was a set up."

I was silent way too long. "What smash and grab?"

"An old pedophile named Winston Tallon. Well, he wasn't there. It was a trap. Three of my men are injured, and one was taken hostage. I forwarded you the video of what they did to him and the warning for someone named Scout."

Fucking Bentley. I saw the signs when he questioned me about what I intended to do with her. He subtly challenged her worthlessness by telling me that she was one of the most brilliant hackers he'd ever come across. I'd seen her photo and had responded with, "More like the prettiest nerd you've ever seen."

He hadn't disagreed, even said Torrid was enamored too.

"I'll handle this."

"I want in. I don't care where these fuckers are based. I want to be there while you cut the tip of his dick off and make him chew it."

He hung up on me, and I went downstairs to view the video.

Our guy was strapped face down on a homemade, wooden spanking a-frame. He was bound with barbwire while a dildo attached to a fuck machine raped his ass.

A masked man stepped into frame. "Now look at what your actions caused, little girl." He stepped aside, and the camera zoomed in on the man's tearful agony. "And this is just the beginning of his punishment for taking orders from a naughty little cunt like you."

The camera zoomed back out, and the masked man stepped back into frame. "I hope this man means something to you. I'd hate for him to suffer for nothing. We'll be in contact with you next, Scout. Don't do anything stupid."

The video cut off, and I snarled as Eden walked in wearing only my shirt. "What was that?"

I took in her sleepy face and bare legs. "*That* was private." Maybe I needed to turn the dungeon into an office to shield her from the horrors of what I did.

I picked up the dummy ankle monitor. "Listen, angel, I've got to handle some things at work. Are you good here alone?"

She rubbed her eyes. "For how long?"

"I'll be back tonight."

She moved to the kitchen to pour herself some coffee. "Sure. Can I set up my art supplies upstairs?"

"Set up anywhere you like." I made a mental note to order some frames for the sketchbook drawings I stole from her when I packed her things to move her in.

She frowned. "I see how you stiffen when Rori gets crazy with your stuff. Paints are messy, Logan. I don't want to cause problems."

"Aw, shit." I ran a hand over my face. "Angel, that's my problem, not yours. I want you to feel comfortable here."

She leaned against the counter. "I'll feel comfortable when *you're* comfortable."

I shut down my computer. "It's going to take some time to socialize me. I've been feral most of my life."

Walking towards the door I added, "I'm trusting you. Please don't touch anything on my desk." I hadn't had the need for passwords and encryption other than the normal shit on my programs until now.

She sipped her mug with a pleasant smile that proved her point about me. "I wouldn't dare, but if I did, you'd probably know. I suspect you have cameras hidden all over this place."

I collected my bag and keys at the door. "I'll show you the footage of us fucking later."

She ambled over and lifted to her tiptoes. I leaned down and kissed her coffee and cream flavored lips. My fingers gripped the hem of her shirt, lifting it off her slowly, giving her time to put down her mug before she spilled it. My gaze fell to the faded bruises I left on her breasts at the meeting. "Stay naked. No orgasms until I get home."

Her lips pulled up. "Yes, Sir."

My gaze narrowed as I bent down and fixed the ankle monitor around her leg. "Use the day to rest, cause I'm going to give you a workout later."

"Okay."

Opening the app on my phone, I switched the signal. "Don't leave the condo."

"What if they come knocking?"

I smirked at her. "They won't. My guy at the PD is a BFR brother."

Her mouth formed an O, and my alter ego pointed out that our cock fit perfectly in that mouth. Our cock agreed wholeheartedly and rose to attention. Fucking hell, if I didn't leave now, I would never pull myself away from her. I set my jaw, opened the door, and walked out vowing to beat the fuck out of Bentley and force him to punish this nosey ass hacker in ways that would forever tarnish how she looked at him.

I sent a message to Bentley telling him to meet me at the warehouse immediately.

His response: **Already here.**

Forty minutes later, I ripped open the door to the warehouse and busted through the inner sanctum. Gaul launched into a fit of barking. I pointed at him, and his mouth snapped shut and he dropped to the floor. The dog knew not to fuck with me.

"Bentley!"

"Over here."

I rounded the corner to the lounge, and my gaze settled on a woman with shockingly green eyes and hair so dark it was almost black. She was butt ass naked, kneeling with knees spread wide. Her pert tits were perfect for the nipple clamps she wore. A delicate chain swooped between her breasts and a third dangled low, leading to a third clamp probably attached to her clit.

"Get that shit off her, put some clothing on her, and bring her to the office."

I spun around and walked out. I hadn't expected Scout to be stunningly beautiful. Bentley scrambled to catch up with me.

"What's wrong boss?"

"Winston Adam Tallon."

He was silent until we entered the office. "What about him?"

"You ordered a smash and grab for a non BFR member."

He folded his arms across his chest. "She agreed to help us if I brought her one of the men who molested her when she was a child."

Torrid opened the office door and prodded a wide-eyed Scout inside. The shirt she was wearing came down past her knees, and it only served to enhance her beauty. While nobody could ever compare with my angel, I could see why Torrid and Bentley were obsessed with her.

Torrid urged her to the chair across the desk from me. "Pet, this is Logan Dalton."

Her spine jolted at my name and terror flashed across her face before she put her mask on. "So?"

My gaze took in the jewel encrusted collar before narrowing on Torrid. He lifted a shoulder. "Goddamn it. Both of you?"

My men opened their mouths, but I lifted a hand silencing them as I returned my glare on Scout.

"Winston Adam Tallon."

Recognition flared in her gaze, and I smiled slightly as I continued, "Dumbass number one sent our Oklahoma team to grab him for you. What exactly did you agree to in exchange?"

Her lips parted and she said, "To help find the girl and exonerate you."

Bentley said, "She means Eden."

"Eden is almost twenty-three-years-old, a woman, not a girl. And your pedophile was a set up. Three were injured and one was taken hostage to torment you."

"What?"

I set my phone down in front of her and played the video Jason sent me. Her eyes bulged, and her jaw dropped open as it rolled on. She gave Bentley a wary glance. "What did you do?"

I said, "The question is, what did *you* do?"

She narrowed her gaze on me. "I take out entire pedo rings. My team would have demolished those guys and brought Winston home for judgment."

"Bentley changed the program, and our guys had no idea what they walked into. That is on both of you. So, I suggest you two work together to get our man out and her team in. I want that masked man strung up in here by his balls, right next to Connor."

Scout added, "And Winston."

I stood up and pinned Bentley with a glare. "I know you want to keep her, so prove her worth to me if you want me to stand with you during the tribunal."

"What's a tribunal?"

"It's your trial, pet." I smirked as I used Torrid's nickname. "It's to determine what your punishment will be." I tapped the still image on my phone.

"That's nothing compared to what I've already survived. So, he might have to have his prolapsed asshole repaired and a few stitches. I've had multiple surgeries to repair damages done to me when I was only six."

Well, that deflated me. "Look, I know you stand for a noble cause and all. But BFR doesn't go after nonmembers who break the laws. We enforce our own."

Bentley cleared his throat. "From the information we got off her latest hack? Out of seven thousand usernames? We suspect nine hundred are society members."

My jaw tightened. "Looks like we have some spring cleaning to do."

I walked around the desk and grabbed Scout's jaw, forcing her to look at me. "You have one shot to right your wrongs to this Society. Fuck us over and I'll make your death the worst punishment you could imagine."

The absolute fire that lit in her eyes caused me to smile. "I'm not afraid to die either, little inferno. But I have the equipment to bring you back to life just to die again, and I promise you it won't be peaceful." I smoothed my thumb across her cheek. "Understand?"

She nodded. "I made a mistake. It won't happen again."

I let her face go and pinned Bentley with a serious stare. "Set up a mobile unit here. I want her under constant supervision while she is working. Someone who is skilled and will pay attention. Preferably someone who won't become beguiled by her beauty, like you two numb nuts."

With that I left the warehouse and moved on to the next order of business.

Dan had moved Mandy into Karla's old home. It was his anyway, and the eviction he filed against Karla was uncontested due to her being missing. I pulled into the driveway and found the man piddling around in the expansive garage. He lifted a hand with a grin that put my mind to Eden.

"Mr. Dalton, what a pleasure."

I shook the man's hand. "We need to talk."

"Sure, sure. Come inside." He walked towards the garage door. "Can we get you something to drink? Tea, whiskey?"

"While it has been a whiskey kind of day, I'll have some tea."

He walked in and said, "Mandy, honey, we have a guest. Can you bring some tea to my office?"

Mandy called out from somewhere deep within the home. "Sure, baby."

We settled in comfortable chairs in Dan's office that still smelled of fresh paint. "So, how's Eden? She settled back in her condo okay?"

Mandy came in wearing a bikini and holding a tray. She set the glasses and pitcher down with a smile and poured sweet tea for each of us. When she went to leave, I caught her wrist. "Stay."

Wide eyes met mine before flashing to Dan. He nodded and she sat down on the arm of his chair.

"We need to bring Eden into the fold."

Dan shook his head slowly. "Her mother—"

"Is dead."

Mandy gasped. "Karla is gone? Poor Eden, I bet she's devastated."

"Not exactly."

I outlined what had happened in Costa Rica while I watched their faces carefully. Mandy had been horrified, while Dan didn't seem surprised by what Karla did. I filed their reactions away and finished with, "Eden is mine. She needs to make an informed choice about joining the Society. I want you two to educate her."

Dan straightened in his chair. "What do you mean by Eden is yours?"

"I don't think I stuttered, Dan. I claimed her long before we stole away on your boat."

"How am I just hearing about this now? BFR has protocol for these things."

"But you let your ex-wife take your child out of BFR. She's free game, and I need someone to sponsor her. I'd prefer it to be someone she trusts, but if you refuse, I can always ask my brothers..."

Mandy's hands lifted as I trailed off. "No. No. We'd be happy to sponsor Eden."

Dan's bewildered face stared up at his girlfriend. "I'm not comfortable with seeing my daughter go through initiations."

Mandy's gaze snapped to Dan. "I don't give a shit about what you are comfortable with. That girl needed us a long time ago, and I'm not about to let her down now. If you don't want to participate just because you might see her tits or whatever, then that's your hangup, not mine."

She got up and held out her hand to me. "I'll be her sponsor, and I know my parents will support Eden if she decides to be inducted."

I took her delicate hand and glanced at Dan as I stood up. "You failed Eden in such a monumental way when she was a kid by being an absentee father. You have the chance to make amends and fix the rift between you. But if you are too selfish to take this opportunity, then I'll pick up the pieces you've broken. I'll keep her safe, and I'll be both father and grandfather to our children."

He stood up too. "You're serious about keeping her?"

"As serious as life and as final as death. She will become Mrs. Logan Dalton, and our vows will be unbreakable."

Mandy said, "You love her."

I met her gaze. "She's the precious angel who saved me from my own personal hell. I adore her."

Her face softened. "Good."

Dan followed me to the door. "I'm sorry—"

I held up my hand. "Save the apologies for Eden."
"Yeah, sure."

Chapter Thirty-Two

Jeepers Screamers

Eden

I sank into the warm water of the massive tub with a sigh. A candle was tucked away on a shelf full of bath salts, oils, and jars of herbs. I lit it; today would be a day of pampering and much needed maintenance. Four days of hair growth, and I was getting stubbly. Not that Logan seemed to mind. I could turn into Sasquatch, and he'd still hit it with the same passion as he had been.

The way he desired me felt liberating even though I was currently stuck inside his condo wearing his ankle monitor. But that was temporary since the attorneys called Logan to tell him that the district attorney was dropping charges.

The evidence they had collected against him had mysteriously disappeared or been corrupted by the collector. The Blue-Frosted Rose Society was vast and powerful. They had members and supporters in every social class. After receiving my statement, they realized they didn't have a case at all.

After my bath, I slipped one of his shirts over my head and padded barefoot through the condo. He had made space for my clothing in his closet, but his t-shirts were ultra soft. I still had boxes to unpack from my old condo downstairs, but there were items I didn't know what to do with. Those would have to wait until Logan got home.

I was getting used to the locked doors and sleek modern interior, but it shocked me how comfortable his furniture was. The condo fit his personality. Cold, rigid, and stern with pockets of *curl up and cuddle* strewn about.

His bed had been the most pleasant surprise. I had never slept in a more comfortable place. It was like the damn thing hugged you with love and warmth. The bed was the heart of this place, and I gravitated to it often to curl up with Logan's scent and the cat.

The sun was setting when I settled on the couch to watch an old horror movie. The front door opened quietly, and I met his gaze from across the room. A gaze that seemed to take everything into account all at once. Like he could actually see the ghost of my presence all over his space.

"Honey, I'm home," I said with a smirk to him as he just stood there watching me watch him.

"You're supposed to be naked."

I adjusted myself on the couch so I could see him better over the back of it. He embodied the stillness of a predator. It made me want to run just to see if he'd give chase.

"Are you going to punish me?"

He walked towards me, fingers unbuttoning his dress shirt. "Not right now."

My gaze soaked up his tattooed chest and ripped abs as he crossed the distance between us. This man was so fine he made my heart flutter. The way he stalked like a feral beast was entirely thrilling.

He lost his shoes and dress pants before he stepped over the back of the couch and settled next to me. His thick thighs were absolutely one of my favorite features, and I gladly let him pull me between them.

His lips pressed against the top of my head as I got comfortable for a cuddle with darkness in the flesh.

"I want to ask how your day went, but..."

He tucked his chin into my neck and said, "I handled some shit and had a visit with Dan and Mandy on my way home."

I stiffened at my dad's name. He hadn't even called me. Well, I didn't have a phone anymore, but still, he could have checked in with Logan. "Oh?"

"I know I said you had a choice when it came to the Society, but I lied. At the time, I thought I was telling the truth, but I was wrong."

My brows knitted as I pulled back, searching his scarred face. "I'm confused."

"I'm not. I *am* the Society for all intents and purposes. You don't have a choice anymore. You are mine, so you belong to the Society. There is no escaping me or your destiny as my wife and Blue Lady."

His arms tightened as he readjusted me against his chest and reclined against the pillows I had propped up. "Mandy is going to sponsor you, along with your grandparents. The education will be rigorous and intense. You'll have to go through initiations, but afterwards, we can perform the marriage ritual and you will officially become *my* Blue Lady in the eyes of the Society."

"Ritual?"

"It involves a lot of symbolism, a little bit of blood, and some public sex, but it will bond our souls together in this life and the next."

"What if I don't want to bind my soul to you?"

His hand stroked my arm slowly as he spoke intimately to me. "Like I said, I lied to you when I let you think you had a choice.

You don't, and I'll chase you into the next life if you ever try to run from me. You. Are. Mine. Forever."

I stilled, searching his eyes for red flags and danger, but only found honest warmth burning behind darkness. "Maybe I enjoy being chased by you."

His lips quirked. "Then it's a good thing that the BFR marriage ritual involves hunting." He leaned forward, "Catching." His lips moved to my ear, "And claiming." His teeth grazed my ear before he reclined against the pillows.

I fought an excited grin as I said, "Then I guess I'm kind of excited to become your Blue Lady."

He pulled the blanket around us and let his long legs curl. "Good. Mandy will start your training tomorrow. Your new phone is being programmed as we speak. Now, what on earth are you watching?"

I smiled. "Jeepers Creepers."

He nuzzled my ear. "A favorite of mine. Did you know it was filmed in North Florida?"

I met his gaze. "Really? I didn't know that."

He kissed the tip of my nose and admitted, "I once drove to all the filming locations. The church was gone, but the diner and the library, where they filmed the police station, were all still there. I was twenty-three."

It took me a moment to get the meaning of his age at the time of his visit. A chill crept up my spine. *Every twenty-three years for twenty-three days, it gets to feed.* "Did you think you were connected to Jeepers or something?"

He lifted a shoulder. "They called me Lurch way before I became a monster. I always sympathized with Jeepers. He was just trying to live. A guy has to eat." Those sensual lips curved into a sexy smirk as dark eyes twinkled down at me.

"If you're a monster that would make me a monster fucker."

His chest tightened with his silent laugh. "I saw the covers on those books I packed."

I sat up and crossed my arms. "Hey, don't judge my love of blue alien guys with horns."

He grinned and added, "And ogres."

My jaw dropped with indignation. "Those are orcs not ogres."

"Angel, I'll paint my entire body blue or green and wear any horns or mask you desire, just to fulfill your book fantasies."

My heart skipped a beat as he stared intensely at me from across the couch. "There was a certain werewolf that never got to knot me."

"Oh, he knotted you, angel. You just weren't present for it."

I smirked as I held his gaze. "I'd like to be awake next time."

"The moment the police return our stuff, I'll let the werewolf hunt you on the next full moon."

He moved to his knees on the floor and hooked his hands under my legs, tugging me to the edge of the couch. "But beware of what you wish for little prey. The monster inside me won't just eat you."

He pushed my thighs wide and hungrily stared between them. He let out a low growl when he saw I was bare down there. "He'll consume your entire soul." My head fell back as his fiery breath fanned my pussy. "You may never be the same."

His mouth closed in, and I let out a gasp at the sensations that skipped through me. Logan ate me with the passion of a starved beast.

But he was *my* starving monster, and I'd happily feed him anytime, day or night.

Logan

Logan Lurch

I made her watch the entire movie as I feasted on her tasty little pussy. She came so well for me, but after thirty minutes, I had to hold her down to continue my meal. Her legs shook wildly, and her pussy throbbed so prettily as she whimpered, gasped, and cried out above me. Her hands kept distracting me, so I made a quick trip to the dungeon for leather cuffs and rope.

She was reclined arms above her, wrists secured to the legs of my couch behind her head. One leg was tied over the back of the couch, and she was spread wide like a four-course meal. I put on Jeepers Creepers Two and got comfortable between her thighs.

"Watch the movie, angel."

"Logan, please. I can't anymore."

I kissed her glistening parts and said, "Oh, yes you can." My tongue traced up and swirled around her throbbing clit, eliciting a squeal from her. I sucked her left labia into my mouth and held it hostage with my teeth before giving it a tug.

"Please, Logan. Just fuck me."

Her pussy had begged to be filled forty minutes ago, and now it was wide open. I toyed with the opening of her vagina as I moved to the right side of her labia. Her soaked pussy sucked my fingers inside, and I filled her up with three as her hips bucked. My cock was beyond control at this point. I was desperate to be inside her the moment she opened for me, but I refused my release until I finished my meal.

"Watch the movie, Eden."

I waited until the scene where Jeepers licks the bus window to unleash my cock from my boxer briefs and slowly climb over her quivering body.

"I own a Jeeper's mask, too," I offered through gritted teeth.

I entered her painfully slowly, pushing just the tip inside and waiting before retreating and starting over. Her body was complete bliss, and I wanted to drag this out as long as I could.

By the time I was fully seated inside her, she was practically feral with need. I gathered her close and held her tightly pinned with my erection deep. She groaned and thrashed, demanding me to move inside her. I rolled my hips, rocking my cock against her pretty little cervix, and she went wild under me with a scream.

"Fucking hell, Logan."

My arms tightened around her as I nuzzled her neck. "I know. It's a lot. But you were made for me, angel."

She turned her bright red face to me. "You're too big."

I licked up the trails her tears left on her cheek. "You just need to let me in, precious angel. Relax that cervix and let me soak in your bliss." I turned her face back to the movie and kissed her neck as I slowly rolled my hips, savoring her heat.

"You feel so fucking amazing."

She whimpered again as I stroked deeper.

I adjusted my lower half, pushing her thighs higher and holding her tighter.

She stiffened as I rolled my hips, driving my tip hard against her most inner parts. Her mouth found my bicep, and I hissed as teeth clamped down around skin and muscle. The jolt of pain almost shook my control. "Bite down and mark your beast as he breeds you."

Her cervix dipped and moved as she bucked under me mid-orgasm, and all mastery of my body left me. The orgasm started at the base of my spine. Electricity tingled through me as I pumped into her.

She screamed a muffled sound and bit down harder.

My cock felt like it exploded into tiny shards of intense pleasure.

My balls painfully tightened. "Oh fuck, fuck, fuck."

I pushed deep and held my throbbing tip as still as humanly possible as I painted her insides with my cum.

"Oh, fucking hell, angel. You flew us to the heavens. Open that womb and receive my demon seed. We're going to create a baby unlike anything this world has ever seen."

My hands found her leather cuffs, and I released my fallen angel. Her arms trembled as they wrapped around me.

She turned her face to mine. "Don't you dare pull out of me."

I grinned. "I'll never leave you unsatisfied."

She kissed my lips and said, "Never leave me period."

My cock jumped at her words, and she gasped. The moment her mouth parted I struck, kissing her with every ounce of feeling I had for her. The way she made my chest tighten without meaning to. The way she looked mid-orgasm as well as in rage hit me deep in my gut. The shape of her hands and the way they touched me. Her mind and the innocence she had. Her creative eye and insane talent. I could go on and on.

She was breathless when I pulled back, and I added stealing her breath to my list of the things I loved about her. "Unlike the beast in the story, I won't turn into a handsome prince. I will always be the monster with a plethora of issues, but you are stuck with me now."

Her fingers moved to my hair, combing through it gently. "All my life I've acquiesced to what others expect of me. I've tried to live up to a standard that I wasn't sure I wanted for myself."

"And what do you want, Eden?"

She met my gaze in a way that told me no one had ever asked her that question before. "I know what I don't want. I don't want a prince with rules of honor and obligations that don't focus on me. I want a monster who is dedicated to hunting, capturing, and consuming everything I throw at him."

"You've got that. What else do you want?"

She let her head drop back with a wistful smile. "A home with a yard large enough for your demon spawn to play and maybe a barn for some chickens and a pony."

"Done."

She lifted her head to gaze down at me. "Just like that?"

My head tilted in a mock shrug. "Well, we'll have to look at some properties and decide if we want to buy or build. Make sure the school systems are top notch..."

She pulled her lips into her mouth, and I lifted an eyebrow. She glanced at the ceiling and then back at me. "I want to continue my education."

"For digital arts?"

Her shoulders lifted. "I want to be an artist. Maybe make book covers?"

I smirked devilishly. "With horny blue aliens?"

She gave me a shove that didn't move me an inch. "Stop. Maybe?"

I leaned in and gave her a quick peck on the lips. "Angel, the world is your playground. Any school, anywhere."

"It's not that easy, especially if you knock me up."

I leaned back just enough to keep my cock from slipping out of her. "I don't think you understand how connected the Blue-Frosted Rose is." I moved my hips slowly. "Or exactly how much money I'm willing to enthusiastically dedicate to making you the happiest angel on earth."

Her face grew serious in a way that turned my stomach to lead. "I'm not ready to be a mother."

The way I stilled had her rushing forward. "When I got my period in Costa Rica, I cried because I was holding on to a piece of you. I believed you were gone forever, and I had been more devastated by that than I allowed myself to feel at the time. I want to have your children someday. But mostly I just want you, and I don't even want to share you with the cat."

She jerked like she just remembered something. Her eyes popped wide. "I left him on the rooftop deck!"

She shoved me back. "He's been up there for over two hours. Go get him."

I lifted off her and tugged my underwear on as she unbuckled the cuffs on her ankles. "He probably fell off the roof or is dying of thirst by now."

I climbed the spiral stairs leading to the deck as she continued, "See? I can't even keep track of a cat. How am I supposed to take care of another human being without fucking it up."

I paused at the door and said, "I'm sure the cat is fine. He's smart and has feral genetics."

The moment I opened the door a gray blur raced past my legs with a growl and down the stairs. I followed him back down and met her wide gaze.

"See? He's fine."

She frowned as she watched him get a drink from his bowl.

Sitting down next to her, I said, "It's not summer yet. He's fine."

I took her hands in mine to gain her undivided attention. "And you're right. I let my alter ego attempt to lock you down with children instead of trusting that I was enough."

"You are overwhelmingly enough, Logan."

"You'd think the older one got, the wiser they'd become, but when it comes to you, all logic is tossed out the window."

She laughed, and my heart jolted at the way her face melted with relief. "I get that, because in the heat of the moment, when you start talking about breeding me, it's such a turn on. I've spent countless hours imagining what our children would look like."

I squeezed her hands. "I'll make an appointment with the medical team for the morning. If I haven't already knocked you up, they can get us back on birth control until you feel ready to have my children."

She hedged, "When you say children, I'm thinking two."

I smirked. "Double that."

"Four?"

I grinned. "That's a good even number for the future."

"What if I'm already pregnant?"

My smile tightened. "My brother, Todd, said babies tend to fit right in with your lifestyle. All the worrying he did about timing and shit was for nothing. Lizzy paused her personal goals for a year after giving birth, but she created the support team she needed to jump back into things. I'd like to think I'm just as dedicated to you as Todd is to Lizzy."

Her mouth tightened. "He sounds like a good man."

"Even Mickey agrees, Todd is the best of us. Look, pregnant or not, everything will be alright."

Chapter Thirty-Three

Pledged

Eden

I wasn't pregnant. As conflicted as I was about finding out, it was ultimately a good thing. For once in my life, I felt like I mattered. That the things I wanted for me were supported and valid.

Logan handed me my new phone with a warning. "Download nothing onto this device. Not even games. I'll provide a separate device for gaming and apps if you want such things. This is your BFR phone, and everything you say or do is monitored so choose your words carefully."

I confessed, "I was going to call Tracy."

"You can call anyone you like, just don't say anything about the Society."

I nodded and he smiled, "Mandy will go over everything you need to know to stay safe when you meet with her today."

"I'll wait to call Tracy then."

I met Mandy at a church in Tampa while Logan went to get his ankle monitor removed and handle some business.

Pilot opened the door to the car he picked me up in.

"Good luck Miss Eden."

I found it weird that all the drivers were called Pilot, but this was the guy who picked us up in the limo the other day for our appointment with the attorneys.

"Will we ever be on a first name basis, Pilot?"

His answering smile was cordial. "I am not a full-fledged member. Most of the drivers are what we call trusted support. It is the best way to stay anonymous."

My gaze narrowed as I cocked my head. "Why wouldn't you become a full-fledged member?"

His smile was compassionate. "If you are still wondering, ask me that question next month, and I'll give you an honest answer."

I frowned. "Is it that bad?"

He laughed. "No. It just wasn't for me."

That didn't help the dread I felt as I climbed the steps of a massive ancient cathedral. It looked like any other old church except for the gated entry with a guard who checked credentials and the overkill of surveillance cameras. I opened the oversized oak door accented in carved symbols and wild roses.

Mandy was waiting for me in the receiving area. "Eden, welcome." She threw her arms around me and added, "I'm so glad you are back."

My gaze bounced around the reception area like I was searching for demons to materialize. But it looked like a regular church. "Me too."

She pulled back, holding on to my forearms. "I'm sorry about your mother."

My gaze settled on her. "I'm sorry about your sister."

Her lids lowered as she looked at the floor. "I lost my sister years ago."

I let the awkward silence marinate, which was not something I would have done four months ago. Finally, I smiled and said, "The same time I lost my dad?"

She let me go and glanced down the hallway before meeting my gaze directly. "There are always two sides to every story, Eden. When you are ready to hear mine, I'm happy to share, but today isn't about me. Let's have a seat in one of the offices."

She led me down a sterile white hallway, into an office with a standard wood desk and a cozy seating area. She chose the seating area instead of sitting behind the cold desk.

She watched me carefully for my reaction. "I know your mother had a change of faith when she divorced Dan."

I lifted a shoulder. "It was one of many changes she went through."

Mandy frowned, but asked, "And do you still have a relationship with Jesus?"

My head shook slowly. "I had a brief relationship with the preacher's son. He stole my innocence, and somehow everyone blamed me when the gossip became too loud to ignore. Karla was so embarrassed by her slutty daughter, she switched churches."

Mandy's frown deepened as her face grew bright with what I hoped was shame. Wasn't this supposed to make me feel better? Instead, I felt sick inside.

"Look, I obviously have some anger issues I need to work through. I'm sorry for making you feel bad about my circumstances. If you are trying to find out if I'm a Christian, I'd tell you that I was 'saved,' but keeping faith when religion is used as a weapon against you is hard to do." I glanced around the room as I said, "This is the first time I've been inside a church since I was sixteen."

She clasped her hands on her lap, and said, "And I have a lot of hindsight guilt when it comes to you. I don't think I'll ever work through the should haves, could haves, and had we knowns."

My smile was tight. "So, what religion is the Blue-Frosted Rose Society?"

Her smile bloomed like a beautiful flower. "We embrace all religions, but our rituals are primarily pagan. Our spiritual leaders have different specialties. Some work with nature while others work with gods and goddesses. We also welcome Christians. I mean, Jesus did perform some magical miracles after all."

I almost laughed. "Logan made it seem like there were a lot of orgies."

"Sex magic is a real practice, and he's always a favorite for the annual Dionysus ceremony, but Logan is involved with more death magic than sex."

My gut tumbled. I could imagine why they'd want Logan for sex stuff. "What is a Dionysus ceremony?"

She shifted in her seat. "As a whole, we follow the wheel of the year. Yule, Imboic, Ostara, Beltane, Midsummer, Lughnasahd, Mabon, and Samhain, but we also have smaller gatherings to bring additional magic for the local members. I'll provide you the exact dates and locations for our sect, but the Dionysus ceremony is held here once a year to celebrate the god of wine, vegetation, pleasure, festivity, and wild frenzy."

Did I really want to know this? "And Logan provides the pleasure for this ceremony?"

"Not exactly. He becomes a vessel for the god to inhabit. I don't think he has as much fun as he does during Samhain." She winced, and added, "But, I can't go into details just yet. Not until you pledge."

"Okay, so your religion is founded in pagan rituals, but you embrace all faiths. What's the big secret? I mean, it just seems so Middle Ages."

Her body relaxed as she laughed. "Middle Ages is perfect!"

She sobered, and leaned forward. "It's a secret because it's real." She lifted her hand as humor bloomed on my face. "No, really. The rituals fuel real magic to our Society as a whole. Once you are a member, you'll gain an insight that you weren't aware of before, and doors will open that you didn't even know were doors."

Logan's voice echoed in my head. *The world is your playground.*

"I'm open, but skeptical."

"Well, it's not wizarding school magic, if you catch my drift, but there's magic in everything you do with intention behind it."

"So where do we start?"

She put her hands on her knees, and stood up. "Rule number one. Before we begin, we must always cleanse."

I followed her out of the office and down the long hall to a locker room. Mandy got a white, sheer, shapeless dress from a shelf and handed it to me. "Put this on, and stow your stuff in one of the cubbies. No one will mess with your personal items. When you're ready, come into the next room. I'll be waiting."

The chemise came to my knees, but it was so thin you could see my breasts and hips if I turned a certain way in the lights. But the next room was dimly lit, and I felt relieved as I entered.

Porcelain clawfoot tubs lined deep rows in the space, but the scent of herbs and flowers drew my gaze to the wall of shelves where Mandy stood. "We need to choose the items that go into your bath, and you need to focus on letting go of any negative energy you might carry with you."

"Does everyone bathe when they come to church?"

"Everyone cleanses in some form or another, depending on why they are here. Pledges must bathe at first."

"Okay."

She had me sit down at a stone table and directed me on what to put into my cleansing. Salts, herbs, flowers, oils, and rocks all benefited this or that, but it was a lot to remember when my job was to mix them while attempting to let go of all my negative shit. I had built up a lot over my lifetime.

But by the time I sank into the tub of hot, fragrant water I actually felt some of that shit just melt away. Granted, it might take a hundred cleansing baths for me to actually feel enlightened enough to shed the thin dress I wore in the water, but that first one was amazing.

An hour later, I was on the fast track for a fledgling membership. Apparently, there were different levels of Blue-Frosted Rose hierarchy. Fledgling was a step above support which took years to reach. A royal like Logan couldn't marry someone outside the Society or even a support member. Typically, royalty wed dukes or above to keep the bloodlines pure or some weird shit like that.

"Heirs are important." Mandy gave me a sheepish smile. "Dan was punished for not taking you from Karla."

My head snapped up from the ancient history book I was reading. A book that was not allowed to see the light of day or be touched without a spiritually clean, and gloved hand. "Punished? How?"

She waved my anxiety away. "Just shunned for breaking tradition."

"By getting a divorce?"

Sad blue eyes held mine. "It's forbidden to break your vows. Punishable by death. Karla knew this."

My gaze narrowed. "What about cheating?"

"If the relationship isn't open, then it's handled by a tribunal. Your mother changed the rules of her marriage. She closed an open door, one she willingly walked through just as often as your father did."

"Are you saying my mom cheated on my dad?" Why wasn't there more shock and outrage in my voice?

Mandy shrugged a shoulder. "All I'm saying is their relationship was open until Dan started pursuing me outside of ritual."

"Try as I might, I can't imagine my mother dancing around a bonfire in a naked sex orgy." I turned the book I was reading so Mandy could see the drawing of exactly that.

She muffled a snort with her hand. "Well, she did. She even signed up for the deflowering ceremony."

"Oh God, do I even want to know?"

"It's patriarchy at its finest. The whole untouched virgin shit, but there is some powerful magic in a blood sacrifice."

I rolled my eyes, and she added, "And your mother enjoyed it so much, she signed up for sex magic rituals often. Well, until she reached the age where she had to play the crone."

"That tracks."

"She waited to have you because she wasn't ready to let go of her youth."

I hedged, "She told me about the breeding ceremony."

"Did she tell you she had her tubes tied during her C section?"

"How did you know? She said it was her big secret."

Mandy folded her hands in her lap, and stared at them. "I kept her secret. Dan doesn't know."

I studied my aunt carefully before asking, "How come you don't have children?"

Blue eyes lifted to mine. "Do you really think Dan would be a better father the second time around?"

I shrugged. "He was a great dad when I was a kid. Before he left."

Her gaze drifted away. "The Society had been pressuring us for heirs, but now that you are pledging for Logan, they'll probably shift their focus to you two."

I huffed a laugh, and returned to my book. "Logan has that covered."

Logan

Logan Lurch

After getting my ankle monitor removed and our things back, I drove to the warehouse in Lakeland to spend the day doing what I could to bring an innocent brother home.

I found Bentley hovering over the pretty little hacker stripped of everything but a jeweled dog collar, and a pink laptop. Her thighs were wrapped in pink cord, and pulled wide, secured to the arms of the computer chair she was in. Her pussy wasn't exactly on display in the recesses of the chair, but I saw enough to make her face bloom with color.

I pointed to the orderly coils, and asked Bentley, "You do that?"

"Yeah. Just because she's helping right her wrongs doesn't mean she gets to skip punishment."

A glance at the array of toys lined up on a shelf next to him, and I shrugged. "Looks more like a funishment to me."

Torrid strode past the door, and said, "Not when you aren't allowed to come."

Her clacking faltered at Torrid's voice even though she hadn't even acknowledged anyone else's presence.

I reached down and tipped her chin up and to the side. Molten hate met my gaze. "How long have they been edging you?"

She jerked her chin away. "Don't touch me."

Bentley chuckled but said, "Two days."

"That explains the bad attitude."

Bentley swiveled her chair to face me. "You owe Mr. Dalton an apology."

A frown developed on her pretty lips right before she reached for the front of my slacks. I grabbed her wrists to halt her. "That doesn't belong to you." Wide green eyes lifted to mine as I squeezed her wrists. I added, "You can apologize by doing your job faster, little hacker."

Bentley said, "We have Connor. He'll be here in three days."

I dropped the hackers' wrists, and she rubbed the pain away as Bentley turned her back to the small laptop desk. Her fingers shook as she returned to typing.

"Where did you learn to rope like that?"

Bentley wandered to a couch lined against the wall. "I've been studying shibari for a few years." Bentley's ADHD made him study many things at once. He was a dancer, writer, leather crafter, and now a rigger too?

"You'll have to give me some pointers."

Bentley sat down. "I'll give you a whole damn class later." His gaze lingered on Scout. "My little hacker loves to be strung up and teased to tears."

A shiver rippled through her like she could feel his eyes on her. "I do not."

"Liar." He grinned at her bare back, and that's when I noticed the change in my second. His knee wasn't bouncing, and he looked completely at ease. Like the constant chatter and music in his head had gone silent. It wouldn't last, but Scout's presence seemed to calm him, even though she was back to ignoring him.

"I don't think your charming personality is working on her, Bentley."

He waved a hand, and scoffed, "She's in love with Torrid."

"Am not."

Bentley snorted. "Are too."

The hacker huffed, and her fingers started moving on the keyboard again. She had pulled back the onion layers of the dark web, and was hot on the trail of the kidnappers who took our Oklahoma brother.

Bentley passed his laptop to me. It was a series of still photos from the torture video. "She is in contact with them, but we already know so much about this ring just from the video they sent." He pointed to the homemade bench the man was secured to. "See that there?" My gaze went to the partial tag still stuck to the wood as Bentley continued, "Home Depot tag."

"There are a million of those around the country."

He laughed in agreement. "Yeah." He flipped to a new still image that was a blurry close up of a reel of barbed wire. "This was purchased at Tractor Supply."

I shrugged my shoulders. "Again, a million."

"But not in Oklahoma, close to Winston's home."

The hacker looked at me over her shoulder. "And I have video surveillance from both box stores putting the same person buying those exact items right after your men fucked up the job." She zoomed in on a still of a man pushing a cart through Tractor Supply. He was too young to be the hooded man in the video.

"Got a name yet?"

Bentley shook his head with a frown. "No. Facial recognition came up blank. He's probably undocumented."

"He doesn't look like a migrant worker."

She swiveled her chair to face us. "He doesn't have to be a foreigner to be undocumented. More than likely he's an aged-out sex slave. Stolen or born into the sex trade like I was."

I studied the young man on the screen. "He appears to be alone. Why wouldn't he run for help?"

Green eyes studied me for a long ass heartbeat. "You've never been abused, so you wouldn't understand."

I dropped my hoodie and tucked my hair behind my ear, leaning in as her eyes widened and locked onto my ruined face. "I've been abused."

She went still. "Yeah, but have you abused others?"

My face must have revealed the answer because she lifted her hand. "As an innocent child? Forced to mutilate and kill other innocent children?"

She lowered her hand, satisfaction showing on her face. "Yeah. It fucks you up for life, dude. They take great pleasure in watching children as young as toddlers kill." She turned back to her little pink laptop and muttered, "I know, I was one of those murderous babies."

Bentley's face pinched. "Don't feel bad for her, boss. She has a fucking feral mouth."

I opened my mouth to tell Bent that I couldn't care less, but Torrid leaned against the door jamb, arms crossed over his thick chest. "She doesn't bite anymore."

Bentley's lips parted on a wide grin. "Yeah, but neither one of us trusts her enough to put our dicks anywhere near that mouth without protection."

I caught the smile that bloomed on Scout's profile before she buried it with her resting bitch mask. These two were in serious trouble concerning her. I hoped, for their sakes, I could stand in her defense during the tribunal.

I checked my smartwatch tracking app and saw Eden was on campus. She said she was going to check in with the school to see if there was anything to be done about her lengthy absence. Since she had been there for hours, I figured she caught up with Tracy to reconnect.

I opened my bag and got out my laptop to work on a few things. Thirty minutes later, Bentley got up and stood behind Scout. He ran his hands over her neck and shoulders before loosening the messy bun she had in her hair. Bone straight, dark hair cascaded over her chair. "It's break time, little hacker."

Her shoulders lifted in a huge sigh. "I don't need a break."

Bentley's hands were already untying her thighs. "Sure, you do. Close the laptop, and drink your water."

"I'm not thirsty."

She stretched her leg as he worked on the opposite side. "I don't care. Drink, or I'll call Torrid in."

With a pout she snatched the water bottle up and untwisted the cap. Tipping it up, she swallowed repeatedly until the water drained out. It crinkled and popped as she slammed it down on the small desk in front of her. "Happy?"

"That you're doing the bare bones to stay alive?" He shook his head. "Stand up."

Her legs shook a little, but her spine was ramrod straight as she lifted her hands to the ceiling and rose to her toes in a long stretch before bending over to touch the carpet.

My gaze went to her round ass, and I noted the green jeweled butt plug she wore with a smirk.

She stood up, and Bentley turned her to face me so I could watch him put the nipple clamps on that he pulled out of his pocket. Not just nipple clamps. Bent kneeled in front of her. "Open up for me, little hacker."

Her face went pensive as she spread her legs. His hands disappeared from my view, but her face told me everything I needed to know as he clamped her clit.

Finally, he stood, and said, "Begin."

Like a pig, I didn't avert my eyes, and she bravely held steady eye contact with me as her face heated. Her titties bounced as she did jumping jacks. Pert nipples jarred the clamps as the chains connecting them jiggled and danced. After several sets of twenty-five, and a few other exercises, Bentley took her into the center of the warehouse, and continued her workout until a fine sheen of sweat covered her body. She whimpered one word as he took the clamps off her.

"Please."

His answering smile was tender. "You know what you need to do in order to stop this."

Her jaw set but her gaze searched the expansive space for someone who wasn't here.

The puzzle wasn't hard to put together. "What does she have to do to Torrid?"

Bentley set a basket of neatly coiled ropes on the floor next to her. "Beg."

One look at her face, and a short laugh left me. "That girl will never beg; her ego won't allow it."

Torrid stalked in with Gaul at his side. "Her ego will crack, and not only will she beg for my cock, but she'll also crawl to it and prostrate herself before me like a good little pet."

I turned my humor on Tor. "Has she even seen your dick? Cause if she has, that might be the reason she isn't begging for it."

Her gaze dropped to the front of his pants, and I said to her, "He's thick."

She jerked her eyes away, and stared at the floor as Bentley taught me a few things about rope.

"Rope can cause severe nerve damage if done wrong." He wrapped the cord around her torso creating a harness of coils and decorative knots. I was entranced by the way he tied her up. It was slow, methodical, and loving. He stopped several times just to put his arms around her and hold her. He leaned in to whisper in her ear often. Words just for her, and she bloomed for him.

The more she was bound the more she went quiet. The transformation from stiff defiance to pliable softness was beautiful to witness. Her jaw relaxed, and she allowed him to manipulate her limbs until her legs were folded and secure, and her arms were tied to the harness behind her back. She was deep in subspace by the time he finished.

Torrid lowered the hoist so Bentley could suspend the entranced girl. Her head hung loosely as she lifted off the floor. Bentley stroked her body with gentle hands as she swayed before him. He hugged and kissed her, still praising her in a voice only she could hear.

My phone chimed as Torrid lowered the hoist. A quick check of my smartwatch told me Eden was on the move. "I gotta bolt. Keep me updated."

By the time I packed up and got into my Dodge Ram, the security system at the condo had alerted me that Eden was safe at home. My heart ached to see her, hold her, and find out how her day went.

Chapter Thirty-Four

Marry Me, Angel

Eden

I had learned to cook a few things while I was in Costa Rica with my mother. Logan found me in the kitchen cooking ground beef for tacos when he came home. He dropped his bag off by his computer desk and washed his hands before chopping the head of lettuce I laid out.

"How was your day?"

I stirred the ground beef and let his question sizzle like the pan before me as I contemplated his answer. I could say fine, but had it actually been fine? After meeting my aunt today and studying the history of the Blue-Frosted Rose Society, one thing weighed on my mind.

"The college needs proof I was kidnapped by my mother."

He made quick work of the lettuce and moved to chopping the onion. "I'll let the attorneys know. They'll send the paperwork tomorrow. How was Tracy ?"

I lowered the heat on the stove and glanced over my shoulder at him. "How did you know I saw Tracy ?"

A smirk was the only answer he gave me.

I smiled, and shook my head slowly. “Shocked as hell to see me standing at her door after all these months. She asked a lot of questions. I told more lies than I was comfortable with, but she pretended to believe them and let me off the hook.”

“She’s actually a good friend who reported you missing after repeated visits to your condo.”

My heart lurched at how much he already knew about how hard Tracy worked to let everyone know I was missing. I swallowed the lump in my throat. Tracy’s hug and grateful tears had made me cry a waterfall already. I didn’t want to cry any more today.

“How was church?”

“Different from any other church I’ve ever attended.” I pulled the pan off the stove and drained the fat before returning it to the heat for seasoning. “It was both cool and awkward at the same time.”

He washed the knife before using it to dice a tomato. “If you don’t want to work with Mandy, I can find someone else willing to sponsor you.”

“I’ll keep her. I feel confident we can work through our shit while I learn about pagan rituals like the Dionysus ceremony you were in.”

I met his gaze and watched him still.

I chewed my lip before asking the question that had been dogging me all damn day. “Has Mandy seen your dick?”

He put the knife down with a sigh. Reaching behind me, he turned the eye off, and moved the meat off the heat.

I frowned, and asked, “What are you doing?”

But before I got all the words out his hand closed around my throat, and he moved me away from the stove. Both of my hands wrapped around his wrist as my heart rate doubled.

My back pressed against the sink. “Logan.” A strangled plea.

His fingers tightened as he leaned in, fire flaring in his gaze. "Eden." A threat.

I lifted my chin, and met his stoney face. "I need to know."

He leaned in. "Not only has she seen my dick, but she's also kissed it."

My stomach dropped, and I tried to swallow but his hand wouldn't let me.

He ran the tip of his nose against my neck, and inhaled by my ear forcing goosebumps to skitter down my arms. "And so has your dad."

He leaned back, and put his face in mine. "They were amongst a hundred others, angel. Many people have seen my dick. Not only that, I've used this dick on hundreds, mostly for punishment, but sometimes in pleasure too. It was a part of who I was, part of my job."

I adjusted my hand around his wrist, and leaned back to see his face clearer. "Was?"

"This dick is yours now. Cage it before I leave for the day if you need to, but it's yours, Eden."

He let me peel his hand off my throat, and I took the chance to rush out of the kitchen. He followed but didn't pounce again. I whirled on him. "It's not just about your dick, Logan."

He fisted his hands at his side, and spoke through his teeth. "You own much more than just my dick." He put his fist over his heart. "You own this, too."

"I know. I just don't like it. My dad? Really?"

He tilted his head. "They wanted to do a threesome right after you moved in, but I passed on the offer."

"That doesn't make me feel better."

"Jealousy isn't supposed to feel good, angel."

"I'm not jealous." I winced as my stomach tumbled. "Maybe I am, but how would you feel in my shoes?"

His grin stole my breath. "Positively murderous."

I wanted to feel his arms around me so badly that I took a step towards him.

He watched my jerky movement, and added, "So much so, that dear old Connor is coming all the way from the United Kingdom to spend his last days in my dungeon."

"You're going to kill him? Wait, you have a dungeon?"

"Not only do I have a warehouse that serves as my dungeon, I'm going to kill that piece of shit and bring him back just for the pleasure of killing him again." He smirked. "Do you want to help?"

"You're serious?"

He didn't have to respond. I knew he was, and as screwed up as it was, my heart expanded with so much love it spilled over in my eyes. I took two more steps, and he folded me into his arms.

"Thank you, Logan."

My morals had been completely upended since Logan came into my life. But the fact that this man would commit murder on my behalf made me feel safe and secure. Not just in my daily life but in this relationship.

He nuzzled the side of my head, and whispered, "You are worth it, angel. I'd kill an entire village for you. If you wish, I'll happily end everyone who has ever touched my dick, too."

A laugh left me but I said, "No. Let them live with the knowledge that they'll never get to touch *my* dick ever again."

He hooked a finger under my chin, and lifted my face. Angling his head, he lowered his lips to mine, and butterflies exploded inside my belly right before he made gentle contact. This kiss was everything I loved about this man put on the tip of my tongue. It was slow passion and burning desire that built into a crescendo of explosive need swirling low inside me.

He pulled back mere inches and cupped my face as my eyelids fluttered open to lock with his dark eyes. I couldn't look away, and he refused to stop gazing into my very soul. So many emotions bubbled up inside me, but I leaned into everything and made myself look back.

"I see you Logan Dalton," I whispered.

He inhaled sharply, like I'd just reached into his chest and snatched his heart.

"I've heard it said that when you stare into the darkness, the darkness stares back."

His gaze shuttered like my words were painful, but I continued, "You once said I was your light, and when the darkness gazes at the sun, it not only gazes back, but it puts a ray of sunshine on you."

His eyes misted but his lips pulled back. "As it burns your retinas and leaves you blind."

A tiny laugh left me. "I'll be your seeing-eye human, even though you busted in here and ruined taco night with your promises to kill for me."

He jerked back. "Ruined?" His gaze dropped down my body. "I bet you're soaked for me."

My head cocked to the side as I smirked at him. "Are you insinuating that I get turned on by your violence?"

His grin bloomed into a smile. "I know for a fact my scary dog vibes get you off, angel. I distinctly remember you coming all over my cock as you gave me the names of every male who touched your pretty little pussy before me." He pressed his forehead to mine. "Don't think for a minute that I've forgotten them either."

He stepped back and reached into the pocket of his slacks pulling out a small box. My heart jumped as he opened it. My hands flew to my face as he went down on one knee.

"Logan?"

The way he looked up at me stole my breath.

"Make an honest man of me, Eden. Marry me."

My mouth opened but full sentences wouldn't form in my brain as I stared at the diamond ring. "Honest?"

My knees went out, and I dropped to the floor with him. "Yes?" I threw my arms around his neck, knocking the box to the floor as I tackled him. "Yes, I'll marry you."

My lips crashed against his as he blindly searched for the ring with one hand while holding me with the other and returned my frantic kiss.

I stopped kissing him to let him put the ring on my finger, like a lady should. However, I beamed like a fiend the entire time. The ring was spectacular. Beyond my wildest dreams.

"When?"

He looked up from my hand. "When do you want to become Mrs. Dalton?"

My fingers gripped the waistband of his slacks. "Right now."

He gripped my wrists, stopping me from unbuttoning his pants. "A few phone calls, and I can have us at the courthouse within days."

He tugged my hands away from his zipper. "In the meantime, it's taco night, and I intend to eat my fill." Dark eyes lowered down my body. "So you will sit in the mess you created until I'm ready to taste everything you've been cooking up for me."

Logan

Logan Lurch

We reheated the meat and finished preparing our tacos. As we sat down at the kitchen bar side by side with our plates, I asked, "You're sure you don't want a traditional wedding?"

She shook her head as she finished chewing. "Who would I invite?"

My angel took another bite of her taco, and the pleasure on her face made me smile. It wasn't that long ago she felt embarrassed to eat in public. "We'll still have a Blue-Frosted Rose ceremony. It will be a huge event if my brothers have anything to say about it."

She wiped her mouth with a napkin, and faced me. "Will they have a problem with us getting married before I become a member?"

"You've pledged. That's all I needed to make it official."

Her brows drew together. "I don't want to get you in trouble."

A cocky grin formed on my face as I reminded her who I was. "Who's going to spank the enforcer?"

A devilish little smirk evolved from her concern. "Me? I might spank the enforcer."

I leaned over and placed a kiss on those naughty little lips. "You can try."

A blush bloomed up her neck and stained her cheeks as she returned to her food. She wanted to challenge me for dominance. How did I feel about that? Half of me wanted to surrender my soul to her whims, but she'd have to convince Lurch.

I changed the subject. "You have three days to decide if you want to participate in Connor's punishment."

Her playful energy fled from her features, and gray blue eyes moved to meet mine. "Participate?"

My gaze moved to my plate. "Your participation is up to you. Face him, tell him off, and leave, or show him how it feels to be a victim. Either way, my hand will be the one to end him." I looked back at her. "Unless you want the honor."

She looked away. "Are you offering to let me kill him?"

"Whatever you need to help you heal from what he did to you."

Her gaze returned. "I survived him. He didn't get to rape me. I'm fine."

"You survived in spite of him, and you say that now, but trauma doesn't always show up so damn quickly. If you have anything to say to Connor, if you want to exact any type of revenge, now is the time to do it."

She ran her fingers through her short hair, and regret squeezed my chest. We should have been talking about buying a new dress or getting her hair done, instead I was offering to let her commit assault and murder. I picked up our empty plates and took them to the sink. "You have time to consider. He'll be alive for five days after we receive him at the warehouse. It takes about a week to line up receivers for his organs."

"You're selling his organs on the black market?"

"I'm not a poacher. We have connections, and everything is above board. People who have been waiting for organs will receive them in a hospital under a doctor's care. His death will save lives."

She passed me the dirty pans to wash and packed up the left-over veggies to put in the refrigerator. "Do they know they are getting the organs of a rapist?"

"He was also a pedophile. And no, they won't know the source, but we'll make sure he's healthy and a good match."

She leaned against the counter and crossed her arms. "How come you didn't bring my mom back and harvest *her* organs?"

I dried my hands, and turned around to face her. "The Cessna was cramped as it was."

That didn't produce the grin I had hoped for.

"Had there been room. Would you have brought her back and punished her like Connor?"

The polite thing to do here would be to lie. But I had made a vow never to lie to my angel. I crossed my arms over my chest as my face turned stoney. "Not exactly like Connor, but yes. I would have put her in the warehouse."

She let out a heavy breath. "And the warehouse is like your dungeon."

It wasn't a question, but I nodded anyway.

"While I love the thought that you'd kill for me, I'm not sure I can handle the reality of it."

My head bobbed with understanding. "You have three days to think about it. I won't judge your decision. But I am ready for another taco."

Her eyes popped wide with exasperation as she looked around the clean kitchen. "But we already put everything away."

My head tilted as I continued to stare at her.

"Oh." A grin broke out on her face. "You don't mean food."

"I want to show you something."

Her gaze dropped to the front of my slacks. "It's about time."

I jerked my chin towards the hallway. "Come on."

She silently followed me down the hall. We went past the first locked door and stopped at the second. I pressed my thumb to the pad, and the lock clicked open. I opened the door and waved her in.

Blue eyes met mine as she stepped inside. A gasp left her as she turned her attention to the blue and silver interior. A brand-new high-end spanking bench, a Saint Andrew's Cross, and sex furniture filled the room. A few floggers neatly lined the walls, but there were still boxes of goodies still to be unpacked.

"It's far from finished."

"Holy crap, you really do have a dungeon," she breathed.

"The moment I got out of jail, I converted my guest bedroom for you."

Her gaze lifted to the chains hanging from the ceiling, a frown lingering on her pretty lips. "So, you did all this before you knew I wasn't selling my snatch in Costa Rica."

"Yes, I did. Every piece of furniture, device, and item was put in this room to remind you exactly who you belong to."

Her finger lifted to her chin as she slowly spun still taking in the scenery. "Do I still need reminding?"

I stepped to the Saint Andrew's Cross along the wall. "Always. Now undress."

Like a doe intentionally stepping in front of the headlights, she held eye contact as she took her clothing off. The expression on her face told me she knew this might hurt, but it also might be the most thrilling moment of her life.

I parted the drapes of the window next to the cross, and the warm glow of the sunset bathed her curves in golden light. The dresser held the leather cuffs with the rings needed to secure my angel the way I wanted.

"Put your back to the cross, and give me your wrists."

After putting the leather cuffs on her, I lifted her hands high. Her breasts jutted out as if they were begging for my attention. They'd have to wait but would get more than they bargained for soon.

Turning my attention to her ankles, I secured them to the cross at the widest points. Stepping back, I took several minutes to admire my Eden, trapped, naked, and vulnerable. My cock had never been so hard.

She shifted under my hooded stare. "Are you going to whip me?"

I had spent countless hours fantasizing about what I'd do to her in this room. I'd spank her, flog her, drip wax over her breasts, AND force so many orgasms out of her exhausted body, but my brain refused to settle on just one thing. I wanted to do it all at once, but we needed to slow it down and talk about what could happen.

Moving towards the small bar I'd stocked with my favorite whiskey, I said, "I think I'll have a drink while I admire the view."

Her brows drew together. "So, you are just going to leave me like this?"

Opening the cabinet that hid the small fridge, I pulled out the ice tray and cracked it, freeing the cubes. "Do you remember your safe words?"

"Green, Logan. I can't get any greener than right now," she said with an annoyed edge to her voice.

I poured the whiskey over the ice and said without looking at her, "Good, because I want you dripping with anticipation by the time we get started."

Her only response was a rush of breath.

I faced her, and leaned against the bar, letting my gaze roam over her body as I sipped from the glass.

"Have you ever worn nipple clamps before?"

Blue eyes widened. "No."

"How about suction cups? I think you'd be so pretty with your nipples pulled tight into sharp points."

"Does it hurt?"

I took another long swallow, and savored the burn of my drink. "Only when you take them off."

I approached her with my glass in hand. "All that blood rushing around your peaks will make the nerve endings go crazy." Lifting the chilled glass to her breast I traced her nipple with it, and enjoyed how it tightened from the cold.

"Do it," her breathy voice shook.

I traced her other nipple with the glass before draining it. "All in due time, angel."

Fingering a half-melted cube of ice, I lifted it to her lips. She opened her mouth, and I pushed it inside. "Suck it slowly."

Her cheeks hollowed for just a second before I held out my hand, and said, "Give it back."

She dutifully dropped the cube in my palm, and I traced down her neck, leaving a cold wet trail over her collarbone down to her right breast. She moaned as I teased her nipple before moving across her body to play with the other.

It melted quickly, and I fished out another cube from my glass and presented it to her mouth.

"Suck."

She sucked the whiskey off it and deposited it back into my palm.

"Good girl."

This cube left a chilled trail between her breasts, down her stomach, and over her parted pussy. She hissed as I held it against her clit.

"Logan."

Her hips wiggled, and she closed her eyes, letting her head fall back against the padded cross.

I made her endure the freeze for thirty seconds before I pushed the ice cube just inside her. Cupping her pussy, I caught it as it came out and used my middle finger to push it deeper. She pulled on the restraints with a shiver. It slipped out again, and I popped it in my mouth before sucking her right nipple.

"Logan!"

I pulled off and said, "That's it. Talk to me Eden. Tell me how this feels."

Eden

How could I put how I was feeling into words? Words could not describe the hurricane of emotions these sensations were creating inside me.

My lips parted. "I, oh god, I'm on edge. Scared, but I'm not."

His mouth warmed up my cold, wet nipple as he continued to suck. One large hand covered my other breast, and his palm felt rough. "I want to come, but I also want to savor the journey."

He pulled off my breast. "And what a journey this is going to be." He moved his hand to suck my other nipple. The sensation tingled all through my body, and pooled low.

"Oh my god, Logan, please."

He lifted his mouth to mine, and I kissed him with all the passion I had in me. He matched my kiss, and took it to another level. My lips felt swollen when he stepped back.

"I think we'll start with clamps."

He opened the top drawer of the dresser on the other side of the window. The clamps were metal adorned with blue gems, and attached with a delicate silver chain. Instead of going to my nipple, he lifted the device to my mouth. "Part those pretty little lips."

When I did, he carefully attached the clamp to my bottom lip. "How does that feel?"

My gaze met his. "Fine." Talking with a nipple clamp attached to my lip made my face heat, and he grinned before he took it off.

He pinched my nipple, playing with it until it tightened for him before he attached the clamp. I swallowed the nervous lump as I adjusted to the sensation. Dark eyes watched my expression intently as he moved to my other nipple. The squeeze of pressure made me feel trapped.

"How does that feel?"

I took a moment to consider. "It stings a little but not too bad."

His smile stole my breath. "Good girl." His hand slid around my throat as he leaned in and kissed me. The second his lips touched mine, my brain fuzzed out, and I whimpered into his mouth. His fingers tightened as he swallowed my moment of panic. I tried to squeeze my thighs together to relieve the throbbing but only ended up jiggling my tits.

He reached between my legs, and cupped my pussy as he continued to devour me until I gave in to his kiss. The moment I submitted, he pushed a finger inside me. I sucked in a breath through my nose and struggled again. His hand tightened around my throat as his kiss grew forceful.

My body was wound so tightly that his finger felt too big. It was too long, and I swore he was stroking my cervix. I jerked my lips to the side, and pleaded, "Logan."

His teeth grazed my ear as he added another finger. "You are dripping wet for me."

"Yes," I hissed, "Oh god!"

"I fucking love it when you are so desperate for my cock you beg me."

He moved incredibly slowly inside me, pushing and pulling, stroking and stretching. I was about to start begging again when his fingers left me. My lips parted as the hand on my neck moved to hold my jaw. Slick fingers slipped over my tongue, and the taste of me filled my mouth. With a lusty groan I closed my mouth around them and sucked.

He pressed his forehead against my cheek and whispered, "My cock is so jealous right now."

He pulled his fingers partially out, and I sucked them back in. He inhaled a sharp breath and said, "But my cock will have to wait, because your thighs will be slick with need before I let him out to play."

His fingers left my mouth and curled around the silver chain connecting my tits. He lifted it, pulling my clamped nipples up until I made a noise I'd never made before. It was somewhere between a cry of pain, a prayer, and a lusty sigh. My eyes squeezed shut as my body trembled.

"Breathe, angel. I'm going to take these off now."

He cupped my right breast. "Inhale, hold, and exhale."

A shout left me as I exhaled, and his large palm covered my stinging nipple. "Logan!" He quickly removed the other clamp, and I shouted, "Oh my god!"

He smoothed his hands over my breasts. "Good girl, such a good, sweet angel."

He lowered his mouth, licking, and gently sucking each aching peak as I lost control over my voice. "Logan, please!"

He pulled his mouth off my breasts and dropped to his knees as my nipples throbbed. "If you come before I'm finished enjoying my meal, you won't stop coming for the next hour. Understand me?"

I nodded, but he wasn't paying any attention to anything but my pussy. He spread me open and licked into me like a hungry beast. His tongue penetrated deep, and my hip jerked forward as it curled and flicked. His lips sealed around me, and he sucked so hard the muscles in my thighs shook violently.

Don't come, don't come. But my body was already careening towards a massive orgasm. His hands smoothed up from my knees to my hips and back down as he devoured me. His nose hit my clit just right, and my spine stiffened as a turmoil of pleasure swirled like a tornado in my lower half.

"Fuck!" It was unstoppable.

I jerked, and locked up as my pussy pulsed, and pounded. I convulsed against his tongue as I moaned and cried out. He growled against my pussy, tongue working overtime inside me, confirming that he tasted my orgasm.

He pulled off and wiped his slick mouth with the back of his hand as he smirked up at me. "Bad girl."

Tears left my lashes, not because I was overly emotional, but because I was overly stimulated, and that orgasm had been intense. "I'm sorry. I tried to hold off but..."

He stood up, still smirking, and winked at me. "You did exactly as I hoped you'd do."

Turning away he went back to the dresser and set a small box on the top. My racing heart paused with trepidation. "Is that my *Soul Sucker 6000*?"

"You didn't think I'd toss your favorite toy, did you?"

I swallowed the lump in my throat. While I loved the clit sucker, it was powerful. I could only go twice before my clit was too sensitive to continue. He had said *for an hour*. "I didn't think about it at all."

"It's all I've ever thought about after watching you barely use it on surveillance."

"Logan, I can't take more than a couple minutes."

He knelt in front of me, and I heard the machine click on. "Oh baby, you aren't using it to its full potential."

Logan parted my pussy and put the small cup right over my clit, and I threw my head back and screamed as my clit rumbled with the vibration. The orgasm that slammed into me was immediate and sudden. He slipped an arm around me, and moved the toy with me as I jerked and shook, forcing me to feel everything.

"Logan, please!"

My cries were ignored. He switched the pulse to a different vibration and held me tight as I screamed again. My legs twisted, and I tried so hard to dislodge the stimulation, but Logan would not be denied. Tears streamed down my cheeks as I came again.

"Please stop."

He pulled the toy off me, but changed the rhythm once more and pressed it against me again.

I struggled in earnest as he moved it around until he found my clit and pressed. "Fuck! Logan." My voice had grown five octaves, and I was fairly sure the police would be knocking on our door in moments.

My clit exploded into tiny shards of pleasure and wouldn't regroup. He refused to relent, no matter how hard I begged. He just kept switching the pattern and intensity as I bucked, screamed, and panted.

It felt like an hour before his mouth replaced the toy. I felt like I'd run a marathon. A fine sheen of sweat dripped down my back as I gasped and cried out. His tongue glided slowly around and over my abused clit. It felt amazing until he hit a sensitive spot, and then it was intense. Sometimes he'd focus his tongue on the spots that had me struggling and pleading before moving away.

My toes were permanently curled. "Please, I'll do anything."

His tongue moved over my clit and stayed there until I exploded again.

Finally, he pulled back. "I'm going to release you, and you are going to crawl over to that *Tantra Chair*. You will bend over the high side, legs wide, pussy open."

It was a good thing he said crawl because my legs refused to hold my weight.

He eased me down onto all fours, and I crawled toward the weird wavy couch as he removed his clothes behind me. My thighs were so slick and messy they sounded obscene as I moved.

"Over the high end, sweet angel."

This thing wasn't a chair at all. It looked like a chaise lounge with humps, one higher than the other. I flopped over the end he pointed at, and went completely boneless. He came up behind me, and adjusted my body, so my ass was at the highest point.

"Grab your knees."

He had to help me find my knees, but I was able to hold my legs forward and open. I stiffened when I felt the cool, smooth metal rim my asshole.

"What is that?"

"Relax," he pressed the object deeper, "it's the perfect size for your first time."

The pressure had my heart rate increasing, and the knowledge that he was staring right at my butthole made my face heat. "Logan."

"I know it feels weird, but you are doing so well, angel."

I felt impossibly stretched, and then, with the assistance of some lube, it slipped inside, and my ass closed around the base. He gently rocked it, and I felt a light vibration inside me. The gasp I released made him chuckle.

"It's a special buttplug, angel. The more it moves, the higher the frequency it emits."

I learned about frequencies this morning at church. Not a lot but the BFR believed that the higher your vibrations were, the more receptive to their magic you became. I didn't think they meant anal sex.

I felt his thick tip press against my slick pussy. "Oh! Logan, you won't fit with that in there."

He slowly pushed inside. "Watch me," he hissed, "Godsdamn angel, it's tight, but you're taking me."

I blew out a harsh breath as my body stretched to accommodate him. The bulb inside me shifted, and electric pleasure crawled up my spine. As if he knew exactly how that felt, he retreated and pushed in again. The vibration from the buttplug reverberated throughout my body.

I lost the grip on my knees as my legs stiffened, and his hands bit into my hips as he held me steady for his tormentingly shallow strokes. "Logan, holy shit, please. I need more."

His deep voice was strained with control. "You're going to get so much that you'll be walking funny and seeing stars for days."

His cock moved deeper before he pulled out and started over. My thighs slammed together, and his legs opened to capture them. Pressing me into the plush mound he seated himself fully inside me. "Brace yourself, Eden."

I grabbed the lower side of the wave just in time to feel him pull back and slam forward.

"Oh fuck!"

And fuck he did. With all his might, he fucked me. Like a beast in a rut, he fucked me, and the vibrations and fullness suspended me in a state of utter bliss. Like my soul moved into a completely different dimension where pleasure and pain swirled in a whirlpool of push and pull. His rough breath was the whoosh of water. The sloppy sounds of fucking were splashes against rocks, and my screams were the shouts of the victim being dragged down to the depths.

This man, who I just agreed to marry, was a machine. His stamina made my eyes cross. I lost track of time in that extra dimension whirlpool, but when he finally came, I swear I felt him in my throat, and tasted his seed on my tongue. The shout of bliss he made had me clamping down on him.

He leaned over my back, and wrapped his arms around me. Warmth bubbled up in me as he kissed my shoulder and panted, "I love you, Eden."

Chapter Thirty-Five

Logan

Connor had arrived this morning looking like he'd already been put through the ringer. I had him stripped naked and strung up like a slab of beef. His face was beet red as he demanded to know why he was there.

I said nothing as I picked a sturdy cane from the wall of torture.

"What are you doing?"

I turned toward the panicked man and tested the reeds' flexibility by giving the air a few strikes. The ominous sound it made had the man begging with all his might. Gods, how I loved that sound.

"Oh man, please. I'll do anything. Just tell me what you want."

I stalked forward as Bentley, Scout, and Torrid wandered into the main area and paused to watch.

"Confess."

I swung the cane, not caring where or what I hit. The impact reverberated up my arm, and the sound of it hitting flesh soothed my raging beast. The scream that followed was pure magic to my soul. I closed my eyes and tilted my face to the skylights as I absorbed his terror and pain like one would enjoy a cool rain in the heat of summer.

I swung again, and it landed across his bare ass. The thud had barely landed when it was followed by another scream. Connor jerked, his buttocks convulsing as a red streak appeared.

I waited for him to quiet before I whispered, "Confess."

"Confess what?!"

I landed another blow along the top of his meaty ass, and the screams started again.

"Confess your sins."

"Wait!" the swinging man cried, "Please, just wait."

I waited until his body twisted just enough to land another blow to his ass.

"Confess."

"I stole millions from my company!"

I struck again.

"Reach deeper, Connor. I'm looking for crimes against humanity."

This time I struck, not once, not twice, but five times as he screamed, jerked his legs, and swayed back and forth.

"Please! I'm not a criminal."

"So, you've never raped a woman before?"

His head dropped. "I'm sorry."

Scout stomped forward still wearing Torrid's oversized t-shirt. "What about children?"

Connor's head swiveled towards her. "Never!"

Bentley pulled her back just as I started swinging again.

When his sobs settled, he heaved his words. "Okay, okay, but it was never rape. She initiated it."

My restraint was impeccable. "What about Grace in Costa Rica?"

His red, swollen eyes shot to mine. "She wasn't a kid."

My lips pursed. "You tried to rape her. She jumped overboard to get away from you."

"How the fuck do you know that? Did her mother blab her fat mouth?"

I closed my eyes, and took several long breaths before I said, "Her mother is dead for selling her to you." Her mother was dead for way more than that, but this piece of donkey shit didn't need to know that.

Scout gasped somewhere behind me. "Karla is dead?"

Bentley whispered something to her, and she went silent.

"Who was she to you?" The talking windbag asked.

"She is my angel. The very thing that keeps me from going over the edge and into the pit of darkness."

My control slipped, and I lit him up good. I lost count at fifteen as my arm cocked back and swung repeatedly until a large fist closed around my wrist.

"That's enough, boss," Torrid said, "you don't want to damage the product too much before sale."

Connor was strangely quiet. He had passed out at some point. His striped body still swung back and forth from the force of my blows.

I nodded at Torrid. "Help me take him down and secure him."

Bentley came back carrying the neck shackle as Torrid lowered Connor to the ground. The beaten man stirred and groaned as he touched the concrete but stayed unconscious.

Torrid had a cell ready for Connor, and we secured him to the wall by his neck. I left him to do my cleansing ritual before I returned home to my angel. I would give the man a day to heal before I came back to punish him some more.

Would Eden be ready to face her attacker by then? She hadn't mentioned him since we last talked about Connor's impending arrival, and eventual death. But my angel had been distracted by my insatiable need for her to be naked under me. I couldn't get enough of filling her up. It didn't matter that we had decided to wait for children, I still loved to breed her.

It was three days before Eden was able to officially become Mrs. Logan Dalton. Mandy and Dan stood as witnesses, and my bride beamed at me as we signed the certificate. She looked amazing after I forced her to spend the day at the spa. I hoped she felt as beautiful as she looked wearing that light blue sundress that showed off her figure and glowing skin. Skin that bore my seal in the form of small bruises and bite marks.

I knew Dan was worried about Eden. She was making unbreakable vows to the beast of the Blue-Frosted Rose, and his gaze traced every blemish and fingerprint that was visible. He knew exactly how freakishly big I was, and I suspected he wondered how his little girl weathered the storm. It made me want to jerk him aside and smack him around. I wanted to scream at him that he should have cared years ago when Eden was enduring abuse at the hands of her mother.

But Eden had greeted her father and aunt with such happiness that I kept Lurch in chains for the day. Mandy and Eden had grown closer over the past three days. They met for four hours every morning, and Eden had taken a keen interest in the use of herbs in ritual. She spoke about the extensive herb garden that grew on the grounds of the church, and the gardeners even allowed her to bring home some cuttings. My home smelled like the Sanctuary, which made me smile when I came home from a long day at the warehouse.

After our courthouse wedding, Eden wanted to go out to eat with her family. Of course, I agreed. I'd break bread with my enemies if that was what she wished, so we chose a restaurant and jumped in my truck to meet her folks there.

I flipped the center console of my Dodge Ram up, and patted the seat next to me. "Scoot over here."

She grinned wildly as she moved over and attached the lap belt before she snuggled against me.

“Open those legs up for me, beautiful.”

The second her thighs opened, my fingers moved her panties over, and started playing. My good girl got comfortable and gave her pussy fully over to me. Two fingers slowly entered her hot body, casually pumping in and out.

“What did Dan say to you when he pulled you aside before the ceremony?”

She turned her lips to my bicep. “He asked if I was okay.”

I curled my fingers stroking her G spot. “Are you?”

Her legs opened wider, and her hips lifted. The sounds of her wetness were loud and sloppy. She was practically laying across the cab as I drove. My thumb grazed her clit, and she arched with pleasure.

“I am now.”

She wouldn’t be soon because I had no plans to allow her to finish without my cock buried deep inside her.

By the time I pulled into the restaurant parking she was a whimpering mess. When my fingers left her, I patted her primed pussy, and said, “Sit up, angel, we are here.”

“What?” She pressed her legs together, and a tremor went through her.

I tsked, and said, “Oh no, sweet girl, keep those thighs open for your husband.”

She pouted. “My husband is a cruel man.”

A joyous laugh left me. “You knew that from the beginning.” I hopped out of the truck and opened the back door. “Stay there, precious angel. I’ll come around and get you.” The gift bag was right behind the driver’s seat. I prayed she’d love the gift as much as I would love to see her wearing it.

I opened the passenger door, and she spotted the bag immediately. "What's that?"

I lifted my arms towards her. "You'll see. Come on, your dad and aunt are waiting for us."

She leaned into my arms, and cupped my cheeks as she kissed me. Fuck, I loved it when she kissed me like that. I pulled her out of the truck and lowered her to the ground as I returned her kiss. She gave me a naughty little smirk as she pulled away and glanced down at the bulge in my dress pants.

I confessed, "There will never be a time in our lives where you don't affect me like this. I'll always want you."

Her smirk bloomed into a lovely smile. "Come on, my family is waiting."

I locked the truck and followed her. "Do you really think that will stop me?"

She glanced back at me. "Are you going to fuck me in front of my dad while we eat dinner?"

"Keep testing me, angel, and find out."

She didn't have time to think of a comeback before we were entering the restaurant and greeting the hostess.

The hostess' smile faltered the moment her gaze found my scars. "Party of four?"

"Back room, please."

A pensive look crossed her face, and I gave her an indulgent smile. "Reservation is under Dalton."

Her eyes popped wide. "Yes, sir, right this way."

Eden's head snapped from the hostess to me. The power I had at my fingertips still surprised her. I gave her a cheeky wink as I put my hand on the small of her back to urge her ahead of me. Her family followed. The hostess seated us in the private room, and servers swarmed us, taking care of our every need.

Once the chaos settled Dan asked Eden, "What are your plans for the future?"

Eden put her drink down. "For now, I'm back at college."

Mandy added, "I don't know how she plans on juggling her schedule, she's so behind on classwork."

Dan frowned as he studied Mandy. "How do you know all this?"

Mandy's brows drew together. "I'm her sponsor, hun. You know this."

He looked down and grumbled, "I didn't know you two talked about more than just history, herbs, and religion."

Eden shifted uncomfortably. "Of course, we talk about more than just..."

My hand drifted up Eden's inner thigh, and I gave her leg a small squeeze as our food arrived.

She briefly glanced at me before finishing her sentence, "You know." A brief smile flashed before she added, "We often grab an early lunch after. You are welcome to join us anytime."

He waited until the servers left before replying. "Yes, of course, I will. I've just been so busy trying to recoup my losses."

I broke the long silence only because I knew my angel wanted a relationship with her father even though the bastard didn't deserve it.

"Now that Eden is my responsibility, you should make up the difference from what Karla stole rather quickly."

Eden frowned as she parted her legs wider, urging my hand to move closer. I gave her thigh another small squeeze but left her pussy untouched. I wondered how long it would be until she moved my hand to where she desperately needed it.

Eden

To say that my wedding dinner was slightly awkward would have been an understatement. The harder I tried to connect with my emotionally unavailable father, the worse it got. Mandy kept frowning at my father like she had some words for him, and Logan's energy buzzed with darkness the longer he was in my dad's presence.

Maybe it was time to give up and accept that he just couldn't fill the role of being my dad. I hadn't cared much before he put me in a condo so he could cut my mother off. I don't know why I thought things could change between us now that I was working on becoming Logan's Blue Lady. So, I treated him like my aunt's boyfriend for the rest of our meal.

Logan's hand never made it past my panties, and I was squirming by the time he put the light blue gift bag on the table in front of me.

"It's about time you stopped teasing me." My face heated from the dual meaning of my statement. The moment I made eye contact with Logan, I felt my blush deepen from the knowing look on his face. I'd pay for that later, and I couldn't wait.

Inside the gift bag was a long jewelry box. I opened it and grinned at the silver chain choker with blue roses winding a circle at the center. "A necklace?"

My dad sat up straight. "That's not a necklace."

Logan's face darkened, and I put my hand on his arm as I looked at my father. He frowned at me. "That's a collar, Eden. If you let him put that on you, he'll own you for the rest of your life."

"I thought that was what we were doing when we got married today."

He glanced at Logan before setting his face with determination. "You know well that marriage can be reversed. It's not too late to back out. You are just a pledge, and freshly married, but this collar symbolizes something that can't be undone. Do you even know the man you married today? Do you know what he does for a living?"

The arm under my hand vibrated with tension. If I let Logan go, he'd annihilate my father, and that might strain my new friendship with Mandy.

"He's a murderer, Dad. He killed a man who drugged and kidnapped me. Then he flew to a different country to bring me home—"

"He killed your mother."

"Actually, no. Mickey killed my mother. Logan held me while my world shattered into a thousand tiny pieces. Then he hunted down the man who assaulted me so badly I jumped ship miles from shore."

The pride that showed in Logan's gaze as I looked up at him took my breath. I didn't need a dad to protect and love me. I had Logan, and he'd burn an entire country down for me.

I swallowed and said, "And yes, I have a few things to say to Connor before you take him apart for daring to touch what is yours."

I lifted the necklace, and handed it to him. "Collar me, Logan Dalton."

Logan turned his chair to face me. "Kneel before me and receive my devotion."

The necklace was cool as he slipped it around my neck. My hair was already up; I just moved a few strands to make it easier for him to work the clasp.

His eyes were almost misty, and his baritone voice cracked. "I belong to you as much as you belong to me, Mrs. Eden Dalton. When you look at yourself in the mirror, remember you own my body, mind, and soul."

I looked at my dad's baffled expression, and said, "You might want to leave now. I'm about to do some filthy things with my owner."

Mandy was the first to move. Her chair scraped the floor, and she reached for Dan. "Congratulations to you both. Come on dear, let's let the newlyweds have some privacy."

I didn't wait for them to leave before I reached for Logan's belt. I had his dick in my hands moments later, and the taste of him on my tongue, stretching my lips around him. He was barely able to shimmy his pants to his knees before a deep moan left his lips. I worked him with both hands, one on his shaft, the other kneading his balls.

He gave me as much control as he could muster before his hand cradled the back of my head. His fingers curled in my hair as he pushed my mouth down on him. "I love you so much, my beautiful angel."

He controlled the depth and speed of the blowjob, and my body bloomed for him.

"But I'm still not going to let you come until I have you home, secured nice and wide for me."

I moaned on him, and he hissed, "Drink me, wife. That's it. Good girl. Swallow my cum because the next time I explode, it will be in your womb."

I had barely stopped swallowing when he grabbed my arm and pulled me to my feet. Empty dishes rattled as he pushed me over the table and lifted my dress. I prayed Mandy said something to the servers as she left and that we wouldn't be interrupted.

"Show me how wet you are, Eden."

His clothing rustled, and I heard his zipper go up. A smile curved my lips as I widened my legs, knowing he regretted wasting his orgasm on my mouth.

He whispered a heartfelt, "Fuck, you are soaked for me."

He pulled my panties off, stuffed them in his pocket, and commanded, "Part your pussy for me, wife. I need to clean this mess up."

I reached between my body and the table and used both hands to open my lower lips for him. Fiery breath warmed my wetness right before his mouth closed in. I let out a long moan as pleasure consumed me. "Oh my god, Logan."

He'd been teasing me all day, and my control was sorely tested. I'd gladly take the punishment later if I could just... "Ah! Yes! Oh my god, yes!" My body stiffened, and I came so hard I saw stars as his tongue found my clit and forced me over the edge.

He pulled back, and growled, "Naughty wife. I told you not to come."

He knew exactly what he'd done. I straightened my dress and faced him. "That was your fault, and you know it."

His answering grin made the hair on my arms stand up. "I'm still going to punish you for it."

I steeled myself for a fiery hot pussy spanking, and thirty minutes of forced orgasms, followed by a dicking down that would have me waddling a hell of a lot worse than I already was. I couldn't wait.

As we left, we stumbled across my dad leaning against the wall just outside the private room. His face was a shade of red I thought only I could get. "I made sure they didn't disturb you." He refused to make eye contact with either one of us.

Logan's lip curled before he said, "Don't think for one second that just because I married the spawn of your loins that the next time you disrespect our relationship, I won't snatch you up and choke you out."

He pushed past my dad as Mandy wandered up. I met her gaze and mouthed, "I'm sorry."

She grinned and waved it off. "I'm so happy for you, Eden."

My smile felt permanently plastered on my face. I was happy, and for once, I wasn't waiting for the other shoe to clobber me. Logan had my back, and I felt brave enough to step outside my comfort zone in so many ways.

Once in the truck, I twisted to face my husband. "I don't know what I'd say to Connor."

"You don't have to say anything. You can just stand there and stare at him, like a snake in a cage."

I thought about that image and said, "That just feels dull."

His lips twisted into a mischievous grin. "I can give you a knife to sharpen things up."

"I might kill him with it."

"Too bad, so sad," he deadpanned as he backed out of the parking space.

"Would that change your view of me if I did? Would I no longer be your sunshine?"

He stopped in the middle of the parking lot, holding up traffic, to meet my gaze. "Nothing you, or anyone else can do, will ever dampen your glow, angel."

"Then take me to see Connor."

A car horn behind us made me jump.

Logan shot the driver a glower through the rearview mirror, but I doubted anyone could see him through the tinted window. He put the big truck into drive, and headed towards Lakeland.

Chapter Thirty-Six

Facing Demons

Eden

We were barely situated on the busy I4 corridor when Logan pulled to the side of the highway and reached into the back seat. He dug around in his duffle bag before pulling out a black cloth. He passed it to me.

"Put this on."

I turned the cloth in my hands before I said, "It's a hood."

He snorted. "Yeah. Even high-level members don't know the exact location of the warehouse."

I slipped the hood over my head, but lifted the edge to grin at him. "So, no peeking?"

He gave me a playful scowl. "Naughty girl. I think you enjoy your punishments a little too much."

I laughed and dropped the edge of the hood, surrounding myself in darkness. The cloth was so dense no light was allowed past the barrier.

The truck moved forward, and I gripped the door beside me with both hands. I jumped when I felt his palm on my shoulder.

"Come here."

I found the buckle to the seatbelt, and his arm wrapped around me as I scooted closer to him. Fumbling blindly, I managed to secure the lap belt before leaning into the comfort of Logan's warm body.

My nose was keen on inhaling Logan's scent. My skin tingled in the wake of his fingertips making lazy patterns on my upper arm. I was more aware of him, his breathing, and energy now that my eyesight had been removed from the equation. Even his voice seemed deeper and more melodic.

"Call Torrid."

The speakers confirmed Logan's order, and a moment later a deep male voice answered.

"Yeah."

"Get my toy ready. I'm bringing company."

"You got it, boss." The line ended, but I stayed silent under my hood. "It's going to get a little bumpy here in a minute, angel. Don't worry, I've got you."

It felt as if he was driving completely off road as the truck bounced and tilted for what felt like forever.

"It's a good thing I don't get seasick."

"Yeah, listen, speaking of sick, I've already had a small go at Connor. He may not look so hot."

I snorted. "He didn't look hot before, so... What did you do to him?"

"I gave him a taste of the cane. My alter ego, Lurch, thrives here. He handles you differently than he does his warehouse victims."

The wariness in his voice had me thinking about how I felt when I said I wanted to come here in the first place. "Lurch won't make me think any less of you, Logan. I love you both."

The road seemed to level out as he said, "We'll see."

I felt him put the truck in park. "Keep the hood on until I tell you."

His door shut as I felt for the seatbelt.

My door opened, and I moved towards my husband's hands. He lifted me out of the truck, but my heels had barely hit the ground before he picked me up like a child and carried me.

I clung to his neck for dear life. "Don't drop me."

"Never."

"I'm just not used to being carried around blind."

He chuckled as a door opened, and a blast of cool air blew by my bare legs.

Logan tensed. "Mind your eyes, Tor."

"You've got her covered, boss."

The door shut with a metallic clang, and Logan set me on my feet. He pulled the hood off me, and I blinked a few times before making eye contact with a beefy, golden-brown man in a military buzz cut.

His smile was warm. "Hello, Eden. I'm Torrid."

I thought Logan had muscles, but Torrid was... I didn't have the words to describe the massive man standing before me. While Logan had height and sharp edges, this man was made to cuddle. Which was an absurd thought since I knew Torrid was an enforcer who was as dark and violent as Lurch.

"Hi."

We were standing in an antechamber. Probably for security's sake. The next door opened, and Logan led us into a reception area with a couple chairs, a couch, and a long hall that led off to the right.

A third door opened to high ceilings, skylights, and cold air. A warehouse. Except for the cells lining the left wall and the naked man hanging by his arms in the middle of the vast space, it was ordinary.

It even had partitions to my right that looked like a cluster of offices. I recognized Bentley standing in the doorway of one of those offices, and I lifted my hand in greeting. His grin reminded me of a golden retriever as he came forward. His wavy blond hair, immaculate dress, and rolling gait helped solidify that image.

A solemn woman with stunning green eyes tracked close behind Bentley, wearing a shirt like a dress. Her frown dug at me. Especially when it deepened as her gaze flicked upward at Logan and then away.

His face remained his usual stoic mask, but I couldn't help but wonder if she feared him because of his scars or for more sinister reasons. My gaze tracked her bare feet and legs before landing on her collar. Unlike my elegant day collar, she wore a dog collar with embedded blue jewels.

"Who do you belong to?" I cringed inwardly at my stupidity.

Her whole body went stiff, but the look she shot Torrid raised my suspicions. "No one owns me. Why the fuck would you ask that?"

Bentley placed a hand on her shoulder, and her glare shot to him. "Don't be rude to the boss's lady, little hacker."

We both looked at each other with renewed interest. I touched my throat as I quickly said, "I'm sorry. The collar threw me. I'm Eden."

"Divina, but you might know me as Scout."

My jaw dropped, and my gaze moved to Logan's tightlipped smile as he nodded in confirmation.

Torrid said, "And Scout has something to say to you both."

Her head snapped to him. "Really? Right away? Like we haven't even shaken hands yet, and you want me to grovel for their forgiveness?"

He merely lifted an eyebrow, and the emotions that played on her face confirmed every suspicion I had earlier. This girl had it bad for Torrid.

"Fine," she turned to me, "I lost my temper with the dumbass and he needed stitches afterwards." With a glance back at Torrid she continued, "I'm sorry he's in the shape he's currently in."

For the first time since entering, I drew enough courage to really look at Connor. His head hung low as he swayed slowly on the tips of his toes. He bore so many bruises that he didn't even look like the man who'd attacked me. Then again, I never gave him the opportunity to get naked before jumping ship. Now he just looked as pitiful as his manhood drooping between his legs.

Logan growled at Torrid as he moved towards the battered man. "You will explain to me later how she got her hands on anything sharp enough to require stitches."

My feet felt like cinder blocks as I attempted to follow my husband. Numbness spread up my body the closer I got to my attempted rapist. I may have felt paralyzed, but my heart was pounding in my ears, and my mind was picking up on every little twinge and breath Connor made like it was a threat to my safety.

The odor hit me immediately, and my nose crinkled at the stench of stress sweat. "You smell."

He lifted his head just enough to look at me. "Grace, thank God. Tell these psychos what really happened." His voice was cracked and rough, but I wasn't sure if it was due to the bandage around his throat or from screaming. Maybe both.

"They know what really happened."

His face twisted in anger and pain. "Then tell them to let me go!" His shout was a gravelly whisper.

"No."

His jaw dropped open in astonishment. He really thought I'd help him. "But you agreed to everything I did to you."

"No, I didn't. I don't care what my mother messaged you. I never agreed to assault. What kind of person wants to do that to someone anyway?"

Scout said from behind me, "A shitty one. Fucking pedo."

Conner could barely hold his head up right. "So, are you going to beat me like he did?" He tried to jerk his chin towards Logan, but it was merely a twitch.

"No. I just wanted to look into your beady eyes one last time before they harvest your organs."

Logan added, "Alive. I'm going to take parts of you while you still breathe. I'll savor your screams as I cut you. When you pass out, I'm going to wake your ass up and continue taking you apart until you no longer wake."

I said, "And I want you to remember my eyes as you die."

Connor let out a sob. "We looked for you in the water. Tried to save you."

"And then you messaged my mother and told her you wanted your money back because I was lost at sea and didn't let you fuck me. Yeah, I read the messages. You knew I hadn't agreed to the terms of that date. I hope you are forever tormented by the horrible things you've done in this life."

I turned my back on him, and he shouted, "Grace, please! Don't do this. Don't leave me here."

I walked straight up to Scout, and said, "You should have cut deeper, so the bastard couldn't talk."

Wide eyes turned to Torrid. "See? I was doing her a favor."

"Pet," Torrid warned as his eyes slipped behind me, "no need to antagonize Logan any more than you already have."

Realizing that my husband wasn't standing next to me, I spun around. "Logan."

He had a nasty looking knife poised at Connor's pursed lips. At the sound of my voice, he turned his head just enough so we could see his scarred face.

"I'm ready to go."

He almost ignored me but Torrid said, "Take his tongue now, and he might reach his expiration date before his time. He's already lost enough blood today."

Logan grabbed Connors jaw, and leaned close. "Lucky sack of shit." Without looking away from the man, he flung his knife, and stuck it into the wall before driving his fist into Connor's stomach.

He stormed towards us but stopped in front of Scout. "He's not yours to punish, little girl. He's mine. Touch him again, and I'll take a finger from you. Understand?"

"Logan."

He spun towards me, and unclenched his fist.

I smiled at him even though the look on his face was absolutely terrifying. "Take me home."

He nodded once, rolled his shoulders, and cracked his neck before he took my hand and led me towards the exit.

In the antechamber, I picked up my hood but pulled him close. "Thank you."

He looked thoroughly confused, but I slipped my arms around his neck and lifted to my toes. My lips crashed into his, and we kissed like desperate lovers.

Logan

Logan Lurch

The following day, I received the call that the Elders had gathered and requested my immediate presence at the Ocala mansion. Mickey had given me a heads up that the tribunal had started a few days ago. There wasn't anything I could do about it then, and there was nothing I could do now, other than show up and pray.

Eden wandered into the room and sat down on my knee. I set my phone face down beside me as I welcomed her into my arms. She smelled amazing, and I dragged her scent deep into my lungs.

She asked, "What's wrong?"

I leaned back in the chair and met her gaze. "I have to go out of town for a few days."

She frowned. "Why?"

My expression made her grimace, but I answered her question. "I have to answer for my failures as an enforcer."

Outrage flared in her face. "What failures? You saved me."

I leaned forward and kissed her forehead. "I shouldn't have had to save you. Scout shouldn't have found any weakness in our security in the first place. That is on me, and I have to answer for it."

She stiffened as alarm replaced the rage. "Answer how? They aren't going to kill you are they?"

"No, angel. My team fixed the issue and have eliminated all threats. No secrets were exposed, but I'll be gone for a few days."

"When do you leave?"

My shoulders folded inward. "Pilot is waiting downstairs."

She placed a hand on my chest. "Is there any chance at all that you won't return?"

"No chance in hell, angel." I put my hand over hers. "Both of my brothers will act as my advocates, and Bentley will be there, too. It's nothing to worry about. I've sat on many tribunal councils, and it's a lot like a congressional hearing with lots of stupid questions and a few disagreements."

"I was a witness, maybe I could help."

I shook my head slowly. "Sorry my love, full-fledged members only."

With that, the little gray terrorist came waltzing into the room with his tail straight, singing the song of his people. Eden rolled her eyes and lifted off my knee, knowing the cat wouldn't stop yowling until he got his breakfast.

"Will you be able to call me?"

"They will take my electronics, but I'll have Mickey touch base with you." I moved to the door. "He won't be able to say much, so don't grill him when he calls."

She flung herself into my arms. "Please be safe."

"Always."

The hardest thing I've done to date was kiss my sweet angel goodbye as she fought worried tears. Should I have lied about where I was going? My gut said no. Lurch, on the other hand, said yes. He knew even less about healthy relationships than I did. I went with my gut but picked up my phone and dialed Tor on my way out of the building.

"Put a trusted man on Eden."

Torrid responded immediately, "I'll keep an eye on her while you are gone."

Some of the anxiety I was feeling eased as I nodded to Pilot and got into the blacked out car. "Thank you."

"They picked Bentley up hours ago."

"This is a standard tribunal, Tor, nothing to worry about."

"I know, but good luck anyway, boss."

I smiled at Pilot, who was patiently waiting to confiscate my phone. "Gotta go, Tor. See you in a couple days." I turned over my phone and got comfortable for the two hour ride to Ocala.

The mansion was located in the middle of several hundred acres of a thoroughbred breeding farm owned by the Blue-Frosted Rose Society. It was the host property of our annual wild hunt and several pleasure parties. The sprawling three-story home towered at the end of a long drive lined with ancient oak trees that shaded the road like a covered bridge.

A plump woman with graying hair rushed out of the entrance, followed by two mousy young men as Pilot opened my door for me.

"Miss Charlotte," I said in greeting.

She did not smile. "You were the last person I'd expected to be the subject of a tribunal, Mr. Dalton."

I nodded. "Normally, I'm in the robes of justice and truth."

Her frown deepened. "Come with me."

Just like the drivers, the young men flanking me were all called Lackey. Their job was to assist and support the woman in charge, Miss Charlotte. The no-nonsense woman lived on site and prepared the entertainment for our parties and wild hunts. Today, it was her job to prepare me to face the tribunal.

"You know the drill, Mr. Dalton. Lackey will accompany you to the purification room."

The androgynous man's face turned beet red as he looked everywhere except at me. There was a tightening in my stomach at his visceral reaction to the thought of being alone with me. I wanted to punish him for fearing me, just to assert my dominance.

"I have no need of help, Miss Charlotte. Tell them I'll be ready in fifteen minutes."

She nodded and grabbed Lackey by his upper arm, pulling him away with her. I heard her whisper harshly, "Idiot. Do you know who that was?"

A chuckle left me as I found my way to the purification room. Poor guy probably wished he was here assisting me instead of facing an annoyed Charlotte. I've seen her bring the most rugged man to his knees with just a few sharp words.

The room was a glorified bathroom with a large soaker tub, herbs, oils, and incense all designed to clean your soul. My soul wasn't here, but I went through the motions with my thoughts on Eden. She'd be fine without me for a weekend, but I wasn't so sure I would.

After purifying my body and several prayers for patience and tolerance, I put on the sheer, pale blue cloak of the defendant and walked through the lavish halls of the mansion to the theater.

Miss Charlotte met me at the door to the stage. I lowered the hood and nodded. She pursed her lips briefly before opening the door and escorting me onto the stage. I knelt on the bare floor in the spotlight and untied the ribbon at my neck.

Miss Charlotte took the flimsy garment off my body leaving me bare to the unseen tribunal. "Gods be with you, Logan."

I didn't need to see them. I knew they sat before me filled with self importance under thick robes and hoods. Our elders were steeped in tradition and chained to ancient thinking. To balance this, Mickey and Todd had gathered with the younger generation of royal members, years ago, and imposed some new rules on the tribunal. There would be an enforcer as well as a few members of my age and class sitting in the dark before me.

A withered old voice said from the dark, "We have called this tribunal to investigate the actions of Logan Dalton, enforcer of our beloved Society."

Most men would tremble and cover their genitals when in this position. My voice was clear, confident and casual as I asked, "What are the charges?"

The voice said, "Disregard of BFR protocol."

Another voice asked, "Is it true you have two non BFR members at your warehouse in Lakeland?"

"It is."

"Care to explain why?"

I lifted my chin and stared into the darkness. "It is necessary."

"And was it necessary to send our Oklahoma brothers to pick up a pedophile who was also not a member of the Society?"

That had not been necessary, but since Bentley had already given his testimony earlier this morning, I wasn't about to throw my brother under the bus. "Yes."

Another voice asked, "So you feel what you have done was in the best interest of protecting our Society?"

Before I could answer another question was put forward. "What about the girl you brought back from Costa Rica?"

My spine stiffened. "My *wife* has pledged. Her mother was eliminated. Ruled as a suicide by investigators in that country. BFR is clear there as well as here. The security breach has been repaired, and the nonmembers at the warehouse won't be a threat in the future."

"What about our missing Oklahoma member?"

"That member is part of an enforcer team. We all know the risks of the job. However, we are close to finding and rescuing him."

"Who do you refer to when you say 'we?'"

A muscle ticked in my jaw, but I kept my voice steady and clear. "I'm sure you already know the girl's role in this fuck up and how she is working to make things right. She has valuable insider experience that we are using to recover our operative."

"And what happens to her afterward?"

"Scout will pledge, or she will be eliminated."

"We vote elimination."

My lips pursed before I said, "Unless you vote to remove me from my position as head enforcer, you have no say on how I run my team and who I decide to add to it. Scout has become a valuable asset. If she wishes to pledge, then she will be allowed to pledge."

I rose to my feet and glared at my audience. "Now fucking vote on what you gathered to vote on. Either remove me or let me do my job, so you can continue living your safe and privileged lives."

Without waiting to be excused, I walked off the stage as the murmuring rumbled behind me. Miss Charlotte beamed at me as she handed me a proper cloak. "Well done. It was nice to see someone come before those old men without cowering like a fool."

My head tilted curiously. "Have I ever come across as a coward to you?"

She snorted. "No. Your brothers are waiting for you in the lounge."

"Thanks."

My brothers were sitting at the bar with Bentley. Todd was the first to notice me. He stood, and I allowed him to embrace me in greeting. It had been a while since I'd seen him in person.

Mickey and Bentley slapped each shoulder as I asked him, "How have you been?"

Todd craned his head back. He was taller than his blooded brother by five inches, but not nearly as tall as me. "I'm living the dream, but you went and got married without telling me."

I shifted and looked away. "I didn't tell anyone."

Mickey slapped Todd on the back, and said, "He was willing to break all the rules to get his girl back. Can't blame him for putting her on lockdown the moment she said yes."

My gaze snapped to him, and hardened. "She's not on lock-down."

Bentley said, "But mine is."

His grave eyes met mine. Fuck, my friend looked positively tortured, though he didn't have a mark on him. He added, "They voted to eliminate her." His wince was positively heartbreaking.

"I can't do it. I can't let it happen. They are forcing me to choose between my brotherhood and the love of my life."

My head shook slowly as I imagined what I'd do if the tribunal had brought Eden into this. "No they aren't. You won't have to choose."

"But she will. You've met her. She'll choose to die over a life of captivity."

Mickey, my dear brother who got off on other people's pain, said dramatically, "There's gotta be another way!"

This earned him a punch in the shoulder from his younger brother, Todd. "Knock it off, asshole. This is serious."

But we all knew that levity and teasing was how Mickey handled uncomfortable shit. So we forgave him immediately. I glanced at the polished wood floors before lifting serious eyes to my second in command. "I truly believe things will sort themselves out with you and Scout. Know that I am on your side, and as long as I'm still in charge, she'll live."

Mickey turned to me. "Are you joining the party tonight?"

"Do I ever join the party during tribunals?"

He snorted. "No, but I thought you might want to put in an effort tonight since they'll be voting tomorrow."

I crossed my arms over my chest, and leaned against the bar. "I'm not changing my behavior just because they have questions about where my loyalty lies."

Todd picked up his drink and corrected, "They don't question your loyalty, just your methods."

I smirked, "Well, if they think they can do the job better..."

Todd slammed his drink on the bar, sending it sloshing over his fingers. "Don't be so smug, there is always someone who wants the power of enforcer. If they feel they can't control you, they'll put someone in your place they *can* control."

I leaned towards him. "Are you asking me if I'm still yours to control, brother?"

He picked up a bar rag and dried his hands off. "Don't be an asshole, Logan. That's all I'm asking."

Mickey picked up Todd's drink and handed it to him. "You're coming to the party with me, and we'll advocate for our brother. Everything will be fine."

Bentley had slipped behind the bar and grabbed a bottle of whiskey as we argued with one another. He knew better than to interject his opinions between us when we got together. As much as we went at each other, we were still family.

"Let's drink this bottle of whiskey, and tomorrow morning before the vote, we work out together."

I lifted my hand and waved away the glass he set in front of me. Alcohol would only encourage the voices in my head to do their worst. I was already dreading a sleepless night without my angel to soothe my soul. It would be better if I could check the cameras in my house and track her phone location, but we all had to turn in our electronics before coming here.

"I'm going for a run. See you all in the gym tomorrow morning."

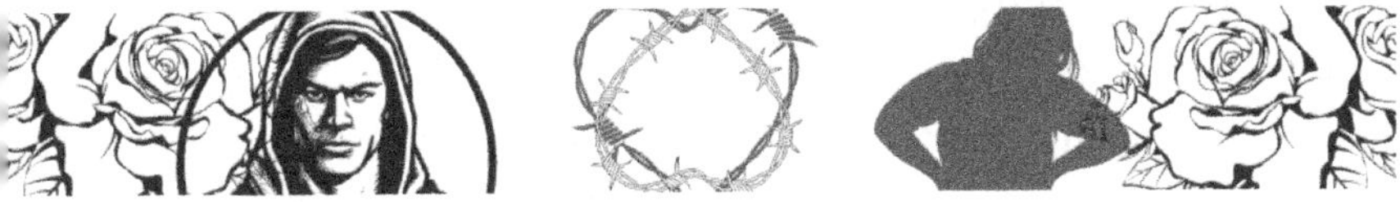

Chapter Thirty-Seven

The Cats Away

Eden

I played with Rori the Terrorist for a few hours after Logan left. It helped pass the time and to curb his destructive behavior. A tired terrorist was a sweet and cuddly kitten. Plus, he made me laugh with his acrobatics.

It seemed like forever since I felt this alone. My brain conjured so many *what ifs* that I was desperate enough to call Mandy to see what her plans were this weekend. Her phone went straight to voicemail, so I called Tracey.

When she answered, I said, "Hey girl, what's up?"

"Getting ready to go out. What are you doing?"

I shrugged. "Nothing much. I'm just bored."

"Wait, where's the man?"

I fingered my collar as my gaze went to the window. "Out of town on business this weekend."

"The cat is away. Do you want to play?" she asked coyly.

"Depends on what you're doing."

She laughed but said, "A new country and western bar opened up in Pinellas Park. Wanna go line dancing with us?"

That sounded fun. "Sure." I got the time and location from her before we hung up.

My mind was on what I had that would fit in at a country and western bar when my phone rang with a private number.

I hesitated before picking it up. "Hello?"

The deep male voice on the other end had my heart pausing. "It's Tor. We met the other day?"

"Is Logan okay?"

He paused before saying, "Yeah, I'm sure he's fine. Listen, a car will pick you up and take you to the bar where you'll meet your friends."

"Wait, you were listening to my conversation?"

He huffed a sigh, like he couldn't believe he had to tell me this. "Someone is always listening, always watching, always protecting you. Understand?"

"Yeah, but I thought it was Logan."

He grunted his understanding. "When they meet they do so without electronics. He asked me to watch over you. And I'll do that for as long as he needs me to."

"Thank you. I won't be a problem tonight."

"I didn't think you would be. I just didn't want you to think you had to call a cab or drive tonight."

I laughed. "I'm not much of a party girl."

"Well, feel free to have as much fun as you want. We'll be watching every unattended drink at your table. Our protection will be unseen, but it extends to your friends while they are with you."

"Thank you." And, I meant that. The anxiety I had about going out for the first time since being drugged and kidnapped disappeared. Even when Logan wasn't here, he was still watching my back.

I threw on a sundress with deep pockets and a pair of cowboy boots that hadn't seen the light of day in way too long. The car was waiting for me as I exited the building, and Pilot greeted me politely as I slipped into the back.

"Good to see you, Mrs. Dalton."

"And you too, Pilot." I fiddled with the diamond ring on my left hand. A gigantic smile grew on my face as I savored being a married woman. It had all happened so fast, but everything about it felt right.

I entered the club and immediately spotted Chandra standing a head taller than the three other girls gathered around a high table. The crowd wasn't too bad, and I made my way towards them. I hadn't seen Tracy's friends since the night of the ball, and I wondered how they'd receive me. Would I be the awkward elephant in the room?

Tracy swung around with a squeal and threw her arms around me. "Eden, my love!"

She turned to her friends. "You all remember Eden, right?"

Lisa, Dulci, and Chandra all nodded with smiles that didn't reach their wary eyes. Like they were all looking for anything physically that screamed *kidnapped girl*, or maybe they were looking for the word *survivor*.

Tracey grabbed my left hand and exclaimed, "What's this?"

I beamed. "I'm married."

Dulci leaned in and shouted over the country music. "Holy shit, that's a nice rock."

"Not nearly as nice as my husband."

Lisa asked, "He's the one who saved you, isn't he?"

I nodded as a cocktail server came up to the table we were standing around. She took our drink orders and disappeared towards the bar. I scanned the room looking for anyone who stood out, but didn't find anyone staring at us.

I asked the group, "Wanna dance?"

Tracy was the only one who knew me well enough to look shocked at my question. She knew I loved to dance, alone, in my room, no audience. I gave her a wink and went to the dance floor even though I didn't know the dance they were doing. There would be no more hiding or worrying about who was watching me. I laughed as I turned the wrong way and tripped over myself as I attempted to learn the steps everyone knew but me.

By the end of the evening, sweat dampened my hair and my cheeks ached from laughing so much. I'd finally let go of my self-induced hang ups and truly enjoyed myself.

As we were walking out, Tracey said, "You've never looked so happy, Eden. I was worried that he had you locked up in that condo keeping you hostage."

My Cheshire Cat grin had her eyes bulging. "I'm a willing hostage. He's so hot, Tracy, and the things he does to me in the bedroom..."

"Fuck, I want one."

"You most definitely do."

Logan

Logan Lurch

I ran and ran until I had looped the property several times, until I was so exhausted the voices in my head were comatose. I fell into bed and slept like a baby who had been fighting sleep for days.

The gentle shake the next morning had me swinging a fist. Bentley was lithe enough to get the fuck out of the way. "Dude!

Do I need to teach Eden how to dodge a punch every morning? Poor girl."

I rubbed my face. "The only thing swinging when I wake up with her are my balls as I pound her sweet ass."

"Ha, well, get the fuck up. They are voting in two hours."

I stretched before sitting up. "What time is it?"

"Almost ten in the morning. Don't worry, we all overslept." He opened the door and added, "Your brothers are already in the gym though."

"I'll be over in a minute."

The gym was located in an oversized outbuilding and was filled with state-of-the-art equipment. Music spilled from the building as I entered. I located Todd struggling through his leg lifts. Unlike the rest of us, his lifestyle didn't require him to be in top physical shape.

I followed the beat of the music and found Mickey attempting to mimic Bentley's warm up routine. They were doing push ups, except Bentley had to be extra and was switching from knuckles to elbows back to knuckles with a leap that seemed impossible. He added some army crawls, flips, and turns all keeping time with the music.

I shook my head as Mickey missed the move and fell flat on his face.

"Haven't I told you not to attempt to keep up with Bent?"

I pulled my shirt off and Mickey's scowl morphed into awe. "Jesus, Logan. When do you have time to do anything but the gym and tattoo shop?"

I gave him an evil smirk as I leaped up and grabbed the top bar. "Fuck off, Mick," I said as I moved my feet like I was climbing stairs until my legs were straight out in front of me, and my abs tensed. I did several sets of pull ups before walking my feet back down to the floor.

Mickey got up and with a shake of his head, he said, "I can't with you two right now." He wandered off towards the machines where Todd was still working out.

Bentley rose from the floor with a grin. "He means he can't keep up, period."

A snort left me as I agreed and moved to the floor to stretch before showing off again. While they were in shape, my brothers ran the corporate side of things. They didn't have to be ready to kill at a moment's notice like Bentley and me, and that was okay in my mind. I never wanted them to put themselves in danger. That was my job.

The elders planned to call for the vote right after we finished working out, so I returned to the purification rooms and cleansed myself there. I took my time with my prayers and chants, allowing my exhausted body enough time to recoup.

I wasn't tense as I strolled onto the spotlit stage and knelt. My freshly washed hair dripped onto my bare shoulders as I waited with my head bowed respectfully.

"Enforcer! Are you ready to hear the results of this trial?"

"I am."

"You lost focus and allowed a breach of security. You abandoned your post and disappeared for three days on a sailing trip instead of dealing with the threat to our Society. We are a brotherhood who comes before all else. You broke protocol by allowing a nonmember to live when she exposed you. Not only did you allow the hacker to live, you allowed her to influence you into missions that were not for the good of the Society. This caused harm to a team of brothers in another state, leaving one captured and tortured."

Another voice took over the first.

"Many have spoken on your behalf, Logan Dalton. You are highly respected among your peers. Therefore in lieu of harsher punishments, you are hereby placed on probation until all threats of this fuck up are eliminated. The terms of probation–"

I stood up. "You do not need to read the definitions to me, I've sat on enough tribunals to understand the terms. I accept my punishment and vow to do my job as I always have." I pressed my palms together and bent at the waist. "I bid you good day, tribunal." I bowed a second time and said, "My elders."

Bentley was waiting for me in the wings. "I'm sorry I put you in that position, boss."

I passed him. "Mistakes happen. Come on, let's get back to work. I need to taste the blood of that pedo ring that handed our asses to us."

The moment Pilot handed my phone back to me, I wanted to call Eden. Instead I called Tor.

He answered the phone. "Hey, boss." Torrid knew better than to ask how things went over the phone. He'd wait until we were face to face.

"Report."

"Eden went out with her friends last night and is spending a lazy Sunday at home."

I found the video footage of my wife laughing as she learned how to line dance. A silly grin formed on my face as I asked, "Any trouble?"

"None whatsoever."

Bentley leaned over to watch the video and said, "Looks like she had a good time."

"I'm glad of it. She's young and deserves to enjoy herself. Do me a favor?"

"Anything."

"Call her and let her know I'm fine, and I'll be home later this evening."

Bentley's head snapped to me and he held his stare as I hung uı with Torrid. "You aren't going to call her yourself?"

The corner of my lips turned up in a devilish smirk. "I want tc surprise her."

Chapter Thirty-Eght

Primal Games

Eden

The relief I felt after Torrid's call was much greater than I let on. Logan would be home tonight, but Torrid couldn't give me a time frame.

The sun was setting when I got back from the pool. I had been checking my phone like a crazy person when a text from an unknown number came through.

Unknown: Do you want to play a game?

Me: Who is this?

Unknown: Answer the question.

Me: No.

Unknown: Answer the question, Eden.

Me: I just did. The answer is no.

With my heart beating like crazy, I opened my call log and called Torrid.

"I just got a strange text. Did you see it?"

He was quiet for a moment before he said, "Yeah. Play the game. We'll get him."

"Are you sure?"

"Ye of little faith. Play his game. We got you." He hung up the phone without so much as a goodbye.

I stared at the texts for a long time before typing. My heart was in my throat, but I trusted Torrid. He wouldn't put me in danger on purpose.

Me: Changed my mind. I like games. Whatcha got?

The response took so long to come back that I had put the phone down and moved on. The chime startled me, and my gut churned as I picked up the phone.

Unknown: I'm dropping a location pin. Meet me at sundown.

The pin came right after and I immediately Googled the park. It wasn't far, but it was a large park that closed at dark.

Me: The gates won't be open at night. How am I supposed to meet you there?

Unknown: Someone will open the gate for you as long as you are alone.

Me: That's not sketch at all. What is the game?

Unknown: You'll see.

My phone rang, and I just about dropped it from fright. It was Torrid, and I let my breath out slowly before answering. "I'm freaking out right now. What if he kidnaps me, or worse? Who is this guy?"

He said, "We've got the location, and you won't be alone."

"Does Logan know I'm meeting some creeper at a closed park in the dark like bait?"

He chuckled-fucking laughed. "Of course he does."

Something didn't feel right. You'd think the enforcers would take my safety a little more seriously. "And he's okay with you using me as bait?"

"Just play the game, Eden."

The line went dead, and suspicion tickled the back of my neck. I put on dark leggings and sneakers. Even though I might be hot, I wore long sleeves and sprayed myself with a natural bug spray Logan had in his bathroom. As I grabbed the keys to my car, my gaze went to the knife rack in the kitchen. A large butcher knife would make me feel safer, but I chose a smaller, more concealable knife instead. I wasn't about to rely on just big, scary men to protect me when everyone except Logan had let me down my entire life. I tucked the knife into my bag and locked up the condo.

It was dark when I pulled into the entrance of the park. An ordinary looking man stepped out of the shadows and into my headlights. He peered at me long enough that I questioned every choice I'd ever made that led up to this moment. Then he used a key and unlocked the gate, opening it just wide enough that I could pull through.

My heartrate picked up as I passed him. What was he wearing again? My mind drew a blank. It was as if it didn't *want* to see the co-conspirator of this deadly game. I needed to get my shit together and pay attention.

It felt like my eyes were so wide as I pulled next to the blacked out car in the main parking area by the lake. I'd been here a couple times as a child for birthday parties, but the park looked completely different in the dark.

I slipped the knife into my sports bra, tucking the fabric around the blade so it safely lay under my right breast before I got out. Other than the crickets and frogs, the park was eerily quiet and still.

There was a note on the windshield of the blacked out car.

It's a full moon, angel. Time to run from the big bad wolf.

My spine straightened at the word 'angel.' "Logan?"

My gaze searched every shadow until a tall cloaked figure wearing a familiar wolf's head stepped forward from behind a small clutch of trees at the edge of the parking area.

I walked towards him, squinting at the jaw under the snarling mask. "Logan?"

He lifted a clawed hand and pointed towards a jogging trail. "Run, little angel."

I hesitated. My breath came in short shallow bursts. "Is this the game?"

He stepped forward, and the moonlight illuminated his feral grin. "You run. I catch."

I reached under my shirt and drew the knife. "I came with claws." I winced. That sounded stupid to my own ears.

He laughed, confirming my silliness. "Run."

Relief mixed with excitement as I spun towards the jogging trail. I was as safe as someone could be, running with knives. The trail was paved, like a sidewalk, but it was darker and more closed in.

There were no pounding steps behind me. No clawed hands reached for me as I sprinted around the bend. The only sound was that of my heavy breathing as I put distance between us. I was the prey, and Logan would stalk me, hunt me.

What would he do when he caught me? The possibilities were endlessly exciting.

Logan

Logan Lurch

After giving her a head start, I pushed off the tree and followed her at a brisk walk. By the time Bentley, and I had arrived at the warehouse, everything had come together, and it was harvest time for Connor. As much as I wanted to torture the fool, we had skilled technicians who handled taking the organs. I was a butcher, not a surgeon. The warehouse operating room was crowded with people waiting for Connor's valuable organs, and our technicians left very little to dispose of.

As we cleaned up the surgery, my alter ego came up with a plan. Torrid reluctantly went along with it even though he thought Eden wouldn't entertain it. When she did, he just shook his head at me in disappointment as I plotted how I would destroy my little angel. Lurch reminded me how wet she got when we played with her at the ball in my werewolf mask.

I knew my girl was too smart *not* to figure this out. I loved that she armed herself, but the fact that she showed up at all deserved punishment.

The thrill of chasing my prey had my primal side pushing forward. I was no longer merely a disturbed human in an elaborate mask. Honing my senses, I stalked my prey in the darkness of the jogging trail. Searching the shadows for movement and training my ears on any sound that might be her. She had run farther and hid better than I gave her credit, but there she was, hiding just up ahead and slightly off the trail.

When I was parallel with her, I stopped and slowly turned the mask to face her. The sudden intake of air that came from her made me smile. She burst from her hiding spot and ran down an unpaved side trail.

A laugh burst from me as I lunged forward and gave chase. This is what my demons lived for, and I let her put some distance between us only to prolong this game of cat and mouse.

"Eden," I taunted, "you can run but I'll always find you."

She fled from another hiding spot, and this time I pursued in earnest. A scream left her as I grabbed her arm and pulled her to a stop. I recognized the knife as it dropped from her hand. "My kitchen knife? Really?"

"Asshole!" She slapped her hand against my chest before I captured it, too. "How dare you set me up like this? I was scared."

I laughed before I leaned close to her ear and growled, "Torric would never use you as bait, for any reason, Eden."

She was sucking air like a fish on a summer sidewalk, and her wide, wild eyes had my cock thickening as she said, "How the fuck am I supposed to know that?"

"You know now. Don't you?"

She struggled against my grip. "Let me go."

Putting both wrists in one hand, I leaned down and picked up my knife. "This game is not over, angel."

She put her defiant face in mine and glared up at me from under my mask. "You caught me."

"And now I get to eat you."

The visible shiver that traveled down her spine told me that was exactly what she wanted. We'd passed a bench back on the jogging trail and I dragged her by the wrists back towards it. She pulled against me until I spun around, dipped low, and put her over my shoulder. The squeal she let out as I lifted to my full height sent the sweetest thrill right to my soul.

Tilting my mask up, I turned and gently bit her thigh with a growl. "Be still," I said around a mouthful of soft legging and tender flesh.

Instead of going still, she did exactly what I wanted her to do. She started kicking, screaming and pounding me in the lower back. "Put me down, you beast!"

I lowered my mask before dumping her onto the bench. She immediately jumped up to bolt, but I was faster and stronger than her. She finally sat back on the bench and glared up at my mask. "What do you want from me?"

Lowering to my knees between her legs, I lifted the knife in my clawed hand and tilted my head before growling, "Just a taste."

I pinched the fabric near her crotch and pulled it away from her sweet pussy. "I hope you aren't attached to these leggings." The knife split both pants and panties like butter as she held her breath. It shuddered out of her when I tugged her hips to the edge of the bench and buried my nose in her pussy for a deep inhale.

"Holy fuck, Logan."

I could only imagine her visual as I parted the fabric and licked into her soaked slit. The mask sat on her pubic mound, like the werewolf had his jaws around her. The mask pressed into my head like she was holding the werewolf steady against her core. My little monster fucker squirmed under my tongue. Her pants and tiny moans confirmed she was into this even though I was purposefully clumsy with my tongue. She'd come with werewolf dick inside her and not a moment sooner.

But the way she gasped and ground against my face filled me with too much need. Need to be inside her, riding her, claiming her. I pulled away and stood up, grabbing her arms and spinning her around. "On the bench, angel."

She was a little too eager as she scrambled up on the bench. I spread her arms wide. "Grip the back and don't let go." Her fingers curled around the wood as I unleashed my cock and lined up.

My fingers slid up her neck and I fisted a handful of hair at the base of her neck. Twisting her head to the side, I growled, "You will watch this werewolf claim you."

"Fuck," she breathed before she pushed her ass against me.

I slammed forward, and her eyes popped wide at the intrusion. There would be no gentle introduction of cock tonight. She knew my alter ego. I drew back and slammed deep once more. Told him she loved him even. Now it was her turn to prove that love as I let him tear into her.

The thing was, she met my violent thrusts with ones of her own. Her grunts matched mine as I drove deeper, punishing her cervix with the tip of my dick. She took what I gave and doubled it before giving it back, and I was running headlong towards an intense orgasm.

"Fuck me harder, you damn beast."

My balls tightened.

I leaned over her and pulled her back against my front. She nuzzled into my neck with a smile as I pumped into her. The moment I felt her teeth pinch my skin I shouted with overwhelming pleasure and spilled into her.

Even as she submitted to the monster inside me, she found a way to win my game. "Gods bless you, Eden. I had plans for this pussy."

She kissed the spot she'd just assaulted and said, "I still have plans for that mask and your dick, Logan."

Gods knew, if I was primed and ready, I would have orgasmed again just from the mischief in her voice. I pulled her to her feet and picked her up in my arms. "You never cease to surprise me, wife."

She stroked a finger along my cheek. "You never fail to meet all my needs and fantasies, Logan Dalton."

"You're still young, Eden. One day you'll grow to hate me, and we'll bicker like old married couples do."

She threw her head back and laughed. "That's because you already are an old married man."

"Fifteen years isn't that much older. One day, you'll be *old*, too."

"Never."

I bounced her in my arms and she squealed. "Okay, Peter princess. Never grow up and keep me young at heart."

She sobered. “Everything go okay at the tribunal?”

I lifted a shoulder. “Yeah. They just like wasting time with formalities.”

Her arms tightened around my neck. “I missed you.”

Those three little words had my chest expanding to make room for the joyous feeling inside me. I’d stalked and captured a rare and precious angel, and she’d never fly away. Not because I broke her wings, but because she chose to stay.

She’d looked into my darkness and found love there. My angel was tough enough to romance the monsters inside me and quiet the voices in my head. I might be on probation with the Blue-Frosted Rose elders, but I finally felt whole.

Change and turmoil might be in my future as an enforcer, but I’d weather any storm as long as I had Eden in my arms.

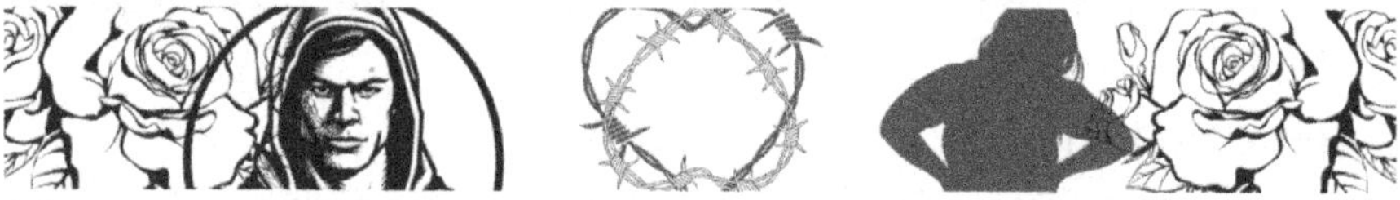

Epilogue

Logan

The past several months had been overly busy for both of us. Eden was on the fast track to becoming a full-fledged member, which demanded a lot of time beyond her normal college courses. I could see the candle burning at both ends and knew she'd burn out soon if I didn't do something drastic.

So, I decided she needed some sea therapy and commandeered her father's sailboat for a weekend getaway. This time, instead of just kidnapping my angel and disappearing, I let everyone know what was up. There'd be no murder this trip, and no accusations that I'd abandoned my post.

Bentley and Torrid were left in charge of the enforcement units and I was positive they had a good handle on things. Scout seemed to be coming around for Bentley, but she still had eyes for Torrid. That love triangle would come to a head in the future, but for now Torrid was still waiting for his pet to grovel for him.

They were a good team when they got out of their own way. Scout was as brutal as they needed her to be. Yet, her life still hung in the balance of the Society, and I could only do so much for her until we were able to rescue the teammate from that pedo ring. We'd gotten close last month, but these guys are quick and smart. They'd lived life on the run for so long that they bolted at the mere hint of capture. It was frustrating to start all over again.

But we had a face connected to them, and our facial recognition software was actively searching for the kid who bought those items from *Home Depot* and *Tractor Supply*. For now, we'd have to wait until one of them fucked up.

We still had our other duties to perform, and since we were still on probation, that meant we had to be on top of our game when it came to protecting our Society. The thing was, we always were on the top of our game.

My darling angel nestled close in the dark of the bed in the master cabin. Her pretty little mouth parted and a soft snore left her, causing my lips to turn up. It wasn't the fact that she snored that lightened my heart. It was watching all the tension melt away the moment those sails popped in the wind and the boat keeled to the side as mother nature took over propelling this vessel forward. I felt the freedom in her eyes as the waves seemed to part before her indomitable spirit. My angel. My life.

My phone lit up from where it lay in the charging station next to the bed. I eased towards it, careful not to disturb my sleeping beauty, but my heart sank the moment I saw who was calling me.

"Yeah," I whispered as I made my way out of the room without smashing my head on the low ceiling.

Bentley's voice made my stomach knot. "She's gone."

"Who?" I knew who but I had to confirm.

"Scout is gone."

I pursed my lips in an effort to keep my voice neutral. "How?"

"We don't fucking know. Torrid said we had a delivery earlier, and she may have somehow gotten help from one of them? I don't know. There's no footage, no evidence at all. Gaul never lifted his head. She just vanished."

I inhaled the salt air of our anchorage. "People don't just vanish, Bent. You know this. Get your fucking head on straight and start thinking like the hacker you are. I'm on my way back. Do not let this security breach go any further than the three of us. We'll fucking find her."

"We have to find her, Logan. I can't believe she'd leave us. I mean, I can, but she seemed almost happy lately."

"Just because she was letting you fuck her, doesn't mean she was happy."

"Letting me? Hell, last night she practically raped *me*." He was quiet before adding, "I should have known something was up."

"That's it. Keep that mindset right there. I'll see you soon."

I scanned the shore we were moored in front of. It was some island that you could only get to by boat or ferry that Dan used to bring Eden when she was a child.

I blew out a heavy breath. I didn't want to be the man to deliver the news that Eden's newest, bestest friend had betrayed all of us. You can't control other people, but Eden had been through enough heartbreak to last a lifetime.

I fired up the boat, hauled up the anchor and pointed the bow towards St. Petersburg. Eden came up from below, rubbing sleep from her eyes and holding her phone. "I just received a text from an unknown number."

She passed the phone to me but when I opened her messages there was nothing there. I turned the phone to face her. "You sure about that?"

Her frown deepened. "I was," she looked around, noting we were moving, "Where are we going?"

"Back. What did the message say?"

"It said, "I'm sorrys."

I pulled her down onto my knee and she wrapped an arm around my neck. "Plural?"

"Yeah, like a kid sent the text." She shrugged, "Maybe I dreamed it. Why are we going home in the middle of the night?"

"Scout is missing."

She straightened. "Missing? Like escaped, or kidnapped?"

"Probably escaped. She covered her tracks well."

She gave me a doubtful look. "If she left, she had a good reason."

I frowned. "I told you not to get too close to her, Eden. She wasn't at the warehouse because she wanted to be. She didn't have the option to just leave."

"I think she's always had the option to leave, she just chose to stay because she was falling in love with Bentley and Torrid. None of you men gave her enough credit. She had a whole ass team of mercenaries at her disposal."

I chewed my lip as I considered her words. "Angel, if we were played by that slip of a girl again, I'll never live this down." It wouldn't be a running joke with a lifetime of ribbing either. Lives were on the line.

"We don't know what's going on with her. Her whole life has been one huge ball of trauma. Just don't jump to conclusions. Okay?"

I nodded and she said, "Everything will work out exactly as it should. You'll see."

Her words didn't help the dread building in the pit of my stomach. Eden didn't know how dense the darkness of Scout's world could be. She might be traumatized, but she could rain chaos, too. Torrid's pet was unleashed and rabid. There was no telling what might happen next.

The End

Keep an eye out for Scout's book on my website. www.amprocto r.com

Hello Pet

About Author

And My Characters

Who created these characters?

I'm a native Floridian, equestrian Gen Xer who spent my summers running feral with her hillbilly extended family in East Tennessee. I say hillbilly with the most respect. My grandmother raised her three girls in a one-room shack in Strawberry Plains when only the tough survived. I grew up on stories of surviving bears and stalking panthers, car crashes where a headless momma got out of the vehicle to carry her child to safety, and shady doctors who profited from the death of patients by life insurance fraud.

I inherited my mother's love of books at an early age and devoured Walter Farley's Black Stallion novels and everything else horse related. My first taboo book was *Flowers in the Attic*, by V.C. Andrews at the tender age of eleven or twelve. That started a tidal wave of discoveries as I absconded with my mother's hidden bodice rippers from her night stand and spent my nights being whisked away to castles and pirate ships only to discover I liked rough men who took what they wanted. I guess that's why my mother put me in charge of the romance section when we opened our bookstore in the 1990s called Upstart Crow in Indian Rocks Beach (later Seminole), Florida.

My mother always wanted to be an author, but passed away in 2015 never achieving that dream. I had been casually writing Spark Bond since my days running the bookstore but never got serious about it until she died. Now, I write full time. I'm not sure if she'd be proud of my books or cringe as she reads them. My mother was a perfectionist and my books are messy. I'm still learning my craft and my backlist is proof of my journey. *Every day, in every way, I am getting better and better.*

My pen name is a combination of my real name and my mother's ancestors. I am related to the Proctors, formally of Cades Cove, TN but they more known for founding Proctor, NC.

I enjoy writing paranormal monster smut the most.

The wolves in Mountain Menace and Mountain Murder are NOT shifters, they are full on lycan werewolves who push the limits of society.

My vampires and fae take what they want and I'm not afraid to go *there* if the story commands it.

Do you enjoy dark, smutty contemporary romance?

I'm a switch. I write what my muse brings to me in unhinged dreams and my over active imagination. If the story calls for human character living abnormal lives, then that's what I provide.

Check out my short, rough romance, Breaking Her Box. It's a secret society dark romance about self discovery and going for what makes you happiest, no matter the cost. There are a few books planned for the Blue-Frosted Rose Society but I don't have release dates at this time.

Cynophobia is a Motorcycle Club (more like Appalachian Cult) kidnapping romance from my back-list that I will eventually fix the tense and grammar issues before sending it to an official editor and re-releasing it on Kindle Unlimited. I'm actually working on that right now.

Wanna hang out and get the scoop before anyone else?

Here's where I socialize.

I hang out mostly on Facebook.

But if you want the inside scoop directly to your inbox then Subscribe to my newsletter. Before you do, if you haven't read my monster romance, I Slept with the Monster Under my Bed, then hit this link to get it free with your newsletter sign up.

Hope to see you around.

Made in the USA
Las Vegas, NV
06 June 2024

90811341R00262